"This part of the world—the Arcnipelago—is the oldest inhabited region of our planet. Why our ancestors endured here for so long is hard to understand when you consider that nine months of the year the rain, cold, and storms make for miserable living conditions. The only way we survived was the profusion of underground hot springs that allowed homes to be kept warm and humid, as most of my kind prefer. So every year, at the peak of the storm season, they had a period of fasting, prayer, and sacrifice to the Water Guardian, begging for deliverance. The symbol on the door was to remind the Water Guardian that true believers lived within and to pass them over. In the old days, it would have been painted in the blood of the eldest *shen* in the house."

Prynn blinked. "Excuse me? Blood?"

"Not for hundreds of years. Long before I was born, the celebration of the Spring Water Festival was heavily curtailed—some of its rites outlawed."

"Fasting and prayer dangerous? Someone should warn the Bajorans."

"Not that part. After the people felt like they'd been preserved from death, they celebrated. Eating, intoxicants," he paused, "*tezha* with strangers—I've read historical accounts of sentient sacrifices: *saf*-induced hallucinations leading to murdering a *shen* or pushing a child off a cliff into the ocean."

"You're kidding me," Prynn said dubiously.

"The finer points of our history—and culture—aren't widely known offworld," Shar said.

"History, I'll believe. But culture? Come on, Shar. I had two Andorians on my floor at the Academy. They never went to parties. Ever. Hardly ever touched synthehol. Never once nibbled at a proposition for an illicit encounter. The phrase 'one-night-stand' wasn't in their vocabulary. What gives?"

"Who we are as Federation citizens living among other species and who we are among our own kind…might be a bit disparate."

"Have you . . . ever been intoxicated? Out of control? Decadent?"

"Yes."

Intrigued, her eyebrows shot up. "Yes to intoxicated, out of control, or decadent? Or all three?"

Shar offered her only an obscure twitch of his antennae.

Prynn studied Shar with renewed curiosity, wondering how much of his true nature he held at bay—and what it would take to provoke it.

WORLDS OF

STAR TREK
DEEP SPACE NINE®
VOLUME ONE

THE LOTUS FLOWER

UNA McCORMACK

PARADIGM

HEATHER JARMAN

Based upon STAR TREK®,
created by Gene Roddenberry,
and STAR TREK: DEEP SPACE NINE,
created by Rick Berman and Michael Piller

POCKET BOOKS
New York London Toronto Sydney Cardassia Andor

An *Original* Publication of POCKET BOOKS

POCKET BOOKS, a division of Simon & Schuster, Inc.
1230 Avenue of the Americas, New York, NY 10020

This book is published by Pocket Books, a division of Simon & Schuster, Inc., under exclusive license from Paramount Pictures.

ISBN 0-7434-8351-0

First Pocket Books printing June 2004

10   9   8   7   6   5   4   3   2   1

POCKET and colophon are registered trademarks of Simon & Schuster, Inc.

Manufactured in the United States of America

For information regarding special discounts for bulk purchases, please contact Simon & Schuster Special Sales at 1-800-456-6798 or business@simonandschuster.com.

CARDASSIA

The Lotus Flower

Una McCormack

ABOUT THE AUTHOR

Una McCormack discovered *Deep Space Nine* very late in its run, but loved it immediately for its politics, its wit, its ambiguity, and its tailor. She enjoys classic British television and going to the cinema, and she collects capital cities. She lives with her partner Matthew in Cambridge, England, where she reads, writes, and teaches. She is the author of the short story "Face Value", which appeared in the *DS9* tenth-anniversary anthology *Prophecy and Change,* and she hopes to return to the worlds of *Deep Space Nine* very soon.

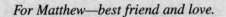

For Matthew—best friend and love.

ACKNOWLEDGMENTS

Love is reading someone's drafts. Thank you, Matthew.

A large number of people have helped me, and I would like to thank all the online and offline friends who have read and encouraged, and been patient with my late replies, extended disappearing acts, and last-minute cancellations. The denizens of Henneth Annûn, Emyn Arnen, and the Lyst have never failed to entertain, educate, inform—and distract.

Two people should here be held accountable for the parts played in setting me on this particular career path. Pat McCormack made me watch *Blake's 7* at an impressionable age and thus must be held personally responsible for all that has followed. Andrew Moul pressed his tapes of *Deep Space Nine* on me, saying, "You'll like this." He was rather more right than perhaps any of us could have imagined.

I would like to extend grateful thanks in particular for all the kindness and encouragement I have received from the following people: M.A.E. has the rare and special skill of being able to come up with names—and the generosity to supply them on demand. Tavia Chalcraft has been enthusiastic and merciless in exactly the right quantities. Andria Laws has provided ice-cream and moral support beyond the call of duty. Brenda Evans has shown me new possibilities in narrative, characterization, and collaboration—and, in turn, has been most receptive to the joys of symmetry. Ina Hark coaxed me, guided me, and pushed me through my first attempts at writing—I cannot measure the debt and can only thank from the heart.

Finally, a deeply heartfelt thank you to Marco Palmieri—for having faith in someone new, for subtle ideas and shrewd editing, for never failing to make things better . . . and for letting me loose on Cardassia Prime.

HISTORIAN'S NOTE

This story is set primarily in December, 2376 (Old Calendar), approximately eight weeks after the conclusion of the *Star Trek: Deep Space Nine* novel *Unity*.

Prologue

"Get that camera over here!"

Teris half-stumbles, half-runs toward the ridge. She waves her hand at Anjen to follow her. "Come *on*!" Then she looks out across the city.

Down below, there's a riot going on. The streets—what's left of them—are filled with people, pressing forward, picking up and throwing whatever they can lay their hands on. Little flashes of fire flare up and there are shouts and cries and sirens wailing.

It's not clear yet what's triggered it, although the city has been on a knife edge for the past week, since that outbreak of *tzeka* fever was announced. The government issued directives, got the medics out on the ground fast, said it was contained—but people are frightened . . . one spark, that's all it will have taken. A situation waiting to happen. And what's happening right now, Teris sees, is that the Cardassian police are overwhelmed, and are pulling back, and the Federation peacekeeper forces are moving in. They have better armor. And better weapons.

They form up in a smooth, professional line, but that crowd's crushing forward. . . .

"You know what, Anjen? I think we should go down there—"

"Have you gone stark raving *mad*?"

"I think we'll get some *amazing* pictures—"

"And *I* think a Bajoran journalist wandering into a riot in the Cardassian capital is a *really* bad idea—"

"You call yourself a professional?"

"Whatever I call myself, it's not stupid! You want pictures from down there—you go and get them yourself, girl!"

"All right, all right, we'll stay here—can you get me and all that in shot?"

"Course I can. . . ." Anjen raises the camera, gestures to Teris until he's got her where he wants her. A foot to the left, an inch to the right. The perfect shot?

Then there is a massive explosion. Someone must've just torched a fuel depot. The blast sends them flying—they throw their hands over their heads, but are back up again in seconds. Anjen is waving the camera about. His hands are shaking.

Fire screams through the night, a red gash ripped in a black sky. It's as bright as day. The whole of the capital is lit up under the unholy glare, the ruins plain to see below them, all for the taking. Teris shields her eyes and looks out at the pandemonium.

"Prophets . . ."

Then the stench reaches them. Teris gags. *Mephitic,* she thinks, marveling. She's always wanted to get that word into a report. Now she can. She pulls herself together. "Did you get that? Did you *get* it? Don't tell me you missed it . . . !"

"I got it, I got it!"

Teris coughs out the foul air, and thinks of the edit they'll do later.

"Beautiful . . ."

The mountains rose sheer and high to the north and the west, their shadows shifting across the valley throughout the course of the day. When you walked around the settlement, you could always feel them. You could usually make a good guess as to the time. *Like living in a sundial,* Keiko thought absently, propping her elbows on the windowsill and resting her chin in her hands, staring up at the peaks that marked and measured out the days at Andak.

The mountains were shot through with black rock, which would glitter when hit by the harsh Cardassian sun, sending sudden sharp shards of light over the base and the settlement. Obsidian, Feric had told her, and then had launched into an impromptu lecture about the volcanic activity that had formed this part of the province. It had been the subject of his thesis.

"Too much information, Feric!" she'd groaned as his eyes, beneath their ridges, took on a zealous gleam. "There's a very good reason I'm not a geologist!" He'd laughed, taking it in the good humor she'd intended, but couldn't resist adding a little bit more information (*"Don't worry—the volcanoes are extinct"*). He was a first-rate scientist, and she hoped that soon enough he might also be a trusted friend. She was sure that she had made a good choice, appointing him as her deputy.

Early evening in Andak brought with it an acute light that, for an hour or more, seemed to settle upon the ancient valley and the new base that lay there in its folds. If you looked at the calendar, it was supposed to be autumn—but the heat had not noticeably dissipated, and it endured even after it went dark. As the year died, Keiko had been told, and winter did come at last to the mountains, the days would become more barren and the nights would be bitterly cold. Cardassia, she suspected, had many cruelties left to reveal.

This evening, the sun seemed to have intensified further, and the efficient gray edges of the buildings were outlined with silver. It was still and hot—and expectant, as if the valley was waiting for something to happen, as if it was waiting for some change. Keiko opened the window, wishing for a little breath of air upon her face. She watched as a small group of people—ten or twelve, perhaps—assembled in the dusty, unpaved square around which the settlement was ordered. Feric was among them. He stood for a while, speaking to one or two of those gathered, and then he and a young woman—Keiko recognized her as one of the junior engineers—moved a little distance away from the others. They each were carrying something, and it was only when they held these before them and then fastened them over their faces that Keiko saw that they were masks.

They turned to face one another, each studying the mask that hid the other from view. The moments slipped past more quickly now, and a hush had fallen over the others gathered there. They were drawn to the scene before them, and stood by unknowing, but eager, watching and waiting. Keiko gazed at this tableau as it held for a long, still moment. The mountains behind at first framed the scene and then, almost imperceptibly, seemed to become part of the composition.

A ripple passed through the onlookers as first Feric, then his companion turned to them. It seemed as if, each in turn, they became connected; whether by their own fascination or some other, more physical charge, they could not afterward tell. The sense of anticipation in the square was growing, the air was becoming slow. If this had been anywhere else, Keiko might have said a storm was coming.

The young woman began to speak, her voice low and rhythmical.

"The power that moves through me, animates my life, animates the mask of Oralius . . ."

There were some children in the square too this evening,

Molly included, playing some game or other—it looked to Keiko as if Molly was organizing proceedings. *Like mother, like daughter,* she thought, with a grin. Growing up on Deep Space 9 had been good for Molly in many ways. She seemed to be able to fit in wherever she was—she certainly had none of her father's difficulties mixing with the Cardassians here, although there were some children hanging back, Keiko noticed, watching the games but not taking part. Well, Molly could be a bit much at first, if you were a shy kid. No doubt they'd get used to her in time, or perhaps get used to each other.

As must we all. . . .

The woman was still chanting:

"It is the song of the morning, opening up to life, bringing the truth of her wisdom, to those who live in the shadow of the night . . ."

Keiko had known even before she'd set foot here that a large part of her job at Andak would be making the staff come together not just as a team, but as a community. Cloistered together, all this way out, it would be easy for feuds to grow, for minor incidents to take on massive significance—for the place to become a hothouse of resentment and intrigue. Keiko was director here—but it was not just the scientific research that would need her attention. A community, that's what she wanted too. And so she'd requested that the team she'd assembled should bring their families with them to Andak. It was only when the requisitions came through—for living quarters, for rations—that she began to realize what a Cardassian "family" might mean. Everyone at Andak had been touched by the war. She, Miles, Molly, and Yoshi—they were the oddities: mother, father, sister, brother. No one else was that lucky. Some of them were the only survivors of their families: Feric, for one, had lost everyone—mother, two sisters, a wife, and a little boy. When Feric looked at Yoshi, Keiko thought her heart would break—another good reason to encourage a community at Andak.

She heard Feric's voice rising, clear and sure in the evening air.

"It is this selfsame power—turned against creation, turned against my friend—that can destroy his body with my hand, reduce his spirit with my hate . . ."

She'd had to fight a hard battle to get Feric's appointment confirmed, right the way up to the advisory board. At least Charles Drury back at the I.A.A.C. had supported her—well, she was *his* appointment, after all, it wouldn't do to lose face and faith in your new research director *this* early on in the project. . . .

"You've got your geologist, Keiko," he'd said, with a twist of his mouth, "Despite his, ah, *fascinating* beliefs . . ."

"He's a member of the Oralian Way, Charlie—and don't raise your eyebrow at me like that. The only reason there's been this much fuss is that he's had the nerve to discuss his beliefs openly. And since when did the I.A.A.C. hire people based on their religion, or lack of it?"

"You make, as ever, a convincing case. But no more controversy if you please, Keiko," he'd said, leaning over to turn off the link. "The budget won't stand for many more emergency meetings. Catering for the great and the good doesn't come cheap, you know. The funding isn't *that* secure. Yet."

Politics, politics, politics . . . We're meant to be doing science*!*

Keiko sighed and leaned her forehead against the cool plastic of the window. It would be all politics again tomorrow, she thought ruefully, with far too little chance for science. Abandoned on her desk, a padd flashed a lonely and unnecessary reminder that the following afternoon, the Andak Project was to be favored with the presence of one Vedek Yevir Linjarin. As if that weren't intruding on her every thought already. A high-profile visitor, putting the project under the spotlight. Yevir, it seemed, never went anywhere without a cavalcade of cameras in his wake. All in the cause of peace—although it didn't seem to be doing his popularity back on Bajor much harm either. . . .

Keiko chewed on her bottom lip. Playing the usual politics was bad enough, but when it meant putting aside all your personal feelings . . . Yevir had hurt a friend of hers, hurt her badly, and Keiko was going to have to spend tomorrow making good-mannered small talk with him. Her friend was a practiced politician herself these days and would understand, Keiko knew, but she would still feel a pang of guilt when she next had to look Kira in the eye.

Welcome to the Andak Project, Vedek Yevir. Here's a punch in the mouth in return for my friend's Attainder.

Now, *that,* Keiko suspected, would get the funding cut for sure. No, she thought with a grin, she'd better steer away from the Miles Edward O'Brien School of Diplomacy and stick with something a little more welcoming.

She cast an anxious and appraising eye around the settlement, at the buildings that seemed to her to sit as yet precariously on the land, and wondered how it would all appear to an outside observer. It was, she would be the first to admit, pretty basic, but there were far worse places to be on Cardassia Prime these days. They had come through the capital on their way out here—that had been a shock. Keiko had *read* about it—had known in an abstract way, the way you think you know things that you see on news broadcasts or read about—but nothing had prepared her for the reality. Nothing had prepared her for the black, blasted landscape, for the dust and the dark, for the hollow eyes of the survivors trying to keep on living in the ruins. Trying to get down one street, they had been held up by workers clearing away the debris—she remembered with a shudder watching as they unearthed a pile of skeletons. . . . She'd only just distracted Molly's attention in time, before the little girl had seen. There had been risks, she and Miles knew, in first moving the family to Deep Space 9, then bringing them here to Cardassia. But there were limits. There were some things you had to protect your children from.

In the square, someone had started humming. Someone picked up the melody, then someone else—and soon the whole assembly had joined in. The sound seemed to build up, seemed to be moving outward from the group, out into the whole of the square, the whole of the settlement, the whole of the valley of Andak. Keiko closed her eyes, listened, found herself thinking of the evening's heat, and the black mountains, and the sharp white light that filled the valley. . . .

"Bloody *hell!*"

Keiko's eyes shot open. She gave a wry smile. That had certainly killed the mood.

She looked over her shoulder and round their quarters with mounting disbelief. *He hasn't . . . tell me he hasn't . . .*

But he had. He'd pulled one of the panels off the wall and was investigating what lay inside.

"What *are* you doing, Miles?"

"I can't get this thing to work properly. Damned Cardassian settings!"

Realization dawned on her. "Are you talking about the temperature modulators?"

He made a noise that she took to be agreement.

"Is *that* why it's so hot in here? *Miles!*" she scolded. "Why didn't you just leave it alone?"

He looked up at her. "You were complaining about the heat again last night, and we had it right down. Turns out the levels have been fixed for Cardassian physiology. I wanted to see if I could get it to go down a notch or two. Should have thought of it sooner."

"But now it's even *hotter!*" She turned away from the window to take a better look at what he was up to and grimaced at the sight. Spread all over just about every available space was a chaos of tools and cables. Yoshi was sitting on the floor, happily absorbed in the vital business of emptying out his father's toolkit and dispersing the contents as widely as possible. Teetering on the edge of a nearby table was a pot of *meya* lilies, paper-thin and exquisitely perfumed, that she had set out only that morning. She stepped across to rescue them, placing them out of harm's way on top of some nearby shelves. Nobody could colonize space as quickly and as thoroughly as Miles, when he put his mind to it.

"Miles," she said weakly, "what *have* you done to my home?"

"Eh?" He looked around. "Oh, don't worry about this. I'll have it all back inside and the panel on again before you know."

But I already *know . . . !* she thought, and sighed, putting a hand to her forehead. From on top of her desk, the padd blinked at her, doggedly.

"Aren't you leaving for the capital in a few hours?" she said. "And are you packed yet?" Something else crossed her mind. "Is your presentation even *ready*?"

He stuck his head again inside the panel and mumbled something.

"I can't hear you with your head in there, Miles."

He twisted his neck a little and glared at her. "I said, I'll finish it on the ride up."

Keiko, who was a mother of two and had once been a schoolteacher, knew guilt the moment she saw it. "So," she said, putting her hands on her hips, "Let me see if I've got this straight. Instead of finishing a presentation on which the whole future of this project may hang, *you* decided you were going to open up the wall, pull out a bunch of cables, and play with them?"

He looked round at her, his expression one of complete bafflement. "To fix the temperature modulators," he explained, as if to someone not quite following something very straightforward, and then he leaned over again. "Don't you know by now that everything I do is done to make you happy, sweetheart?" he added, and then quickly, and wisely, put his head back inside the panel—where he bumped it, and swore again, under his breath.

Keiko came away from the window, and cleared a space on the couch to sit. Yoshi climbed up beside her, and put his hand in hers. "Don't play the innocent with me," she said, stroking his hair. "I know you two—you're both in this together." He gave her a wide and guilt-free grin. Keiko tucked him under her arm, looked round at the anarchy into which her home had descended, and sighed.

Earth, Deep Space 9, Cardassia . . . Nothing really *changes. . . .*

2

Miles O'Brien is by no means the only person making a journey around Cardassia this night. As evening claimed the day, he packed and repacked an overnight bag. It is almost as old and tired as its owner feels right now, a little frayed at the seams, but still serviceable. A padd sits within it, pressed between the underclothes and the clean shirt. It contains almost half of a presentation. Almost. There is a faint hope that it will somehow have written itself in the morning. Not very rational, of course; but then improbable desires will persist, even in a modern man. Now it sits silent in the bag, which sits silent on the knee of the man who sits silently staring at his fellow travelers, rattling along in a curious vehicle, inhaling unburned hydrocarbons from an antiquated combustion engine that someone . . . how might he have put it . . . rescued from a museum, and put to more profitable use. With a few modifications, of course, to deal with the problems of fuel. Miles would be fascinated, if the night weren't hot, and the driver weren't the tiniest bit drunk.

Eventually, this torment will end, of course; he is among a very few on the planet with access to Federation technology, and soon the starship orbiting Cardassia will relay him from the transporter station to which he is headed, passing him molecule by molecule to his destination in the capital.

Others—no matter how elevated their status or urgent their business—are making do with more traditional means of transportation. One man, anxious to be home before full dark takes the capital city, nevertheless must pick his way cautiously over what was once the Department of Rhetorical Administration at the university. Eyes to the ground, flashlight casting thin rays before him, he is alert in a particular way, and so it is that he spots something most other men would miss. He stoops, and scrabbles at the debris, and exhumes it—a book. Most of the cover is torn off, the pages are blackened and a little charred at the edges. He turns it reverentially, as if fearing that further handling may cause it to disintegrate entirely. Enigma tales, he sees, and enjoys a fleeting moment of triumph. He does not have a copy of this one. He slips the book inside his jacket, and moves on. The oily blackness of the lake laps against the rubble, and his unsteady feet tingle at the thought of slipping beneath the cold ripples. In better days he never failed to enjoy this journey—perhaps that is why he had chosen this place for his business tonight—and as he stumbles on he takes some comfort in his find.

Another traveler, slightly luckier, is nonetheless unused to the combination of broken roads and antiquated vehicles that passes these days for infrastructure. One hand clutches at a plastic cup while the other manipulates the contents of a padd, and he has braced himself by planting both feet firmly—if inelegantly—against the seat in front. And then his carriage jolts forward, and he lurches with it, and he hisses in pain and irritation as the hot liquid of his fish juice slops and spills upon his lap. He looks around for something to use to wipe up the mess, and then tuts as he must make do with dabbing it away with his sleeve. How, he wonders, can one meet a valued colleague and friend when one is . . . mired?

It is no mean feat, then, to make a journey around Cardassia these days—and all these gentlemen are, in fact, exceptional. For most of the populace elects not to risk the new perils that the streets present, and on the whole choose to remain indoors—or, at least, under shelter—from the dark, and from the rain. On another night, even these men would have remained in the peace of their homes, offering what hospitality they can to their friends, and what comfort they have for their families. But the call has been put out and, ever dutiful, they must prepare themselves. They must brave the streets, and all their intractable ways.

This, then, is how things are set tonight upon Cardassia. The ordinary folk are hunkered down and hoping for nothing more than the sight of another gray morning. Some are more ambitious, and they move about, and take their business onward with them. And Miles O'Brien sits at a makeshift desk in a wreck masquerading as a hotel room, drafting and redrafting until, long after Keiko would have despaired of him ever coming to bed, he is finished, and the dawn is clawing at the window.

3

A forlorn morning light touched what remained of the capital city. Garak raised his face for a moment to savor the rays of the pale sun, and then hurried across the street. He chose the short-cut over the flattened ruin of Victory Square (something of a mis-nomer now, he thought), rather than taking his usual route and following what had once been the boulevard itself. Now, *that* was a strange habit, he decided, as he picked his way expertly over the rubble, always choosing the path that was no longer there—as if walking along the lost paved ways of the city would somehow conjure them up, as if mapping out the geography of the place would somehow bring it into being once again.

A damp breeze began to lift, picking up a bit of rubbish just ahead of him. Garak contemplated stopping and clearing it up, and then kicked it out of the way instead. He was already late, and not much inclined to engage in futile endeavor this early in the morning. Better to save that for later.

He hopped over what was left of a wall, and spied O'Brien already waiting for him outside the squat, gray block of offices. He was looking in the other direction. A smile crept across Garak's lips. It was . . . *unfortunate,* what had happened between himself and the chief on Empok Nor. O'Brien had always been so *exceptionally* polite about it, indeed had never mentioned it again, although it was—perhaps inevitably—always *there*. . . . Garak slowed his pace to move more quietly, came up behind O'Brien in his blind spot, and tapped him on the shoulder.

O'Brien nearly went into orbit. He swung round, and then glared when he saw who it was. "*Chrissakes,* Garak—are you *trying* to give me a heart attack?"

"My apologies, Chief," Garak said cheerfully, and without a hint of contrition, his mood much lifted. "I didn't mean to startle you, I'm sure."

"You've got a bloody strange sense of humor, do you know that?"

"You wouldn't deny me a little joy, now would you?" he murmured, and held out his hand. O'Brien took it, shook it. "Welcome back to the capital," he added. "How was your journey down?"

"Fine, thanks." O'Brien hesitated before releasing his hand. "You're looking tired," he said, frankly.

"No doubt because it's far too early in the morning," Garak responded smoothly. "And—I confess—the thought of the day ahead does weary me a little. . . . Shall we get some breakfast? There's still time before the session starts."

The sky was clouding over and it was starting to rain—thin, black rain. O'Brien grunted his assent. Garak led him round the side of the office block, down what had once been a side street and was now an uneven patchwork of temporary buildings, and toward an odd structure put together from larger pieces of stone and metal that had survived the Jem'Hadar onslaught. A welcoming smell of cooking emerged from this odd place, getting stronger as Garak pushed the door open. O'Brien sniffed appreciatively.

"A lot of the Federation staff from the embassy come here," Garak told him, leading the way in and picking a table next to the window. "So you won't have to suffer Cardassian cuisine." And it was warm, and it was dry. And, in addition to these advantages over much of the city, it was also a good place to sit and listen to what government officials—onworld and offworld—were talking about. Garak didn't bother to add that. He took the seat in the corner, put his back to the wall, and surveyed the room. Old habits died hard. O'Brien sat down opposite.

They exchanged pleasantries as they ordered and then waited for the food, Garak asking about O'Brien's family, hearing the news from Andak.

"Big day for Keiko today," O'Brien said. "Vedek Yevir is paying the base a visit."

"Ah yes," Garak said softly. His eyes lit briefly in amusement. "The turbulent priest. Try not to mention him when you see Ghemor later—he does tend to start grinding his teeth rather when the vedek's name comes up. Our beloved but harried leader would like even a little of his favorable press coverage."

"Yevir certainly knows how to make a splash."

"All for the glory of the Prophets, I'm sure," Garak said, sitting back as the plates arrived, and noting with some relief O'Brien's evident satisfaction at what had been put in front of him. "And in selfless pursuit of peace between our peoples. We're all on the same side these days, it seems. Although I do wonder sometimes if I preferred it when I knew precisely who my enemies were."

O'Brien looked at him, furrowed his brow, and didn't answer.

Garak made a preliminary assault on his breakfast, and brooded a bit. "This place is on the site of what was an Obsidian Order facility," he said after a moment or two, in a conversational tone. "Well, its cellars were, at any rate—I think the offices on top dealt in transportation logistics. I often wondered, after the Order collapsed, whether there was anyone still Down Below—" He put the capital letters on for O'Brien's benefit; no one at the Order would ever have been so vulgar. "—whether they languished on for a while, waiting for someone who would never come . . ." He waved his fingers suggestively.

O'Brien stopped to look at him, his fork halfway to his mouth. "Remind me never to take you up on that offer of a tour of the city," he said. "I'm not entirely sure I want your, ah, unique perspective." He took the forkful, swallowed, stared at his companion, and frowned. "I think you should get away from the city for a bit, Garak. Go offworld. You're getting morbid."

Indeed, I seem much possessed by death these days. When I look at my fellow citizens, all I see is the skull beneath the skin.

"My apologies," Garak said, meaning it this time, and shifting the food around on his plate with his fork. He looked out of the window. The rain was coming down more heavily. Across the way, there was a medical center, and a queue already stretched outside, despite the early hour, despite the rain. *Tzeka* fever was not a killer—if you could get the drugs and the water filters out quickly enough. *If* you could. Now how would O'Brien put it? Oh yes, that was it. *Bloody depressing.*

"Do you ever regret leaving the station?"

Garak looked up sharply, but O'Brien's attention was firmly fixed upon his breakfast.

"Where I could have spent the rest of my days sewing? Not quite my style, wouldn't you agree?" He glanced out of the window again. "Anyway, Cardassia doesn't let go that easily . . ." he murmured, and then forced out a smile. "Better to be directing events on a ruined world than directing nothing at all, don't you think?" He sighed, overdramatically. "What a fate! At my time of life, to be reduced to upholding democracy."

O'Brien snorted. "How is the castellan?"

Garak raised an eye ridge. "Alon?"

"Oh, first-name terms, I see!"

"Old school friend," Garak murmured, and then admitted defeat—as far as his breakfast was concerned, at least—and put down his fork. "The same as ever. Shrewd. Dedicated. Perhaps a little too sincere for his own good . . ." *Reminds me a bit of Damar, in fact—although his oratory is not so interminable. Nor impromptu, thankfully.*

"I would have thought a little sincerity would go down well these days."

"I think a decent supply of water would go down better."

"Early days yet, Garak," O'Brien said gently.

"He's appointed a new political advisor," Garak said, changing the subject. "A youngish man, name of Mev Jartek." He frowned. "I'm not too sure of . . . his background—not yet, anyway. He wasn't military, at any rate."

"What do you think of him?"

Garak tapped his fingers for a moment on the salvaged plastic of the table, and stared at the queue outside. It didn't seem to have moved. And the rain was still falling. "He wears bad suits," he said.

O'Brien choked slightly on his coffee. "Surely you can't hold that against him . . . !"

"What else do you need to know about a man?"

"Well—friend or foe?"

Garak gave a dry smile. "But I thought we were all friends these days," he reminded O'Brien, then shrugged. "You'll see him for yourself later. I wouldn't mind hearing your opinion of him, to be honest."

"Will he be at the committee meeting?"

Garak nodded.

"I'll keep an eye out for him then." O'Brien set down his cup, suddenly businesslike. "How do you see this session playing out, Garak? Anyone I need to watch out for? Any foes?"

Garak glanced round the room again. No one to worry about that he could see, but he leaned in a little further, and lowered his voice. "You'll be giving the S.C.E.'s recommendation that the funding goes to Andak, yes?"

The conclusions of O'Brien's report were technically embargoed until he had made his presentation to the appropriations committee—but he *was* among friends, after all. He inclined his head.

Garak took that to mean assent. "Well, I should hope so," he murmured, with a curve of his lips. "You're in a strong position as the representative from Starfleet—well, few of us on Cardassia are overly keen to get on the wrong side of you these days; hardly unreasonable of us, as I'm sure you'd agree—but there are still some fairly strong opponents of the Andak Project on the committee. There's Entor, for one."

"Entor?"

"Former gul. And the Directorate's main representative on the committee." Garak drummed his fingers on the table again, impatiently this time, and pursed his lips. "I'm sure it's not the case that the Directorate go out of their way to oppose each one of Ghemor's policy initiatives, but it certainly seems that way. The cut and thrust of the democratic process seem to have gone straight to their pompous heads. Entor will be tough in his questioning."

"I can cope. And the S.C.E.'s recommendations are perfectly clear, after all." O'Brien had taken care to lower his own voice, Garak noticed. Well, he'd done covert ops too, of course.

"Starfleet won't be pleased if funding is diverted from Andak into a project like the one at Setekh."

"Well, don't expect Entor to roll over and agree just because Starfleet says so. And . . ." Garak hesitated, lowered his voice further, "don't be surprised if he gets in a few shots about your wife being director of the Andak research."

O'Brien nearly spluttered his coffee over the table. "He wouldn't *dare*—"

"Be prepared—I *mean* it. Ghemor's staked a lot of political capital on getting the Andak Project funded, and Entor won't shy away from using anything at his disposal to undermine him. He'll count blackening your name and that of your lovely lady wife as a good day's work." Garak shifted in his chair, leaned forward again to emphasize his point. "This man is hardly committed to the cause of Cardassian democracy, O'Brien. He sees quick solutions as the most desirable solutions, and he sees the military as the ones to deliver them. So have your answer to that one ready."

O'Brien nodded. "You're the expert, Garak."

"Indeed I am." *And will he spot that lie?* Garak wondered. *This game is new to me, although I seem to recognize many of its rules. . . . Or am I just mapping the old city onto the new one, hoping to find something familiar? That could be a mistake. . . .*

"Anyone else I need to watch out for?" O'Brien asked, dragging Garak's attention back to him.

"For the moment, no. Ghemor wants to talk to you after your presentation—you're not hurrying back to Andak, are you?"

"No particular rush. Keiko's got everything under control—well, I hope she has, it's her job, after all."

They stood up, paid, left. Outside, the rain and the queue had settled in for the day. A Federation patrol passed by, four young officers, peacekeeper forces. They eyed the queue warily. The queue eyed them back, balefully.

"I thought Cardassia was meant to be hot," O'Brien mused, as they hurried back round the corner to the offices, trying to keep dry. "Like up at Andak. But it's barely stopped raining since I got here."

"It's all the dust," Garak replied, shortly. "Our Cardassian heritage. This rain contains much of what was once our art, our architecture, our books . . . much of what was once our population, too, come to that."

"Bit ghoulish." O'Brien shuddered. "You *are* getting morbid, Garak."

"Like many of us," Garak replied, shouldering open a door and letting O'Brien duck inside first away from the rain, "I'm just a product of my environment."

4

"Now, don't run away screaming, Keiko," Feric said under his breath, "but I think Naithe has just spotted you."

"Oh *no* . . ." Keiko groaned, putting a hand up and pinching the bridge of her nose. "That's *all* I need this morning. . . ." She drew in a deep and steadying breath, put on her best *I am always here for my team* smile, and looked up to see the little Bolian huffing toward them. Once he started talking, Naithe had a tendency not to stop—and Keiko still had most of the base left to check over this morning.

"Good morning, Director, good morning!" Naithe said cheerily. "A fine morning, is it not? And I am assuming, based on the evidence presented to us each day, that this means it will continue to be a fine afternoon, which surely must alleviate some of your concerns—"

"Thank you, Naithe, yes it does. It's always good to know that the weather at least is going to be supportive—"

"Rest assured that we are all of us one hundred per cent behind you, Director, one hundred per cent. All of us here are very proud of Andak and the work that we're doing, led by your good self, and each one of us knows just how important the vedek's visit is to the future of the project. I myself am looking forward to discovering what effects this important day will have on our blossoming little community—"

Keiko and Feric glanced at each other, and both of them suppressed smiles. Naithe had a tendency to think the entire project at Andak had been set up just for the purposes of his studies.

"—particularly whether such a high-profile event throws up any fractures between senior staff—and, of course, whether the presence of such a controversial figure—and a Bajoran at that!—as the good vedek might even put stresses on the relationships between the Cardassian and Federation staff members here—"

Feric coughed slightly. "I'm sure, Dr. Naithe, as you say, that we're all one hundred per cent behind Keiko today."

"Undoubtedly! Undoubtedly!" Naithe looked at them both, and then blinked. "Well, I've no doubt that you've plenty to do this morning, Director, plenty to do." He smiled brightly. "Carry on! Carry on!" He trotted off back across the square.

"Did he say anything helpful at all then?" Feric asked, looking after Naithe in complete bewilderment.

"No, although he did make me slightly more anxious about this afternoon." Keiko sighed. "I'm sure he meant well."

"Isn't he supposed to understand people?"

"He must, he's written books about them."

Feric shook his head. "It's a strange idea for a subject—what does he call it? Xeno-sol . . ."

"Xenosociology," Keiko said automatically. "The study of alien social systems."

"Here on Cardassia, that was called military intelligence."

She laughed, and they carried on walking, companionably, toward the east side of the square, where the accommodation blocks were to be found. They walked alongside them for a while and then turned into the makeshift street that ran between the lines of small gray units. Outside one or two of them she saw that some plants had been put in. There was even a little girl digging away, turning over the dry soil in front of her home. Keiko smiled and waved, and the girl grinned back. So that class she had given was having an effect on one of the kids at least—although Keiko didn't expect to see many more running out to take up gardening. She doubted she'd ever catch Molly doing it, for one. This part of the settlement was as new and bare as the rest of it, the soil thin and powdery from the lack of moisture—but those little bits of brave green hinted how there could be something here, given what it needed to grow.

There's so much we could do here—so much we could all learn from each other.

She felt the press of the mountains behind her, and thought that perhaps next year she and Yoshi could try to make a water garden. He would still be too small to understand *much* of the principles behind the design of efficient irrigation systems—but she was fairly certain that he would like the mud.

"Tell me about the service you held last night," she said to Feric.

He frowned. "I was wondering when we'd come round to that." He rubbed a finger along the ridge below his eye, a gesture she had come to recognize meant that something was worrying him. "Did you mind that we met in the square?"

"Did I *mind*?" The question puzzled her. "Why on earth would I mind?"

That response seemed to surprise him. "The Oralian Way is not an entirely popular group on Cardassia at the moment, Keiko. Not even all that popular here at Andak. But the evening was so beautiful, and not to be a part of it seemed so wrong. . . ." He frowned. "It's not our way, really, to make such a public display of our beliefs. I was afraid that you might be worried about the ramifications of that. Given what some people here think of the Way."

"Feric, you can believe what you want wherever you want! When I asked you to tell me about the service, it was as your friend, not as your boss!"

He laughed a little. "Of course," he said. "You're Federation." He gave her a dry, sidelong look. "You know, Keiko, when you're brought up to think carefully before you dare to utter even a single word, suddenly being free to say what you like is . . ." He had to grope for the right words to express himself here. "Well, it's *terrifying*," he said, at last.

"I don't think you've once shied away from that in your life," she replied. He smiled, looked down at the ground, seeming to want to evade the compliment. Keiko knew that he would have been unusual on Cardassia in choosing to pursue a scientific career—most men went into the military, or into politics (or both, this was Cardassia after all). And Cardassia had hardly been the kind of place that encouraged or rewarded individuality.

"Tell me about the Way," she said. "What it means. What it means to you."

"Start with the small questions, why don't you!" he grinned. They had turned to head back to the square, and when they reached the edge of it, he stopped and looked at the mountains, vast and black.

"Botany, Keiko," he said, with a perhaps just a hint of humor lingering in his eyes, "is in quick time. Two seasons—and you're done. But geology . . ." He wagged a finger at her. "Geology is in slow time. If you spend long enough looking at rocks, you get a different perspective on things." He stared back at the mountains. "A different perspective on people, on how they fit into the world."

He stopped for a moment, and when he began to speak again, his voice was quiet. "My mother was a geologist. She used to bring me here, when I was a child. I'd sit and watch her working—sifting through her samples, cleaning off the dust, listing, cataloguing . . . it's slow work, it needs patience. Anyway, I remember once, she told me that those mountains had been there long enough to see one civilization fall and another rise. I thought that was an amazing idea, the most exciting thing I'd ever heard—that the land was older than the people who lived upon it."

He bent down and excavated a stone from the soil. Then he examined it closely, and began to polish away the dust between his fingers. The stone had flat smooth planes that came to jagged edges, and beneath the dirt the color was turning out to be a glossy black.

"Because that means we're not at the center," he continued. "We're just part of something much older, something much bigger. That's what the Way is about, Keiko; about how everything connects—across time, across place. About how we change when we can no longer see ourselves at the center." He twisted the little rock expertly, and its edges caught sharply in the white sunlight.

"And that's what the work we're doing here is about too, isn't it? What we want Cardassia to be. What we as Cardassians want to be. If we're brave enough to change our land and so change ourselves with it—or if we just want to keep on fighting it, and fighting each other, and anyone else unlucky enough to find themselves in our path. Those mountains have seen two civilizations rise and fall now." He put the stone in his pocket and then sighed. "I brought my son here once. He was bored before the end of the first day. We ended up hiding behind the rocks and playing soldiers—"

He came to a sudden halt. Keiko glanced away from the mountains and back at him. He was looking across the square and frowning. When she turned to look she understood why it was he had stopped.

Crossing the square was a tall Cardassian woman, moving with grace and purpose toward them. Feric straightened himself up and tensed, folding his arms behind his back—almost, Keiko thought, as if he was preparing for battle.

"Don't worry," she murmured to him. "I know Tela's difficult, but she doesn't mean any harm. . . ."

"She may not mean harm, but I fear she does not mean *well*, Keiko. . . ."

The woman was practically within earshot now. They'd have to leave the rest of this conversation for later. *Tomorrow,* Keiko thought. *We'll talk about this tomorrow. I don't need anything else on my plate today, although given Tela's expression, I'm afraid that's going to turn out to be wishful thinking. . . .*

Tela looked at Feric first. "Dr. Lakhat." She acknowledged him with a precisely measured tilt of the head. Just enough respect, but not too much of it. Cardassians, Keiko thought, were so precise with their courtesy it was as if they were wielding just another weapon.

"Professor Maleren," he replied, quietly, politely—but as steadfast as the objects of his study.

She turned her attention to Keiko. "Director O'Brien—"

"Please, it's been almost two months now—call me Keiko."

"Very well . . . *Keiko.*" She sounded almost unhappy saying it. "I appreciate that you are particularly busy today, but I would like—if I may—to speak to you on a matter of some urgency." She flicked her gaze over at Feric. "In private."

Feric gave a wry smile. "How about," he said, turning to address Keiko, "I carry on checking everything's in order for this afternoon, and you come and join me when you're ready?"

Keiko smiled back him—her deputy, her friend. "Thanks, Feric," she said warmly, and then she turned to the other woman, feeling her heart sink.

"Let's go to my office," she said—and so they went off, walking side by side across the square, in silence.

This really is all *I need this morning. . . .*

5

There were very few office towers left standing in the capital; most of those had been occupied by organs of government, the various aid agencies, and those fortunate individuals whose wealth seemed miraculously unaffected—perhaps even increased—by war. Of those that remained, even fewer had not been touched by the rioting. Wealth drew resentment, and resentment focused into fear and hate and fire and death.

In one of the quieter parts of the capital, a single building stood strangely untroubled by anarchy. Four or five men had made their way to the place that morning, arriving at intervals—five minutes, ten, seventeen. No regularity. The routes they had taken were planned with care. A pause at a particular pile of rubble to check for a chalk mark; a momentary halt as if a thought once forgotten had been suddenly remembered, and a reversal of direction. The routine that was no routine, well practiced, instinctive, safe.

There were two ways into the building—front and back. The larger, double doors at the front had admitted two men, over thirty minutes apart. The first was younger. He pulled both doors open—one in each hand—and strode in swiftly, resisting the giveaway temptation to cast a furtive glance about himself. The second was older. He had adopted the half-hunched walk of the average citizen, picking his way unsteadily over the rubble, and sliding through a single doorway. A third had, perhaps, entered via the rear—shifting a pile of garbage cans to make his way through, spilling some liquefying detritus. It poured over his well-made shoe, and he cursed. Two never even approached the anonymous façade. The remains of a bakery stood at the end of the street, twisted, metal reinforcements reaching naked from the crumbling concrete. They had passed into its dusty interior, and made their way through newly connecting cellars to join their colleagues.

They met rarely, these men. They would normally contact one another through more covert means: an encrypted data rod left in some innocuous location, for an untraceable lackey to collect. (One amused himself by using a safe-deposit box in the bombed-out ruins of the old central post office.) But occasionally, if events threatened to run out of control, for example, or they wished to propel them forward, they would feel the need to convene.

The first to arrive had surveyed the room in which they were to meet and, with a curl to his lips, had set to work beating dust from well-stuffed if shabby chairs and pulling them into place around an ancient, scarred table. He timed the operation to perfection and was seated comfortably, with a good view of all the entrances and with all his padds laid out neatly before him, by the time the second made his way in. This man only nodded a quick greeting and then shuffled into place, aiming for inconspicuousness at one dim corner of the table. The next two arrived in quick succession. When the first of these came, he was already thumbing his way through the files, and simply took his place without acknowledging his associates' presence; the other took his seat and began to fuss over his shoe. A wayward elbow dislodged the items that had been fastidiously arranged by his more timely colleague. Having taken the trouble to arrive early, he favored the new man with a distempered look.

When the fifth at last made his entrance, the four were settled in their seats, waiting. Not a word had passed between them. This man, the last, took his time to walk across the room, each footfall measured out with care. With slow and scrupulous attention, he made his way to the head of the table, drew out the chair, brushed some invisible dust from the seat, and then took his place. Whereupon, with the same meticulousness, he drew out from inside his jacket pocket a single padd, which he laid down before him and straightened until he was apparently satisfied that it sat in perfect alignment with the edge of the table. Only then did he look up to consider his colleagues.

"Well, gentlemen. Let's begin."

6

"The trouble with democracy," Garak murmured into Miles's ear, "is that it takes up too many mornings."

Miles grunted, but gave no further answer. After a while, you got to be able to tell when Garak wanted a reply, and when he just wanted an audience. Anyway, Miles was finding out that he had more than a little sympathy with his point of view.

The session of the grandly titled Technological Appropriations Committee was taking place in a considerably less than grand meeting room in the temporary buildings that currently housed the offices and staff of Castellan Ghemor's administration. An administration which Miles, and most of the quadrant with him, most fervently hoped was not as temporary as its surroundings. An administration for which Miles was hoping to provide support in his presentation later today. When he finally got the chance to speak. He rubbed at the back of his neck. Stationed on Deep Space 9, he'd forgotten just how long committee meetings like this could take, as everyone made sure they had as much say as they possibly could. Which they frequently mistook for saying as much as they possibly could. Sisko had had no patience for these kinds of lengthy proceedings, Miles thought, with a certain wistfulness.

He sighed to himself and glanced up. One of the light strips on the ceiling was flickering slightly, and Miles had a strong suspicion that four or five hours of that—never mind all the blathering from a bunch of self-important politicians—would be enough to drive him mad, or at least to jump up and take a screwdriver to the damned thing. *Tempting to take a screwdriver to some of this lot too,* he thought, glancing around the room, but he put that notion aside regretfully. Cardassians liked the sound of their own voices after all. And when on Cardassia . . .

Well, the day was certainly shaping up to be a long one. Two rival projects chasing the same bit of funding. Andak or Setekh. Miles was objective enough an engineer to know that it was not just—not at all, in fact—because Keiko headed the Andak Project that he was backing it. The Setekh Project, in Miles's opinion, was a quick fix, and not even a good one—like slapping some sealing tape over a volcano, and hoping it would hold back the flow of lava. The idea was sound enough—the people at Setekh were working on new soil-reclamation technologies—but the way the project was being implemented . . . Well, that was the rub.

Unfortunately, it wasn't just a question of may the best project win. There was a whole host of political agendas surrounding this decision, some of them to be explicitly aired in these sessions, some of them remaining very strictly implicit. . . . Miles grimaced and remembered Keiko's frequent complaint: *Forget the science, Miles! Don't you know that what* really *counts is the politics?*

Alon Ghemor himself was presiding over the session. The committee room was arranged with rows of chairs lined up behind a single chair and table, where a spokeswoman from an independent scientific team was drawing to the conclusion of her report. The committee members themselves sat in a row behind tables facing the rest of the room, representatives from the Directorate sitting to Miles's right, representatives from the government to the left. Ghemor was sitting at the center. He had steepled his hands before his face, and was tapping his thumbs thoughtfully against the ridge on the base of his chin, listening intently. His gaze was fixed on the woman before him but, every so often, Miles saw him cast a swift, sideways glance at his fellow committee members, monitoring their reactions. As Garak had said, Ghemor did look dedicated, and determined too. The news transmissions picked up all that. What they didn't pick up so much was that he also looked very tired. Miles hoped at least some of that was just an effect of the artificial light.

Although keeping this whole show on the road must be taking it out of him. You'd think at least he'd be able to delegate this hearing out to someone else.

But then Ghemor *had* publicly and repeatedly spoken in favor of the Andak Project, after all. It was no wonder he was chairing these sessions. However he might prefer to fill his day, he was stuck with this one, no question about it. If Andak lost its funding after all this debate, it would be a very personal humiliation for the castellan.

The light flickered again. Miles pressed his fingers against the bridge of his nose. He was up next and, if what Garak had said about the types of question he could expect were true, he could definitely do without developing a headache before the whole thing was done and dusted. The coffee that he'd had at breakfast had been a lot weaker than he liked it. And the technical discussions so far—the details of which he knew at least as well as anyone in the room—were hardly stimulating. Still, he tried to force his concentration back on Dr. Remar as she made her closing comments in support of the work being done at Andak.

His attention was pulled away from her again almost straightaway when a door slid open just behind Ghemor, and a Cardassian slipped in. He handed a padd to Ghemor and then went to sit down at the far side of the room.

Garak tapped Miles's arm. *Jartek,* he mouthed, nodding his head in the man's direction.

Ghemor's new political advisor. Miles looked at him with interest. Youngish, thinnish, with hooded eyes that darted about him, and bearing a bland expression that was just a shade too studied. Garak could teach him a thing or two about that, Miles thought. Jartek seemed to be trying to blend chameleon-style into his surroundings, but he wasn't quite succeeding. Garak could probably teach him a thing or two about that as well.

Remar had finished speaking. Ghemor set his hands down before him on the table, sat up straight, and addressed her. He was a tall man, and knew how to use this to his advantage. And his voice was strong, and he took care to make it carry.

"Dr. Remar, thank you for contributions this morning. I'm sure I speak for all the committee when I thank you for the clarity of both your presentation and your conclusions."

Remar inclined her head gracefully in acknowledgment.

"I'd now like to open the floor to my colleagues," Ghemor continued, gesturing to either side, "who no doubt have some questions for clarification to put to you. First of all, I'll call upon Merak Entor, who is the senior representative on the committee for the Directorate. Merak," he said, in very neutral tones, turning to address the man seated at his far left, "I imagine you have some things you'd like to ask . . . ?"

Ah, so this *is the infamous Entor?* The light flickered again. O'Brien ignored it, and stared at the former gul.

You could tell a mile off he was ex-military. Despite his civilian clothes, he was holding himself like he was still in uniform, and when he spoke it was as if he was addressing a roomful of cadets. *Did they train them particularly to swagger in the Cardassian military?* Miles wondered, and not for the first time in his life.

Remar folded her hands on the table in front of her as Entor made his opening—and lengthy—remarks. At least he remembered the common courtesy of thanking her again for attending the session, although perhaps barking it out like an order wasn't entirely in the spirit of things.

Miles watched as Ghemor glanced over at Garak, a faint smile twitching across his lips. Garak rolled his eyes in response. *Get* on *with it, Entor!*

"Dr. Remar," Entor said at last, "you have been a remarkable advocate for the Andak Project."

"I strongly believe," she replied, leaning forward in her chair to emphasize her point, "that the research being conducted there has the potential to transform Cardassia's future—"

"Yes, yes—we've heard this argument from you already this morning, in detail and at great length."

A couple of the panel members from the Directorate smirked. Remar pursed her lips. "When explaining difficult technical matters," she replied mildly, "it is important to take into account the . . . level of expertise of one's audience."

She smiled, almost demurely. Entor scowled. Garak chuckled. *And does everyone on Cardassia learn how to do the verbal tango? Must be on the curriculum at their schools.*

"What I would like to know, Dr. Remar," Entor continued, undaunted, "is precisely how objective you have been in coming to these conclusions."

Remar blinked at him. "I beg your pardon?"

"How objective are you in your support of the Andak research?"

"Objective? I was asked—as a former member of the Science Academy—to provide a comparative report of the two projects on the basis of their scientific strengths, the respective quality of the teams concerned, the potential benefits to the reconstruction of Cardassia . . ." She ticked the points off on her fingers, and then shook her head. "To be perfectly frank, Councillor Entor, I'm not sure I entirely understand the purpose of your question."

Entor gave her a cold and predatory smile. "Then let me make an explanation which takes into account your . . . level of expertise of political matters. Is it not true that the deputy director of the project to which you have given such unequivocal and eloquent support was once your lover?"

Miles raised a hand to his mouth and just managed to turn his laugh into a cough. For a moment, he felt like he'd entered into some kind of cheap holodrama. Beside him, Garak seemed to be thinking much the same thing. He folded his arms and leaned back in his seat. "Oh, *please!*" he muttered.

Remar, however, was not laughing. In fact, she looked humiliated. *Can't be pleasant,* Miles thought, *having your personal life dragged out like that.* And in front of the cameras. He shuddered slightly. Would Entor do the same with him? He thought again, fondly, of that screwdriver. . . .

"Almost *twenty years ago* . . . !" Remar said, and then collected herself. "How could you *possibly* suggest that I would—"

Entor ignored her, turning to address the members of the panel from the Directorate. "Dr. Feric Lakhat—we heard his evidence at the start of last week. A follower of the Oralian Way, I understand," he said. Several of the panel nodded, as if that bit of news explained a great deal. O'Brien heard Garak draw in a hiss of breath.

"Councillor Entor," chimed in Neret, sitting at the other end of the panel, "I have to say that I don't believe that this line of questioning is either helpful or relevant."

"I believe it is of *extreme* relevance," Entor shot back.

"You're implying a degree of corruption on the part of Dr. Remar which would run counter to all her principles as a scientist—"

"That's correct," Entor replied, squaring himself aggressively.

Remar had now regained some of her self-possession, but was quite plainly furious. "Councillor Entor," she said, "I believe that your question says a great deal more about the mind-set of the former military than it does about the scientific community. My recommendations were based solely on the scientific evidence and on the merits of the two projects concerned!"

"And I believe," added Neret, "that Councillor Entor has overstepped himself. I sincerely hope he intends to retract that obnoxious accusation and apologize to Dr. Remar—and to the rest of this committee. As ever, the Directorate appears to be bent upon sabotaging rather than participating in the democratic process—"

"And as ever," Entor replied angrily, "that process is shown up as the *sham* that it is!"

At that, it seemed to Miles that the whole committee broke in, their voices rising as they each struggled to be heard. It took Ghemor a good couple of minutes, but eventually his voice overpowered the rest, drowning out the uproar. His eyes were blazing and his lips were thin with fury.

"This is *unacceptable*! I will *not* have these hearings reduced to the level of a barroom brawl." He stood up abruptly. The rest of the room followed protocol and did the same, some rather more shamefaced than others.

"We'll continue this afternoon," he said, giving the assembly a rather sour look. "When perhaps we might aspire toward constructive debate rather than outright farce." He turned on his heel and made his way out through the door behind his seat.

Jartek stood up smoothly. "I think we can take it that the meeting is adjourned." He reached over and turned off the transcription devices. "This time, Councillor Entor, I think you may have gone a little too far."

The room erupted into a frenzy. Jartek slipped after his master.

Garak swung round to face Miles. "You see now what I mean about Entor?" He was seething, Miles saw, actually seething.

"I most certainly do." Miles eyed the former gul uneasily. No shamed face there—in fact, Entor looked pretty pleased with himself. A couple of cronies had gathered round and seemed to be encouraging him in this. "He's hardly subtle about it, is it?"

"And yet somehow he manages to create chaos. It's idiots like that," Garak ground out, "who will cripple Cardassia before she's even had a chance to get up off her knees. And all in the name of her greater glory. Well, we tried that once, and where did that get us?"

Was that a flash of idealism, Garak? Didn't think you had it left in you, if it had ever been there in the first place. . . .

No, that was unfair, Miles decided. Cardassia had always been the one thing that had mattered to Garak.

He watched as Garak sighed, and composed himself—and then nodded to O'Brien to follow him. "I think we should seize our window of opportunity and have you meet with our illustrious leader. If he's not crawling up the walls, that is." His eyes narrowed; his expression sharpened. "So, before we go in—what did you think of Jartek?"

Miles stared at the closed door and barely noticed as the light strip guttered one more time and then went out. "Not really got much to go on yet," he answered. "But you're dead right about one thing. It's a *terrible* suit."

7

Keiko pressed her hand against the security panel to unlock the office door, and then stepped back politely to allow Tela to enter first. The older woman hesitated for a moment on the threshold, and then went in ahead. A draught came out through the open door, and Keiko drew in a quiet sigh, relieved to feel the fresh air again upon her face. She always kept the temperature fairly low in her office—it was her haven from the heat of Cardassia. Feric complained about it all the time, amiably, but Tela never had—although, as Keiko stepped past to take her place behind the desk, she thought that she saw a frown briefly trouble the other woman's cool, set face.

"Please," Keiko said, gesturing to a chair, "do sit down."

For one fraction of a second, Tela remained standing—upright, proud, with the apparently instinctive bearing that made so many Cardassians appear overwhelming. Then she nodded slightly and lowered herself into the offered chair, smoothing a nonexistent crease from her skirt and still seeming very tall. Dealing with Tela was like participating in a dance, Keiko thought—a very precise, formal dance . . . and sometimes Keiko felt as if she were being forced to improvise, making up her moves while Tela sidestepped her, again and again.

We should be friends, Keiko thought, a little sadly. *We're both scientists, both women, both mothers . . . and yet we shift cautiously around, neither of us able to take a first, real step toward the other.*

Tela was casting an eye around the room. Was she imagining herself in this office, behind this desk? Tela had applied for the directorship of the Andak Project, Keiko knew, and the decision not to give the post to a Cardassian had been deliberated long and hard by the I.A.A.C. But if Tela was bitter about Keiko's appointment—and then Keiko's choice of Feric as her deputy over Tela—she had never shown it. She had, in fact, kept a thoroughly professional distance. But, nevertheless, whether intentionally or quite unconsciously, Tela contrived to give the impression that she was on the wrong side of the desk, as if she had been somehow dispossessed from what was rightfully hers. *This office. My office,* Keiko told herself firmly.

After a moment, Tela leaned forward in her chair. She reached out a long, thin hand and, with a cautious finger, tapped the school bell that stood on one side of Keiko's desk. It made a dull sound.

"What *is* this?" she asked. It seemed to be genuine curiosity. *We* are *both scientists, after all.*

"That's my school bell," Keiko said, and laughed a little. "A relic from my former career!"

Tela looked up at her, an eye ridge raised in surprise. "You taught school?"

"For a while—on Deep Space 9, when Miles was posted there. The children had nothing to keep them occupied and were getting into trouble and . . . well, there was hardly much call for a botanist on a space station. A happy combination of circumstances."

Well, not always entirely happy. . . .

Tela's eyes widened, as if something had suddenly become clear to her. "Ah—now I think I understand better about these classes you've asked us all to give."

"On the station, we found that the school was a good way of bringing very different and diverse communities together," Keiko explained, deciding that perhaps it would be good politics at this point to pass over some of the difficulties. "So yes—that's why I'd like us all to take some part in educating the children here at Andak. Not so much that it interferes with the work we have to do, of course," she said quickly, "but there are some brilliant, gifted people here, and I think it would be a real opportunity for the children on the base to be exposed to their ideas, to learn from them."

Tela had listened to this speech impassively. Her eye fell upon the bell again. "May I?" she said, touching the handle.

"Please do," Keiko replied.

We are so very *courteous to each other. . . .*

Tela picked the bell up, carefully.

"It's quite solid," Keiko assured her. "It's meant to be rung vigorously, over the noise of children playing!"

The bell clanged a little. Tela quickly reached for the hammer. She turned the bell upside down and examined the mechanism, tapping the hammer against the metal, recreating the dull sound. "Did you *really* use this on the station?"

"Oh no, of course not—it would have deafened everyone! Resounded all along the Promenade. I wouldn't have been popular if I'd done that first thing every morning!" Keiko smiled in what she hoped would be taken as a friendly manner. "No, it was a joke on Miles's part, really, when I started the school. I was very nervous about the whole project."

"Nervous?" Tela gazed up at Keiko, pinning her with an inquisitorial stare. Keiko berated herself inwardly.

That was a little bit too much information. One of us has to take the first step, make the first move forward, yes—but I'd rather have Tela unbend!

"The whole project was a risk," Keiko replied firmly. "We didn't know whether the Bajoran parents would accept a school that didn't teach their faith as an explicit part of the curriculum."

"And did they?"

"With time, and with effort—yes, they did."

With a surreptitious glance, Keiko checked the time on the display. It was several hours yet until Yevir was due to arrive, but she still had much of the base to check on. It wasn't fair to leave it all to Feric—it was her responsibility. Why, Keiko wondered, did Tela have to pick this morning—of all mornings—to indulge in small talk?

Tela set down the bell, brushed away another crease in her skirt that Keiko, at least, couldn't see, and then folded her hands before her. When she lifted up her gaze again to look at Keiko, she was a study in composure. Plain but perfect clothes; her long dark hair held up in an intricate style which seemed effortlessly achieved—although, when Keiko looked a little closer, she could see the strands of gray flecked among the black. Very few of the Cardassians at Andak other than Feric had spoken to Keiko of their experiences during the war and Tela Maleren most certainly had not. She had a daughter here, Nyra, but had never mentioned a husband or a partner. Keiko didn't even know if there had been more than one child. And she had to wonder, as she often did, how much of a toll the brutalities of the war had taken upon such a cultured, civilized woman as this.

"I used to love teaching when I was younger," Tela said, simply. "When I became principal of the Science Academy, I had less and less time for it. I regretted that." She looked at Keiko coolly. "I'm sure you understand about administrative burdens. Do *you* miss teaching, Director O'Brien?"

"I *do* miss it, a great deal," Keiko said, marking the shift back from first names to titles. "And I'm sure," she added, doggedly, "that we love teaching for the same reasons."

A very small smile, like a fault line, crossed Tela's face. "Do you think so, Director O'Brien?"

"Well, I love to teach because I love to give children and students new ideas—to see their minds opening. To see them take what I have and to make something new from it, which is their own."

"Then—as I suspected—we are not in accordance. When I taught, it was to pass on to my students their tradition, their heritage. Everything that made us Cardassian, which had been given to me, which I loved and wished to give to them in turn." Tela had begun to finger a silver bracelet around her wrist. With a flash of insight, Keiko grasped that she was very distressed.

And confused. . . . Surely the Oralian Way is all about Cardassia unearthing her lost past . . . ? Shouldn't she welcome it . . . ?

"Professor Maleren . . . *Tela*," Keiko said carefully, although she could not keep some urgency from creeping into her voice, "we've worked alongside each other now for nearly two months, and you've never chosen to speak to me like this before. I'm glad that you're talking to me now but, please, you *must* tell me what it is that's brought you here this morning."

"There is so little left," Tela said, tracing the filigree and the small red stone on the bracelet and looking beyond Keiko out of the window. "And yet there seems to be no will to protect it; worse, there seems to be a desire to destroy even the little that remains. You say that you taught in a school which did not let belief pass through its doorways. And yet here, in Andak, you allow the open practice of religious faith."

Suddenly, again, Keiko understood. "You're talking about the service yesterday, aren't you? The Oralian Way?"

Tela's lips thinned. "It has no place in public here at Andak. No other groups or affiliations at this base practice their faith or air their views as openly as the members of the Oralian Way did yesterday. It is *not* acceptable—"

"Professor Maleren, I'm not going to use my authority to bar any adult here from expressing their beliefs however they choose—privately or publicly!"

"Where there are *children* watching, Director O'Brien!"

They stared at each other across a desk which now seemed to be cavernously wide.

"I have a daughter, you have a daughter," Tela said softly. "Can you care so little about what she learns? Do you see so little of worth in your own traditions, your own values, that you have no wish for those to be hers too?"

"Molly has lived most of her life among other cultures. Her own mother and father are from different cultures. Of course I'm happy for her—and for Yoshi—to learn all that they can from everything around them. *Those* are my values."

Again, the fault-line smile. "Infinite diversity is a luxury—and one among many that Cardassia has never been able to afford. All that I have left now to give to my own daughter is ruins, Director O'Brien. Perhaps if that was all you had, you might wish to protect it too." She frowned. "At the very least, if I cannot make an appeal to you on these grounds, let me appeal to your sense of pragmatism. There are many, many people here who are not happy with what took place in the square yesterday. You are serving neither yourself nor the project if you ignore this."

Keiko had to look down for a moment to collect her thoughts, but when she could face the woman opposite again, it was with determination in her eyes. "Tela, I don't underestimate your concerns, and I do understand them. I won't hide away from this, that's not my style. I want us to find a way to solve this, to everyone's satisfaction. But, for the moment at least, while the project isn't yet secure, while—today!—all of Cardassia, and beyond, is going to be watching us, we *have* to pull together."

Tela sighed a little. "I must not leave you doubting my commitment to this project," she said, and then she smiled. But her smile was sad, and it touched only the very edges of her eyes. She looked out of the window. "You know, don't you," she said, softly, "that if our work here is successful, it will change Cardassia forever? And not just Cardassia, but its people. We will change the air we breathe, and the land we use to grow the food we eat—and so we will be changed ourselves."

Keiko did not answer, but waited for Tela to finish.

"You do realize that even if we *could* return to how we were—that I have committed myself, committed my *work,* to that change?"

"I know, Tela. I know."

"But still, there is so little left," Tela explained again, raising her hands in a hopeless gesture. Then, with a swift and elegant movement, she rose, and made for the door. When she reached it, she stopped before touching the panel, and turned.

"There is one other thing that I have to say—that you will be making a mistake, Keiko, if you try to treat us as if we were Bajorans. We are not superstitious—we are rational; too rational, perhaps. But we *are* alike in one way, I'll grant you. Alike because of what they learned from us—to be hard, to be obdurate."

"I understand that, Tela," Keiko said. "And I'm not dismissing this, nor underestimating the gravity of your concerns. This is something all of us will have to deal with, if we really want to be a community here at Andak."

"Ah yes, the community. . . ." Tela gave a dry smile and opened the door. "It's a worthy vision you have—but I fear you may be building castles in the air."

"I hope not," Keiko replied. *And I can be adamant too,* she thought, as Tela nodded a courteous farewell and left.

8

The overwhelming sensation gained on entering Ghemor's office was one of information overload, from the viewscreens taking up most of one side of the room. Six of them, stacked three by two, and each, so far as Miles could make out, tuned to a different channel. Two were streaming out information on foreign markets—it was close of business in at least three different places and it looked to Miles's admittedly untutored eye as if the Cardassian *drokna* was continuing its stately decline in all of them. The other four channels were all broadcasting news, from various parts of the quadrant.

The excess of data that was bombarding him meant that a moment or two passed before Miles noticed something odd about the screens themselves. They were square and plain and ordinary—not the oval and too-ornate displays of distinctively Cardassian design that Miles had become accustomed to on DS9. Here, at what was supposed to be the center of his power, the castellan relied on Federation technology to keep his office running. The news was brought to Ghemor from around the nation that he now led via six screens just like any that you could see anywhere in Federation territory.

Ghemor had not, Miles noticed gratefully, chosen to *listen* to all six channels at once. Right now, he seemed to be focused solely—and very intently—on the Federation News Service, which was transmitting a report from . . . wasn't that Andak? Miles looked a little more closely at the screen. Yes, that was

Andak. He recognized those mountains and that particular shade of gray to the buildings. *That* was Vedek Yevir arriving. And there was Keiko, greeting him, and looking grand! Miles smiled at the sight of her, and wished once again that he could be there with her, but he knew Keiko would cope admirably. She always rose to the occasion. And there was no way he could have missed coming to this meeting—which he could only assume *was* going to reconvene that afternoon. Bloody annoying to come all this way and not get to make the S.C.E.'s presentation, and this such an important day for Keiko . . . He looked again at the display. The report was wrapping up.

" . . . *And with the future of the project currently under discussion, Vedek Yevir's presence here can only be seen as a boost for the team working at Andak, and for their political backers, including the Cardassian castellan Alon Ghemor and his struggling administration . . .*"

Ghemor made a slight noise at the back of his throat, which sounded to Miles to be ominously murderous.

" . . . *this is Teris Juze, reporting from Andak . . .*"

"Don't worry about it, Alon," Jartek said. His voice was smooth and soothing, and easily smothered the sound of the broadcast. "Federation news, remember? Yes, it's the best—but, still, you can't be surprised if all the good in the world is attributed to the vedek."

"It'll be laying on of hands next," Ghemor said morosely. "Vedek Yevir Linjarin heals the sick. I'd give my right arm for just half of his favorable coverage. No, strike that—I'd give my right arm for just half of his coverage period, favorable or not."

"These things take *time*," Jartek said patiently, reaching out to turn down the volume on the display. "And effort. Don't worry about it, it's all under control."

"Who's the elected leader around here, anyway?"

This all sounded, Miles thought, like an habitual grouse. Garak seemed to think so too, pushing himself up from the wall and stepping forward to cut off the flow.

"Before you launch yourself into that one again, allow me to introduce Chief Engineer Miles O'Brien, of the Starfleet Corps of Engineers. You might want to *try* to give a good impression. . . ."

Ghemor gave Garak a half-smile that combined more than mild irritation with something that Miles suspected might be verging on affection. Then he turned to Miles, and offered his hand. Miles took it. Ghemor's grip was resolute; Miles returned it, and managed not to recoil at the sensation of the scales of the other man's skin. *Friend,* Miles told himself firmly, *not foe.* Ghemor did look genuinely pleased to be meeting him. And, this close, he looked even more determined—and even more tired.

"Welcome to the capital, Chief O'Brien—"

"Miles, please."

"Miles." Ghemor nodded in acknowledgment of the courtesy, and then waved a hand toward a chair, and took his own seat. "I appreciate your coming all this way. Is there anything you'd like? I myself thought it was a . . . *dry* session this morning, and I can't think hearing all that scientific data again can have been fascinating for you."

"Wouldn't say no to a coffee," Miles said, with a grin, settling back into the chair. Straightaway, without being prompted, Jartek pressed a button on the com on the desk, and murmured a few instructions. Then he sat down, on Ghemor's left, regarding Miles from beneath heavy-lidded eyes. Garak remained standing— Miles could just see him out of the corner of his eye. He had returned to his place by the wall, folding his arms and with his head leaning back. Something seemed to be amusing him, or why else would he have that slight smile? Miles watched Jartek look over at Garak, frown, and then lick his lips. For a split second, he was thoroughly and overpoweringly reptilian. Miles shuddered. *A pit of vipers,* he thought.

He pulled himself together.

"Does Entor regularly break up sessions in that way?" he asked.

Ghemor did not try to conceal his frustration. "Too damned often."

"He's not subtle, but he does seem to be effective."

"Were I a different man, and this a different time, I'd trump up treason charges and have him executed," Ghemor said bluntly.

Just beside him, Miles felt Garak shift forward slightly. Jartek's pale eyes were on him in an instant.

I'm guessing Ghemor doesn't know about my brush with Car-

dassian law. I'd like to know how Garak knows. Actually—no, I wouldn't.

"Different place now, Cardassia," Miles said, equably. Garak leaned back. Jartek uncoiled a little. "Or so they tell me. This is a democracy now." He quirked up an eyebrow at Ghemor.

Who threw his head back and laughed. "So they tell me, too!"

You know, I think I actually like *this man.*

Ghemor seemed more relaxed now, and was looking at Miles as if he had also decided that this was a man he could do business with.

"Let's get down to it, Miles," he said, putting his elbows on the desk, and leaning forward. "I'm hoping you're here to tell me that the S.C.E.'s recommendation is that we fund Andak over Setekh. My secret dread in the dark watches of the night is that Starfleet has suddenly had a change of heart."

"Then rest easy," Miles replied. "There's no way we'd support any resources going to the work being done at Setekh." He hesitated, and then went ahead and broached the matter uppermost in his own mind. "You're aware, aren't you, that the technologies being developed there have military applications?"

Ghemor curled his lip. "That is, I think, perhaps the worst-kept secret on Cardassia Prime at the moment. Yes, I've read Remar's secondary report—so's everyone on the committee. Half the damned capital knows the contents of it, although it's supposed to be classified. Which means, so far as I can tell, that so long as it's not reported in the press, everyone can *talk* about it to their hearts' content."

"Ah, those are the perils of freedom of speech, unfortunately," Miles said. "Do you know who leaked it?"

Ghemor looked over at Jartek.

"We've got a very good idea," the younger man said, "but no proof. An aide to one of the Directorate representatives on the committee."

"For all their dislike of it, the Directorate seem to be remarkably competent when it comes to the democratic process," Ghemor said. "Or remarkably competent in subverting it, at any rate. And even if the committee votes in favor of Andak, you can see, I assume, where the Directorate will go afterward?" He gave a short laugh. "Give them their due, they've played this one very

well. It's a no-win situation for Ghemor and his government—
leaned on by the Federation and other aliens, blocking a project
which, as everyone knows, had certain . . ." He waved a hand.
" . . . *ancillary* benefits—"

Miles looked at him in disbelief. "Who the hell in their right
minds wants to see Cardassia armed to the teeth again right
now?"

"That could be considered something of a Federation perspective . . ." Garak murmured.

"Whole bloody quadrant more like!"

"A fair point," Garak conceded, "and one I'll grant you. But
you have to look at it from the ground here on Cardassia. There's
the military—dispossessed, more than a little disgruntled. But
most of all . . ." He shook his head. "Democracy is slow, Chief,
and sick and hungry people are not so patient."

"There's a great deal of will for change, Miles," Ghemor said
quietly, "but there's also a great deal of fear. These are delicate
times. Dangerous, too. The word 'security' has a lot of potency."

"And what does a democrat do," added Garak, "when the popular will is not for democracy, or the people don't care enough
about democracy to protect it?"

"When did you take up philosophizing?" Miles said, twisting
his head to get a proper look at him.

"Exile," Garak replied dryly, "not only broadens your hori-
zons, it also gives you time to think."

There was a silence, broken only when the door opened and
an aide came in bearing a tray of drinks. They all feigned ease.
The aide set the tray on the desk and left. Ghemor pushed Miles's
cup toward him and began to pour from a pot. Miles caught the
distinctive tang of redleaf tea. Garak came and took a cup and
then withdrew to his station by the wall.

Miles stared at the window. Rain was beating down upon it,
heavier and heavier, and the morning was fighting a losing battle
against it, and against the pictures streaming from the
viewscreens. Jartek reached out, hit a control on the desk, and the
strip lights came up, bathing the room in mock-yellow. He sighed
as he did it—the first completely involuntary thing he'd done,
Miles thought, as he picked up his own cup. He sipped gratefully
at the hot coffee. On DS9, he had downed mug after mug of *rak-*

tajino, but since he had come to Cardassia, he seemed to crave instead the food and drink of home.

This time the coffee was strong enough and he felt it begin to push back some of the heaviness still lurking behind his eyes. All this weak artificial lighting was playing havoc with his head. God only knew how the Cardassians put up with it all the time.

Miles sighed. "What I have to make clear, Castellan," he said, "is that if the Andak Project is voted down, that sends a message that it doesn't have the support of the Cardassian government. And that won't be looked upon favorably by either Starfleet or the Federation."

The rain drummed on against the synthetics of the window.

"If I wish to look plausible as a democrat," Ghemor said at last, seeming to weigh each word carefully, "I cannot ride roughshod over the decision of the committee. Particularly the members of the Directorate."

Miles looked straight back at him, and didn't answer. He didn't have an answer. Which was why he wasn't a politician.

"The Federation makes for . . . an interesting ally." Ghemor said. "As I said before, it's a no-win situation for Ghemor and his government." He stared at the displays before him. The Federation news had switched over to a live feed from Andak, where Yevir was about to make a speech. "You know," he continued thoughtfully, tapping his thumbnail against the ridge on his chin, "if the committee does vote against Andak and the project is killed, I think I'll resign. Point of honor."

"That's the first I've heard of *this*!" Garak levered himself up from the wall and took a step forward, wielding his cup with menace. Jartek too looked like he had something to say, but Garak got in first. "Need I tell you *just* how bad an idea that is?"

Miles quickly hid his own alarm at the prospect. It would be chaos. Ghemor was the one holding the political scene in Cardassia together—and he was only just managing it. If Ghemor went down, the democratic reform would go with him. And what was there to replace them?

"Sometimes it seems like a very good idea," Ghemor replied softly.

"I can't imagine *any* circumstances under which that particular piece of insanity could seem a good idea," Garak persisted.

"During those dark watches of the night."

There was a pause.

"Keep it there," Garak advised, but his voice was almost kind, Miles thought.

Ghemor laughed ruefully. "Very well, Garak!" he said, tapping his fingers on the desk. "We'll strike that from the plan, then, shall we? No resignations on points of honor."

"*Better* idea," said Garak. They stared at each other for a moment longer, and then Ghemor smiled and shook his head, looked over at the display, and waved a hand.

"Turn the sound up will you, Mev," he said. "Looks like the vedek's going to start talking soon. Let's hear what he has to say for himself today."

9

Vedek Yevir was not, Keiko reflected, turning out at all as she had expected. The ogre responsible for Kira's Attainder was a tall but unassuming man who still seemed in many ways to be rather like the minor military officer he had once been.

I don't remember him from the station at all, Keiko thought, anxiously brushing from her face a stray piece of hair that had been picked up in the light breeze. *Which must say something about what he's like—well, what he* used *to be like.*

Because there was certainly something else to Yevir now. Keiko would not have forgotten *this* man if she had met him before.

The previous night, after Miles had set off for the capital (leaving their quarters *almost* tidy), Keiko had bitten the bullet and contacted Kira on Deep Space 9. Once they had caught up with each other, swapping news of the station and of the family, Keiko had got to the point of her call.

"You're going to be seeing pictures of me shaking hands with Vedek Yevir, Nerys," she admitted. "I'm sorry about that."

"Don't be, Keiko. The Prophets know, I've had to extend the hand of friendship often enough in the past to people I'd rather be strangling!"

They'd both laughed, and exchanged a few cheerfully grumbling and mutually sympathetic remarks about the way politics intruded on the real business of life. Then Kira had gone rather thoughtful.

"Yevir might not be what you expect," she said, biting her lip. *"I . . . don't know if the Prophets have touched him, but I do know that that's what he believes. And it shows—it comes through, Keiko. Whatever I might think of the man himself, I can't deny that."*

And she was right. It was as if there was some kind of light within Yevir, Keiko decided. Most of the time it was veiled, but when he was listening intently—and he did a lot of that, listening intently—something would flicker behind his eyes. It unnerved Keiko, but it also drew her to him. She thought she understood a little more now why this man had such a following, why he had once been favored to be the next kai. Like Kira, Keiko had no idea whether the wormhole aliens really were guiding Yevir on his path, but there was no doubt that the man had that self-belief, and that in itself was a powerful and attractive force. Like a moth to a flame.

It would be an awful lot easier if I could just detest him. . . .

The photographs and the formalities seemed to take an age. It was with relief that Keiko could finally introduce Yevir to Feric, and switch off her public smile, even if it was just for a few moments.

"Dr. Lakhat," Yevir said. He was softly spoken but his voice too had that same self-assurance, that same lack of doubt. "It is indeed a pleasure to meet you. I am always glad to meet more followers of the Oralian Way." And then he took the unusual step of reaching out his hand and placing it upon Feric's ear, as if to judge or embrace the Cardassian's *pagh.*

A ripple of murmuring behind her made Keiko once again conscious of the reporters nearby. They were lapping up this little display of cross-cultural unity.

Feric bowed his head slightly, granting Yevir full permission to give the blessing. "Welcome to Andak, Vedek Yevir. It's an honor to meet the man who has placed so much faith in my own faith."

Yevir smiled. "I could not be here on Cardassia were it not for the Oralian Way. And Cleric Ekosha's willingness to take upon herself the mission to Bajor was the act of a brave woman. One with vision."

Ekosha, Keiko remembered—the kind of woman whose faith

might bring peace where the politicians had failed. An uncomfortable thought came to her. *Doesn't the vedek have the same kind of faith? Might he be the same kind of man? Feric seems to think so. . . .* Unsure where to put the thought, Keiko turned back to Feric, hoping her face did not betray her.

"I went to a gathering led by Ekosha once when she was still here on Cardassia Prime," Feric said. "She was remarkable. She's a fine ambassador, not just for the Way, but for all of my people. As you are for yours, Vedek."

Yevir bowed his head in acknowledgment and, the friendship established, he turned back to Keiko, folding his hands before him. "Director," he said, "I would be honored to learn more about the work you are doing here at Andak."

"And I'd be delighted to show you, Vedek," she said, loud enough for the reporters to catch her. "Please, step this way, and I'll tell you a little bit more about the project and about the settlement."

As they moved off, the crowd of staff members and their families that had been assembled for Yevir's arrival dispersed. A handful of them were going back to their posts, but most headed toward the lecture hall on the north side of the square. Yevir, Keiko, and Feric would join them there a little later—Yevir was going to give a speech to the whole community after his short tour of the base. There was to be a reception afterward. . . . All in all, Yevir was taking a fair amount of time out of his schedule to see Andak.

I'd better not waste this opportunity then. I want everyone to see just how important the work is that we're doing here. Just how much it matters to Cardassia.

A breath of wind was coming down from the mountains, easing the heat of the day, following them as they walked southward across the square.

"I noticed," Yevir remarked, "how many children there are here."

"That's right," said Keiko, nodding. "Andak isn't just a scientific project, Vedek. We're a long way from anywhere out here, and so the scientists and the technicians on the team brought their families out with them."

Or what's left of their families. Keiko left it unsaid. Feric knew it well enough, and Yevir too was a survivor of an occupation. They both knew the cost of war, better than Keiko did.

"And so we're trying to build a community here as well," she concluded. "There's a school, for example—" She gestured to her right, over to the west.

"And Keiko," Feric interjected dryly, "having once experienced life as a teacher, is very eager for us all to be tested in the same way."

Yevir smiled. "You're to be applauded, Director. That kind of work is as difficult and as valuable in its own way as the scientific project you are carrying out."

Keiko nodded her thanks. She glanced back over her shoulder and saw that only a handful of the press was following them—most had gone to set up in the lecture hall.

"What I want to show you first, Vedek," she said, "is the very heart of the work that we're doing at Andak." She pointed ahead, south, toward a long, low gray building that ran the length of the square. "That houses the equipment that we use to measure and intervene in precipitation levels here."

"That is the heart of Andak?" Yevir asked.

"Almost—but not quite." She smiled in anticipation. "That lies just the other side."

She led him past the long laboratory building, to a low fence. There she stopped and pointed out across the plain. "This is what Andak is about, Vedek," she said.

He looked out over the fields, shielding his eyes from the glare of the white sun. The lands ahead were yellow and barren, and the soil was poor and dusty. Anything here would be scratching a living, and barely surviving. He turned to Keiko, his face puzzled.

"If our work goes according to plan," said Keiko, "then you should come back here in two years' time. Because then that plain will be green."

"Can you feel the breeze upon your back, Vedek?" Feric said softly. "The mountains at Andak, and the shape of the valley and the plains, produce some unusual atmospheric effects. Effects that we're hoping to be able to harness, and then to replicate."

"Preliminary work on increasing precipitation levels has been extremely encouraging," Keiko said.

Did Yevir understand? Could he glimpse a little of the vision that Keiko had, that Feric had—that all of them at Andak shared, whatever their other differences?

When Yevir spoke again, it was slowly. He had clasped his hands before him once again. "I . . . *believe* that I understand what you are telling me, Director O'Brien, and I have to marvel at it." He looked up at the sky, which was vast and bright and empty, but behind them was the ever-present shadow of the mountains. "Here, in the desert, where there is only sun and stone, where there is no water—you're going to make it rain." He looked sharply at Keiko, and the light flickered again behind his eyes, like the shards of black glass that sometimes gleamed on the mountains of Andak.

"That's right," said Keiko. "And I'm sure you can see what the benefits are for Cardassia. If the work we do here is successful, we'll have taken a major step toward making the planet agriculturally self-sufficient. These few fields here," she gestured out to the enclosures beyond, "may look bare now, and it's true that they won't be able to provide enough of a harvest to sustain the whole of Cardassia. But if we can expand our work—not just here, but elsewhere on the planet, at other places where the population is too great and people are struggling to subsist on poor land—then this could be a long-term solution to what, historically, has been Cardassia's greatest lack. The lack that drove them to invade—and occupy—other, more fertile worlds."

Yevir raised his eyebrows. "So you are looking to address a *social* problem, not just an agricultural problem."

"It's not just that," Feric said quietly. "For some of us, this is about cultural change. Cultural regeneration. A commitment to a new way for Cardassia."

Yevir stopped and looked all around him, at the dry yellow fields and the bare black mountains; looked back toward the dusty square and the fragile settlement clustered around it.

"Only the Federation," he said at last, "would conceive of a project on this scale. Cardassia lacked water and so became an aggressor? Then the Federation will bring them water, and with it peace." He looked at Keiko thoughtfully. "I do not know much about Earth and its philosophies, Director, but one word, one idea, comes to mind now. *Hubris.*"

"Excessive pride and ambition," said Keiko, squaring her chin and looking straight back at him.

"When mortals try to take on the aspect of gods," Yevir said, and then he smiled at her, and his mood lightened. "Do you see yourself as a miracle worker, Director O'Brien?"

She laughed and shook her head. "Hardly! This is a scientific and technical project, Vedek," she said firmly. "We've defined a problem, and we're designing and implementing solutions for it. That's all that we're doing."

"Although your solutions could well have extraordinary effects—"

"Well, I certainly hope so!" Keiko said, and then laughed again. "It's a big team to put together to achieve something small!"

She gestured to him to follow her, and they went back alongside the laboratory. The wind was on their faces now, still no more than a whisper, but enough to make the heat endurable.

Yevir listened closely—intently—as they walked back along the square and Keiko pointed out the offices, the accommodation blocks with their hopeful green, the smaller labs on the north side; but as she spoke she watched him, and she could see how his mind was turning over what she had told him.

When they reached the entrance to the lecture hall, the other members of the senior staff were there to meet them. The little group of reporters that had been following them lined up nearby as Keiko made the introductions. A tall and graceful woman stepped forward first.

"Vedek Yevir, this is Professor Tela Maleren. She was formerly principal of the Cardassian Science Academy and now heads our team of physicists. She is one of the most eminent scientists in the quadrant, and we are very glad to have her here at Andak."

"Professor," Yevir said, bowing his head in greeting. "It is an honor to meet you. May I ask what the phrase on your badge means?"

With rising alarm, Keiko took a proper look at Tela.

Sure enough, the woman was wearing a small badge. In clear white Cardassian characters upon a black background were the words *Protect What Remains*. Keiko glanced around the rest of the senior staff. Two others were wearing the same badge. Beside her, Keiko heard Feric let out a soft sigh of exasperation.

"Thank you for asking, Vedek Yevir, and I hope that your visit here to Andak is proving an informative one," Tela replied. Her tone, Keiko noticed, was one that she used when addressing meetings—well modulated, carrying. Once again, Keiko became very aware of the reporters gathered round. A young Bajoran woman was signaling to the man with her wearing a camera headset to move in closer.

"These badges," Tela continued, "are a formal protest. They are intended to express the concerns of many at Andak that certain members of the community are permitted to worship in public here, while other individuals extend the courtesy of expressing their beliefs in private."

Keiko kept a bland, pleasant expression on her face and fumed inwardly. *So this is how you show your commitment to the project, Tela? I'd hate to see what you'd do if you were against it!*

"When you speak about worship, am I right in thinking that you are referring to the Oralian Way?" Yevir asked.

"That's correct, Vedek. A public gathering of the Way was held here at Andak yesterday. I would like to see this prevented from happening in future."

"Cardassia is now governed according to democratic principles, Professor. Why should these people not be free to express their beliefs publicly?"

"I don't think," Keiko said, with a slight edge to her voice, "that this is either the time or the place for this discussion—"

Yevir raised a hand—politely, but to stop her speaking nevertheless. The cameras remained fixed on them. "On the contrary, Director—I would very much like to hear more about Professor Maleren's worries. Professor," he said, addressing Tela directly once again, "I believe I understand now the nature of your protest, but," he pointed at her badge, "I do not understand what you mean by this. *Protect What Remains?* Do you truly see the Oralian Way as such a threat?"

Tela's glance for a moment passed over Feric. "When something has been weakened, it's easy to damage it beyond all repair."

"But the Oralian Way seeks to restore to Cardassia a past that had been lost. A history that had been forgotten. It too wishes to protect what remains—*all* that remains." Yevir's voice was soft. "Are you not being inconsistent, Professor?" He left the gentle accusation in the air for a moment, and then carried on. "Change *is* inevitable."

A wave of sorrow passed over Tela's face. "If I thought otherwise, I would not be here at Andak. But not all change is for the best." A wisp of hair had come adrift from the intricate styling, and she brushed it away. Again, Keiko noticed the threads of gray among the black.

"Vedek Yevir," Tela said sadly, "there is so little remaining of Cardassia, and I fear that what there is might be lost. I would ask you, please—respect what we have left and return to Bajor. Let us find our own peace, among ourselves."

Keiko stepped forward. It hadn't, thankfully, turned into the scene that she'd been dreading, but it was time now to put a stop to it. "People will be waiting, Vedek," she said, gesturing past Tela.

Yevir nodded, and then looked once again at Tela. "Perhaps we might finish our discussion later, Professor?"

Tela inclined her head. Gently, but firmly, Keiko guided Yevir onward, out of the Cardassian sunlight, and into the cool, modulated air of the lecture hall.

10

Garak leaned a shoulder against the wall at the back of Ghemor's office, watched the broadcast from Andak, and turned over in his mind the state of play on the *kotra* board on which he now found himself.

He felt—not for the first time in recent months—a certain frustration at the disordered and protracted way in which the game had to be played these days. Far too many of the pieces were beyond his control for his liking. Worse—*far* too many of them seemed to be moving according to their own will. He glanced quickly and surreptitiously about the room. Ghemor, Jartek, and O'Brien were all engrossed in the broadcast from Andak.

And you're only as good as the pieces you have left. . . .

Keeping half an eye on the display screen, he reached out and picked up a stylus from Ghemor's desk, and began toying with it absently, twisting it between his fingers.

"There's Keiko again!" O'Brien said, not quite managing to keep the pride and excitement out of his voice. Really, O'Brien could be almost endearing at times.

And yet he had also, in the past, showed not inconsiderable skill as a *kotra* player himself. Garak tapped the stylus impatiently against the palm of his hand. Whatever its manifold charms, the Federation was hardly lining up to fall in with Garak's priorities—not that that came as much of a surprise to him. In Garak's extended and not always entirely enthusiastic experience, the Federation seemed to specialize in saying one thing and doing another. One might almost call it their Prime Directive. Yes, it might give them something of a predictable quality—but that was not *quite* the same as being dependable. And while Garak would be the first to agree that he was hardly in a position to reprimand the Federation for showing a certain . . . *elasticity* toward truth—indeed, while trapped on Deep Space 9 he had yearned for at least one of those earnest Starfleet officers to show just a little glimmer of corruptibility—still, right at this point, he would have liked to have counted on the Federation's unequivocal support for Ghemor. It would be infinitely preferable to their current offering of sympathetic noises combined with lofty disinterest.

Garak looked thoughtfully across at the broadcast. Yevir—now, *that* was someone moving at will around the board. And with plenty of others moving around in his wake. Garak tapped the stylus against his lips. It was exasperating how the peace process had lost its political momentum, how it had become solely the province of Yevir and Ekosha and their followings. What Garak wanted—what he would *like,* if everyone would just have the common courtesy to arrange themselves precisely as he wished—would be to find or, failing that, to engineer some point of connection between the two, between Yevir and Ghemor.

Is there any *way that they could be brought together?*

He turned the pen again between his fingers, and then sighed to himself. It was a fantasy, of course, and Garak had long since learned not to indulge himself in those. Ghemor was too far out already—he was perceived as too reliant on the Federation, and he was certainly too compromised by the need to juggle all the demands of the domestic political scene. Reaching out a hand in friendship to the Bajoran religious leader would only increase rather than lessen Ghemor's growing reputation for weakness. And there was no gain for Yevir from courting the castellan, not that Garak could see. Not when Yevir was doing so well all by himself. . . .

On the screen, the vedek was speaking with quiet fervor about the work being done at Andak, praising the team and its leadership, and the willingness shown by so many people there, from such different perspectives, to work together for the good of Cardassia. Give him his due, Yevir's speeches always conveyed his conviction.

"There is one thing you can say for him," Jartek said. "He knows how to please a crowd. And all without sounding the least bit false."

"Yes, but, you know," complained Ghemor, "if *I* could make speeches like this, instead of ones about which agricultural reclamation technology has garnered my support, I think *my* popularity would rise markedly."

O'Brien grunted. "Well, *some* people get excited about technology," he muttered.

"And anything can be turned into a vote winner," Jartek said, with confidence.

Garak—safely hidden away at the back of the room—looked at him with loathing, but stopped short of baring his teeth. Jartek seemed to awaken his hitherto unsuspected inner Klingon, and Garak had quite enough on his mind at the moment without learning to embrace *that*. . . .

Covertly, anxiously, he took a good look at Ghemor, and he worried to see the stress lines that were more and more deeply engrained on his face, fretted again at how much the man had aged in only the past few months. Ghemor's threat to resign had frightened Garak—plain and simple. Part of his motivation for saying it, Garak knew, had been for O'Brien's ears, to send a message back that the castellan would appreciate a little leeway from his Federation allies, a little room to maneuver. But on some level, Garak was sure, Ghemor had meant it. On some level, Garak didn't really blame him. But if Ghemor went, who could replace him?

The fact of the matter—whatever others might wish—was that there *was* no one else. No one else with the determination, no one else with the will. Or, to put it another way, no one else mad enough to push themselves forward as the focal point for all the griefs and the grievances that currently beleaguered Cardassia. Once again, as he did from time to time, Garak thought of Damar; once again he regretted him. And then he suppressed the thought as quickly as he could. Another fantasy. Garak had accumulated many regrets over the years, and not one of them had ever helped him in a crisis.

No, there was no real candidate to replace Ghemor. And so *that,* Garak decided unilaterally, was not an acceptable outcome to this game.

At least he has some allies. . . .

Garak's eye fell again upon Jartek. He felt a moment's uncertainty, and then a contemptuous smile curled across his lips. Whatever Jartek might tell himself in those long silences of the night, he was not and never would be a match for Garak. Not with that neckline.

Anyway, there were other, more troubling competitors around, and those were far more deserving of Garak's attention than Jartek . . . Entor, for one. Now, he really *was* a threat. And an increasingly confident one, if Garak's instincts were to be trusted—and they were, after all, the only instincts that he *did* trust. Entor's little scene this morning had been one in a long line, but it had been so blatant, so outrageous . . . Entor didn't think he could lose this battle, Garak realized, with a sinking heart. Entor was convinced that the Andak Project's days were numbered. Garak pressed the metal of the stylus against his cheek. It was cold. His hands had not warmed it.

You're so very sure of yourself, Entor. You know something that I don't know—and I do rather tend to take exception to that. It really is not courteous of you at all.

Back on the screen, Yevir was talking about his mission to Cardassia, about his hope that, between them, the Cardassians and the Bajorans could find a lasting peace. About how glad he was that the Oralian Way had been willing to take the first step with him toward that peace.

Ways and means, Garak thought, his attention wandering away from the transmission. *It's all about ways and means.* He drummed the pen against the palm of his hand again, thought about his frustration, about the way he felt the pieces were lining up against him. . . .

If you don't like the rules—there's really only one answer. So what's the plan, Garak?

He frowned for a second, and then allowed himself a small smile. After all, he loved a good game of *kotra*—and he really hated losing.

The plan? I don't know yet—but when I've got one, I guarantee you, it will be the work of a master.

He flipped the stylus up in the air with his left hand, caught it expertly in the right, and turned back to the broadcast.

People, he observed, were careless in their use of color. The crowd was like oil on water, a heliotrope ripple round the bright orange of the vedek's robes, swelling and breaking with his oratory. He allowed his mind to fall in with the pattern of the words.

And then everything went black.

Ghemor swore under his breath. "How," he said, looking up beseechingly to the heavens, "am I supposed to run a government when the damned *power* keeps cutting out!" His voice had risen too.

O'Brien had gone over to the screen and was trying the time-honored engineer's technique of thumping it hard. "And there was I thinking government *was* the source of power," he said dryly.

Ghemor growled. "I think you'll find that the People have something to say on that score."

Jartek tipped his head.

"The lights are still on," Garak said flatly. Everyone turned to look at him.

"What?" said O'Brien, puzzled, his brow furrowing.

Garak jabbed the stylus upward at the yellow strips on the ceiling. "The lights are still on. And look at the display." He pointed toward it with the pen, at the control panel on it, which was flickering away, calmly and unperturbed. "This isn't a power cut. My guess is that someone's pulled the broadcast. Or is blocking it."

Garak gritted his teeth and felt the frustration rising up within him again.

There is someone else playing on this board. Someone I missed. Someone I know nothing *about. . . .* He threw the stylus onto the desk, bitterly.

Ghemor straightened himself up in his chair. O'Brien was still staring at Garak, his confusion beginning to turn into alarm. "Why would anyone—?"

And then the com on Ghemor's desk chimed, urgently.

"Everything appears to be going rather well."

Redleaf tea in an antique cup is passed from one hand to another.

"Would you say so? I take it you've read the report on what

happened at the committee meeting? After the official transcriptions ended?" A nervous gesture toward an untidy pile on the nearby desk. *"Jartek is pushing Entor very hard—perhaps too hard. I'm afraid he . . . he might be cracking. And then where will we be?"*

"Indeed . . . that could be a problem. . . ."

"He cannot be allowed to become careless. There's nothing to establish a direct link, of course?"

A crease is smoothed out of a stained but well-tailored suit. *"Of course not . . ."* Then the hand reaches out and picks up a book resting on the arm of the chair—a battered volume of stories by Shoggoth. *"Another of your finds? This one has certainly been through the wars. . . ."*

"You like enigma tales?"

The book is set back down.

"Do you know, I always found them rather tiresome."

Somehow Keiko managed to keep the smile going, but inwardly she was still fuming as she accompanied Yevir through the lecture hall, past the crowd assembled there, and toward the dais at the far end. He himself was quiet and contemplative as he walked alongside her, hands folded before him, completely unreadable. She wondered what he had made of Tela's appeal, wondered if it had altered his perception of the project—wondered if it would make him change the content of his speech. . . .

Of all the times for Tela to pick to let us know she'd seen the blinding flash of light and converted to democracy! And I could hardly stop her from giving her opinion, now, could I? But couldn't she have waited until later—perhaps spoken to Yevir at the reception? Couldn't she have just waited until there weren't any reporters around, hanging on every freely expressed word . . . !

Keiko sighed. If she was being brutally honest with herself, what she was angriest about was that she had missed it. Tela had given her a warning—in a typically elusive, Cardassian fashion, yes, but a warning just the same—and Keiko had not heard it.

I should have guessed something like this might happen. I admit it—I misread her. I thought we'd come to some kind of understanding. . . . I thought she knew I was taking her concerns seriously. . . . Well, Tela, I'm taking you seriously now. Very seriously.

Walking just behind Keiko, to her left, was Feric. She glanced at him, quickly. Feric was good at presenting a calm face to the world, but Keiko saw that his eyes were slightly narrowed under their ridges, saw the tightness around the edges of his mouth, saw that his hands were clasped firmly behind his back. Keiko had gotten to know Feric well and there was no mistaking how he felt. He was angry. She gave him a small, encouraging smile, but he couldn't quite manage one back.

Keiko looked over her other shoulder. Next to Feric walked Tela. She too seemed outwardly unruffled, although she was fingering the badge that she was wearing, just as earlier in the day she had twisted her bracelet around and around.

Well, I hope you are *feeling unsure about what you just did.*

The four of them went up the steps and onto the dais, where four seats had been set out, just behind the lectern. Courteously, gracefully, and yet both moving with a great deal of purpose, Feric and Tela put Yevir between them. It was, Keiko thought, a very Cardassian maneuver. At least they had that in common.

Keiko went up to the stand to introduce their guest to the community at large, keyed up the notes for her little speech on her padd, and then looked out across the hall. The two rows nearest the front were filled with the children from the school, and she caught sight of Molly among them, sitting on her hands, rocking back and forth a little, excited to see her mother up on the stage. She gave her a quick grin in return. Behind the schoolkids, almost the whole of the team from Andak was assembled—the scientists, the technicians, all the support staff—mostly Cardassian, but with Federation people here and there among the rest. Naithe was sitting at the end of one row, near the aisle, chattering away at one of the young Cardassian engineers who was looking slightly frayed by the Bolian's attentions. There were even one or two Bajorans here and there—an agricultural specialist from Keiko's own team; a physicist that Tela had appointed . . . Even Tela, Keiko thought, had picked the best people for the job, regardless of their backgrounds.

It was, Keiko realized with a rush of excitement, the first time she had seen all of the team gathered together at once. And this picture before her was so much what she had hoped for, so much as if her dreams for a community had come real, that Keiko forgot Tela, forgot the press lining the sides of the hall, forgot all of her worries, and remembered to be proud once again of all that was being done—of all that there was to be achieved—at Andak. She smiled at her team gladly, a smile that would make her husband—half a continent away—exclaim with barely concealed pride at the sight of it. And then she set her padd aside and spoke from the heart.

"I don't need to tell all of you how important today is for Andak. I know I don't need to tell you, because in the past few days you've all shown—with all your help, all your support—just how much you understand what today means to the project, to the community. You've all shown me how proud you are of the work we're doing here, how you want the whole of Cardassia, and beyond, to understand the significance of our project. To understand that what we're doing—and how we're working together to achieve it—can stand for Cardassia's future in the quadrant."

She paused. The first rush of adrenaline that she always got from speaking in public was leaving her, and she felt a surge of nerves in the pit of her stomach. But when she looked round the hall, people were smiling up at her, encouraging her.

"When Vedek Yevir first approached me to come and visit Andak, I knew at once that he, of all people on Cardassia today, had to come here to learn more about our work and our community. Because Vedek Yevir, too, has the future of Cardassia at heart. I knew that he would understand all that this project is about, all that it means for Cardassia and, so, the rest of the quadrant. I'm very glad that so many of us—Cardassian, Bajoran, human—have been able to come here to Andak. I'm very glad too that the vedek has come today, to meet us, and to speak to us, so that we can all learn from each other how we can build Cardassia's future. Please, all of you, join me in welcoming him here to Andak."

She stepped back from the lectern and began to clap, and the rest of the gathering followed suit. Yevir took his place at the stand, but it was a minute or two before the room went quiet enough for him to begin speaking. Keiko didn't hear much of what he said at first. Still nervous from having given her own speech, she took in a deep breath and sat down. Feric, sitting next to her, leaned in and whispered, "Nice speech, Keiko. I hope he appreciates you warming up the audience for him."

I hope he does too—and forgets about all that nonsense with Tela.

She began to listen.

"—cannot praise highly enough the principles behind the work being done at Andak—"

She heaved a sigh of relief. It looked like he was going to stay on script, and leave any discussion of Tela's intervention until a more private moment.

"—in particular the direction being given by Professor O'Brien—"

The applause from the audience that met this touched Keiko much more than Yevir's words, grateful though she was for them.

Well, it's always nice to be appreciated! And nice to know I'm doing something *right!*

"—the willingness of all of you here, from so many different backgrounds and persuasions, to work together for the good of Cardassia, and the vision that you all share for the future of this planet—"

Keiko began to relax. Yevir was a good speaker—and all of this praise was very timely for the project. . . .

"Because," Yevir continued, "as I have seen and learned from my visit here today, projects like this one represent not just the physical but also the *spiritual* regeneration of Cardassia . . ."

In the capital, Mev Jartek too was admiring Yevir's style, and wishing to himself that he could persuade Ghemor to be perhaps a *little* more crowd-pleasing, perhaps a *little* less hard-hitting. . . .

"—it has been a great inspiration to find that you all share so much in common with my *own* vision, my *own* mission to Cardassia." Yevir paused, and looked around the hall. "When I came here to Cardassia, it was in the hope that—between us—we Bajorans," he pressed his hands against his heart, "and you Cardassians," he gestured around the hall, "could finally find the way toward peace between us. I was most glad that the Oralian Way," he nodded at Feric, "was willing to take the first steps with me toward that peace."

Well, Keiko thought, *that was a pretty explicit demonstration of support for Feric. I'm going to enjoy hearing what Tela will have to say about that later. . . .*

Suddenly, Keiko noticed a Cardassian girl. She looked no

more than fourteen years old, and she was loosening the fastenings on her jacket. A little farther along the platform, Tela Maleren shifted forward and murmured, "Nyra?"

Half a continent away, in the capital, Elim Garak was staring at the colors on the screen, staring at them hard until their pattern shifted and they merged into one another. As is the case with nearly all so-called live broadcasts, there was a minute or two delay between event and transmission, between the motion and the act; and because of this he had not yet seen—when the screen went black—Nyra Maleren walking steadily down the hall and up onto the stand. He had not cast an expert eye over the device that was strapped to her chest beneath her jacket. And neither was he there to confirm what Yevir Linjarin had said when he took a step back and muttered to Keiko O'Brien.

"Director, I believe that girl is carrying a bomb."

12

Miles watched as Ghemor cut the com channel. The castellan let his hand rest before him on the desk. He appeared to sit, simply staring down at it. One of his fingers was beating out a rapid tattoo. Miles couldn't tell if he was doing it voluntarily, but it was definitely making him edgy. *Edgier.* He sucked in a breath of air—hoping to calm himself down a bit—and then put the question that was uppermost in his mind.

"What in the *bloody blue blazes* is going *on* there?"

Ghemor looked up at him, his finger still tapping an erratic rhythm. "Miles," he said, "I'll be frank with you—it's not good news. I'm sorry. From what we're able to make out, it seems there's a siege situation unfolding in the lecture hall. Someone in there has a bomb, and is threatening to detonate it—"

Keiko . . . Molly . . . Yoshi . . .

Miles raised a hand to his forehead. That blasted headache had come back. The pulse of the fake light and the drum of the rain seemed to have started up a pounding against his temples. He felt a slight pressure against his back, and swung round to look. But it was only Garak, resting a hand upon his shoulder—just for a moment, and then he withdrew it.

"What do they want?" Miles said. His lips seemed a little numb. *Strange feeling,* he thought, as if from a distance.

"Well, it appears they have a whole series of demands," Ghemor answered. Miles watched distractedly as his finger tapped and tapped against the tabletop, "but I don't yet know in detail

what they are. Internal security are having trouble finding someone in authority to deal with down at Andak. There's a whole
bevy of reporters inside the hall but all the transmissions coming
out have been cut and it isn't really clear why—"

"Well," Jartek said, "at least that's a bit of good news."

Garak, standing next to Miles, shifted forward slightly.
"That's an odd remark," he said mildly. "Perhaps you might like
to elaborate on it?"

Now, that's not a good tone of voice, Miles thought absently,
his hand still pressed against his forehead, trying to sift some
sense from everything going on around him.

"What I *mean*, Garak," Jartek said, and now he didn't dis-
guise his irritation, "is that while the situation isn't under our
control, at least *that* isn't being broadcast across the whole of the
quadrant. We've got time to find out what's going on, time to *get*
things under control, sort out a proportional response, and get the
message out that Alon deals promptly and effectively with
threats like this. *That's* what needs to be done."

"Is that right?" Garak said. He was smiling now, just a little.

That isn't good either. . . . Miles closed his eyes.

"Garak—" Ghemor said, the warning clear.

"There are *political* implications to all of this, Garak," Jartek
shot back, "whether you like it or not. If this all blows up in our
faces, it'll be a disaster for this government. And *someone* has to
be thinking ahead to what capital we can make out of it—"

Miles felt a cold stab of fury slice its way through the haze in
his head. His eyes shot open. The next thing he knew he had one
hand around Jartek's throat, and the other was pulling back to
thump the little snake all the way to Andak.

"Mr. O'Brien." Ghemor's voice rose—and Miles suddenly had
more than a glimpse of why it was that Ghemor was in charge. "I
feel I ought to remind you that Mev is the chief political advisor
to the Cardassian castellan. And since you're the Federation's representative here—I don't think you really want to do that."

"Let him go, Chief," Garak murmured. "He's not worth it. It's
not a . . . proportional response."

"You're not helping, Garak," Ghemor said sharply.

Miles stared at Jartek—at the ridges on his face, at the strange
and alien skin—and loathed him, and all of Cardassia with him.

*We shouldn't have come here. This place and its damn people
turn on you and* bite. *It really is just a pit of bloody vipers. We*
shouldn't *have put our kids in the middle of this!*

Jartek was staring back at him, eyes wide, mouth open. His
tongue slid nervously around his teeth and his lips. Miles shuddered in distaste.

"Mr. O'Brien," Ghemor said again.

Keiko always said I'd make a terrible diplomat. . . .

Out of the corner of his eye, Miles could see that Ghemor had
risen from his chair. And that Garak had taken one preparatory
step forward.

Keiko. . . .

"Bloody *hell!*" Miles said, and let Jartek go. The young man
pulled back quickly, jerking up a hand to rub at his neck. Bluish
bruises were already appearing against the gray of his skin.

"Well," said Ghemor, letting out a slightly ragged sigh, and
sitting back down in his chair, "that's *one* crisis resolved, at least.
Mev," he said, more calmly, and glancing over at his aide,
"you've said some helpful things—thank you. I'll be bearing in
mind everything you've drawn to my attention. But why don't
you . . . why don't you go and have a chat with security and find
out how soon they think they can raise someone at Andak for me
talk to? I really need to know exactly what's going on down
there, and I need to know quickly."

Jartek hesitated, and Ghemor nodded toward the door. Jartek
slid out, giving both Miles and Garak as wide a berth as he could.
As the door shut after him, Miles turned to Ghemor.

"I'm sorry," he said, sitting down heavily, "I shouldn't have
lost my temper. Don't know what came over me—"

Ghemor waved a hand to stop him. "Well, I do. Mev's sharp
and he gets done what needs to be done—but he can be a bit
single-minded. And—as a result—he does sometimes lack tact."

Garak snorted. Ghemor glared at him. "He also doesn't know
when to *shut up*," he added, pointedly.

Garak raised his hands, accepting the admonishment. "Can I
say this at least? You need to get someone down there to Andak
as soon as possible. Someone you trust—"

"Offering your services, Garak?"

"Well, I'm most flattered to learn that you hold me in such

high esteem, but I *was* going to suggest Macet." Garak frowned. "Much as it pains me to say it, Mev does have a point—and whether or not it *seems* you can deal with this promptly and effectively, you do also *need* to deal with this promptly and effectively. I think Macet's the man to do it. He's experienced, and he's good in a crisis." Garak gave a wry smile. "He's also the military man least likely to score political points off you should he bring this to a satisfactory conclusion."

Ghemor eyed him for a moment, and then nodded, and opened up a com channel. "Get hold of Gul Macet for me, will you?"

The rush of adrenaline had passed, and Miles had listened to all this through the haze which had descended upon him once again.

Keiko . . . Molly . . . Yoshi . . .

He was dimly aware of Macet voice's coming through the com, was dimly aware of Ghemor ordering Macet out to Andak to resolve the situation. And then he became aware of a hand on his shoulder again. It was Garak, looking down at him, a concerned expression upon his face.

"Macet really is very competent, Chief," Garak said softly. "It's impossible to make any promises, but if anyone can end this safely, I'm sure it's him."

Miles nodded wordlessly.

"Might I make a suggestion?"

"What is it, Garak?"

"That you go back down to Andak with him? I hardly think that the committee will be reconvening this afternoon."

"Long way to come for nothing." Miles stood up, and then gave a short bark of laughter. "Well, we knew the project's future would be decided one way or another this afternoon. It's just all a bit more literal than we'd thought, isn't it?"

"I think you can leave that to us to worry about here."

"You know what the worst thing is? That there's nothing I can do. I just have to sit it out and watch and hope for the best." He paused. "These situations are very unstable, you know. Are you sure Macet would want me breathing down his neck? It's not as if I can do much there," he finished, bitterly.

"I'd beg to differ on that score. Not to put too fine a point on it, but almost all of the authorities on the Andak Project are stuck inside that lecture hall. You're about the only person *outside* with the requisite expertise. Macet's bound to find that useful."

"I'm just an engineer—"

Miles stopped speaking as the door opened and Jartek came back in. Jartek glanced across at Miles and Garak and then bypassed them and went straight over to Ghemor.

"You, Miles," Garak murmured, "are just an engineer in exactly the same way that I am just a tailor."

He stretched out his hand and offered it to Miles.

Miles shook it.

13

Keiko, trying her best not to move, felt a chill creep down her spine, and suppressed a shiver. Her shirt was sticking to her back, but the sweat was cold. *The temperature modulators must be set too low,* she thought—and then her heart clenched as she thought of Miles, his head stuck behind the panels of the wall, trying to put off working, trying to make their quarters cooler for her.

She looked over at Molly, a few rows from the front, sitting with all her classmates. Molly wasn't excited now—she was pale-faced and very still, with her arms wrapped around her. Keiko swallowed hard on the lump that had risen up all of a sudden in her throat and carefully, ever so carefully, risked giving Molly a slight smile. Molly didn't return it, just stared back at her mother with eyes gone wide and huge with fright.

Shock, Keiko thought. *I think she's in shock. Why on earth did we bring our children here?*

She looked fearfully along the row at the other schoolchildren, and then at the row in front of Molly, at the little ones. All of them school age, not as tiny as Yoshi (*Yoshi!*—and her heart clenched again), but small nonetheless. After Nyra had delivered her speech the first time, Keiko had seen the teachers whisper hurried instructions to their charges to keep very quiet and very still, and since they were mostly dutiful little Cardassians, they had all done exactly what they were told. All together, from the small ones up, there were twenty-three children of school age in this room.

Or twenty-four, if you counted Nyra Maleren.

Cautiously, as cautiously as she could manage, Keiko twisted her head so that she could look at Tela Maleren's daughter.

Nyra was standing at the far side of the dais from her. Her jacket was open, which meant that Keiko could see, that they could all see, a package strapped across Nyra's chest. It seemed so innocuous—it was almost like something you might use to play pass-the-parcel—except that when you looked more closely, you could see a steady, an ominous, pulse of red light.

She said it had to be triggered—but would she even know *if there was a countdown? She can't have made that herself— someone must have done it for her. . . .*

While the rest of the room watched her, Nyra herself was rocking slightly on her feet, back and forth, back and forth. Every so often she seemed to mumble something to herself. Her lips were parted and dry, her gaze darting around the hall.

Who could have put her up to this? She's just a child. . . .

Keiko's instinctive reaction, when Nyra had first come up onto the platform and set out her demands, had been to assume that Tela was behind all this somehow. Hadn't she already said much the same? That Yevir should leave Cardassia Prime? That she disapproved of the Oralian Way? It had not come as much of a surprise to hear the same sentiments coming from Nyra's lips. And then all of Keiko's angry preconceptions were blown away (she winced to herself slightly at that expression), because then Tela had tried to speak to her daughter—had asked her what she was doing, had begged to know why she was doing it. And Nyra—although she had not screamed, had not shrieked—had obviously, from her shaking, which had gotten worse as her mother murmured haltingly at her, been close to losing control. It had taken Yevir, of all people, sitting back in his chair next to Tela, to set his hand gently upon the woman's arm and whisper to her that it would be better if she stopped speaking. Keiko noticed that he had kept his hand in place for quite some time.

Tela had been silent since then, her head dropped low, her hair coming loose in long strands. She was all but motionless, save for one fingertip that had not stopped stroking, stroking, the red stone on the bracelet around her wrist.

And, against Nyra's chest, a red light flashed on and off, on and off.

Someone in the hall coughed, and hurriedly tried to smother the noise. Nyra started a little. Her hand clenched and raised, and then she dropped it. She ran her tongue over her lips, and then started speaking. She had quite a small voice (*because she's just a child* . . .), but tension was making it come out shrill and, in any case, the hall was so deadly silent that her words carried across it quite easily.

"I am here today," she said, staring out across the hall, concentrating hard on her words as she enunciated them with great care, "to speak out for the future of Cardassia. Because that future is in danger, and because no one will act to preserve it, *we* must act. Cardassia is being polluted by alien influence and alien ideas, all of which threaten to destroy what little remains of our own ideas, our own culture . . ."

Keiko shifted backward in her seat. It was the same speech Nyra had made twice already. It was clear she had learned it and rehearsed it many, many times.

"So this is a message for Alon Ghemor—who claims to be our leader, who *pretends* to be our leader—but who is really diluting us further and further, who is giving away all that we have left piece by broken piece—"

The little red light beat in time with the rhythm of her words. She was rubbing her thumb along the edge of the device on her chest, up and down, just like her mother, caressing the bracelet on her wrist.

"It is time for this to be stopped. It is time for us to become pure again. . . ."

Keiko felt Feric move in his seat until he was leaning close to her.

"What do you think is going on outside?" he muttered from the side of his mouth, watching Nyra closely as she carried on with her speech.

Keiko kept her eyes on Nyra too as she answered. "They'll have people here as soon as they can," she whispered. "I'm sure they'll try to start talking to Nyra soon; they'll try to talk her down. . . ." She stopped for a second, as Nyra glanced in their direction. When the girl looked out across the hall once again,

Keiko continued. "What we need to do in here is *nothing*—we just need to keep quiet. Most of all, we mustn't startle her. Let her keep on making this speech. As long as she's still talking, she's not blowing us all to little bits."

"How long," Feric said, from between his teeth, "do you think it'll take for them to get someone here? And who are 'they' anyway?"

"The police? The military?" she suggested. *Miles,* she hoped, and tried to put that thought out of her head. This was not the time to be thinking about herself—she was in charge here, with two hundred people looking up at her, two hundred people her responsibility. "And I know they'll be here as soon as they can, Feric," she murmured, hoping it sounded reassuring. "I know they'll be doing all they can."

If for no other reason than because Andak means so much.

"These, then, are our demands; this is what Ghemor's false and treacherous government must do. Firstly, we wish to see that government dissolved. It is the idea and the instrument of aliens—of Bajorans, of humans. It does not speak for any true Cardassians. It is not part of the Cardassian way. Second," and at this point she stared at Feric, who could not help but press back a little into his seat, "the Oralian Way claims to show the way back to our past. But true Cardassians are not taken in by their lies and superstitions. We want these people stopped; we want their practices forbidden. They are polluting our way of life." She stopped for a moment and frowned, as if struggling to remember the next part of the message. The red beat against her breast urgently. "Finally," she said, turning and pointing at Yevir, "all aliens," and then she gestured toward Keiko too, "must leave Cardassian soil. Cardassia must find its own, true way. They have come here pretending to offer us peace, but they've lied to us! All that they have to offer us is slavery!"

There was a bit more to come yet, Keiko remembered, the bit where Nyra explained about the bomb she was carrying.

But this time round, Nyra wasn't going to get there.

Keiko jerked up her head at the sound of a chair scraping across the floor.

Miles, she thought, always had the right words for any occasion. And Keiko had been married to Miles Edward O'Brien for a long time now.

What the bloody hell does he *think he's playing at?*

Because Naithe, sitting at the end of a row just by the aisle, had pushed back his seat, stood up, and now he was walking toward the front of the hall.

Nyra stopped speaking and froze to the spot. She stood staring at Naithe as if she couldn't comprehend what he was doing, as if she couldn't quite believe that he was doing it.

This isn't in her script, Keiko realized—which didn't make her feel any better. *If she feels threatened, she's going to trigger that bomb. . . . Oh, Naithe! I don't know what you think you can do, but you're way out of your league here! Sit down and shut up!*

"Now, my dear little lady," Naithe said, stretching out one of his hands, not looking anywhere near where Keiko was shaking her head at him, as frantically as she could without startling Nyra, "I think that you should listen to me. . . ."

14

The shimmer of the transporter haze diffused and the world all around Miles resolved itself. He blinked and shook his head, disoriented for a moment by the dissonance between the lowering skies of the capital and the sharp, stark light of Andak.

Strange how quick you get used to things....

And then he came into focus.

The base was like a ghost town, emptied of life. Only the mountains remained, patiently watching all that happened. During the days, the square was often quiet—the children were at school, the scientists were in the labs—but it never felt deserted as it did now. You could always hear, even if only faintly, the heartbeat of work and the pulse of conversation, you were always aware that life was going on in the little buildings gathered around the square. At night, people would be passing to and fro, and all the little houses to the east of the square were lit up and alive, and you could usually see a light on in one of the labs, as someone pressed on with their work in the early hours.

But this quiet was unnatural.

Beside him, Macet too was taking in their surroundings. He muttered something to his second-in-command, and then troops began to materialize in the square. Fifteen or twenty blocks of uniform and weaponry, solid black-and-gray in the bright light, shifting into action as soon as they arrived to deal with the equipment they'd brought with them. Miles eyed them cautiously. Armed Cardassians tended to make him a bit jumpy. Even looking at Macet only added to Miles's underlying sense of unease. Macet was just like Dukat—and yet completely unlike. The face was the same (well, near enough), but the voice and the bearing were markedly different. Friends who looked like foes. Cardassia turned things upside down.

Miles turned away from his confusion to look toward the lecture hall. Someone was hurrying across the square to join them. It was one of the handful of Starfleet personnel stationed at the base—Jack Emmett, a security officer, very young, very keen. He had a padd in one hand, and his other was twitching nervously around his phaser.

"Chief O'Brien," Emmett said, rather breathless. He was obviously very glad to see someone senior, but he was also looking at Miles with trepidation. Miles felt a stab of sympathy for him.

Poor lad. Can't feel good to let a siege happen on your watch.

"This is Gul Macet, Emmett," Miles told him. "He'll be taking charge here."

Emmett looked even more relieved at that.

Macet addressed Emmett directly, and skipped the formalities. "Can you give me a rundown of what's been happening?"

"Well," Emmett took a deep breath, "we were watching the vedek's speech on the monitors, and then she stood up from the back and started walking forward—we thought it was odd, you know, while the vedek was talking—but it *was* her mother up on the stage after all, so we thought that maybe it had something to do with that—"

"Her *mother*?" Miles said. *Molly?* he thought for a moment, thoroughly bewildered.

Emmett shook his head. "No, no—Tela Maleren's daughter, you know, Nyra. She's the one with the bomb."

"*What?*" Miles looked at him in disbelief. He'd been assuming it was one of the staff—one of the adults.

"Would someone explain the significance of that to me?" Macet said.

"Nyra's just a kid, Macet," Miles said. "She's . . . what, fourteen years old?"

Emmett nodded. "Something like that."

"Ah," Macet said. His hand went up to his chin, and he began slowly to smooth down his facial hair. "That could certainly complicate things. . . . Well, let's not worry about it for the moment. What happened next, Emmett?"

"Nyra went up onto the stage, starting talking, issuing all these demands, said there was a bomb." He swallowed. "There were just a couple of us out here—we didn't know what to do— the security chief's in there, and all those reporters . . . I knew there was a few minutes' delay on the broadcasts, and I figured if *that* started going out across Cardassia, it might mean panic, you know, wide-scale . . . so I pulled the transmissions." He looked at Macet nervously.

"Good move," Macet said. "Are you still getting anything from in there?"

"Yeah . . . there's one journalist, seems to have got herself and her colleague right up near the front, right near the stage—we're getting good pictures from them. We've been monitoring them from the security office—" He gestured to a building on one side of the square.

"I'll come and take a look at that in a minute," Macet said calmly. "What else has been happening?"

"Not much—she just keeps on making this speech . . . making these demands . . ."

"I see." Macet stared past Emmett toward the lecture hall. "First things first," he said at last. "Can we transport into the building?"

Emmett shook his head. "Nyra's told us that if anyone tries to use transporters, it will trigger the bomb."

Macet turned to Miles. "I've not heard that one before. Is that even possible?"

Miles nodded. "Easy enough to rig up a transmitter calibrated to work on the same frequencies. She wouldn't even need to activate it herself—it would all be automated."

"So we lose even the small window of opportunity we might have had between beaming in and her reacting to it. . . ." Macet tugged at his beard thoughtfully. "She could be bluffing about that, of course."

Miles raised an eyebrow. "You want to bet on it?"

"No."

"And even if she isn't," Miles pressed on, "there's some very sensitive bits of equipment in the labs right next door to the lecture hall. If you use the transporters too close to them, chances are you'll be destroying much of the first two months' work done here. And I'm guessing Ghemor has asked you to resolve all this *without* finishing off the project."

Macet gave him a shrewd, closed look. "Good guess," he said. "All right, transporters—regretfully—are not an option." He looked about him, taking in the square, the lecture hall, the land around. Sunlight hit the pure black of the mountains beyond and they shone back fiercely. Macet shaded his eyes and stood in thought for a moment. "So," he said, turning back to Miles and lowering his hand, "that leaves us with two other options. Either we get her to stand down by means of persuasion, or we get her to stand down by means of force."

"What—storm the building, you mean?"

"It's not a subtle response, but it would certainly resolve matters."

Miles sucked in a breath of air, pushed it out slowly. "What was that you said about a small window of opportunity? Bashing the doors down won't give you the same element of surprise as beaming in. Think you'll have enough time to stop her?"

"Well, that's the risk, isn't it? Of course—we'd have to vaporize that bomb completely, or . . ."

No need to be so damn casual about it!

"You're in command, Macet—but I *would* like to remind you that my family is in there—"

"Along with about two hundred other people. *None* of whom I wish to get killed—including this Nyra."

Miles stared down at the yellow dust of the ground, all at once very glad that he was just advising here. Macet would make the best decisions, he told himself—and the most objective decisions.

"All of which," Macet concluded, "means we should try talking to this girl first, I think. It's just possible she's regretting finding herself in this position, and that the offer of a way out might be exactly what she wants to hear."

It's also just possible, Miles thought, *that someone mad enough to strap a bomb to her chest is mad enough not to care whether she lives or dies—never mind whether anyone around her lives or dies—and that talking to her is a complete waste of time.*

But it really was their best option at the moment.

"Well, Emmett," said Macet, clasping his hands together, "how about you show us these transmissions you're getting from in there? And I wouldn't mind seeing the schematics of the hall as well—exits and entrances in particular."

They followed Emmett toward the security office. He was already punching up the plans of the hall on the padd he was carrying. He passed them over to Macet, who reviewed them silently as they walked along, and then Emmett took his chance to have a quiet word with Miles.

"The younger kids—they aren't in there, sir. They were all in the crèche. And when this all started we moved them all out as far from the hall as we could."

Miles closed his eyes for a moment. So Yoshi at least was safe. He mumbled gruff thanks to Emmett, patting the young man's arm gratefully.

When they reached the door to the security office, Macet handed the padd over to his second-in-command. "Get people stationed at each point of egress," he said. "I want them ready to go in." He looked at Miles. "You know this girl, yes?"

"Well, by name—"

"That's the closest thing I've got to an expert. So that'll do fine."

They went into the security office, Emmett close behind them. It was a small room with a few viewscreens to one side and a desk littered with the cartons and debris of a recently abandoned meal. Emmett cleared this away hastily, as well as the pack of cards dealt out across the desk. It looked to Miles that Emmett had been teaching someone how to play poker. Almost certainly, Miles thought, this had been the other young security officer in there, a Cardassian, sitting staring at the display. He glanced up anxiously, and took in straightaway the blunt authority of Macet's insignia. "I think this has just got serious, sir," he said.

Miles looked at the display and saw Naithe taking slow steps toward Nyra. The Bolian advanced with an indulgent, paternal smile. Nyra herself was sweating, her face becoming more flushed by the second.

"The bloody idiot, he's going to get everyone killed!"

"Emmett," Macet said, calm but firm, and stepping forward decisively, "can I speak to them?"

Emmett swallowed, nodded, and hit a few controls. "That should be working now," he murmured.

Macet leaned over the display.

"Nyra," he said.

On the screen, the girl jumped. Her hand jerked up.

"Wait, Nyra," Macet said.

It was a good thing that the instinct for obedience ran deep in the Cardassian nature, Miles thought, watching as Nyra's hand halted, although it was still trembling.

"Thank you, Nyra," Macet said. "Can I talk to you for a bit?"

The girl was looking round as if she couldn't work out how this voice was talking to her from nowhere. *She's losing it,* Miles thought, and folded his arms around himself.

"I'm outside the hall, Nyra, in the security office. Do you know where that is?"

Slowly, the girl nodded.

"Good, so you can picture me, in the security office?"

She nodded again.

"Good! Can I tell you my name, Nyra?" His voice was smooth, but not condescending. *Well judged,* Miles thought.

Nyra licked her lips. "*Okay . . .*" she whispered.

"Thank you, Nyra. I'm Akellen Macet. I'd like to talk to you, if that's all right with you."

Nyra touched her throat with her fingertips. Her expression sharpened under the ridges. "Why?" she said, her voice charged with suspicion.

"I've just arrived here at Andak, Nyra. I haven't heard what it is you want. Will you tell me?"

Nyra paused, her fingers playing around her throat, and then: "All right," she said.

As she began to speak, looking up, Macet closed off the channel, so they could hear Nyra but she could not hear them. "I think the castellan should be receiving all this," he murmured, still focused on the display. Someone in the hall, taking advantage of the fact that Macet's intervention had distracted Nyra, had had the presence of mind to grab Naithe and make him sit down.

"Emmett—sort that out for us, will you?" The young man nodded, and set to work.

Macet glanced at Miles, wiped his hand across his mouth, and looked back at the display.

"Well," he said, taking a deep breath, "at least she's talking to us now."

15

"Stalemate," Ghemor said bitterly. He rubbed at his eyes with his fingertips, and finally brought his head to rest on his hand. Quietly, almost unnoticed, Jartek refreshed the contents of the cup on his desk. The infusion allowed little curls of steam to escape into the still air and perish.

Garak appraised Ghemor with the cool, calculating eye of the expert observer. He measured the extent of Ghemor's fatigue against the likely duration (and outcome) of the crisis. And then he chewed hard on his lower lip. All the redleaf tea on Cardassia—however sycophantically supplied by Jartek—would not alter the fact that whoever was calling the plays on Cardassia Prime right now, it was emphatically not its democratically elected leader. Nor would it prevent a teenage girl from blowing herself up or being cut in half by disruptor fire, and the moment when that order would be forced from Ghemor was approaching all too soon.

"Stalemate?" Garak murmured. "So it seems." He stared at the display. The castellan's office had been receiving the transmissions from Andak for a little while now. They'd seen the recording of Naithe's somewhat ill conceived intervention, and then Macet's cool handling of the situation—

And he deserves a medal for that.

—although right now, all was quiet inside the lecture hall. Not tranquil—hardly—but quiet. Nyra was standing on the stage, just a little way from Keiko and Yevir. She seemed to be murmuring to herself, her body shimmering with the passion behind the muttered words. Probably just repeating what she'd said before, the thoughts she had been given—what she (or her masters, at least) wanted from this whole fiasco. The usual xenophobic routine. What troubled Garak more was just how bright her eyes were. Nyra Maleren could not stand up to this strain for much longer.

Long enough for Macet to reason with her?

Garak considered the evidence on the screen before him, weighed it carefully—and suppressed a sigh.

I doubt it.

Which meant that Ghemor really *was* going to have to give that order to send the troops in. Against, most unfortunately, a teenage girl.

A teenage girl about to blow a Bajoran ambassador for peace all the way back to his Prophets.

Garak hissed under his breath. Whoever was choreographing this whole farce really had done an admirable job. It was just possible that he was left with no way out. . . .

Ways and means . . . It's all about ways and means. . . .

"Play the transmission back," Garak said suddenly. "From about . . . fifteen minutes ago. Just after she stopped talking about her demands and when she started spouting all that overblown nonsense that someone has clearly been feeding her about Cardassia's future."

Jartek opened his mouth, instinctively ready to object, to raise a question, to delay. Garak gave him a stare—not the full version, he was saving that for another occasion, but it was enough for his immediate purposes. Jartek closed his mouth, cleared his throat, insinuated himself a little closer to the console on the desk, and jabbed at a couple of buttons. The recording went into reverse, the figures on the screen flickering backward into the past.

"There," Garak said, pointing his finger at the display. "Play it from there."

Jartek fiddled unwillingly with another control and the performance began over again.

The usual xenophobic routine . . .

" . . . *must leave Cardassian soil,*" Nyra said. "*Cardassia must find its own, true way. . . .*"

Ways and means . . .

"That's *it!*" Garak slammed his hand down flat upon the desk. A couple of padds jumped up slightly.

Ghemor grabbed out to stop a stylus before it leapt off the table. "Care to put Mev and myself in the picture, Garak?"

Garak turned to him and, as he did, he realized that his other hand was clenched into a fist. The skin was stretched taut over his knuckles, and he could see the fine vessels pulsing triumphantly. He let it fall slack to his side, relaxed, and then smiled beatifically at Ghemor. He could, he thought, almost be described as happy. This situation was under control now; under *his* control—which was the only one that mattered, after all.

" 'Cardassia must find its true way,' " Garak repeated softly, pointing at the image of Nyra on the display.

"I heard her. But neither of you are making much in the way of sense—"

"The True Way? You haven't heard of them?"

Ghemor shook his head.

"*Ah . . . !*" Again, Garak smiled at him, and clasped his hands together in anticipation of the largesse he was about to bestow.

"You're starting to unnerve me, Garak—and I have to say I'm not much in the mood for that right now—"

"The True Way," Garak said, "was a . . . *curious* little organization with which I had some dealings in the past."

"You mean you spied on them?" Ghemor said bluntly.

Garak tutted and pursed his lips in distaste. Really, people had *no* appreciation of the delicate handling that was involved in such matters; they were always so very *crass* about things—

"Yes, I spied on them."

"And?"

"It was a radical group opposed to peace with Bajor, and very firm in its belief that all the woes of Cardassia could be blamed on the Federation. A doctrine that would play well these days, as I'm sure you can imagine. They tended to prefer the direct approach—bombs, assassinations. This," he indicated at the screen, "is just their kind of thing. As I say, only a small outfit, but quite effective—for fanatics."

He smiled coldly. They had once even targeted the senior staff of Deep Space 9, Garak recalled, trapping them in the holosuite, inside one of Bashir's more preposterous fantasies. . . . There was a nostalgic twinge in his shoulder as it remembered the occasion. Over one of their ambiguous breakfasts, Odo had revealed to him that the True Way had been responsible for that particular melodrama. It really was rather a pity that Odo had never seen fit to ask him directly about the nature of the organization, given that Garak was almost certainly the quadrant's leading authority on the subject. . . . Effective, yes—but the True Way had also proven disappointingly easy to infiltrate.

"What happened to them during the Occupation?" Ghemor prompted.

Garak shrugged. "What happened to *you* during the Occupation? Dictatorships are hardly discriminating, Alon, you know that. Fanatics, moderates, enemies, allies—the Dominion took them all."

The great leveler. All of us equal in their eyes. Well, most of us.

Garak stared for a moment at the image of Nyra Maleren. Jartek had switched the transmission back to real time, but there was no perceptible difference. She was still standing there with her hand reaching up across her chest, whispering what she had been taught.

"Ah," he amended, "they took *almost* all." He sighed a little. "There's a legate—forgive me, a *former* legate, I should say—who survived the Occupation. His name is Korven. He was key to the True Way's operations when I had them under observation. He lives right here, in the capital. And he . . . well, let's say that he owes me a favor or two."

Yes, let's say that.

"A favor?" Ghemor gave him an unreadable look. "How do you know he's still alive? Did you look him up or something, Garak?"

Garak thought for a moment of evading that particular question, and then remembered Jartek, standing by and listening most attentively.

"I looked up a lot of people when my exile ended," he said quietly, then rallied. "You never know who's going to be able to provide assistance, or require some assistance in return. It's good, I think, to have friends in need."

"And Korven is such a friend?"

I think he could be. With a little . . . encouragement.

Garak shrugged again, committing himself to nothing. "Well, I won't really know until I ask. . . ."

"Why didn't you arrest him?"

Garak turned to look at Jartek, caught momentarily off his guard by the sudden intervention. "I beg your pardon?"

"If Korven was so important to the True Way—a terrorist group, you say—why didn't you arrest him? Why did you leave him free to commit more crimes?"

Trying to sow seeds of suspicion, Jartek? Even now?

"Sometimes," Garak said, imbuing his voice with a patient weariness, "it is helpful to keep people in places where they are less likely to surprise you. Or," he added, more cheerily, "as my father used to say—keep your friends close, and your enemies closer."

Or dead, as Tain had been most usually wont to add. But Garak saw no need to endow Jartek with *that* particular piece of Order wisdom.

No need to squander all *my inheritance.*

His sense of purpose restored, Garak turned his attention away from Jartek, and away from the display, and looked out of the window, out onto the real world. Night had fallen on the city, and the rain was falling too, falling as if it would never stop.

"I think," said Garak softly, watching the patterns made by the rain on the plastic of the window, "that it's time I paid Korven a little visit."

16

"To be honest, Macet," Miles said, "I'm surprised she's not gone and done it yet. I thought suicide bombers just went in and did the job."

"That's true," Macet murmured, "which tells me we'd do well not to consider her a suicide bomber." He looked up from Nyra to Miles. "There've been a couple of explosions in the capital recently. No one was killed and, well, let's face it, there's not all that much of the city left to blow up these days. So it could just have been resulting from damage from the Jem'Hadar purge."

Miles nodded. "Power supplies left damaged and unattended, that kind of thing?"

"Exactly. Or," Macet continued, and looked back at Nyra, "it could have been stage one of something. And this," he tapped the screen, "could be stage two."

"Do you really think so?"

"I'm not an expert by any means, O'Brien, but if the people behind this girl just wanted to make some news, surely she'd have been told to take the place out straightaway, and the vedek with it. But all this time spent making demands?" Macet shook his head. "There's a political agenda here. One that we're going to hear more of, I suspect. But that, thankfully, is not my concern—rather it's the concern of my political masters. *My* business is with Nyra."

"So what about her?"

"Well, in the eyes of *her* masters, young Nyra is completely expendable. And I imagine they'll have done their best to convince her of that too." Macet gave an odd smile. "As I'm sure you know, it's not that hard to persuade a Cardassian to give up her life for some greater good." He focused on the monitor again. "I'm sure I can get Nyra to understand that she's being used—but what would be the outcome of that? Would it just tip her over the edge, if it makes her feel betrayed or let down? Am I better pointing out that she has other loyalties too?"

"*Other* loyalties? Like what?"

"Well, for one thing, she knows all the people in that room, I'd guess—or many of them at any rate. Relatives. Children she's been to school with. Do you think she *really* wants to see them dead?" Macet took a deep breath. "Well, there's only one way to find out, isn't there?" He reached out to switch the com back on.

"Nyra," he said, softening his voice. "Nyra, can you still hear me?"

Framed within the screen, Nyra twisted her head, almost as if she was trying to ward off Macet's words. Miles swore under his breath and rubbed a finger behind his collar, letting some warm air in to touch the back of his neck. *Talk to us, girl!*

Macet remained impassive. "Nyra, can you tell me if you can still hear me?"

There was a moment's silence, and then: "Yes!" the girl shouted back, angrily.

"Good," Macet said, his voice remaining smooth. "Can I ask you to do something for me, Nyra?"

"What do you want?"

"I'd like you to keep on talking to me, Nyra—please."

"Why?" she shot back. "Why do you want me to keep on talking? We've been talking for ages. I don't want to talk any more! When are you going to do what I want?" Her hand crept up along her chest to where the red light was still burning on and off.

Miles went cold with fear. His hands clenched at his sides. He risked taking a look at the far corner of the screen. Keiko, only just in shot, had closed her eyes. But the line of her jaw was set.

"I will do it, you know," Nyra said. The shaking in her hands had reached her voice. "I mean it!"

"I believe you, Nyra!" Macet said quickly. Miles winced.

Take it easy, Macet! Don't panic her. "I believe you! But are you sure it's what you really want to do?"

"What?"

"Look around you, Nyra. Look at all these people in the hall. You know them all, don't you?"

Nyra whispered something, but they couldn't make it out.

"What did you say, Nyra?"

"Yes . . . yes . . . I know them. . . ."

"Can you tell me some of their names?"

Nyra shook her head.

"You don't know their names? There, at the front, aren't there some people you go to school with? Can you tell me which of them are your friends?"

"Can't . . . I don't want to!"

"All right, Nyra, that's quite all right. You don't have to do anything you don't want to do—remember that. You don't have to do anything you don't want to do. But tell me—isn't that your mother there on the stage next to you?"

Suddenly, Nyra's shaking got a whole lot worse.

Wrong move, Miles thought, and glanced over at Macet. He was rubbing anxiously at his beard. He knew it too.

Damn! How are we going to get back from this?

Miles looked at the other pictures, on the smaller display screens lining the main screen. There were three entrances to the lecture hall—the main entrance and two emergency exits up near the dais itself. There were four men stationed at each one, plus another six men up on the roof. All had their weapons out, all were ready and waiting to act as soon as Macet gave them the order.

Macet had checked on them too. His hand was now right above the control that would cut the sound link to the main hall, cut the link so that Nyra wouldn't hear him give the order.

Miles held his breath. Macet's hand was hovering over the com. Nyra's was shaking and you could see red through the translucence of her skin.

And then, as if a prayer was speaking itself, someone said Nyra's name. As if offering the response, the image on the screen juddered and, for a moment, all that Miles could see on it was the blank brown of the fake wood that covered the floor of the hall.

"Don't tell me we've lost it . . ." Macet growled.

For an age that in reality lasted bare seconds, the world behind the screen was unknowable. And then the picture slipped back into focus, resolving itself slowly into the figure of Vedek Yevir Linjarin, sitting upright in his chair.

"Nyra," he entreated her, again.

She turned to stare at him, the sweat beading cold upon the ridges of her face. It was getting late now. The automated light system had activated in the lecture hall. To Miles's eyes, it gave Nyra's gray skin an even more ghastly hue.

"That is your name, is it not?" Yevir said. "Nyra."

She nodded. Her fingers twitched, syncopating with the votive light upon her chest, which pulsed on, untroubled by all that was happening around it, entrenched in its purpose, in its promise.

Watching her—watching Yevir—and thinking of Naithe, Miles was twitching too. "*Bloody hell—not again!*" he muttered, his hands steepled before his face.

Until this moment, Yevir had been sitting with his hands clasped under his robes. He drew them out now, slowly, and set them down at rest, flat upon his knees.

"My name is Yevir, Nyra, Yevir Linjarin."

And then he sat still. Nyra watched him as if in a trance.

He's like a snake charmer, Miles thought, rapt himself.

Macet leaned forward to speak into the com. "Vedek Yevir," he said, his voice so relaxed they might have been meeting at the long-forgotten reception, "I am sure that your intentions are good, but Castellan Ghemor has asked me to speak on his behalf to Nyra—"

"That may be so, Gul Macet." Yevir turned his head away from Nyra, and his face stared out directly from the monitor (*and how the hell does he know which way to look?*) and said, "But it is my distinct impression that Nyra no longer wishes to speak to *you.*"

Macet cut the com. "What I am . . . *hoping,*" he said, his tone rather more taut than Miles had heard it so far, "is that Yevir has just got on the right side of Nyra."

"Good cop, bad cop, huh?" Miles tapped the side of the console.

Macet stared at him. "I beg your pardon?"

"I mean—you had just turned into the villain, hadn't you? And now Yevir's stepped in between you and Nyra, he might have taken some of the pressure off her."

Macet nodded. "Well, that's what I'm hoping. For a little while, at least." He stared at the display. "Provided the fact that he's an alien doesn't count against him. She didn't exactly like Naithe very much, did she?"

"Well, she was just showing a bit of common sense there."

"Yevir *is* Bajoran," Macet pointed out. "And a particular focus for her discontent." He glanced at his waiting men and listened to the shorthand of the communications passing between them, stating positions, status . . . His eyes narrowed.

"D'you really think they could make it in time?" Miles asked.

Macet gave a noncommittal grunt. "Well, it's what they're being paid for," he muttered. "Not that keeping them on standby like this for hours is going to be good for their reflexes." He straightened himself up. "For the moment, they're going nowhere. The surest way to keep everyone in there alive is to talk this girl down. So she won't talk to me any more? Then let's find out what she has to say to the man she claims she wants to kill. Let's find out if she really can kill him after talking to him. Violence tends to become just that bit harder," he said, "when you can put a name to your enemies. When they stop being faceless. There aren't that many people with the nerve for it."

17

Garak had frequently found himself entertaining the notion that a joke on a cosmic scale was being perpetrated against him. A joke perpetrated, most likely, by some trickster-god, whose peculiar sense of humor seemed to be matched only by a regrettable taste for the melodramatic.

To pluck an example from out of the dead, night air . . . Throughout his exile, Garak—while never wholly abandoning the hope of the triumphant restitution of his birthright—had struggled not to remember Cardassia. It was a mission that had necessitated some formidable acts of will, which, he had to confess, he was not always entirely capable of performing. Nonetheless, he had applied himself to the task with his characteristic zeal, had negotiated the occasional lapse of concentration; and had, finally, caught sight of Cardassia again. Viewed upon a screen, it had been distant, it had been tantalizingly out of reach, but it had been subtle and beautiful. It had been everything that he had tried not to remember.

He had then spent the next few weeks buried away in a cellar and glimpsing the elusive grail of his homeland only at night. And when, at last, he came back up from the underground, he surfaced to look upon a city burning and to the rising awareness that it was not just the city, and not even just the planet, but his whole civilization going up in flames.

So you did not want to remember? the gods said, as they turned the sky black and blotted out the sun. *Then look upon our mercy! We have answered your prayer!*

It seemed that those whom the gods wished to destroy they first made Cardassian.

It was at this point in his ruminations that Garak would most usually come to the decision that he really was taking himself far too seriously. For one thing, if there were gods, it seemed highly unlikely that they would be taking so much time out of their celestial pursuits to devote such particular attention to the fate of Elim Garak. Garak rather feared that this might constitute the inexpressibly vulgar sin of vanity. Nevertheless, he could not rid himself entirely of the suspicion that if there *were* gods, it seemed that they were capricious. They were not to be propitiated. And they frowned upon the just and the unjust alike.

Take Korven, for example. When Garak had first encountered him, Korven had been the very model of a Cardassian military man. He had been an exemplary cadet. He had accelerated through the ranks, and was among the first in his cohort to acquire the coveted insignia of a legate. He had put down a civilian insurgence in Lakarian City with such aplomb that he had briefly acquired a soubriquet (although it couldn't have been particularly memorable—certainly Garak could not call it to mind now). He had taken command of the Twelfth Order and turned the garrison on Sarpedion V from one of the least regarded in the Union into arguably the most effective. He had served his term with the expected and requisite ruthlessness on Bajor.

Unfortunately, somewhere along the way (and Garak secretly suspected the baleful atmosphere of Bajor), Korven had also managed to acquire some rather idiosyncratic political beliefs—thus providing more evidence for Garak's long-standing and as yet still thoroughly robust theory that the military should never, *ever* be encouraged to think for itself. And it was the perhaps inevitable expression of these beliefs—in the form of a bomb planted outside the offices used by the Obsidian Order for intercepting and decoding transmissions from Starfleet Intelligence—that had initially drawn Korven to Garak's attention. Nobody had been killed in the blast and very few injured—in fact, compared with the rate of attrition being inflicted at the time by the resistance on Bajor and taking into account the fact that the offices had been due for an expensive refurbishment, it counted almost as a net gain. But it had been more than enough to attract the

ever-watchful eyes of the Order. And when, after a deftly conducted investigation, Legate Korven had brought himself to
Garak's particular attention, Korven's military record, his exemplary service, and his unmemorable nickname had counted for
precisely nothing. The Obsidian Order, after all, derived a certain
amount of professional pride from not being easily swayed.

From thereon in, it had all been really rather unexceptional.
Korven had had more of a desire to live than die a hero. And so,
with the application of no more than his usual methods, Garak
had very quickly succeeded in persuading Korven to tell him
everything he knew. Whether Korven similarly considered the
experience unremarkable, Garak seriously doubted. Because
when Korven and Garak finally parted ways, Korven had been
left with the (quite accurate) impression that he had only narrowly avoided a most unpleasant execution. He had been firmly
reminded that obedience to the state was by far the truest way for
any Cardassian. And he had been left in no doubt that he would
be very wise to consider Garak a mouthpiece for that state. And
so Korven went back to the True Way, this time with a leash
around his neck, with Garak at the other end.

Garak had seen no particularly urgent need for Ghemor to be
apprised of all this. But not even Garak himself was entirely able
to judge the full extent of his reasons why. It was true that it
suited him, as it often had in the past—and particularly in front
of Jartek—to derive a certain mystique from the rumors and the
uncertainty surrounding his former profession. Moreover, habits
died hard and Garak—trained in the old school when it came to
deniability—still stood firm in his belief that there were certain
aspects of the political process from which the world at large
(and Ghemor in particular) was best kept protected. Discretion,
you might say, was the better part of good government. And
when information had been acquired—or extracted—with so
much care and attention, it seemed a shame to pass it on casually.
Indeed, it seemed almost disrespectful of the source.

And yet . . . and yet . . . it was just conceivable, it was just
within the realms of possibility, that there was another reason
why Garak had not told Ghemor all that he had done to Korven,
why he had buried this fragment of history. For when the balance
was weighed, when the account was drawn up and laid out, it had

to be conceded that Korven—for all his crimes—had not deserved Garak. Just as Cardassia—for all her crimes—had not deserved the intensity, the implacability, of the fire that had
consumed her.

And yet here Cardassia was, and the city at her heart smol-
dered—charred black and raw—with Garak passing through it
like a shade. Passing through it with his hand set upon his
weapon, while dust-filled rain clouds spread out against the ruin
of the sky, obscuring the gaunt light of the Blind Moon. Passing
through it, seeking restitution.

The rain had thinned to nothing more than an acrid dampness
in the air, and it tasted sour upon his lips. As Garak continued on
his pilgrimage down through the lost ways of the city, he heard,
carried toward him upon the air, the distant chorus of disruptor
fire, the plaintive falling harmonies of a siren. He saw the smoke
and the fumes rising from burst pipes and the metal wreck of
buildings still twisted into their death throes. He caught the bitter
stench of the burial pits.

This is Cardassia, nor am I out of it.

And so it was that when Garak reached his ultimate destination his mind was verging upon the metaphysical. He made his
descent down the final few steps to where Korven lived. And
there he would have to concede that it was one point of evidence
in favor of some fundamental unity of purpose at work in the
cosmos that certain things were understood universally. There
were certain truths one might call self-evident—that a red flashing light meant danger, that punishment had very little to do with
crime, that a knock on the door in the middle of the night is always feared within.

Concealed by the darkness, with only that blind moon as his
witness, Garak stood upon the last step and hammered hard upon
the door. Two or three minutes passed, within and without.

I do believe I may be expected. . . .

A particularly thick black cloud scudded across the dimmed
sky and the moonlight fractured. The world waited in anticipation before a harsh, artificial light went on inside. Then Korven
opened the door—and his skin grayed further at the sight of the
man leaning against his doorframe, smiling at him and blocking
his exit. His face was transfigured into that of a man who had

once told everything he had to know, and was ready to do it all over again.

"Korven!" Garak said, with an almost paternal warmth. "Long time, no see!"

Korven did not answer. He did not move, either. He just stared at Garak as if he were looking at a ghost. He stared at him as if Garak had risen up from the dead, and had come back to haunt him.

"Don't worry. I'll let myself in." Garak stepped past him, inside, then looked back at the man still standing on the threshold, to summon him within. "You will join me, won't you, Korven?"

18

Tired beyond imagining, Keiko sat with her eyes closed and her head dropped a little way down onto her chest. As this hellish day had progressed, and the slow minutes had turned into endless hours, it seemed to her that the whole world had been reduced to just this room. At first she had tried to keep on looking around the hall, to try to reassure people, but many had pulled back into themselves. As the evening drew on, and the buzz of the lights had insinuated itself behind her temples, she had started to feel almost as if she was going into a trance. She had sat and watched the children for a long while, remembering how it had been her idea to encourage people to bring what remained of their families here to Andak. Many of the children had become exhausted from fear and from being forced to sit still for so long. One or two had fallen asleep, leaning upon each other for support. But, when last Keiko had looked, Molly had still been wide awake, still hugging herself, and she had been staring down at the floor.

Now that her eyes were shut, it seemed to Keiko as if the world had shrunk even further. It was down to no more than two voices—one as taut as a cord that was about to snap; the other soft and flowing, like rainfall on a warm spring afternoon.

"I wonder if you have heard very much about Bajor, Nyra," Yevir said.

There was a dark, brittle silence. "I've heard enough," the girl replied at last.

"What have you heard?" he asked her, almost urging her, although his voice remained soft. "What have you learned about us?"

"I've heard all about your superstitions for one thing. And about how *you* are trying to bring them here. But we don't want them here! Cardassia doesn't need them. Cardassia doesn't need your lies!"

Keiko listened to Nyra's voice with a sad bewilderment. How could Nyra feel so much hatred? It was beyond Keiko's comprehension. How could someone so young—and Nyra seemed still to be a child to her—have been twisted so far out of recognition? How could she have come to this point, to want to cause so much chaos and destruction?

Keiko herself had been the kind of child that liked order. She liked to have things settled. In her room, when she was very small, the toys each had their particular place. The books, which rose steadily in number year by year and quickly outnumbered the toys, had all been shelved alphabetically, and her name had been carefully inscribed inside each. A set of little pictures—watercolors, landscapes—that her grandmother had painted as gifts for her had hung on the wall symmetrically on either side of a square mirror.

"It seems to me to be such a shame that's all you've heard about Bajor. Did no one ever tell you what it looked like? How green it is? What the rivers are like, and the waterfalls? That in our cities there are gardens between all the buildings, and that the gardens have pools of water in them?"

"If it's so perfect on Bajor, then why don't you go back there?" Sharp, angry, suspicious. Close to breaking. "Why are you *here*?"

For quite some time in her otherwise ordered youth, one thing had troubled Keiko, had disrupted the sense of definiteness that she preferred. For a long time, longer than she generally admitted, Keiko had had no idea what it was she wanted to do. Whenever people asked her—and people tended to take a great deal of interest in this bright and talkative girl—she would say that, like her grandmother, she wanted to paint pictures. It sounded neat and tidy in her ears, to carry on a family tradition. But, in her heart, Keiko had known that it was not for her. Her grandmother spoke of the pleasure she took from placing the dark lines upon the white page; she spoke of seeing underlying patterns in the world and then describing them. But, when she thought about it, this made Keiko worry, that she might put a line in the wrong place, and then not be able to change it, to put it in its proper setting.

"Why am I *here*, Nyra? Oh, that's quite simple—because from far away Cardassia is unfathomable. Close up, perhaps I can find out more about you. And I'm hoping that I might find that we have something in common."

"We're *nothing* like you!"

Keiko was not able to settle to her satisfaction the matter of what she should do with her life until she found herself taken out on a school field trip. She had not been looking forward to the event, suspecting it would be hot (it was the middle of a very humid summer), and that it would leave her so tired it would ruin the rest of her week. She sat and sweltered bad-temperedly for most of the afternoon, until an exasperated teacher (and Keiko understood more of the frustrations of teachers these days) lost patience, and demanded an essay on the life cycle of the lotus. Keiko took on the assignment with the grace to know it was probably deserved and settled down to finish it as quickly as possible.

"Are you so very sure about that, Nyra? Have you heard of the Occupation? I wonder what you know about that?" Yevir murmured, more to himself than to her. "I doubt you're old enough to remember anything about it." He sighed, lost for a moment in his own memories. "If you ever came to Bajor, Nyra—and I'd like to think that one day you will—you'd see a lot more than rivers and gardens. You'd see broken buildings too, just like you can here on Cardassia. You'd see monument after monument raised to remember where a hundred people or more were shot by soldiers. You'd see places where the fields will never be green again, because an army once went there and poisoned the land."

The lotus had captured Keiko's imagination. As she read more about it, she found herself secretly admiring the flower, which sat in murky water and yet remained delicate and pure, untainted by its surroundings. She drew picture after picture of its fine-hued petals and green stems. She came to love the feel of digging at roots, came to love the sight of soil beneath her fingernails. She found out that flowers had special names, and learnt that these were just part of a larger system of description and designation. She grasped that even if things *looked* different, they often turned out to have more in common than a superficial glance could tell you. And that was when Keiko understood for the first time fully what her grandmother had meant when she spoke of the patterns that lay behind the everyday world, and the pleasure to be taken from perceiving them, and describing them. The study (by the end you could hardly call it an essay anymore) took away a prize that year, and Keiko's future was settled. She was going to be a botanist.

"What happened?" Nyra whispered.

A moment or two passed before Yevir began again. "Bajor was occupied, Nyra, just like Cardassia was. And the Car . . ." He hesitated, bit down upon the word. "These occupiers stayed on Bajor for years. For decades. People were born and grew up on Bajor who could not remember anything else other than that Bajor had been an occupied planet. Can you imagine what that was like?" He paused for breath. "There is one thing that I'm sure that you can imagine. Because these occupiers were there to exploit Bajor, and they were very cruel—as cruel as the Jem'Hadar were here on Cardassia. So—yes, I think we have a lot of things in common, Nyra. But knowing about cruelty isn't the only thing we share, I think."

Keiko had lived in many risky places, had found herself in many dangerous situations. But she knew that compared with those of Yevir and Kira, or Feric and Tela, her life had been a safe and a happy one. Compared with theirs, hers could even be called sheltered. She knew that was the difference between them—but how could she wish it any other way? Nyra's life had been ruined by war, to an extent that Keiko could not really conceive, to an extent that she did not want to conceive. There were some things she didn't want to come too close to, some things she didn't want her children to come too close to. Keiko knew when to look for similarities that were hidden out of sight—but she was enough a product of her training to value diversity, enough a product of her culture to understand how vital different perspectives could be. She knew that she had talents—and not just scientific ones—that were needed on Cardassia. And that if she was given time, then what she was doing here could change things, for the better.

"Some people on Bajor," said Yevir, "began to lose hope. They started to believe that the occupiers would never leave, that Bajor would be kept prisoner by them forever. But they *did* leave, Nyra. We made them leave. Do you know how we did that?"

Bajor came through. Cardassia can too.

"How?"

I don't know if we're going to survive this. I don't really know how we can. But I know that if we do—there's nothing, and no one, that will drive me off Cardassia. Because what we're doing here is right.

Keiko opened her eyes. And when, at last, Molly looked up too, she saw that her mother was gazing at her and smiling at her radiantly, just as if everything was going to work out fine.

19

The room Korven was inhabiting was ill lit and small, but every surface was covered and every corner was filled. Garak took it all in. He saw books and paintings, pieces of sculpture, piles of padds. . . . There was even a superbly worked tapestry, framed, and propped up in front of the window, blocking out whatever light there was left to come into the room. Korven seemed to be establishing a one-man museum. Altogether, the dimness of the place and the layers upon layers of cultural detritus gave the room a strange intimacy. Korven stood to one side, stooping slightly, and as close to the wall as he could manage.

There was a viewscreen set into a recess and partly obscured by a small painting. It was a Tarinas: characteristic of her, but a minor work. A passable enough piece of propaganda commemorating the Relief of Rakantha. Tarinas had specialized in depicting the glories of the Occupation but, while the Cultural Conservation Committee had honored her with prize after prize for her efforts, she had always been rather bland for Garak's tastes. But it fitted well in this place. Even from where he was standing, and without closer inspection, Garak was fairly certain that it was not a reproduction. He imagined Tarinas was dead now. There were other artists he regretted more.

Garak pointed past it, to the screen.

"Switch that on."

Korven shifted slowly across the room. He picked up the painting and placed it with care to one side, and then pressed a few controls on the console. The device whined and flickered, and then resolved itself into an aerial view of the settlement at Andak. Garak smiled as he realized that Korven had obviously been tracking the day's events, although he seemed to have kept the sound muted.

The square was floodlit, and something of a crowd had assembled there, all attention focused on a large building at one end which Garak took to be the lecture hall. Expertly, he picked out the dark shadows stationed on the roof of the hall, caught the occasional flash of what he knew was a weapon being shifted to track a target. On the ground, a barrier had been set up to keep people safely away from the building, and a handful of soldiers were stationed along it at intervals. Security at the base was being taken seriously, Garak noticed approvingly—he could see, blending into the crowd, agents moving about, keeping an unobtrusive eye on the civilians there. These themselves seemed to comprise the few people from the settlement not inside the hall, a small group from Yevir's office, some medical teams, and a large number of reporters.

" . . . *and at least forty reporters, including our own Teris Juze and Lamerat Anjen. A spokesperson from Alon Ghemor's office has said that the situation is sensitive but currently under control.* . . ."

Garak followed the report for a little while, reassuring himself that—for the moment at least—Andak was going nowhere. He found that he was slowly flexing the fingers on his right hand. Korven watched this exercise closely. When Garak finally turned to him, he pointed at one of the two chairs in the room. Korven had still not looked him in the eye, and his stoop had become a little more pronounced.

"Sit down," Garak told him.

"Hell of a time for a history lesson," Miles said through his teeth. "What's he going to tell her about the resistance, do you reckon? Think he'll mention how successful they were blowing things up to achieve their political ends?"

"He has already passed on drawing her attention to Cardassian involvement in the Occupation," Macet noted. "Perhaps he's a little more skilled at this than Naithe was."

"He *is* a priest," Miles acknowledged. "And a politician. I suppose that somewhere along the way he must have picked up a thing or two about how to inspire belief."

Macet checked on his troops. The comlink chattered back at him.

" . . . *four-five—target has moved, repeat, target has moved. No shot.*"

". . . *copy, four-five, I got that . . .*"

". . . *three-seven—target coming into view; repeat, target coming into view—collateral estimated at two . . . correction, three others . . . three-seven—I now have a shot. Waiting. I still have a shot. Waiting. . . . Target has moved. No shot.*"

A green light winked at them, drawing attention to one of the smaller screens on the display. There was an incoming transmission, from the capital. Macet reached back to the console, and accepted it. The urgent, military squawk was silenced, making way for the smoother tones of the executive.

"Care to give me some on-the-spot analysis of this turn of events, Macet?"

There was Ghemor, leaning back in his chair, arms folded. It was a good approximation of nonchalance, but the persistent tapping of one fingertip against his forearm gave the lie to it. Standing behind him, only just in view, was Jartek. He had changed jacket, Miles noticed, to one with a much higher collar. Probably to cover up the bruises he'd put there earlier, Miles thought, with a grim satisfaction.

"Your guess is as good as mine, Castellan," Macet said.

"I was hoping for a little more than that—"

"Well, Yevir has her talking," Macet replied, then raised his finger. "Correction—Yevir has her *listening,* which is the next best thing. And if she's talking—or listening—she's not blowing anything up."

"My next question has to be whether the topic of conversation is likely to encourage her to blow something up."

"Well?" Macet said, turning to Miles, with a twist to his lips. "You're the expert."

Miles shook his head. "Don't look at me!"

Macet stared at Yevir, checked once more on the position of his men, and then turned back to the screen. "He's Bajoran, sir, and he was the particular target of this attack. I . . . believe that the longer he's left talking to her, the more likely it is that she'll activate the bomb. I'm ready to order them in whenever you want."

"How?" Nyra whispered. "How did you make them leave?"

"We fought them, Nyra—we fought them with weapons. We shot them and killed them and blew them up and, in time, we drove them out. And once Bajor was no longer occupied, just like Cardassia is no longer occupied—then we put our weapons down, and we tried to live in peace."

"But Cardassia is *still* occupied!" Nyra said, suddenly angry again. "By the Federation, by all kinds of influences—*alien* influences—that want to destroy the little we have left—"

"Nobody wants to destroy Cardassia, Nyra! Cardassia has seen enough destruction! All that people want to do is help—"

"We don't *want* your help!"

"Are you quite sure of that?" Yevir's voice had clouded, like the sudden change of light on a cool spring day that signals thunder, when the sky becomes heavy, and darkens. "Can you be so certain that you speak for everyone on Cardassia, Nyra? Do you speak for all of the people in the cities fighting off the fever they caught from the water? All those who lost everything and everyone they loved and yet still struggle on to live another terrible day, for the sake of what they've lost? All the people in this room who are only here at Andak because they wish to make life on Cardassia better—"

"What *I'm* doing will make things better—"

"How? By killing *more* people? By leaving another part of this planet stripped of anything except dust? There's enough of that already, Nyra. Is that really all you have to offer Cardassia?"

"There's nothing else left!" Nyra shouted back.

"No," he answered. "You're wrong."

And then, very slowly—very purposefully—Yevir Linjarin stood up.

Ghemor jerked forward in his seat. Jartek blinked and hissed. Macet cursed. Standing at the back of the security office, Jack

Emmett invoked the gods of three different worlds and swore he would give up gambling.

"What the *hell's* he doing?" Miles whispered.

Garak shifted some padds to one side and found what he was looking for—a bottle and a couple of glasses.

Someone—Garak didn't care to remember who—had once told him that fear of death would always overmaster the desire to serve the state. Which was something of a heresy, actually, now he came to think about it. At any rate—Garak, who had an instinct for the perfect comeback so unerring that many people suspected (or hoped) it would one day get him into serious trouble, had retorted, *Maybe, but there's no reason why the two can't be aligned.*

Garak poured the *kanar* and set one glass down just within Korven's grasp. He settled in the chair opposite, swished his own glass round, and then breathed in the scent. It was hardly vintage—Korven's predilection for preservation obviously didn't stretch as far as his *kanar*—but it was sufficient for the task at hand. He took a sip.

Korven spoke, his voice husky and hesitant. "What do you w-want, Garak?"

Garak could recall exactly when Korven had acquired that stammer. He observed Korven carefully, watched his face become a little clammier, and looked down into the swirling depths of his drink.

"Well—what do you have for me?"

"I c-can't . . . can't think why you're here. Not after all this t-time. After all that's h-happened—"

"Stop talking."

Korven obeyed. He reached out to take his drink, and downed most of the contents of the glass. Garak measured every detail—the attempt at precision marred by the slight fumbling, the shake of the hand as it set the glass back down.

"This," Garak gestured at the pictures on the screen, "bears the unmistakable imprint of the True Way. You *were* the True Way, Korven. It wouldn't have existed without you then, and I don't believe it could exist without you now. So don't try to tell me you're not involved." He stared at the other man. "You can start talking again now," he added.

Korven picked up his drink once more, and peered down at it. "Ever since G-Ghemor took power, the True Way has been re-forming," he said, and raised his eyes to look at Garak. "This d-democratic project's going nowhere—you must realize that. It's holding back the relief work, slowing up the process of g-governing the planet—You know as w-well as I do that what C-Cardassia needs is f-firm leadership—"

Garak held up his hand to stop him. "I'm not interested in your justifications. I can make them up for myself—justifications do tend to have a tedious uniformity. In your wisdom you have decreed that there is no place for democracy on Cardassia and also, no doubt, that you and your kind are best qualified to re-place it. See? I can make all that up for myself. So skip it—and give me some facts."

"Andak," said Korven, after taking another drink, "was a n-natural target, at least it was once Ghemor had s-staked so much on it. And when we h-heard that Yevir was going there . . ." He shrugged.

"Yes, that must have been very exciting for you," Garak mur-mured. "Two problems tidily disposed of, all at once. The peace mission finished, and Ghemor's government destabilized and discredited." He tapped his finger on the arm of the chair, and waited until Korven had the glass up against his lips before he spoke again.

"So," he said, "what else, precisely, has the True Way got planned?"

"When the Occupation ended, Nyra," Yevir said, as he went toward her, "Bajor celebrated. Everyone around me was jubilant, everyone was happy. Because we were free at last—as we had al-ways hoped, had always dreamed. But I . . . I was not happy. When *I* looked around the world, it seemed to me that everything was drab. That there was no purpose to it, no point. I didn't feel free at all, Nyra, I felt lost."

He stepped a little closer. "And then I found what was miss-ing, Nyra."

She stared at him, mesmerized, as he moved toward her.

"What did you find . . . ?"

He took a deep breath, and then his face, which until now had been so serene, so tranquil, was transfigured. It lit up as he spoke.

"Purpose, Nyra! Meaning! And then . . ." He had to stop for a moment to collect himself. "And then the whole world was transformed, before my eyes. It was as if I could see colors again, all the colors around me. All that drabness, all that grayness—suddenly I could see what was truly there! And I understood my place in it all, Nyra. I understood that I was part of it, and that I had a purpose in it." He smiled at her, lovingly. "You understand all of this too, Nyra, don't you? You understand how it feels to believe in something. You understand what purpose is. Do you not want to live to see it fulfilled?"

He was very close now, perhaps an arm's length away. Slowly, he opened out his hand, unfurling the fingers like the petals on a flower, and offered it to her.

But she did not seem to notice. She was looking up into his eyes, and she was crying.

"It's not the same," she whispered to him, shaking her head. "It's not the same. I saw it."

"What did you see, Nyra . . . ?" he urged her.

"Where she taught," she said, and nodded at her mother. "The Academy. It was everything she stood for, everything she loved. I was going there too, I was going to study there and be like her. It was what the women in our family did. Our tradition. And now it's ruins. It's all gone," she said. "There's nothing left. There's no future. No future left, for any of us."

Her hand began to move again.

Just for an instant, at the very core of his being, Yevir Linjarin understood what it was like to feel doubt. And then he prayed to his Prophets to guide him and to use him and to deliver him. Behind him, on the stage, Keiko O'Brien was smiling at her little girl and marveling at how beautiful she was. Feric Lakhat was thinking of the mountains, and of his son, and was mouthing the words of a prayer. And Tela Maleren had covered her eyes and was shedding silent, bitter tears that ran down her hand and onto the silver bracelet about her wrist.

*   *   *

"There's never a right decision, Castellan," Macet told him quietly. "Only the best one in the circumstances. You just have to act in good faith. Let me send them in."

Garak absorbed all of this new information. He sifted through it, assessed it, started to make connections, started to see patterns where before there had only been chaos and confusion. He drank the last of his *kanar.* And then he stood up.

"It's time I went," he murmured, setting down his empty glass. He took a single step toward where the screen flickered on, and watched the broadcast for a moment or two, confirming that there was as yet no more news. From the outside, Andak was still there. Who knew what was going on inside?

He picked up the painting by Tarinas. As he had guessed, it was the original. He studied it for a few moments, considered the composition and the brushwork, the overall effect of the piece. He still didn't like it. She had been too glib, he decided; she had lacked the subtlety of a true Cardassian.

"It was good to see you," he said to Korven, and was surprised to discover that it wasn't a lie. "It's good to know that you survived. Not enough of us made it." He put the picture back, facedown, and turned to look at his host. "I'm sure we'll meet again."

Korven nodded his acquiescence.

Garak walked past him, across the room, and over to the way out. He felt a little tired, and told himself it was probably the *kanar.* Whatever it was, he felt a sudden need to leave this tiny room, overfull with the fragments that Korven had taken from the ruins. He was anxious to get out of here, even if only to taste the bitter rain outside. Recent events—recent realizations—had persuaded Garak to set a lot of the past behind him.

Still, there were *some* trade secrets that you learnt and never forgot. It was just the same in tailoring.

Measure twice, cut once.

"Before I go," he said, mildly, unambiguously, and resting his back against the door, "tell me about Entor."

In the capital, Ghemor ordered Macet to proceed into the lecture hall.

At Andak, Macet relayed that order to his troops.

Inside the hall, Nyra—hearing the sound of the doors breaking down—committed her hand . . .

. . . And found it held by Yevir.

"Have faith," he said to her. "Have hope."

Teris leans her head on Anjen's shoulder. "Did you get that?" she whispers.

He puts his arm around her.

"Of course I did, Juze."

20

The lecture hall was the biggest space under cover at Andak, but you could hardly blame people for not wanting to remain in there. As a result, the square outside became frantically busy as the hostages piled out of the hall, and looked around anxiously for their friends, and for their loved ones, or just for someone to tell them what they should do next. The medical crews that had been waiting moved into action rapidly, to steer them into blankets and to give them something to eat and drink, to make sure that the stress of the day had not taken a critical toll upon anyone.

The first thing that Keiko did, when it was clear that their ordeal was truly over, was to run down from the stage and embrace Molly, swinging her up into her arms and kissing her. They sat for a while together on a seat at the end of a row, holding each other tight, waiting for the hall to empty, so that they could leave. When mother and daughter finally emerged into the square, the bright lights set up outside blinded them both for a moment, and they felt, rather than saw, Miles grab them into a bear hug.

"Where's Yoshi?" Keiko whispered, as Miles took Molly from her. The little girl hooked her arms around her father's neck, and her legs around his waist, and then laid her head upon his shoulder.

"Safe and sound. That Jack Emmett's a good lad, he made sure all the little ones were okay." Twisting round so that Molly was not between them, Miles leaned in and kissed Keiko on the cheek. His eyes had gone oddly bright.

"God, love," he murmured, chewing at his lip, "I'm glad you're all right."

She smiled at him and held on to his arm, then reached up and stroked the face of their daughter. "I'm going to be stuck here for a while," she said to him, tiredly, and he nodded his understanding.

"Yeah, I know . . . Macet—he's in charge of the operation—he said he'd need to talk to you as soon as you could. There he is," he nodded over at a distinctively tall and uniformed figure standing only a few yards away, and talking earnestly to some of the troops that had just come out of the hall. "I'll take the kids back home and put them both to bed," Miles said. "Come home as soon as you can get away."

Keiko watched regretfully as her husband and daughter went off across the square toward their quarters, and then she began to walk toward Macet. On her way over, she heard someone's voice rise above the mêlée, calling out her name. She turned round—it was Feric. She did not hesitate to hurry over to him, and they embraced each other. No words were necessary at first—they were two good friends who were very glad to see the other safe and alive.

"How are you?" she said at last, pulling back a little, but still keeping her hands upon his arms.

"The same as you, I should imagine—absolutely exhausted." He gave her his small smile.

"Are you going to go home? Go to bed?" she suggested, worried at how tired he looked.

"No . . ." he answered, and gave a deep sigh. "I think I'll stick around awhile. Some of the kids are still pretty upset and their parents aren't quite in a state to cope with them yet . . . I'll see if there's anything I can do there."

She hugged him again. "Just don't overdo it," she said softly. "I'll need you. Tomorrow—and all the days afterward."

"Don't worry," he said; and then, just before he pulled away, he added, "They won't beat us, Keiko. We won't let them. We're here to stay."

Whether he meant the project or the Oralian Way Keiko wasn't sure, and she didn't care. Right now, either sounded fine to her. She patted his arm, and nodded—and then he went on his way. Keiko carried on toward Macet. As she got nearer, she called out to him. He stopped talking to his men and turned to look at her.

He had a padd in one hand and a mug in the other, and the resemblance to Dukat was thoroughly disconcerting. She suspected that she was so tired that she hadn't managed to cover her surprise quickly enough, but he did not react to her lapse. *That's very polite of him,* she thought. *He must be fed up with it—but I'm starting to fall asleep on my feet, and this day has been too surreal already. . . .*

"Director," he said, calmly. "Thank you for your time—I appreciate that you must be anxious to get back to your family." He took a sip from the mug, and nodded a dismissal to the men standing nearby, and they withdrew—solid, reassuring figures that stood out even as they dispersed among the crowd.

"Well, that *is* what I'm here for," she said. She watched the steam rise from his mug and caught the aroma of *rokassa* tea. Her stomach lurched a little. Feric insisted on drinking that noxious potion every morning, when they met for their daily meeting. She swallowed, and remembered her own manners. "Thank you for all that you've done today," she said, fervently.

"Well, that's what *I'm* here for," he said, with a dry smile. He lifted up the padd. "I won't force this on you yet, but I thought you might like at least a preliminary report on all that's been happening here. It seems—according to some of our sources back in the capital—that the base was targeted by a radical terrorist organization called the True Way. Nyra Maleren—and, again, you have to bear in mind that this is only after a very preliminary discussion with her—appears to have been recruited by them in some way. I'm not sure of the details of how that happened yet, and that will be the priority for the investigations I intend to conduct over the next few days." He took a little more of his drink.

"Where is Nyra now?" Keiko said, a little faintly, her mind reeling at all this news. *Recruited? Here? How?*

"We're using one of the base offices to hold her, and we've been asking her some questions there. I hope that's acceptable, Director."

"Of course . . . whatever you need . . ."

What's the protocol for dealing with minors in a situation like this? Keiko wondered. It was not as if it was something she had ever had to think about before.

"Is her mother with her?" she asked.

Macet shook his head. "Nyra refuses to have her in there."

"Is there *anyone* with her?" Despite all that Nyra had done, Keiko couldn't bear to think of the girl by herself right now. Who knew what kind of state she was in?

Macet raised an eye ridge and gave Keiko an odd look. "Yes, in fact, there is . . . Vedek Yevir, of all people. Nyra seems to have acquired a great deal of trust in him. When I was last in there, Nyra hadn't even let go of his hand yet."

That piece of information did not surprise Keiko at all. When she had heard the doors crashing in, and thought that it was all over, she had glanced across at Nyra and had seen the look of sheer despair that she had given Yevir, a look that had been begging him to help her. Keiko could well imagine how Yevir might now seem the only certainty in Nyra's collapsing world.

Keiko gazed around, searching for Tela, but the square was chaotic, and the Cardassian woman was nowhere to be seen. As she looked round, however, she did catch sight of Naithe—and before she could look away their eyes met. The Bolian waved, and began to hurry toward her.

Oh no . . . not now . . .

Tomorrow, Keiko decided grimly, she and Naithe were going to have a long talk to find out just what he had thought he had been doing when he had approached Nyra. Right now, though, she really didn't have the strength for it—and there were other, much more pressing questions on her mind. She turned back to Macet.

" 'Recruited,' you said. What did you mean by that?"

By now, Naithe had come to stand by her elbow, and he was listening in on the exchange, his head bobbing about between them both like some kind of little bird chasing after seed.

Macet looked down at him impassively. He tapped his fingers against his mug, and the sound came out hollow.

I suspect Macet would like a word or two with Naithe as well. . . .

"These kinds of organizations prey upon people's vulnerabilities, Director," Macet said. "They prey upon people—the young, usually—who are afraid, and afraid above all for their future. Hearing what she had to say earlier, it's not hard to see how they might have settled on Nyra as being particularly susceptible to their tactics. The impression I've got from what Nyra has told us so far—although, unsurprisingly, she's not really very coherent at the moment—is that once Andak was picked out as a target by the True Way, someone was placed here. This person has been recruiting one or two of the teenagers to their cause. Oh," he concluded, with a curl of his lips, "and, at the same time, teaching Nyra how to make a bomb and plan a siege."

Keiko's hand shot up to cover her mouth. "*Who?*" she whispered.

Who at Andak could have done such a thing?

"Unfortunately, Nyra isn't being very forthcoming in that respect. I think she feels she's done enough betraying this evening."

"Are they still *here?*" Keiko shuddered, thinking of all the people milling about her in the square. . . .

"Oh, no—I doubt that very much, Director! They'll be long since gone—"

"Oh dear," interrupted Naithe suddenly. "Oh dear me."

I'm not going to throttle you yet, Naithe, but I might have to, soon. . . .

"Oh dear," Naithe said again, and his eyes were almost popping out of his head. "Director, I . . . I do believe I might know a little bit about this."

Keiko felt her hold on her temper start to slip. *Really, Naithe—not everything is about you and your bloody research—*

"Please," said Macet silkily, "do continue. . . ." He raised his mug, concealing most of his face, but not his eyes. The resemblance to Dukat became striking.

"Oh, well, you see—in the course of my studies here, I sat in on some meetings of a little discussion group run by one of the junior staff. . . . It was for one or two of the older children, you know. . . . An interesting little group, they talked a great deal about Cardassian culture and history and philosophy—"

"And what did they have to say?" Macet said, his eyes reptile cold. Had she been standing in Naithe's shoes, Keiko would have been feeling more than a little afraid by now, although the Bolian seemed blithely unaware of Macet's fury. And, what was worse, Keiko could feel her own heart sinking too.

It was my idea to encourage everyone at Andak to take part in teaching the children. Which means that whoever it was holding these meetings could do it and not arouse a single suspicion. A sick and helpless anger surged up in her as she thought how something she had valued so dearly, something she had been so proud of, had been so callously used. *These people really do warp everything. . . .*

"Oh, well," Naithe said, "you see, Cardassian culture isn't something I know a great deal about; really, I couldn't say, I was watching the group *itself,* you understand, how it interacted, and how it would fit in with the rest of the community here. . . . Oh, but, you see, I'm quite sure—*quite* sure—that these meetings were completely innocent, the young man who was leading them was quite personable—charming, in fact; he was very interested in my research—"

"Naithe," Keiko said, and was amazed at how patient her voice sounded coming out, "who was it?"

"Oh yes! Of course!" He gave the name of one of the junior researchers.

"Do you know him?" Macet asked Keiko.

"Not very well . . . he was on the statistical analysis team." She frowned, cast her mind back to when she had stood up on the stage and looked round the hall. "You know, thinking about it, I'm not sure he was at the lecture. . . ."

"That doesn't surprise me," Macet said. "If it is him, he'll have left hours ago—probably before Yevir even arrived here. But we'd better not jump to conclusions. . . ." He shoved the padd into his pocket, and then thumbed on his combadge and issued a few quiet instructions to his men to start searching the base.

Keiko, feeling suddenly even more weary, put her hands up to her head.

"These people are experts at infiltration, Director," Macet said quietly, and even kindly. "Your recruitment procedures wouldn't have been set up for this—I suspect not even your security protocols would have picked him up. It's certainly not your fault." He turned to the Bolian. "Dr. Naithe," he said, rather dryly, "I wonder if I might take a look at your records concerning these meetings you attended."

"Oh, well, you know, these interviews *are* meant to be confidential. . . ." Naithe caught Macet's expression. "Although perhaps I might make an exception in this case—"

"That would be very generous of you, Doctor," Macet replied. "It would certainly save me the trouble of arresting you for impeding my investigation."

"Oh dear me, no," murmured Naithe, indistinctly. "No, that certainly wouldn't do. Er . . . come along with me, please, we'll go over to my office straightaway. . . ."

As they turned to go, Keiko addressed Macet one last time.

"Gul Macet," she said, "do you know where I can find Tela Maleren?"

"Last I saw, she was waiting outside the room where we're holding Nyra." He gestured across the square toward the office blocks. "Be gentle with her," he added.

Keiko nodded.

Should I go? What would it achieve?

She looked across the square to where her quarters were.

Really, I ought to go back to Miles and Molly and Yoshi. . . . But I have to see her. I can't not. . . .

The decision made, she started to cross the square, stopping now and again to speak to members of her staff, to hear their stories and share in their relief. It was some time before at last she reached the offices, and she stepped out of the noise of the warm night into the quieter, cooler corridor.

At the far end, Keiko saw Tela Maleren. She was sitting with her head resting back against the wall, staring up at the gray ceiling. The door next to her was closed. As Keiko approached, her footsteps sounding along the corridor, Tela raised her head and turned to look at her. The intricate styling of her hair had come unbound, and she had tied it back, very simply. It gave her an odd look, Keiko thought, almost as if she had been stripped down to no more than the bare essentials.

"Director," Tela said, and her voice came out much calmer than Keiko would have thought possible. "Was there something that I could do for you?"

Keiko was momentarily taken aback. Did this woman never

lose her poise? Her gaze fell upon the silver bracelet around Tela's wrist. Tela was not twisting it now. Her hands were resting flat upon her lap, and they were still.

"I thought . . ." In her confusion, Keiko stumbled over the words. "I thought there might be something *I* could do for *you* . . . ?"

"No," Tela said simply. "No, thank you, I don't think so."

They fell into silence. Tela rested her head against the wall again. Muffled noises came from the square, but nothing could be heard from beyond the door.

There's nothing I can do here, Keiko thought. *And I don't think I'm wanted. I should be with my own family.*

"Nyra will not see me," Tela said suddenly, and as if reporting nothing more than a very simple fact. "Nor will she speak to me."

"I would imagine she's very confused at the moment," Keiko offered, carefully.

"Indeed, I imagine so. In addition, I believe that in some way she holds me responsible for what has happened today."

Keiko could not think of a response to that.

"Which, I have to say," Tela continued, in the same terrifyingly objective tone, "I am coming to believe has a great deal of truth to it."

"Oh, no, Tela." Keiko shook her head emphatically. "That's just not true—"

Tela stopped her with a look. "Not true? Where, precisely, do you think, Director, that Nyra learnt to be suspicious of humans, or Bajorans—even the Oralian Way, Cardassians, all of them? Where did she learn this, if not at home? Where, too, did she learn the idea that she should protest against them in some way?"

"But whenever you had a problem with the way things were being run, Tela," and Keiko was struck with the realization that she was speaking as if Tela's part at Andak was already in the past tense, "you always followed procedure. You were always willing to discuss things. Surely it was clear to everyone that you had no desire for any more violence—"

"And yet the evidence before me leads me to conjecture that such subtleties may well be lost on children." Tela gave a very bitter smile. "I have no doubt whatsoever that Nyra proved to be easy prey for the people who persuaded her to do this insane, destructive thing. They would have found that much of their work had been done for them already."

"Tela," Keiko began, shaking her head—but then stopped at the sound of the nearby door opening.

Vedek Yevir came out, folding his hands within his robes. He nodded at Keiko, but it was Tela he spoke to first.

"Nyra and I have been talking for a while, Professor, and I believe that she is willing to see you now."

Slowly, Tela stood up, smoothing down her skirt, trying to draw together some remnants of her dignity. "Thank you, Vedek," she said. "I hope that you'll remain outside. No doubt Nyra will want to see you again shortly."

"Of course, Professor. I'll be here as long as I'm needed."

Tela went inside and closed the door.

Yevir turned to Keiko. He looked as exhausted as everyone else at Andak.

"Well, Director," he said, his voice very low. "I must say that this was a rather excessive response to my visit. If you had not in fact wanted me to give a speech here, all you needed to do was refuse my request."

Keiko could not help but laugh—even if she could only manage a little.

Nobody said he had a sense of humor as well.

"How does it feel to be a miracle worker, Vedek?" she asked.

He glanced back over his shoulder at the door and sighed. "I have worked no miracles here," he said. "All I did was find a little common ground. The Prophets guided my hand. And the Prophets will have to take care of the rest."

He looked at her, very closely, and for just a second she caught that veiled intensity once again, the power that he seemed to have to lead people, to persuade them to his purpose. "You look very tired, Director," he murmured. "I wonder if you should go home, to your family. Too many at Andak are not able to do that tonight."

Count your blessings, Keiko—that's what he means.

She nodded her agreement and, before she turned to go, she said, "You'll always be welcome here at Andak, Vedek."

And she prayed that Kira would understand.

21

Garak stood for a moment outside the door to Ghemor's office, examined his nails, and contemplated the nature of accountability. There was, he decided, a strange and—in his experience—not always entirely fathomable relationship between deed and punishment, between merit and reward.

He opened the door quietly and slipped inside.

Ghemor was half-sitting, half-leaning upon his desk, grimly eyeing one of the screens in front of him. "They're going to win prizes for this, aren't they?" he said. "What's that thing called, Mev?"

"The Wurlitzer, Alon," Jartek murmured, as he poured Ghemor a cup of redleaf tea. It appeared silently on the corner of the desk by Ghemor's hand.

"That's the one, the Wurlitzer." Ghemor took the cup and drank some of the tea. "They'll win the Wurlitzer for this."

"That depends," said Jartek pointedly, "on how—and if—you let these pictures out."

Garak leaned against the door frame and folded his arms. "Ah, the freedom of the press! Another watershed for Cardassian democracy, eh, Jartek?"

Jartek jumped a little, surprised by his sudden appearance, and glared at him. "Just making sure the right message gets across."

Garak smiled at him mirthlessly.

"I'm sure it's not called the Wurlitzer," Ghemor muttered. He looked at Garak, eyes very sharp. "Well?"

Garak pushed the door closed behind him and walked over to stand by Ghemor's right hand. On the display screen—as he could, really, have predicted—the footage of Yevir talking to Nyra was playing, over and over again.

"Very nice," he said, nodding at it. "I bet they win the Pulitzer for it." Jartek shot another glare at him, unsure, as always, whether the humiliation was deliberate.

"And what prize do we take away this evening, Garak?" Ghemor took a sip of tea, and his eyes glinted as he looked at him from over the rim of the cup.

"Oh, all manner of trophies," Garak said cheerfully, joining him on the edge of the desk and stretching out his legs. "Korven turned out to be as informative as ever he was. And as accommodating." He paused.

"Don't stop on my account," Ghemor said.

"It *was* the True Way behind today's events," Garak confirmed.

"And do I need to have Korven arrested?"

"No," said Garak. "I don't think that will be necessary." He smiled. "We've come to an agreement, Korven and I. He had all manner of interesting things to tell me—and I don't doubt there'll be more—but, perhaps most satisfyingly, I was delighted to discover that during his erstwhile career in the military, he was once Councillor—formerly Gul—Entor's commanding officer. . . ." He left the corollary of that hanging in the air.

Ghemor caught up with him in a split second, Garak was pleased to see. "You've *got* to be joking. . . ." Ghemor said. He put his cup down on the desk with a clatter.

Garak shook his head.

Ghemor began to laugh, very softly. "Mev," he said, turning his head slightly, "get me Councillor Entor on the com, will you?"

Jartek frowned. "Are you sure? It's pretty late, Alon—"

"Oh, I think he'll speak to me!" Ghemor was grinning from ear to ear now.

"I think he will too." Garak smiled. After he had left Korven, he had taken the trouble to check for any outgoing communications, and he knew for a fact that Korven had contacted Entor directly after Garak had left him. "In fact, I rather imagine he'll be waiting for your call. . . ."

And less than pleased that that *link has been established.*

Jartek began to punch through the communication. He looked miserable, Garak thought. Which was in and of itself a happy thought. Garak filed it away lovingly for future contemplation and enjoyment, and then turned back to Ghemor.

"It's not *substantial* proof of a link between Entor and the True Way," Garak told him. "But it's good enough for our purposes, I'd say. Embarrassing enough."

"Good enough—*embarrassing* enough—for the Directorate to drop their opposition to Andak?" Ghemor looked at him hopefully.

"Well, given all the Directorate's recent lip service to the democratic process, I would think that being found to have even the slightest possible association with the terrorist group that tried to wipe the Andak project off the face of Cardassia would hardly inspire confidence in their claims to be committed to that process." Garak curved his lips into a hungry smile. "I suspect that our good friend Councillor Entor will be very anxious not to have that particular piece of information broadcast widely about Cardassia Prime. And, I should imagine, he will be very keen *genuinely* to become a good friend."

"Garak," said Ghemor, with undisguised admiration, "you are a miracle worker."

"Perhaps," Garak replied, with a reasonable attempt at modesty, examining his nails once more. "I prefer to think that I'm merely . . . attentive to detail. And to loose ends." He gave Ghemor a sly smile. "They're talents that serve well in tailoring—and in all manner of other occupations."

Jartek coughed politely, softly but surely inserting himself into the conversation. "I've reached Entor's secretary, but she says he left his office several hours ago—"

"Then try his home, Mev!"

"Alon, we *really* should be thinking about what we're going do about those pictures—"

"We will, Mev, in a minute! Get me Entor first. Wherever he is, whatever he's doing—I don't care. He can damned well fit in with me for a change instead of the other way round!"

"I doubt, somehow, that you'll be dragging him out of bed," Garak said dryly.

"Pity," Ghemor said bluntly. "I'd have enjoyed that. He's given me enough sleepless nights."

Jartek sighed and turned his attention back to the com.

That's right, Mev—you keep yourself busy. While I have a quick and quiet word with Alon. . . .

"It's a strange thing," Ghemor said, contemplatively.

"What is?"

"Well, just that while I'm delighted this situation is resolving itself so well—"

"*Very* well," Garak corrected.

"*Very* well," Ghemor conceded, "but still, I do find myself wondering what part democracy played in it. We're going to get the funding for Andak confirmed—but not because of any argument I or anyone else made at the committee. It's all because of Yevir, and because of what you knew about the True Way—because of a whole set of lucky circumstances, really. . . ."

Garak shook his head. "No, that's not right. Because when it comes down to it, what matters is that we won through negotiation. We didn't win using the same tactics as the True Way were trying. We didn't win through resorting to violence."

Well, except to Korven. But that was *seventeen years ago.*

On the monitor, Yevir received Nyra's hand again.

Garak contemplated the image for a moment. It was sublimely iconic. "You know," he murmured, staring at the display screen, "Your messenger boy over there is right about one thing—these pictures are going to have a profound effect."

"You're not actually *agreeing* with Mev, are you, Garak?" Ghemor's voice too had dropped to be close to a whisper.

"Well, not *entirely*—"

"I'm glad to hear that. I'm fairly certain my system can't take too many more shocks today."

Garak pursed his lips. "I've said this to you before, but *why* you keep him around, I'll never understand—"

"And I've said this to *you* before—it's because he's useful. Let's skip this argument tonight, Garak, I'm too tired for it." He sighed, and gestured at the display. "What do you think I should do about the footage?"

"What grounds are you using to hold it back?"

"State security."

"Ah yes . . . *that* old favorite. . . ." Garak stared at the picture, of the zoom-in on the Bajoran hand holding the Cardassian hand, and shrugged. "Why not just let them do whatever they want with it?"

Ghemor looked at him in surprise. "You mean that?"

"Well, why not? Really, Alon, what have you got to lose? Politically, your name is pretty much synonymous with the Andak Project. And now, thanks to Yevir's quite divine intervention, Andak—and by association, *you*—have his unequivocal blessing. So why not bask in some of his reflected glory?" Garak glanced over to where Jartek was still trying to raise Entor on the com and jerked his thumb in his direction. "In fact, I think you should get Mev the Messenger there to fix up a meeting between you and Yevir. Get the cameras on both of you, side by side. Shaking hands, preferably. *Ghemor greets Yevir; says, 'When it comes to peaceful solutions, we are all united.'*"

Ghemor laughed out loud. A little of the permanent air of strain that there was about him dissolved.

Garak waved his hand in the air vaguely. "I know the prose is hardly polished. Ask Mev to write you some headlines, that's what you're paying him for, isn't it? My point is that *finally* you've got some common ground here. There's no need always to be in competition."

Ghemor chewed at his thumbnail. His eyes were thoughtful, and alert.

"Besides," Garak added, "you're starting to get tiresome about the whole thing. And possibly verging on the neurotic."

And trust me—I recognize the signs.

Garak sighed. Something about the whole day was troubling him still. A loose end somewhere . . . He knew he wouldn't be able to let it go.

I'll sleep on it—if I can. It'll make sense in the morning. I'll make it make sense.

"I have Councillor Entor waiting to speak to you, Castellan," Jartek said.

"Thanks, Mev," Ghemor said. "Oh, and one last thing, before you head off home—contact that Bajoran reporter, will you? Tell her she can do whatever she wants." Then he reached over and switched off the display.

22

"Now, what was the very last thing I said to you when we spoke the other day?" Charlie Drury's words and his tone belied the relief that was transparent in his eyes. *"Ah yes, that was it—'No more controversy if you please, Keiko!'"*

"I know, I know. . . ." She smiled back at him. "But look at all the press coverage I got for us, Charlie! Surely it was worth it all just for that?"

He snorted. *"Hardly. Anyway, I'm assuming you don't plan on making a habit of this?"*

"Oh, I think we can safely say that you can rest easy on that score." She sighed deeply and pushed her hair away behind her ears. "Tell me, Charlie—how is this going to hurt the project? Do you think we're finished?"

"For heaven's sake, Keiko—don't worry about that now! Let me worry about it. Take a couple of days off, play with your kids, and we'll talk about all that later in the week." He smiled at her fondly. *"I'm glad you're all safe, Keiko,"* he said quietly, and then cut the com.

The room was quiet at last. Keiko slumped back into her chair. A couple of unread messages were still waiting for her, but she decided she wasn't even going to look at them until tomorrow morning. She sat and listened for a little while to the faint and comforting hum of all the equipment in the house—the com on standby, the temperature modulators, some gadget or other belonging to Miles. She had dimmed the lights before contacting

Charlie and, when she looked round, everything seemed to have taken on soft shapes and shadows: the desk, the table, the couch, Miles's toolkit, her papers, the children's toys. At the other side of the room, on top of the shelves, was the pot of *meya* lilies she had put there to keep them safely out of Miles's way. Had that really only been yesterday?

The flowers were drooping a little now, and in the half-light they looked sad and forsaken. With a sigh, Keiko pulled herself wearily up from her chair and went to fetch them. Sure enough, the soil was dry—*meya* lilies sucked up moisture. She watered the plant generously, liberally, and then took the pot back with her over to her desk. She sat down again in her chair, set the lilies in place before her, and leaned in close to them. She breathed in the sweet and subtle scent and admired once more the beautiful colors and clever fractals of the flower.

Each *meya* lily had three thin petals. From a distance these seemed to be pure white, but when you examined them more closely and, particularly, when you looked at the center, you could see, hidden away inside, a fine pink line that deepened to a dark and bloody crimson as it descended toward the stem. Then, if you traced the long, fragile petals back upward, you saw that at the top they each had three points. The leaves of the lily, clustering dark green and glossy beneath the petals as if to cradle them, also opened out in this way. The *meya* was indigenous to Cardassia, however unlikely that seemed. It was so needy for water, so thirsty, that you could only find it near the coast, and these days only in a few very remote places. It was impossibly fragile, Keiko thought, and desperately unsuited to the heat and aridity of its native land. *Stupid, stubborn thing,* she thought. *And each year it just keeps on flowering.* She gently touched the thin stem of the nearest lily. It quivered beneath her fingertip, and then was still. *One day,* she resolved, *they'll grow here at Andak. I'll grow them here at Andak.*

She heard a soft footfall behind her, and then felt Miles rest his hands upon her shoulders. After a moment or two just standing still, he began to knead at the muscles at the bottom of her neck. She dropped her head forward, gratefully.

"They're both asleep now," he said, and leaned in to kiss her softly on her hair. "You're not working, are you?" he added, his voice rising a little in surprise.

"Just thinking about flowers," she murmured, shifting her shoulders around so that they followed the motion of his fingers.

"Oh—so you *are* working!"

"Can't help myself," she said dryly. "It's a vocation."

He carried on with his task for a little while, and she closed her eyes, and began to feel the strain of the day depart, piece by piece. Then Miles began to speak again.

"I'm still so angry with him, you know."

"Mm? Angry with who?"

"Yevir . . ." He stretched the name out as he said it, making it sound like an accusation.

She opened her eyes. "You're *angry* with him? But he saved our lives—"

"He took a bloody stupid risk talking to Nyra like that. He was lucky he didn't get you all killed—"

"Is that what it looked like to you?" she said in surprise. "Because from where I was sitting it seemed like Yevir knew *exactly* what he was doing."

His hands halted at their work. "Do you really think so?"

"Oh, yes," said Keiko, softly. "I think the vedek judged the effects of his intervention very carefully. Almost scientifically, you might say," she murmured, and then raised her shoulders up to demand his attention back. Miles began massaging them once again, and the knots and the tension dissolved a little further.

"The people *I* despise," she said eventually, "are those from the—what did Macet call them?"

"The True Way," Miles muttered. Another accusation.

"That's it. The True Way—what a terrible, terrible name that is! What's true about their way? What's so true about using children like pawns to . . . well, to die, and just because of their hate? It's despicable. Poor Nyra . . ."

Miles grunted, noncommittally.

"What does that noise mean, Miles?"

"Just that . . . well, I have to wonder whether Nyra actually thinks she's done anything wrong."

"Miles, she's only a kid!"

"I know that, sweetheart! I'm not saying I don't feel sorry her—and God knows I feel sorry for that mother of hers all right—"

Keiko nodded her agreement vigorously.

"—but I think that if Nyra was given half the chance, she would just do the same thing all over again."

"But Miles, what she did is . . . well, it's incomprehensible!" She twisted her neck to look up at him. "Can you imagine Molly, when she gets just a few years older, doing something like that?"

"No, sweetheart, I can't—but then Molly's not Cardassian, is she?"

Keiko opened her mouth wide in disbelief. "*Miles!* That's an *ugly* thing to say!"

"Now, hang on a minute!" he came back. "Don't get me wrong. I'm *not* saying Cardassians are all mad, or evil, or anything like that. Macet's someone to respect, that's for sure; so's Ghemor—I can even put up with Garak, when he's not trying to give me the creeps. What I mean is . . . Of *course* I don't think Molly's going to hit her teens and start planting bombs under people. But that's because Molly's not from a culture that's spent the last ten years in decline, fought and lost a brutal war, and then been burnt to the ground. And I have to wonder too," he finished up, his hands working faster on her back as if to emphasize his point, "just how much trouble's being stored up as a result for Cardassia in the future."

"It's in enough trouble as it is," Keiko murmured, wriggling beneath his touch.

"Well, what I mean is—if there's a whole generation of Nyras growing up. A whole lot of kids who see violence as natural, and reasonable, or the only answer. Fifteen, twenty years' time—these will be the people running the place. I just . . ." He hesitated again. "I just can't see how kids can live through all of that and not be affected by it. Not grow up thinking that killing is a good or a normal response to a threat. And I wonder—what kind of society can you make out of children who've been traumatized like that?" The rubbing at her shoulders became gentle again.

She thought hard about what he had said, and what he had left unsaid.

"Do you wish we hadn't come here, Miles?" she asked him at last. "That we hadn't brought *our* children here?"

He didn't answer her, just kept on working at her muscles.

"Miles?"

"Well, Deep Space 9 wasn't exactly safe, was it?"

"That's evading the question, Miles—"

"Oh, I don't know, love! What do you want me to say? If it meant that you and Molly wouldn't have to go through what you've gone through today, then of course I'd say I wish we hadn't come here!"

"Do you want us to *leave?*"

"No . . ." he said eventually, his voice quavering a little. "No, I don't think so."

"You don't sound very sure about that."

"Well, that's because I'm *not* sure—how can I be sure? But *you* don't want to leave, and so . . . so we'll stay. For a while, at any rate." He stopped what he was doing, and leaned over her shoulder, to get a better look at her. His expression was a little worried. "You don't want to leave, do you, Keiko?"

She gazed at the lilies in front of her upon the desk. "I did, at one point this afternoon," she admitted. "It was when I was looking at Molly, and she was just sitting there with her arms around her . . . And I thought—what do we think we're doing? I thought—we must have been mad to come here. To *Cardassia,* of all places!" She reached out to touch the green velvet of the leaves.

"And?" Miles prompted her. He had straightened up, and his hands were at work again, this time rubbing gently at her temples.

"And as I listened to Yevir," Keiko said, sighing as she leaned back against Miles's chest, "I realized that it would be wrong to go. That there were things that you and I could do here that would really make a difference. That I *could* change things here, for the better. And that it would be . . ." She hunted around for the right word, "Well, it would be *irresponsible* to leave. Do you understand what I mean? That it wouldn't be right for us to sit back and do nothing, when there's so much that needs to be done. I guess . . . because we'd be storing up trouble for our own future then."

"So we keep on going with our work here—whether Cardassia wants it or not?"

"Well, even Tela knew things had to change. . . . We spoke about it . . . was it really only this morning? And she said then that she knew that change had to happen. Even though there's so little left, and even though she regretted it, she knew that there's just no going back for Cardassia."

He stroked the hair upon her brow, and sighed.

"You, don't believe me?" She smiled to herself. "You know, Miles, you should listen more to Garak!"

"Now, there's something I never thought anyone would say to me!"

"I mean it! The wiser people on Cardassia—"

"Well, I suppose he counts," Miles muttered.

"The wiser ones," she carried on, ignoring him, "the ones who *really* love it—they know that if Cardassia is going to survive, it has to change. And so they're committed to that change, completely committed."

"And the unwise ones? The ones who—I suppose—only *think* they love it?"

"Well," Keiko said, "I've heard it said that actions speak louder than words." She pushed the plant pot to the center of her desk, straightened herself up in the chair, and turned to look at him. "Which I guess means we'd better make sure we get results, hadn't we?"

23

As a grubby dawn scours the morning sky and leaves it grimed, three gentlemen set out to take counsel with each other once again. They approach their meeting place like stars aligning in some maleficent conjunction or—to the more scientific mind— like lines converging at a point upon a graph. But whatever their nature, here they all are now, gathered together at the top of a hill, watching as Cardassia wakes to a new day.

In the past—before recent events altered the landscape irrevocably—this was a favorite vantage point for those who wished to gain a sense of the lay of the city. The hill itself is not especially high, but it stands on the edge of the town and, by a fortunate confluence of geographical contours and architectural planning, it offers a particularly comprehensive view. A path leads up to the very top, where the hill is paved, and there has been placed a plaque, mounted upon two iron posts, showing in metal a representation of the skyline ahead. Each monument and building is clearly indicated, and a few notes about their history and purpose are offered for the edification of those who take the time to pass this way. The plaque is still there, even though the places it describes are not, and the eldest of the three men gathered stands with one hand resting upon it, looking out.

The youngest man is eating from a carton of hot canka nuts he bought from an enterprising old woman selling them out of a box she had turned into a stall and set up on a street corner. At regular intervals, he draws out a nut, crunches it open on his back teeth, retrieves the kernel, and then drops it on the ground, where a small pile of debris is accumulating next to his right foot. Then he chews and swallows the nut, and sighs out his warmed breath, watching as it curls through the dank morning air. His colleague, the middle man, observes this ritual for a while with a curiosity that threatens to become exasperation. And then he shakes his head impatiently, and turns to their elder, standing motionless, and surveying the ghost of the view.

"We ought to come to a decision about Korven," he says to him, briskly.

The senior turns his head almost imperceptibly. "A 'decision' . . . ?" He rolls the word around in his mouth, as if he does not much care for its taste.

"What I mean is—can we depend upon him now? Is he still reliable—?"

"We shall see."

"Is he—forgive me, I have to ask this question—is he now to be considered . . . surplus to requirements?"

"We shall see."

A little chastened, the first speaker falls quiet, and turns his attention back to the progress being made with the nuts. The older man continues to watch the gray morning light spread out further across the soiled sky. The youngest of the three takes out his final canka nut, and pops it into his mouth. Then he carefully folds up the empty carton, and places it into a pocket. His colleague's eye ridges shoot up, almost as far as his slick hairline.

"Why," he asks, inexplicably vexed by this action, and tapping the toe of his boot at the husks on the ground, "did you throw all those away, and not the carton?"

The young man chews meditatively at his nut. "Well, it's not quite the same, is it?" He pats his pocket. "This is plastic." He nods down at the ground. "Those are organic."

The other sighs, and decides it is hardly worth his while pointing out that the shells have fallen onto stony ground. His colleague swallows his mouthful of nut, licks the salt from his lips, and then sniffs at the morning. There is a sharp smell that catches at the back of the throat, as if something had been burning, and was then put out.

"What about Garak?" he says bluntly.

*His words steam up in the cold, and then they seem to hang
there. They seem to acquire substance. And so does the doubt—
and the fear that always arises from doubt. It becomes an almost
tangible thing. The hand resting upon the edge of the plaque
grasps it more tightly, the knuckles whiten, the sinews stiffen.
Cardassia gasps for air within that clutch.*

*"Who can say?" the older man murmurs, at last. "Who can
say?" He releases his hand, and runs his finger—lovingly, rever-
ently—along the lost metal skyline. Then he turns slowly to face
his colleagues. "But you may leave that . . . decision . . . to me."*

*His voice is like nails being drawn slowly down stone. The
youngest of the three stares back coldly for a moment or two, and
then nods as if to accept the rebuke or, at least, the authority of
his senior. The other merely shifts the nutshells about with his toe
again, shivers, and sighs. The old man rubs his hands together a
little to warm them. Then he places both hands in his pockets.*

*"Gentlemen," he says, and inclines his head. His friends are
both blessed with enough experience to recognize a dismissal
when they see one. And thus, with no further farewell, all three
depart, heading off down the hill in different directions, each
back upon his own trajectory, each the hero—and so the villain—
of his own enigma tale.*

It was late afternoon, and by some miracle it wasn't yet raining. Garak stared down at the padd in his hand, and thumbed his way diligently through a report from the Cultural Restoration and Reconstruction Commission. Next week's business.

Something flickered, and Garak glanced up and out of the window. Outside, the streetlights were coming on—now, *there* was a rare sight. Garak blinked, feeling somehow oddly heartened by this approximation of normality, and then he went back to his industrious assessment of the contents of the padd. As he read on, he listened closely as Entor, sitting in his place at the far left-hand side of the panel, finished his statement to his colleagues on the Technological Appropriations Committee.

"—and as a consequence of the events of the past twenty-four hours, and because of my desire to see a safe and a stable Cardassia, it is my conclusion that the project at Andak requires the committee's unequivocal support—"

Too many words to say something very simple, Entor. You lost. We won. Garak reached the end of the report, came to his own conclusions on cultural conservation, and then allowed himself to stretch out lazily in his chair. *But I'm content to let you talk on awhile if it makes you feel better.*

"Thank you, Councillor," Ghemor said—really rather graciously, Garak thought, all things considered—when Entor at last drew to a close. Then he called for a vote. Two members of the panel from the Directorate voted against Andak, but it was a formality. The project's funding and so its future had been secured.

With evident satisfaction at the outcome, the castellan brought the meeting to a close. As he stood up, he glanced over at Garak and inclined his head almost imperceptibly. Garak knew the signal.

I'd like to talk to you.

Give Ghemor his due, Garak reflected, as he made his way across the meeting room, he never tried to make it an order. He weaved past all the people offering each other their opinions, and through the door that led to Ghemor's office. Ghemor was standing with one hand pressed against the window frame, the other holding a glass, watching the light withdraw from the city. He shifted his head slightly on hearing Garak's approach, and then twisted the blinds shut. The room became closed, suffused with the false yellow of the strip lights. Ghemor turned, leaned back against the wall, and regarded Garak thoughtfully.

"Korven owed you a favor, you said. Do I want to know exactly how you did all this?" He downed the contents of the glass.

Nothing to tell, Alon. Just the same old story. I tortured a man seventeen years ago, and now he does what I tell him.

"Almost certainly not," Garak replied.

After a moment or two, Ghemor moved away from the window, walked slowly behind his desk and sat down, his eyes all the while fixed on Garak. He poured another drink for himself.

"We got what we wanted," Garak reminded him.

"Indeed we did," he said. There was a bitter edge to his voice. "Strike up another victory for democracy. What did Entor call it? A sham."

"If you wanted the luxury of leading an ethical life, you really shouldn't have gone into politics," Garak pointed out. "And if you're not prepared to do what it takes to secure the future of Cardassia, neither should you have accepted it as your responsibility." He moved carefully toward the desk, pulled out the chair and sat down. Ghemor didn't answer.

"What's brought this on, Alon? This isn't like you. This isn't what you were saying yesterday."

Ghemor rubbed at his eyes. "I'm tired," he said frankly. "And more than a little disheartened." He glanced at the blinds shielding the window and the room. "And I'm sick of the rain."

Aren't we all? I don't think I know anyone in the city who isn't desperate to feel the sun upon his face again. But Garak didn't reply, just waited.

"These are the days that count, aren't they?" Ghemor continued, softly, still staring at the covered window. "What we do now—what we choose to fight for, how we choose to fight for it—that will make all the difference, won't it?" He looked back at Garak, with eyes intense and more than a little troubled.

You're asking me for moral guidance? Oh Alon, you're going to be sorely disappointed! I've played the part of the loyal lieutenant before—to Tain, to Damar—but neither of them made that mistake!

"Yes," Garak said instead, wearily. "The fights we choose now will make all the difference. But how we choose to fight them?" He shrugged. "Bad men seize power because—" The words "good men" stuck in his throat. "—because better men will not do what it takes to stop them."

And we are the better men—whatever that tells us about Cardassia. Whatever that means for Cardassia.

"Yevir stopped that girl just by talking to her," Ghemor answered.

"From what I've observed of our good friend the vedek, he doesn't trouble himself unduly with doubt. A luxury that he shares with Entor, with the True Way, with the puppeteer that pulled the strings on that poor child Nyra Maleren . . ." Garak stared down at his hands, smoothed out the creases on his jacket. Then he looked at Ghemor. "Stop flattering yourself that this has all taken some kind of moral or ethical toll. You *enjoyed* watching Entor this afternoon!"

A smile tugged at Ghemor's face. And then he began to laugh. "Oh, I most *certainly* did . . . !"

"Well then." Garak smiled at him. "Remember to relish your victories, Alon. Because no one else will. And because otherwise you'll drive yourself insane."

Ghemor poured him a drink. "Celebrate this victory with me, Garak?"

Garak took the glass and raised it, and they drank—and then the door to the office opened. Both of them straightened up in their chairs, pushing away what remained of the doubts before they might be seen.

Jartek came in, holding some padds. Ghemor relaxed a little, resting his elbows on the desk. Garak didn't move a muscle.

"I have first drafts of the press releases about the committee's decision if you want to take a look through them, sir."

"That was quick, Mev." Ghemor reached out to take them.

"Well, I didn't have any real doubts as to the outcome," Jartek replied. "Not once Mr. Garak here had taken charge of the situation."

Garak responded with a smile which he didn't allow further than his lips.

Ghemor scanned through the data. "These are looking fine, Mev—go ahead with them. Whatever we owe him, I'd still be more than a little pleased if we could dislodge Vedek Yevir from his customary spot as chief newsmaker on Cardassia Prime—if only for an evening. Do you need some quotes?"

Garak stood up. His particular expertise was no longer needed here, and he wanted to get out of this shut-in room, even if only into the dead air of the city. He set his glass down on the desk. Ghemor looked up at him, raised his hand in farewell, and nodded his thanks.

Outside, Garak stood for a minute or two and surveyed the world beyond the offices. The streetlights cast an orange haze that failed to diffuse the gray dusk encroaching on the city. Before him lay the black hole that had been Victory Square, where memorials to Cardassia's greatest guls and legates had once stood, now no more than rubble on the ground and dust in the sky above.

They poisoned Cardassia. . . .

Garak shook his head to free himself of the thought. O'Brien had been right—he *was* getting morbid. He really needed to put a stop to that.

He walked out briskly into the wreck of the square. Within watching distance of the office block there was part of a statue still standing, the base of a monument, with a piece of an arch offering a little shelter. There, in the lengthening shadows, Garak stood and watched and waited, and thought about all that had been lost—Cardassia, with her bright skies and dark dreams; and he thought too about all that remained—all the certainties, all the doubts. The sky went black. After forty minutes it began to rain.

Fifteen minutes after that, Garak's vigil and his patience both paid off. He stepped out from his cover into the partial, artificial glow of the streetlights.

"Jartek," he said.

The younger man slowed down and turned. "Garak," he replied, his pale, hooded eyes blinking once, twice, dismissing a frown, and watching warily as Garak lengthened his stride to catch him up. "Have you been waiting for me all this time?"

"It was no trouble." They fell into step alongside each other. "You're going in my direction, it seems." Garak watched from the corner of his eye as Jartek considered asking him why he'd waited, and then didn't. Jartek seemed always not quite to be as smooth as he would wish, Garak thought. And the stripes on his jacket were just a shade too wide.

"It's raining . . ." Jartek tried.

"It's usually raining in the city these days."

They walked on in silence.

"So tell me, Jartek," Garak said, as they rounded the corner by the offices, "are you content with how events have turned out?"

Jartek swiveled his head to look at him. "All things considered, I'd have to say yes, really. It could have been an awful lot worse. Imagine if that bomb had gone off. Disastrous for the government."

"It's certainly been something of a triumph for Yevir—again."

"The castellan too," Jartek said with a frown. "He ordered a prompt and effective response—"

"Macet did his job there very well, I thought."

"It was Alon giving the orders—that'll be clear enough, wait until you see the news later. It matters to people who's running the show. And—even better—it all comes with the added benefit of securing the Andak funding." Jartek smiled. "Yes, I think we can say the past few days have been a success for the Ghemor government." He was almost preening. Garak pursed his lips.

They were beyond the reach of the streetlights now or, at least, the ones that had been rigged up here had no power. There were a few halfhearted buildings, but no people to be seen about. Given the many dangers that they might face in the streets these days, people tended to stay under cover after dark. The rule of law was such a *precarious* thing, Garak thought. Even after such a good day for Ghemor and his government—and it had been just that, a *very* good day—there would still be parts of the city that *really* weren't safe to walk through late at night. . . .

With one quick, expert movement, Garak had Jartek by the throat and pressed up against a wall. The younger man's eyes goggled and he started choking.

"What the—!"

"Shut up!" Garak hissed, tightening his grip just a little further. Jartek clawed at his hand. Garak grabbed his wrist and slammed it hard against the stone of the wall. "Now you listen to me," he said, very softly. "You'd better be just half as good as you think you are, because if you've left a single fingerprint, *anywhere,* we can kiss goodbye to Ghemor—"

"What d'you mean? I don't—"

"Don't lie to me! I've played this game for years, Jartek! *Tell* me what you did!" Garak gripped a little harder. "What did you give Korven? Information? Money? *Both?*"

Jartek nodded, as much as he could.

"So the True Way would make a move, yes? And you'd be there, a step ahead, ready to discredit them?" Garak's eyes widened in sudden alarm. "Korven didn't know it was all coming from you, did he?"

That would put a rather different complexion on our little talk. . . .

Jartek shook his head. Garak concealed his relief.

"You're not that stupid, then. What else?"

"Nothing, I swear, nothing. . . ."

"Are you quite sure of that? You didn't, to pluck an example out of the air, leak Remar's report on Setekh?"

Jartek stared at him, his eyes widening, paling. Garak tightened his grip and the choking noise started up again.

"Yes, yes, that—that too!"

"And tell me—and you'd better be very, *very* certain of this, Mev—have you left *any* fingerprints?"

"None, none, I'm sure of it—please . . . !"

"Oh, you'd better be right." Garak gave him a cold smile. "Anything more to confess?" he asked. "While we're both here—and no one else?"

"No . . ."

Garak stared at him, at his unshielded terror, stared hard. Jartek's hair was wet from the rain and his eyes were bright from fear and panic. Garak took it all in, and judged what it meant. Sometimes you knew when you couldn't get anything else. You knew when there wasn't anything else to get.

"*You're choking me . . .*" Jartek pleaded.

Garak leaned in, close. "The next time," he whispered into Jartek's ear, "that you get a clever idea, you talk to me. Do you understand that? You do *nothing* before you've told me *everything.*"

"*I swear, I will. . . .*"

"Oh, and I believe you!" Garak replied, his voice soft and benign. He let go. Jartek slid down the wall, rubbing at his throat and coughing.

"One other thing," Garak said, as he turned to head off into the night, "Get yourself a new suit."

And *that,* he decided, as he left Jartek spluttering on the ground, was a proportional response.

Garak made his way back home through the rain and the ruins. There was a hazy red glow off in the distance—maybe the lights had come on somewhere, maybe something was burning.

Dark skies and darker dreams, but still the city of crimson shadows.

And as Garak walked along, his hand in place upon his disruptor, he remembered again all the lost ways of his city, remembered again all the rules of the game and just how well he played it. And he knew he'd not been this satisfied at the end of a match since he'd shot and killed Weyoun.

Epilogue

Spring came as a surprise to Andak, and it surpassed all expectations. As each day dawned a haze would settle on the mountains, softening their edges, and for an hour or more they would be sheathed in cool, translucent gray. Then the rain would fall—clear showers of pure water that came punctually mid-morning, and that freshened the air for the whole of the day. Spring had come to Andak, as it had never done before, smoothing the shift from harsh winter to stark summer; a third season, a proof of change.

Keiko watched all of this progress, and she marveled at it. In the plains to the south of the base, a gentle but ineluctable transformation was being wrought, as the barren yellow fields became fertile and grew. The first shoots of the crops they had planted were appearing. Monitored every minute, both day and night; surely nothing had been watched so proudly, discussed so thoroughly, nurtured so tenderly? The models from the physicists, the projections from the statisticians, the data from the geologists and botanists, the sheer bloody hard work of them all, as Miles put it—all these complex strands had been woven together, and now the plains of Andak were embroidered green.

The gardens at the settlement were growing too—and this made the houses seem less temporary, as if their roots were finally taking. Here, it had to be admitted, lay one of Keiko's few regrets—that she had not planted her *meya* lilies last year. *But even I didn't think that there would be so much water . . . !* And it seemed to Keiko that even this lack was more like a promise—a promise that there would be a second year of growth at Andak, and that it would be remembered as the spring that *meya* lilies blossomed in the Cardassian desert.

Keiko sat up from where she had been kneeling, stretched her back, and then tucked her legs under her again, watching closely the work being done in front of her.

"Is this right?" the girl next to her asked, tentatively dripping water on the row of sprouting green. Keiko leaned in and checked the moisture levels.

"They'll cope with a little more," she murmured. "And you'll need to watch them—they'll need watering each day throughout the growing season."

The girl nodded, and poured from the container much more abundantly. Having enough water for all their tasks still took some getting used to, particularly for the Cardassians here. Keiko set down her measuring tool, and wiped at her forehead with the back of her hand. Then she looked around the square.

The evening was golden, the light soft and warm. Children were out playing, Molly among them—or, rather, at the head of them. Even Yoshi was out, sitting near one edge of the square, down on the south side, where it was quiet. He was fingering the leaves of the *aramanth* bushes that stood there. These were already showing their first bright yellow buds. Feric and the other members of the Oralian Way, under Keiko's tutelage, had planted these—two lines of bushes, four in each line, meeting up in one corner of the square. A small, secluded grove, set right at the heart of the busy settlement. In an hour or so, judging by the quality of light and the shadows being cast by the mountains, the Oralian Way would be coming out to hold their meeting there. Feric's plan for later in the spring, he had told Keiko, was to put something permanent at the point where the bushes met. He had spent what time he could spare during the winter months working on a carving, chipping away slowly at a large piece of black Andak stone.

For the winter had been long . . . and there had been points during it when Keiko had come close to despair. Even when the aftermath of the drama in autumn had died down, even after the work at Andak had been financially secured, there had still been the not inconsiderable matter of making the project a technical success. Once the politics were out of the way, there was still the science to be done.

Keiko had been warned repeatedly—by Feric, by many others among her friends at Andak—that the winter would almost certainly be harsher than she was expecting. "Whatever you're thinking it'll be like, Keiko," Feric had told her, "double it. Triple it."

And they had all been right. She would never have imagined that a place this hot could become so cold. Most of all, she would never have guessed how quickly the winds could whip up and in from the plains. Miles upon miles of flat, open land across which they could pass without hindrance, gathering speed and vengeance until they came to a sudden, whirling halt as they hit the mountains—and the settlement, huddled below. Winter had seemed to Keiko to consist of nothing more than day after day of salvaging and fixing broken equipment that had been ripped up in the gales; week after week of looking out at the plains and wondering whether anything of what they had planted there could possibly stay alive through such an onslaught. Winter had been long, bleak, and barren. Each day she had wondered how anything could survive it.

And not all of the community had come through. Naithe, for one, had gone well before the year turned. "Frontier life, my dear director," he had said to her—and to anyone around who was willing to listen—"has turned out to be rather too exhilarating for my tastes, I'm afraid." Keiko would have liked to think that Naithe had left here a little sadder and a little wiser—but at a conference she had recently attended, she had heard someone say that he was dining out on the story of how, when he was at Andak, he had single-handedly talked down a Cardassian terrorist. She had no idea how he was managing to spin a story like that out of the real events of that day . . . but some people would never change. At least he was as irrepressible as ever, she thought—and found that she could remember him almost fondly.

Tela Maleren and Nyra too had gone, of course . . . bound for the capital, at first, Macet had told her; it seemed that there were many people there who wished to know all that Nyra knew. Keiko had had no news of either of them for months now. For all she knew, they might well no longer be on Cardassia—and she was not sure who, or even if, she ought to ask to find out more. And others had left Andak in their wake—mostly friends of Tela and several among the staff who had been sympathetic to her views. There had been no overt antagonism that Keiko knew of—and certainly there had been no formal requests from others for them to leave. It seemed they had gone entirely of their own accord.

"We have to be realistic about this, Keiko," one had said to her, regretfully. "After all that happened—how can we possibly stay here? What credibility do we have? Who would ever trust us?"

Keiko knew that many people at Andak had welcomed these departures, but she herself viewed them with ambivalence. She was honest enough to admit that on some level she was relieved that the divisions which had once threatened to undermine the settlement would no longer be there. But these losses were the source of her other, main regret too—that all the very different people that had come together at the outset, all with such great hopes and plans, had not been able to reach an accommodation. Not everyone who had made the journey out to Andak had found they had a place there.

Keiko had had no trouble filling the posts that had been left empty, at finding people willing to come out to this remote part of the planet. There were still too few places like Andak on Cardassia; too few places where such highly trained people could use their skills, and live an almost normal life, rather than scratch around for survival. And, these days, Andak was a by-word for success. It signified hope. It signified the future. Keiko looked around the square again, at the gardens and the labs, at the kids playing and the people working, at the grove and at the mountains, and she felt proud of all that she could see, of all that had been done and would be done. She thought of the rain that would fall in the morning, sweet and clear. . . . And, before she could quite stop herself, she thought too, as she still sometimes did, of that day when it looked like everything would be lost; the day when the whole place seemed about to go up in flames. . . .

Keiko turned back to the girl still working alongside her.

"That should be enough for now," she said. "We'll come out and water them again tomorrow."

A file is closed and set upon a table. "Well, gentlemen. I think that's done."

"Fade to black . . . and hold . . . and *cut.*"

ANDOR

Paradigm

Heather Jarman

ABOUT THE AUTHOR

Heather Jarman grew up fantasizing about being a writer the way many little girls fantasize about being ballerinas and princesses; she had all the lyrics to the Beatles' "Paperback Writer" memorized by age 6. But in her wildest suburban childhood dreams, she had no idea how Saturday afternoons spent lazing in her beanbag chair watching *Star Trek* would dramatically impact her lifelong aspiration.

Indeed, the *Star Trek* universe played host to her professional fiction debut, *This Gray Spirit,* the second novel in the critically acclaimed *Mission: Gamma* series of *Deep Space Nine* books set after the TV series. She's also written *Balance of Nature,* part of the *Star Trek: S.C.E.* series, and contributed "The Devil You Know" to *Prophecy and Change,* the *DS9* tenth anniversary anthology. With Jeffrey Lang, she collaborated on "Mirror Eyes" for *Tales of the Dominion War.* She's also currently writing an original young adult novel.

She lives in Portland, Oregon with her husband and four daughters. She rarely finds time to lounge about in beanbag chairs these days, much to her deep regret.

To my sisters and girlfriends: they are one and the same.
Laurie, Jane, Julie
&
Bethany, Dena, Kirsten, Mikaela, Susannah

ACKNOWLEDGMENTS

First, to the rangers at Capitol Reef National Park, Torrey Utah: Thanks for answering my questions. Second, I drew much inspiration for Andor's neoromanticism from *The Letters of J.R.R. Tolkien* and other biographical and scholarly writings on Oxford's Inklings. The films of Hayao Miyazaki and Akira Kurosawa provided visual and cultural context.

Thanks to my fellowship of writers, especially Andy Mangels, Mike Martin, and Danelle Perry, who provided a wonderful setup for this story in their novels *Cathedral* and *Unity*. Keith DeCandido, as usual, was a dear friend and should consider a second career as a therapist. High fives to Terri Osborne for joining the crazy gang and giving me another girl to hang out with at Shore Leave. Special thanks to Dean Smith, Loren Coleman, and Kris Rusch for giving such great advice.

Besides being a soulmate, Kirsten Beyer provided me with brilliant insights into this alien world of Andor and the best beta-reading a writer could ask for. Bethany Phillips provided invaluable support all along the way.

There wouldn't have been a book without my honorary big brother, my Jem'Hadar boy, Jeff Lang, who, on a daily basis, held me together and offered this wise admonition: "Put one word in front of the other."

The deepest thanks to my family, who endured simultaneous remodeling and novel writing coupled with piles of laundry and no food in the house. My incredible husband Parry is a candidate for sainthood. My daughters are the light and joy of my life. No woman is more blessed than I am.

And a special thanks to my editor, Marco Palmieri, who is friend, counselor, cheerleader, and an all around good guy. *Lunghi in tensione e prosperano!*

HISTORIAN'S NOTE

This story is set in November, 2376 (Old Calendar), approximately four weeks after the conclusion of the *Star Trek: Deep Space Nine* novel *Unity*.

We all begin with good intent
Love was raw and young
We believed that we could change ourselves
The past could be undone
But we carry on our back the burden
Time always reveals
In the lonely light of morning
In the wound that would not heal
It's the bitter taste of losing everything
That I've held so dear.
Though I've tried, I've fallen . . .

—Sarah McLachlan

From *The Tale of the Breaking:*

Thirishar rose up with sword in hand and challenged the gate-keeper of Uzaveh, saying, "I have done as your Master com-manded. The tasks are completed. Now let me pass or face the same fate as those who were sent forth to stop my quest."

But Uzaveh the Infinite, watching from the Throne of Life, was amused that this creature, made of little more than the dust of the universe, dared demand entry at the gates. To spare the gatekeeper from the warrior's death-blade, Uzaveh bid Thirishar enter.

Thirishar walked proudly down the Path of Light, believing that as the first to complete the tasks of Uzaveh, the Empty Throne beside the Infinite, the Throne of Secrets, now belonged to the Greatest Among Mortals. Had Thirishar not earned the right?

But wise Uzaveh, omnipotent and omniscient, Eternal and In-finite, knew that the warrior possessed the power and knowledge to conquer all challenges, save one.

Uzaveh held up a hand, and Thirishar halted.

"Are you Whole?" whispered Uzaveh in a voice that shook the universe.

But the warrior did not understand the question. "I am Thirishar. I claim the Empty Throne."

"No," answered Uzaveh. "You are unworthy, for you are not yet Whole."

Thirishar trembled and knelt before the Uzaveh, for the first time understanding the arrogance and the vanity that had misled the mortal to this moment.

Still, Uzaveh had mercy.

Death was not to be Thirishar's fate.

"Instead," decreed Uzaveh, "from one, there shall be four.

"To one shall be given wisdom to be a protector—the cunning warrior who shall fight for the future.

"To another shall be given strength, providing a foundation upon which the others can build.

"One shall be given blood, the river of life that shall flow among the others, providing nurture and sustenance when the flesh longs to yield.

"And to the last shall be given passion, for the flame of desire will bring change to the others and warm them when the chill is bitterest."

So Thirishar became four: Charaleas became wisdom; Zheusal became strength; Shanchen became blood; Thirizaz became passion. Together, the four are the First Kin.

Uzaveh banished the four to the farthest reaches of the kingdom and upon seeing them there, so far from the Thrones and utterly alone, appointed for each a guardian.

For Thirizaz, the Fire Daemon fed the soul-consuming passion. Loving Shanchen became a vessel for the Water Spirit, forever bound to the Eternal love flowing from Uzaveh's Throne. For strong Zheusal, Earth became protector. For wise Charaleas, the Stars became guides, their light defying darkest night.

"When you are Whole, as I am Whole," Uzaveh said, "then shall you return to my presence and assume your place at my side."

—From The Liturgy of the Temple of Uzaveh;
Third-Century Codex

I

At the crossroads of the universe, Prynn Tenmei looked up and suddenly felt insignificant.

From its broad sloping base on the docking ring to the tiny airlock port suspended nearly a half-kilometer above, the great arching tower of upper pylon one began as an enormous wall of metal, narrowing dramatically as it curved up and away from Prynn. Its gray plated surface stood out in stark relief against the angled light of Bajor's distant sun.

Now, that would be a zero-g walk to remember, Prynn thought before she reluctantly tore her attention away from the station and back to the matter at hand.

Striding slowly across the hull of the *Defiant,* Prynn decided that she'd found the one place where no one would look for her. "No one" being Shar. If he couldn't be bothered to show up for their date—their holosuite reservation, she was quick to amend—then she couldn't be bothered to hang around Quark's waiting for him. Having spook parents proved to be good for something, after all: over her lifetime, she'd developed a finely honed sense of how to disappear, and going EV was one sure way to do just that. The odds of her accidentally running into anyone *(Shar!)* in the vacuum of space—not exactly the station's hot spot—were next to nil. Besides, the *Defiant* needed her. She'd noticed an anomalous reading the last time they'd taken the ship out. If she waited for the engineers (who'd said it was nothing) to see it her way, she'd be tapping her toes until B'hava'el went cold.

Prynn wasn't one who liked waiting.

Halfway across the ship's topside, she stopped and adjusted the settings on her gravity boots, allowing for enough pull that she wouldn't drift off into nothingness but enough give that she could practice acrobatics. A little bounce in her step when she was in zero g made the occasional somersault and standing back tuck much easier. She had a hard time understanding some people's phobias about extravehicular operations. Sure, there were minor worries about damaged air supplies and being set adrift, but such mishaps occurred maybe one walk in fifty. And last time there had been a problem, the transporter chief was able to beam her aboard before hypoxia set in. From her perspective, the pleasures of zero-g work outweighed the risks; she relished the feeling of near complete liberation from terrestrial constraints. Given the choice between going out in a work bee or a space suit, she'd take the latter every time. Besides, the *Defiant* was her baby. As senior flight controller, she knew the starship's needs better than almost anyone—including the engineers, who liked to believe that *they* knew better. When she'd told them about the temperature fluctuation on hull grid Z-47 and how she thought an extravehicular diagnostic was in order, they'd waved her off. Actually, *Senkowski* had waved her off. She suspected that he was the kind of engineer who didn't get the fun side of EV repairs.

The first time the fluctuations appeared, she'd explained to Senkowski how she believed she'd be able to identify the problem if she saw it up close. He'd blanched (and for a pale guy, that was saying something) and muttered about recalibrating the sensors. During their last patrol two days ago, the same readings in the same grid showed up on her board. When she confronted him, he had told her the fluctuations were statistically insignificant and to stop being so neurotic. Okay—he didn't use the word "neurotic" but she could tell he was thinking it. Noting the look on his face, she figured the prospect of an EV repair shift scared him. *Statistically insignificant fluctuations my ass. Coward.*

Prynn bent down and caressed the starship's skin. A visual scan of the ablative armor didn't immediately yield any evidence of a problem. But she had a pretty good idea of what was ailing the old girl and where she should start, so she took a step, somersaulted, touched down on the starship's surface on the toe of her boots, and somersaulted again. Much faster—and more fun—than walking the remaining distance. Still . . . this time it wasn't as much fun as it normally was. Orbital skydiving in the holo-suite would have been better.

More like, orbital skydiving with Shar, dammit.

Ditching their plans wasn't his style. Nog had been known to occasionally shop around for a better offer, but not Shar. He usually arrived early whenever they had plans. Which was why Prynn had been so taken aback when he didn't show up tonight—without so much as a page! She'd been sitting on the balcony level of Quark's, nursing a Core Breach, then another, not really thinking about how much time had passed, when it occurred to her to check the time; Shar was forty-five minutes late. Trying to reach him over the com turned into a waste of time; he wasn't accepting her calls. Then Treir had materialized, prepared to take a third order, and exuded something suspiciously like pity. Prynn had taken the cue, thumbed her bill, and hightailed it out of there. Her ship needed her, even if Shar didn't. Prynn was once again reminded why she typically avoided relationships: stable, rational individuals resorted to mind-boggling, time-travel-paradox-level logic to justify their behavior. And she was done with it. *Done.*

Maybe it was males in general. Once, in outraged humiliation after a roguishly handsome cadet she thought was interested in a relationship with her—not just sex—made it clear she was just another conquest, she'd screwed up her courage to approach a fellow pilot: a female cadet. She'd reasoned that perhaps the romantic problems she'd had thus far might not be colossal bad luck but more like an irreparable defect in the entire male gender. Males tended to be emotionally stunted when it came to romance. Avoid the gender, avoid the defect. Reasonable thinking. When an opportunity had come up to ask the woman out, Prynn found herself saying, "Can you believe what a jackass that Jack DiAngelo is?" and they'd sat at the bar having an all-night bitch-'n'-bull session about their relationship horror stories. She'd concluded from that experience that the old adage—*Men: can't live with them, can't kill them*—would follow her to the grave.

She was loath to admit it, but she'd cherished an unexpressed hope that Shar, being a male (of a sort) member of a different species, wouldn't exhibit the same obtuse stupidity she'd come to expect from males of every skin color, planetary affiliation, and physiological variation.

The odd part was that up until tonight, he'd been perfect. She'd never sensed that he was uncomfortable with their evolving relationship. Predictably, a brief awkwardness ensued when Prynn had first raised the idea of a romantic liaison a couple of months ago, but they'd quickly overcome it, moving into a rhythm of shared meals, gym and entertainment time, and holosuite visits.

After a few weeks of Prynn doing the asking, he'd started taking the initiative, tonight's holosuite appointment being his idea. He seemed to enjoy her companionship, gradually opening up about himself. More recently, he'd shared his feelings about losing Thriss and why he'd let his bondmates return to Andor without him. Her heart had swollen painfully in her chest as she listened to him; she understood what a gift of trust he offered. Prynn couldn't remember the last time she'd felt as close to someone as she'd felt to Shar in those moments. Their losses and their messed-up family lives gave them plenty to talk about, but it was a sense of being known as you could be known only by one who had passed through—and emerged—from suffering that bound them together. He mattered to her now. *A lot,* she admitted to herself. And it irritated her to realize it. *I can't believe I've let myself get in this deep,* she thought, unclipping the tricorder from her hip and beginning to scan the *Defiant*'s hull. *If I've let it progress to this point and am just figuring it out, what's Shar feeling?*

Pressured. Trapped maybe. And after she'd reassured him that all she expected from him was friendship? *Don't kid yourself, Tenmei: You saw this holosuite time as a date; he sensed it and he didn't want to hurt your feelings so he conveniently "forgot."* She hissed a curse, clenched her teeth, and sighed in self-disgust. She deserved to be stood up. Self-imposed exile in space was suitable punishment. *You're stupid, stupid, stupid, Tenmei.*

She found the section her tricorder identified as grid Z-47, squatted down, and initiated a scan. Submicroscopic pores had opened up in a two-centimeter-square section of the ablative armor, making the metal more susceptible to microfractures.

Technically, Senkowski was right: such a small vulnerability wouldn't impact the *Defiant*'s performance any time soon. Prynn knew, though, that this section would become more porous over time and would have to be replaced. She grinned. She loved being right.

She performed an in-depth scan of the damaged plating, mapping every micrometer so that Senkowski, Leishman, and the others could perform the repairs.

"Prynn."

She flinched. That was Shar's voice over the comm in her helmet. She was debating whether or not to ignore his call when a shadow moved over the hull in her field of vision. Startled, she spun around and saw another figure in an EVA suit standing behind her. The glint of blue behind the faceplate told her all she needed to know to identify her visitor. She stiffened. "What are you doing here?"

"It seemed like a nice time of day to go for a walk."

"Very funny."

"Nog's teaching me sarcasm. Apparently utilizing such an inflection is a critical component of Ferengi interpersonal communications."

"How clinical of you."

They stood facing each other for a long, silent moment. Prynn refused to give in to her impulse to ask him what the hell he was up to.

"While the view of the Denorios Belt is lovely from here, could we move inside to continue our conversation?"

"Conversation. Hmmm. I was working. You intruded."

"I apologize for my earlier lapse. It was unintentional. . . ."

"No big deal. Like I said, I had work to do. Pores in the ablative armor."

"That can be serious. Is it safe to take the Defiant *out?"*

"For now . . . and about"—she paused, gulping, feeling ridiculous—"another six months."

"I'm glad you took care of it tonight. Since it was clearly so urgent."

Prynn exhaled through gritted teeth. "Give the sarcasm a rest, please. I'll tell Nog you've mastered it and can move onto something new—like pseudosincerity."

He paused.

She knew he was studying her, trying to read her and not having any luck. Bless the EVA suit. Dropping her eyes to the tricorder, she studied the readings, and then uploaded them to the *Defiant*'s engine room. Too bad she couldn't put flashing lights around Senkowski's console and a big full-spectrum banner on his screen proclaiming, *I told you so.*

"Zhavey *contacted me via subspace tonight. She asked me to come home to Andor.*"

Her eyes flicked up. Shar had stepped closer to her. Their gazes met. She searched his face. "Really?" Since Charivretha zh'Thane had left the system following Bajor's induction a month ago, no communication had passed between *zhavey* and child. Never mind that Shar had left no doubt that he had severed his ties with Andor. "You're not going, right?"

"*I would like to talk it over.*" A long pause. "*With someone I trust.*"

She flushed, ashamed, relieved, and overjoyed all at once. "Oh. Okay."

"*The shuttlebay's empty right now. Join me?*"

She thought she heard a smile in his voice.

Prynn shrugged out of the EVA suit sleeves, dragging a tanktop strap off her now bare shoulder. Without seeing him, she knew Shar, who had only removed his helmet, watched her. She stood still for a moment, feeling the weight of his gaze, enjoying the attention. *He'll break your heart if you let him.* Self-consciously, she pulled the strap back onto her shoulder, shimmied out of the rest of the suit, and replaced it in the supply locker built into one wall of the shuttlebay.

"So," she said, turning to face him. "What's up with your mom?"

He took a deep breath, his antennae curved and quivering with nearly invisible tension. Otherwise, his inscrutable composure revealed nothing. "The Andorian Visionist Party, the most vocal opposition to *Zhavey*'s Modern Progressives, is very close to procuring enough votes in the planetary districts to recall the ruling Progressive cabinet and with it *Zhavey*'s Federation Council seat."

"That's too bad—I know how much the councillor's political career means to her." *About as much as Vaughn's Starfleet career means to him,* she added mentally. "But what does this have to do with you?"

As he continued shedding his EVA suit, Prynn noticed a square-linked, gunmetal chain around his neck, disappearing into his tank. Shar explained, "The opposition is claiming that my *zhavey* has lost touch with the Andorian people, that she's become the Federation's tool, not Andor's representative looking out for our people's interests. As part of their case, they're using my refusal to return to Andor for the *shelthreth* as proof that she's not only failed as a councillor, but also as parent."

Prynn whistled. "That's harsh."

Shar nodded.

"So what business is it of theirs if you consummate your bond or not? Isn't that *your* business? Your choice? I don't see what that has to do with Vretha."

"As some see it, failure to reproduce impacts the Whole, Prynn, not only the individual. Each lost opportunity adds to the burden faced by my people. Besides, whether I like it or not, I have a high profile on Andor."

She looked at him, questioning.

"Yes, I'm Charivretha's *chei,*" he said. "But I've gained some additional notoriety since Anichent delivered the Yrythny ova to my colleagues back home on my behalf. Then there's Thriss's *zhavey.* A thousand years ago, Sessethantis zh'Cheen would have been the First Princess in one of Andor's ruling families. We haven't had government by hereditary gentry for five centuries. But there are many—including the Visionists—who still acknowledge the position of those families and pay their descendants honor. Thriss's suicide was a blow to more than her kindred."

"Let me guess. Thriss's *zhavey* is also a ranking Visionist."

"The regional party chieftain of the Archipelago, one of our most populated regions."

"So Vretha wants you to come to Andor to help her save face with Thriss's influential family," Prynn said. "And to prove to her constituents that the Visionists are misrepresenting her."

Shar nodded, hanging up his suit and closing the locker.

"What do you get in return?"

The first hint of a smile touched his eyes. "On my behalf, she will publicly invoke the Whole Vessel Law, which legally allows bondmates to separate. She will then remove herself from any and all positions where she can influence my career. I agree to see her when she's nearby on business. Otherwise, I am left alone."

"No strings attached?"

"That's what she promised."

"Do you believe her?"

"I want to."

"But . . . ?"

Shar said nothing.

He didn't need to. Of course he wanted to believe his *zhavey*, wanted to trust that she had his best interests at heart; experience had taught him to expect differently. Prynn intimately understood the internal war he fought. As far back as she could remember, she'd struggled to define life independent of Vaughn, but the relentless magnetic craving of wanting his approval, to please him, had never abated. That was the problem with parents. Of course they gave life and that earned them the right to expect a lot, but in Prynn's experience, parents didn't hesitate to run roughshod over their children when their own needs required attention.

The edge of her anger blunted, Prynn moved closer to where Shar stood and gestured for him to sit down. They both dropped to the deck, cross-legged, shoulder-to-shoulder. Turning her head, she sought his eyes. He sensed her and met her gaze. Prynn probed his expression for evidence of deceit or manipulation and found nothing. *He's exactly what I thought he was.* She sighed deeply, leaned back against the wall, her arm inadvertently brushing his. She felt him stiffen at her touch, and her breath caught in her throat as she waited for him to react.

He didn't pull away.

They sat in silence for a long moment, Prynn's mind racing between choices, impulses, and memories. She could sense what a burden Vretha had placed on him by asking him to come home, and she wanted to relieve him of that weight. Tell him to claim his life without thought to what his *zhavey* wanted. Peeling away

the surface layers of her protective instincts, however, Prynn realized she wanted him to defy Vretha because of her own fear:
that if Shar left Deep Space 9, he might finally connect with
Andor in a way that would keep him there. She wasn't ready to
lose him—to lose the potential of *them*. The pain of losing her
mother again, of Vaughn's choices, receded when she spent time
with Shar. She believed she helped him in the same way. They
couldn't walk away yet. *But he trusts me to advise him. Whatever
I think, whatever I'm afraid of . . . he has to come first.*

"Tell me the truth," she said. "Will she keep her word?"

"Truth? I am not entirely certain that I need what she has
promised. My life here is comfortable. I can meet my career
goals. I know Captain Kira respects me for myself—not as an ancillary to my *zhavey*. I have"—he turned his gaze on
Prynn—"friends. Friends that mean a great deal to me."

The *Defiant*'s atmosphere suddenly felt dry and thick, leaving
Prynn speechless. She swallowed hard. *Maybe he's closer to
feeling what I'm feeling than I thought he was.* She looked into
his face and leaned closer to him. His eyes, gray and haunted, en-
tranced her.

"Prynn?" he whispered.

She maintained eye contact, willing him to see what she felt.

A throat clearing. "Excuse me, Ensigns."

Startled, Prynn and Shar flew apart and pushed off the floor,
snapping to attention.

Lieutenant Commander Phillipa Matthias, Deep Space 9's
counselor, stood still just inside the exit on the opposite side of
the flight deck. Prynn hadn't even heard the doors open. *And
once again Prynn Tenmei makes a fool of herself in public. . . .*

The corner of Matthias's mouth turned up—perhaps a touch
of amusement at what Prynn imagined they must look like, sitting on the deck, still out of uniform. She wished her ability to
bluff her way through a card game carried over to more personal
situations.

Before either Prynn or Shar could speak, the commander said,
"At ease. I know neither of you is officially on duty, and I'm
sorry to intrude, but a situation's come up. A personal matter
concerning Ensign ch'Thane."

Prynn nodded and said, "I'll go—"

"No," said Shar, grasping Prynn's hand before she could turn away. "I'd like you to stay."

"Are you sure about this, Ensign?" Matthias asked.

"Quite sure, Commander," Shar answered. He gave Prynn's hand a reassuring squeeze; she squeezed back.

Squaring her shoulders, Matthias linked her hands behind her back and narrowed her eyes, focusing intently on Shar. "I've just come from speaking with Captain Kira. You may not be aware of this yet, but an official request from the Federation Council has come in for you to take personal leave to travel to Andor, which the captain has granted."

Shar's antennae tensed. Prynn could feel the rising heat of his embarrassment traveling down to his hand. Vretha's bullheaded way of pursuing her own agenda astonished her.

Matthias continued, "I'm also slated to travel to Andor."

"Sir?" Shar whispered.

"Shar, I—" She broke off, closed her eyes, and took a deep breath. Her lips parted; no words emerged. A contemplative pause became a resigned expression. "I apologize. I'm finding that the right words escape me right now. I've been asked to run a rather unpleasant errand on behalf of someone I'll be visiting on Andor. I'm hoping that if you're traveling there yourself that I . . . well . . . won't have to do it."

"What is the errand, Commander?"

"Sessethantis zh'Cheen invited me to Thriss's Sending."

Color drained from Shar's face. "I'd assumed the rituals would have been held before now."

Matthias shook her head. "One of *Zha* Sessethantis's bondmates has been on deep-space recon for six months. He returns to Andor next week."

The merest mention of Thriss stirred up Prynn's protectiveness toward Shar, but she wasn't sure she understood what they were talking about. "Sending? Is that Thriss's funeral? Wouldn't her family have attended to that as soon as Anichent and Dizhei returned to Andor?"

Shar shook his head. "Not necessarily. For those who observe the old traditions, as long as the body's integrity can be preserved, the Sending is postponed until all the pieces of the deceased life—family especially—can be reassembled." He looked at Commander Matthias. "And as Thriss's caregiver in the final month of her life—"

"Her *zhavey* felt I held a critical 'piece' of Thriss—that my participation in the Rite of Memory was needed or Thriss might not be complete in the next life," Matthias finished for him. "Under the circumstances, I could hardly say no. Still, I know that this is a family time . . . and there are other . . . issues."

"Like me?" Shar said quietly, his voice edged with bitterness. Matthias smiled sadly and nodded.

"Will there be time for you to help your *zhavey* if you're attending Thriss's funeral?" Prynn stroked the back of his hand with her thumb; he remained unresponsive. "Shar? Is everything okay?"

Matthias frowned at him. "You didn't know, did you?" Shar shook his head, and through gritted teeth, Matthias grunted, "Dammit."

"I assume that your unpleasant errand involved obtaining this from me?" Shar reached behind his neck and unfastened the square-linked chain, pulling out a diamond-shaped pendant from beneath his shirt. He held it out, dropping it into Matthias's hand.

"*Zha* Sessethantis asked me to—I mean I—I couldn't think of a way to ask. I thought if you were going to Andor that you could—"A deep pink flush tinted Matthias's porcelain complexion.

"No, I understand, Commander," Shar said neutrally. He held out the chain for Matthias to take. "Thantis is nothing if not a keeper of tradition. Honor your commitment to the *Zha* of Cheen-Thitar clan."

"Wait a sec—" Prynn looked from Matthias to Shar and back again, her eyes slowly widening. If what she thought was happening here was actually happening here, it was too outrageous to be believed. She looked at him again, hoping she'd misunderstood; his hollow expression left no question in her mind. "You're not invited. Are you, Shar?"

He said nothing.

Shar wouldn't be excluded from grieving with Thriss's family—*his* family. He couldn't be! To prevent him, the one closer to Thriss than any of the others—she'd been the love and light of his life . . . Dropping her eyes to her floor, Prynn thought she finally comprehended the crushing weight of Shar's self-imposed exile. "There's no way you should go. You don't owe them anything. They can all go to hell."

"Prynn—" Shar said.

"No." She refused to look at him. "All of them—Vretha, Thriss's mom, your bondmates—they're punishing you for daring to defy them, to be who you are. They don't deserve you. Stay here—with people who care about you."

Gently taking both her hands so she would look at him, he whispered a thank-you before turning back to Matthias. "When do you leave, Commander?"

"In two days."

"If I decided to travel with you, is there room on the transport?"

"You don't have to do this, Shar," Prynn insisted.

"At minimum, I have to consider it."

"Why?"

"Because sometimes," Shar said, "what is just and what is right aren't the same."

She bit her lip, sighed. *Say it like you mean it.* "All right. Whatever you choose, I'll support you. That's what friends do."

His eyes smiled at her again.

"If you're thinking about coming, why don't you take this back—" Matthias held the necklace out to Shar. "We can work something out."

"No. You take it. Thantis will never receive it from me." Shar pushed Matthias's hand away, sending the necklace clattering to the floor near Prynn's feet.

Prynn bent over to retrieve it. Furrowing her brow, she studied the pendant, running her thumb over the surface. The silver-toned diamond shape was small enough to fit in the palm of her hand. A cross etched into the surface sectioned it into triangular quarters. Each quarter was engraved with an ornately embellished geometric symbol, paired with a string of runelike characters—words, she assumed—beneath each symbol. It was surprisingly lightweight and delicate. A clasp along one edge suggested that it wasn't merely a pendant, but a locket. Prynn said, "I don't understand why something of yours is so important to Thriss's mother."

"A token—a *shapla*. At the Time of Knowing each bondmate receives one. It bears the traditional icon for each gender"—Shar pointed out the geometric symbols—"and our names in old Andorii script." Lifting it from her hand, he unfastened the clasp, revealing its contents—four locks of white hair woven together. "Mine, together with one from each of my bondmates. With Thriss's death, she must be made Whole, so this weaving, along with hers and those of Dizhei and Anichent, will be sent with her on her journey to the next life."

Still struggling to process the notion that Shar wasn't invited to the funeral, Prynn felt this latest indignity reignite her simmering anger. "You're returning your engagement gift to the person who won't even let you come to the funeral?"

"It's what's done, Prynn. Spiting the rights of the dead because I have arguments with the living dishonors Thriss's memory. It was naïve of me to think that I could keep this for myself, that Thantis would overlook it." Shar passed the *shapla* back to Matthias. "I believe I have decided."

Prynn tensed, bracing herself for his words; she knew, though, without being told what his decision would be.

"Regardless of whether or not I participate in the Sending, my remaining on the station will lead to speculation among my people. Some may choose to believe that I am sulking. Or worse, that I am vindictive. Some will believe that I am ashamed of my choices and I am *not*. I will go back to Andor and help Charivretha because she is my *zhavey*—it is the right thing to do; then I will return to Deep Space 9." Shar let a breath escape slowly through his nose before he looked at the commander. "I'll discuss my leave with Captain Kira before my next shift."

Matthias closed her hand around the *shapla*. "And I'll send my travel plans to your personal database. We can coordinate later. Good night, Shar, Ensign Tenmei." After a slight nod, she exited the shuttlebay.

When she had gone, Shar turned back to Prynn, his expression veiled. "I know you believe I am mistaken."

Prynn shook her head no. Halfheartedly, she paced a few steps back and forth in front of the shuttlecraft *Sagan*. She struggled for the right words—how to tell him that she couldn't bear the thought of him having to endure any more disappointment and sadness, how to say *your happiness matters to me,* to let him know that no matter what, she would be there for him—and then suddenly she knew what was required of her. "If you have to do this, you're not doing it alone. I'm going."

"Prynn—"

"No! Don't even think about trying to talk me out of it. I'm owed some leave time, and I'm going with you to Andor."

For once, his emotions were laid bare—surprise, relief, and something else, something she didn't dare name; Prynn's throat tightened.

"Thank you," he whispered. "I cannot begin . . . Thank you."

That face . . . She longed to touch his cheek and fold him in her arms. *That beautiful, sad face.* "Of course," she said simply. "That's what friends do for each other."

2

Still feeling odd in his civilian clothes, Shar crossed the rounded observation deck of the interstellar transport *Viola*, weaving in and out of socializing passengers who quaffed beverages and sampled cracker-and-fruit appetizers, and slowly made his way toward the viewport wall. Before he was thrown into a whirlwind of *Zhavey*'s public-relations events, he wanted a single private moment. The *Viola* was next in line for docking at Andor's Orbital Control Station, so he couldn't linger too long. Easing into the spot being vacated by a pair of Ktarians, Shar looked out on his homeworld for the first time in six years.

Through a break in the silver clouds, he saw patches of the Zhevra continental mass, dull in its variegated browns and blacks, spreading like the massive relief maps he'd crawled all over as a young *chan*. Squatting down over the Vezhdar Plain, he'd caressed the knobs and crests of the Great Rift Range, memorizing the geological markers with his fingers, impressing each corner of his planet upon his memory by touch. *This is where I live,* he'd said while pointing to the terraced benches of Hill Country. *This is where I belong!* And the teacher had nodded approvingly, as if to say, *Good chan !*

Now, studying Andor from far above, he traced the smooth railing, the memory of gritty slot canyon walls filling his fingertips, the warm wind caressing his face. *How much the same it seems from up here,* he thought. *But I'm not the same, am I?* As close as home appeared, he had never felt as disconnected from this place as he did now.

He had expected this moment to feel different. He wasn't sure *exactly* what he'd expected, but this wasn't it. A gush of nostalgic affection, maybe. An appropriate sense of loyalty, of duty, to the people whose plight had defined his life—such an emotion would be understandable.

Instead he felt nothing. Numbness.

Wait. His thoughts paused. "Remoteness" was a better word; he felt far away and he took this understanding as affirmation of the choice he had made to sever his personal ties to Andor. Anichent and Dizhei would be better off without him. Whatever tether had once bound him to Andor's destiny had been pulled so thin, he could scarcely sense its existence anymore. Perhaps it was not *what* had bound him, but *who*. She who had made this home to him was gone. Without her . . .

What is wrong with me?

The comm system clicked. "*Viola on approach. Stand by for docking. Travelers to Cheshras Island and the eastern Archipelago, please check with central ticketing about potential storm interference. Travelers continuing on to Vulcan should remain aboard. Thank you.*"

Storm? That wouldn't be good news for Phillipa. He turned back to the viewport. Sure enough, vivid gray-green whorls churned sedately over the cobalt blue Khyzhon Sea, the delicate cloud cover effectively masking the violence of a spring typhoon. The population centers on Cheshras Island might already have storm shields up. Phillipa would have to reach Thelasa-vei province before Deepening or face further delays. If Shar's schedule had allowed them to leave a day earlier, as Phillipa had originally planned, the commander would have arrived before the storm system. Now, she would most likely be late. Thantis would be disappointed, yet again, and of course it involved the *chei* of zh'Thane, who had been the source of her *zhei*'s suffering. All knew the old aphorism "As is the *zhavey,* so is the child." There would be no question in *Zhadi*'s mind as to whose fault this was. Since Sessethantis and Charivretha had spent most of Shar and Thriss's early years circling warily around each other, Shar was certain Thantis now took perverse pleasure from *Zhavey*'s latest career ordeal.

A slight tingle in his left antenna heralded the approach of Prynn behind him, mere seconds before she called his name from across the lounge. He turned to greet her. Her short green jacket and matching boots were easy to spot in the crowd, as were the vivid autumnal colors of Phillipa's Bajoran-style tunic and trousers. Shar himself had chosen a baggy gray shirt and black leggings, then covered them with a floor-length black cassock. He hadn't reckoned how strange it would feel to shed his uniform and travel with crewmates who had done the same.

From appearances, Prynn and Phillipa had retrieved their travel bags and appeared ready to start on the next leg of their journey. He left his place at the railing and met them halfway.

"You heard the announcement?" Shar asked Phillipa as he took his bag from her.

"I did," Phillipa said. "I take it that there might be storm delays for me?"

Shar nodded. "I should have realized—it's typhoon season in the region you're traveling to. Ionization of the atmosphere rises dramatically, to a degree seldom seen on Class-M planets, making transport impossible. Public travel is delayed or suspended owing to dangerous meteorological conditions. It's less of an issue in Zhevra Continent, where the climate is usually more accommodating."

"So Phillipa is stranded in orbit?" Prynn asked. "For how long?"

"It depends on how well the climate controls can manage the more violent arms of the storm. However," Shar said, turning again to Phillipa, "Prynn and I won't transport down to Zhevra until we know that you're on your way."

They felt a slight shudder as the transport's engines powered down. A low clang sounded beneath the passengers' ambient chatter, the sound of docking clamps attaching to the ship's hull.

"Prepare to disembark."

The trio allowed themselves to be propelled along by a crowd that appeared to have origins in every corner of the Federation. For his part, Shar didn't remember Andor being such a popular tourist destination. He didn't make frequent trips offworld while growing up, but he didn't recall any return trip that was as crowded as this one had been. The three of them had squeezed into a two-person sleeper compartment with Shar, who needed less sleep than his human companions, and napped on the floor as necessary. Under those circumstances, the superior/subordinate protocol quickly gave way to all of them being on a first-name basis.

They walked three abreast through the airlock and down a sloping gray corridor into the gate lounge of Orbital Control. Though he hadn't been to the station in many years, his recollections of it as a straightforward, Federation-style public facility proved to be correct: utilitarian beige couches and chairs; high, drafty ceilings; replicator stations and information kiosks distributed evenly through the gate area. Helping Phillipa find her way around shouldn't be difficult.

"Prynn, if you'll check the departure monitors to find out which transporter station we're queued to"—Shar waited until she'd nodded in acknowledgment before shifting his attention—"I'll take Phillipa to the main desk to straighten out— *what?*"

Without warning, an intense, white-yellow light beamed into Shar's face and blinded him. Raising an arm to shield his eyes, he squinted past the light, but saw only dark silhouettes.

The verbal barrage began, assaulting him on all sides.

"Sat 2 newsnet, we're live from Orbital Control with Starfleet Ensign Thirishar ch'Thane. Ensign ch'Thane, how is it being home on Andor?"

"What? It's fine. But I don't—"

"What did Councillor zh'Thane have to do to get you to agree to leave Deep Space 9? Sat 6 had a report—"

"Is it true Councillor zh'Thane will be invoking the Whole Vessel Law on your behalf?"

"I'm not going to discuss—"

"Have you spoken recently with your mentors at the Andorian Science Institute and if you have, do you have any comment on the rumored research under way?"

"I don't know what you're—"

"Do you have any greetings to send out to friends or family?"

The unexpected cacophony overwhelmed Shar as the reporters pressed in, the lights from their headsets hitting him from all sides. None of them were giving him a chance to speak.

Twisting to look behind him, Shar caught Prynn's confused expression as she fought to get through the pack of reporters. He reached out, trying not to become separated from her, but she was already too far away. As his frustration grew, so too did the instinct to lash out. His body tensed—

"That's enough!" a voice declared. A uniformed sentinel—a *thaan*—pushed his way through the crowd toward Shar, followed by several other security personnel, who were forcing the reporters back despite their hisses of indignation. "You people should know better—this area is off limits to nontravelers. If you want to speak to Ensign ch'Thane, you'll need to make other arrangements. You have thirty seconds to comply or face charges."

Without asking for Shar's consent, the *thaan* grabbed him by the arm and steered him away from the crowd. Another guard had affixed himself on Shar's other side, and together the pair guided him to a different part of the facility. Confusion and anxiety gave way to anger as questions raced through his mind. Foremost among them: How would a swarm of reporters have known his travel plans? Unless . . .

Zhavey.

Sighing with annoyance at the reporters' herd mentality, Charivretha switched off her monitor. *Hand them a story gift-wrapped and they ruin it*, she thought. *All they had to do was wait until he'd cleared the gate area!* Her intention hadn't been to have him attacked; she had hoped to show Andor a pleasant homecoming scene. Instead? Chaos. Thirishar would be justifiably furious. Charivretha touched her desk's compad, signaling her aide. "Zhende, contact Satellite Station 3. Thank them for their restraint, and let them know they can have a sit down after my press conference."

Hand to chin, she leaned back in her chair and contemplated the view over the octagonal Plaza of Freedom and its glorious fountains: Serpentine streams of water leapt over towering leaves of nearly transparent green mica, imported from the Archipelago region. In the distance, the cerulean obelisk of the Shran monument stood out against the crisscross skyline of slanted office towers and high-rise residences that so identified the Andorian capital. Years of work had earned her this view. The thought gave her pause. Thinking of passing time as "years" instead of "cycles" testified to how far she'd come from Hill Country.

Her first visit to this office had been in her fourteenth cycle, before her Time of Knowing, when her *zhavey* had brought a petition to Andor's Federation representative, protesting the border conflict with Cardassia. She now sat behind Councillor th'Vrash's very desk; she remembered how the morning light gleamed on the highly polished, petrified *eketha* wood, the glyphs and runes of Andor's ancient iconography carved into the surface. When she'd taken up residence, she'd brought her personal belongings from her parliamentary office, assorted holos and awards, a sculpture given her by the children of Shayel Island, a room-sized rug woven by Sessenthantis zh'Cheen in one of her rare, generous moods. . . .

Thantis. Why had she even allowed the *zhen*'s name into her thoughts? Doing so immediately assured she'd slip into a foul mood—especially since Thantis had deliberately neglected to invite her to Shathrissía's Sending. Granted, Shar had been closer to poor Thriss—fragile child that she was—but his decision to place his duty to Starfleet above his duty to his people had directly contributed to her suicide. Thantis rightly excluded him, but Vretha had done nothing to earn such a snub. Whether or not they liked each other was beside the point! Protocol demanded that all family members attend a Sending—not only those who maintained amiable relations.

A perfunctory chime, then Zhende poked his head inside the door. "A gong has sounded, Councillor. The Presider has convened a party Enclave."

Vretha's hand fell from her chin. "He promised he wouldn't!" Rising from her chair, she grabbed a crimson robe from a hook on the wall and hurriedly pulled it over her clothes. The Presider's aide had assured her that she would have until Deepening to present her strategy to the party leadership. Why had the Presider gone back on his word? She was still waiting to hear from Progressive activists in a number of districts—

Racing past Zhende's workstation, through her chair-lined waiting area—gratefully empty of constituents and press—she stepped out onto the open-air ramps that sloped down the sides of the Parliament Andoria building. Vretha moved quickly along the nearest route to the lower levels. As she walked, she scanned the plaza, noting a gathering crowd; she guessed someone on the opposition side of parliament had organized yet another rally. The Visionists were evidently stepping up their campaigns. Across the plaza, issuing from the other visible wings of the government complex, she spotted several officials in brightly colored robes headed to the subterranean Enclave chamber.

"Charivretha."

Wincing inwardly at the familiar voice, Vretha stopped and turned, waiting patiently for Representative th'Tethis, who was robed in distinctive purple, to waddle up to her. The delay was unwelcome: Appearing before the Enclave at the last minute might send a signal of disrespect to the Presider; failing to honor the demands of an elder *thaan* would also be disrespectful, so she was caught between two duties. *No positive outcome either way,* Vretha thought. It briefly occurred that perhaps th'Tethis was slowing her down on purpose to make her look bad before their senior party officials. She'd heard rumors that he was mentoring a young *shen* out of Wethesa who he hoped would eventually take her seat. *I'm not finished yet,* Vretha thought.

Th'Tethis held out a quivering, flattened palm; Vretha touched her hand to his and bowed from her shoulders. "How can I serve you, Elder *Tha*?"

"Keep an old *thaan* company, Charivretha. We will go to Enclave together."

"As you ask," Vretha said, and took his proffered arm.

Together, they followed the down ramp to the next level. She was forced to stop again when th'Tethis paused to retie his ceremonial robe. Several more levels awaited them. All around, parliamentary representatives with their aides made their way to meetings. Glancing out of the corner of her eye, she saw that most of the bright-colored Enclave robes had already vanished, presumably to the lower levels.

They walked in silence for several minutes before th'Tethis asked, "And how fares your clan, Charivretha?"

"It endures, Elder *Tha*," she answered automatically. "And yours?"

"Those of us who remain endure as well," th'Tethis said with an odd expression, almost as if he'd made a joke. Before she could inquire further, he said, "I understand that your *chei* has come home."

Ah, so he saw the newsnet report. "He comes to help his *zhavey* during a troubled time."

"Indeed," said th'Tethis. "Better troubled times with family than without, wouldn't you agree?"

What is he playing at? "As you say, Elder *Tha*." Vretha looked ahead. The final corridor was empty. As she had feared, she and th'Tethis would be the last to arrive.

"What awaits you is not what you expect," he told her.

"Excuse me, Elder *Tha?*"

"Let me speak frankly, Charivretha. Do not rush to face your fate. Soon enough it will find you."

Vretha's eyes narrowed. "May I speak frankly as well, Elder *Tha?*"

The *thaan* smiled, revealing a mouth of copper teeth. "You know I do not judge my colleagues on their adherence to dusty traditions. Otherwise, I'd join the Visionists."

"Then hear this." Vretha dropped her hold on his arm and took a long step forward, placing herself squarely in his path. If he had no use for manners, she would behave accordingly. Brashly, she forced eye contact with him, violating the boundary of his inner world; his antennae tensed. "I will not be shuttled aside for some ambitious *shen* you are grooming to replace me."

"My protégé has cycles before she will be qualified to assume the Federation Council seat," th'Tethis said, the corners of his eyes crinkling kindly. "It is not I who wants you replaced."

Vretha stood stock-still, stunned by the magnitude of her mistake: she had no response for th'Tethis. She had exhibited the naïveté that would be expected from a first-cycle provincial representative.

Sliding his arm through hers, th'Tethis whispered, "Be glad that you confronted me, Charivretha. You now know you have one less enemy within the party. But remain on your guard."

Vretha hesitated. Finally she asked, "Can I count on your support, Elder *Tha?*"

"You can count on *no one* to sacrifice their political career on your behalf, Charivretha. Remember that. You must convince your fellow Progressives that your usefulness is not at an end, and that they have more to gain than to lose by continuing to support you."

Vretha allowed a sigh to escape her nostrils. So she was in for a fight. She'd expected as much, but had not anticipated having to battle her own party. Had she gone into Enclave expecting its full support, her political end would have been swift. Th'Tethis had armed her with the knowledge she would need to have at least a chance at survival, and for that she was grateful. She told him so.

The old *thaan* patted her arm. "Fight well," he advised her in his soft, rasping voice, "and others will fight with you. Ah, here we are."

Entering into the Heroes' Antechamber never failed to evoke awe in Vretha, no matter how many times she'd walked through this, the oldest room in the Parliament Andoria complex. She imagined the great ones who had gone before her, smoothing the flecked gray stone floor with their sandals, symbolically purifying themselves with water and oil before they undertook the sacred business of governing Andor. From four walls of the eight-sided room, the faces of the mythological Guardians studied all who approached the Grand Chamber, judging their worthiness. Before the vaulted archway that led within, Vretha and th'Tethis removed their shoes, then paused to wash their foreheads and palms in the mineral water bubbling up from the ground into the ritual basin, also carved from stone. Dabbing their fingertips in ornate vessels of sweet-scented oil, they touched their eyelids, noses, tongues, ears, and antennae, sealing the vessels of their senses from receiving or offering treachery. Pulling their hoods up from their shoulders to cover their heads, they approached the entrance.

Four *chan* warriors, clothed in the dark padded armor of the old Imperial Guard, stood at the archway, ceremonial blades drawn in defense of the Enclave. Vretha announced her intent to join the gathering, and the guards stepped aside, pointing the tips of their weapons to the ground. She crossed over the threshold into the Grand Chamber, a room hewn entirely from a dark, almost black granite; as she'd anticipated, a full Enclave had con-

vened around the diamond-shaped well in the middle of the
room. Progressive leaders from Andor's sixty-four electoral
provinces knelt around the lip of the depression, facing the center, and leaving open spaces among them for her and th'Tethis.

Striding toward the gathering, Vretha paused and bowed at
the shoulders before the Empty Throne, situated between the
archway and the Enclave. Legally, Andor was still a constitu-
tional monarchy, despite the fact that no single ruler had reigned
over the planet in centuries. Thalisar the Last, who first united
her people centuries ago, had deliberately died childless—but
not before implementing the parliamentary system that she had
created to succeed her, and which had governed Andor ever
since. The Empty Throne, unlike its namesake in the myths of
Uzaveh, was kept to honor what Thalisar had achieved. In a single lifetime, she had utterly abolished the clan warfare that kept
Andor divided for so long. Charivretha wondered grimly if she
had envisioned the altogether different struggles that had replaced the clan conflicts.

Eyes averted politely, Vretha knelt three places down from
Presider ch'Shelos, while th'Tethis assumed his place on the opposite side of the well. On a signal from the Presider, those gathered around the Enclave basin moved to a sitting position, their
legs dangling over the edge. Vretha glanced discreetly at the figures around the well, wondering how many friends she had left
among them.

"I apologize for the suddenness of this meeting, Charivretha,"
ch'Shelos began, "but the party leadership felt it was critical that
we have a dialogue before your press conference."

"You've called me here to ask me for my resignation," Vretha
said, determined to gain the upper hand quickly and unwilling to
grant ch'Shelos the privilege of trumping her. "Let me be clear,
then: I won't do it. At a time when Andor needs an experienced
voice in the Federation, there is no one who knows better how to
represent our interests than I." She would not gloat at the surprise
the Presider projected.

He recovered quickly from her opening. "You've honored us
with your service, Councillor, but certainly you are wise enough
to see that our present circumstance requires drastic action. Our
administration is under siege from our political adversaries, the

Visionists. The Progressives, as a whole, are fighting to keep our agenda moving Andor into the future. In that equation, Vretha, you are a divisor, a liability, because the Visionists have managed to put your face on their attacks."

"And you propose to balance the equation by subtracting me, is that it?" Vretha asked, holding her chin high. "I'm disappointed, Presider, that my own party, which has always fought passionately for the least of causes, would capitulate so easily to Visionist pressure."

Ch'Shelos's eyes narrowed. "There is the larger vista to consider, Councillor. Even you can see that a strategic sacrifice may derail the Visionist attacks sufficiently to buy us the time we need—"

"So you wish to buy yourselves time," Vretha said. It was a risk, daring to interrupt the Presider, but she judged that now was the time to take a few risks. "That seems fitting in a way. Our entire agenda has been about buying time, after all, whether it's the time to weather the political crisis of the moment, or the time to search for a genuine solution to our ongoing reproductive crisis. Buying more time has become an end unto itself. What do a few small sacrifices along the way matter—careers, relationships, lives—as long as we have more time?" Where had *that* come from? Vretha felt her inner heat rising, images of Thriss entering her mind unbidden.

A representative in azure blue—she didn't recognize him with his hood—spoke up. "A dramatic critique, Councillor, but a hypocritical one, since you have supported the strategy you now condemn throughout your career."

"I've not merely supported it," Vretha countered forcefully, "I've helped shape it. Such is my point, *Cha* Presider and honored colleagues. History and experience have shown us that Andor has ever been a world of complexities, requiring that we be a patient people, reluctant to act in haste, determined to find the best solutions to our problems, not merely the most expedient ones. Eliminating me is the expedient solution. Time can truly be bought by allowing me to continue my work on behalf of our people. I therefore ask for a chance to counter the attacks against our party."

"Against yourself, you mean," the blue-hooded one said.

"You argue for *your* political survival, not ours, Charivretha zh'Thane. And you channel the voices of radicals such as your *chei* in your desperation."

A hiss escaped Vretha's teeth. Murmurs rose among the members of the Enclave as she glared at the blue-hooded representative, fighting to hold back her rage. Her anger wasn't for him alone, though. He was right about what she said—that Andorians might be sacrificing too much to buy time was Shar's old argument. How many times had he said the same things to her to justify his defiance of the Andorian way, of her? Her preoccupation with their long-standing quarrel and all that it had wrought was splitting her focus. She'd made a mistake, she realized, that was about to cost her.

Presider ch'Shelos suddenly held out his hand in front of him, palm down. "Enough!"

The chamber fell silent. But Charivretha's glare remained fixed.

"This discord wastes our energies," ch'Shelos said. "Councillor zh'Thane, as admirably passionate as your arguments are, they do not change the political realties we face. Your request for time is denied."

"I ask the Presider's pardon," a soft voice said, "but I wish to speak."

All heads turned in the direction of the speaker and ch'Shelos said, "Representative th'Tethis is recognized."

The old *thaan* inclined his head. "You honor me, Presider. Thank you. I wish to say merely that I believe Councillor zh'Thane has, perhaps without realizing it, raised a point in this debate that we should consider before this august body does the bidding of its enemies and removes her from her post."

Charivretha's anger yielded to surprise. The murmurs resumed among the other members of the Enclave. Despite his kindly, humble manner, th'Tethis was unmistakably on the attack. And more, he was actually taking the Enclave to task on her behalf, making himself a target for reprisal if the majority remained against her.

"I see that I have everyone's attention," th'Tethis said with amusement as the murmurs died down. "Good. Then let me speak plainly. I am old. In the view of many, I know, I have overstayed my welcome, not only in parliament, but in this life. So be it. I will make no apology for that. For I am the last of my clan, our line having dwindled as so many others have in recent centuries. I have clung to my life fiercely for one reason: to delay the day of my clan's extinction." He looked around the Enclave, allowing his gaze to fall on each face. "It is a familiar paradigm, is it not?"

No one answered. Vretha's shock was absolute. She had known that the Tethis clan was small, but she never imagined—

"I say this," th'Tethis went on, "because what Charivretha has dared to say here about our buying time is true: We are consumed by it. So much so that we don't give it much thought anymore. It comes to us naturally now, to put off inevitability. It pervades every aspect of Andorian life because, both as a species and as individuals, we see our death."

"Presider, enough of this," said the blue-hooded one. "This rhetoric is off-topic and has nothing to do with—"

"It has everything to do with why we are here," th'Tethis interrupted, his flashing eyes fixed on the speaker. "And I remind you all that I have the floor."

"Continue then, Elder *Tha*," ch'Shelos said.

Th'Tethis reached out with a gnarled, trembling hand to the shoulder of the *shen* at his left and slowly rose to his feet, breaking the Enclave. It was a serious breach of protocol, but Vretha could not help but admire the old *thaan*'s audacity. The tactic's symbolism was clear: *Push me,* th'Tethis was saying, *and I will push back harder.* Perhaps, like her, he felt that he had little left to lose at this point by offending the Enclave in order to make his point. But where she had stumbled, th'Tethis walked confidently.

"Representative th'Sivas," he resumed, addressing the blue-hooded one as he began to circle the Enclave, "you believe I spout rhetoric, that what I say has no bearing on the reasons for this gathering. I tell you that Charivretha zh'Thane's political future and the plight of our people are inexorably linked. But like you, I did not truly see it—not until the councillor herself brought the two thoughts together.

"As all of you are aware, there are rumors flying about radical new research under way at the Science Institute, ostensibly to explore the possibility of reengineering our biology. Andori-

ans would be altered at conception in such a way that the four
sexes would be reduced to two, making subsequent conceptions
viable among pairs instead of quads. Our reproductive crisis
would be solved in one generation."

Vretha's stomach lurched. Wild conspiracy theories intruded
on legitimate political discourse from time to time, but the revul-
sion she felt at such a monstrous idea made her wonder how anyone could give credence to it. She wasn't sure if it was sheer
fascination with the thought of such radical reengineering, or
horror at the notion that some Andorians were desperate enough
to be willing to alter the species fundamentally in order to insure
its survival.

"This is a vicious rumor devised by extremist factions in
the Visionist Party to cast aspersions on Progressive integrity,"
th'Sivas went on. "We should not dignify such gossip with discussion."

"On the contrary. We need to discuss it," said th'Tethis, "because I believe you are correct, Representative th'Sivas. These
rumors are, I think, part of a much broader strategy on the part of
the Visionists to take control of the government by discrediting
Progressive ideology. Or does anyone in this chamber truly think
it is an accident that these rumors started surfacing at precisely
the same time that the attacks on Councillor zh'Thane, and by
extension, the Progressive Party, began?"

Whatever protocol framed the discussion collapsed as representatives heatedly debated the implications of th'Tethis's state-
ments. Even ch'Shelos had become caught up in the debate with
those nearest him. Vretha merely watched, trying unsuccessfully
to get a read on the Enclave. Then, after several minutes, a young
shen in a jade robe spoke up.

"I have a question," she began. "What if these aren't merely
rumors fabricated by the Visionists? What if the research is real?"

Silence fell. Into it, ch'Shelos asked, "Do you have reason to
believe that it is, Representative sh'Yethe?"

"I have reason to wonder if we should dismiss the idea out of
hand, Presider," sh'Yethe said. "Especially after all that has been
said so far today. . . . I wonder if this wild rumor isn't exactly the
solution we've sought for generations?"

Vretha saw th'Tethis narrow his eyes at the young *shen*. Not disapproving, she saw, but thoughtful.

Th'Sivas seemed incredulous. "You're talking about a crime against nature."

"Some would argue that what has happened to us is a crime against nature," sh'Yethe countered. "Or perhaps a crime *of* nature. We all know the stakes here. For centuries science has sought answers to our dilemma and failed. In our desperation, we implemented the bond-matching programs to maximize the chances for successful conceptions. To that end, we've altered our culture, our values, our ways of thinking about bonding and how we raise our young, and the best we've done is to slow the decline. But how long can we truly endure this way? The best minds among us believe that we have ten generations, perhaps fifteen, before the light that is Andor is extinguished. Am I the only one willing to consider that this may well come down to choosing to die as we are, or to live as something else?"

"This monstrous extremism," th'Sivas began, "is precisely why the Visionist attacks are succeeding. Our party is riddled with radicals who will rationalize any idea, no matter how extreme, without considering the consequences. They want immediate results but fail to recognize that some lines should not be crossed. I put it to you, Presider, that these efforts to dilute the matter at hand must not succeed. There is one real issue before this Enclave: Charivretha zh'Thane's political future."

"They are linked," th'Tethis insisted. "If we dismiss zh'Thane now, we are guilty of seeking the same immediate results you claim are espoused by radicals."

Ch'Shelos stared into the well for a long moment before turning his gaze on her. "Is there anything you wish to add, Charivretha, before I put the matter to a vote?"

Vretha met the Presider's eyes; then she rose to her feet, facing him. "Our human associates have a myth: an intricate knot that could be unraveled only by the true ruler of the world. Many tried and failed to untie the knot, until one came with a sword and cut the knot in twain.

"Andor has no analogue to this tale. Seldom do we act in haste, for we believe that to do so would be to blind ourselves to the possible consequences of our actions. Yet we know inaction is equally perilous, carrying its own share of consequences. So we have always tried to find a balance." She paused to take a deep breath. "I will find the answers. Allow me to continue in my fight for my council position, and I will expose this matter of reengineering our species for the myth it is. And by so doing, I will reveal the deceits the Visionist Party has attempted to perpetuate on our people. I ask that I be allowed to *act*, with care and sober thought, not on my own behalf, but for all of Andor." She glanced briefly at th'Tethis, whose eyes were again crinkling at her. Then she searched the faces of her colleagues, many of whom had sought her counsel or asked for her endorsement in their campaigns—and dared them to defy her.

A chime sounded. The Presider picked up the executive padd from its place at his side, excused himself, and read the incoming message. He studied the data for several minutes, during which Vretha could sense a change in him. His antennae had tensed, and he radiated profound concern.

The Presider tapped out an acknowledgment to the sender and then dropped the padd into an inner pocket of his robe. "As is my prerogative," he told the Enclave, "I am tabling this discussion owing to an unfolding situation. Details are still scarce, but I will share what is known.

"As some of you may have noticed on your way here, a rally was being organized in the Plaza of Freedom, outside the Parliament Andoria complex, presumably by our Visionist colleagues across the aisle. While we've been here, nearly sixteen thousand protesters have gathered in the plaza. They have been calling for the present administration to step down, and for new representation to be sent to the Federation Council."

Vretha braced herself. The number of protesters was distressingly higher than usual, but not dangerously so for the plaza. And the demands were much the same as in other recent rallies. There must be worse news coming. . . .

"Similar demonstrations have been reported throughout the capital and in nearly every major population center on the planet, all taking place simultaneously. Current estimates are that as many as eight million protesters are involved. Homeworld Security is attempting to maintain order, but we are receiving reports of violence and property damage sweeping through several cities, including this one."

The Enclave sat in stunned silence, until Vretha asked, "Casualties?" The word seemed to catch in her throat.

Ch'Shelos looked directly at her. "No figures are available yet. But a number of deaths are already confirmed."

"I'll be blunt, Ensign ch'Thane. Andor isn't safe for you at this time."

Shar was in a dark mood. Being accosted by the newsnet swarm had been bad enough. But the wait he had been forced to endure in the cramped security office—alone except for the uncommunicative *thaan* who had saved him from the reporters— with no knowledge of Prynn's or Phillipa's wherabouts, had made him wonder if he was under some kind of secret arrest. The *thaan* had told him only that Shar was waiting for Sentinel zh'Nastha, Orbital Control's chief of security, who had apparently been in no great hurry to arrive. Shar tried to keep himself occupied by discreetly studying the data being displayed on the surface of the security desk; reading upside-down was a skill he'd mastered in his youth, for amusement's sake. As an adult, he found it had its uses. For a few minutes, he followed streaming lines of sensor data, discovering such scintillating facts as seventy-five percent of the station's current population of eighty-five hundred staff and transients as of an hour ago were Andorian. But he was no closer to understanding why he was here, or why he'd been separated from his friends. Whatever security's reasons, they were determined to keep him here.

Zh'Nastha was all business when she finally arrived, took her place behind the desk, set down a padd, and made her pronouncement.

"I don't understand," Shar told her.

"You're perhaps aware that Andor is politically volatile at present," zh'Nastha said, in a manner that suggested she knew he was acutely aware of it. "What you may not know is that your arrival has coincided with a series of demonstrations all over the planet, and some of these have erupted in violence, including those at the capital in Zhevra. We believe your *zhavey* and other prominent Progressives are the targets of these protests. Within the last hour, Homeworld Security intercepted a group armed with a homemade explosive attempting to infiltrate our transport station in the capital. We also have intelligence of a possible terrorist threat to this facility."

Shar took a moment to absorb this new information. "You think *my* arrival catalyzed all this?"

Zh'Nastha's antennae turned toward each other: a shrug. "It may be part of something on a much bigger scale. On the other hand, their attack on our Zhevra station at the precise hour of your arrival might indicate that you were being targeted. Either way, we don't believe the timing of these events is coincidental."

Shar's eyes narrowed. "Are you telling me I cannot travel to the surface?"

"No. You're a private citizen, and are free to do as you like . . . up to a point."

"Meaning?"

"Meaning you won't be transporting anywhere. Because of the threats issued against this facility and the incident on the ground, operation of the transporter systems has been suspended until further notice. Passenger shuttles are being made available for travel to the surface, but for your own safety, I must strongly recommend that you avoid the capital."

Shar paused to think. If he'd learned anything during his time in Starfleet, it was to take security concerns seriously. "Can you suggest an alternative?"

Zh'Nastha consulted her padd. "One of your companions, Lieutenant Commander Matthias—she's traveling to Thelasavei, correct?"

"You can't be serious," Shar said before he could stop himself.

Zh'Nastha's antennae pulled back in surprise. She continued, "It's a busy time of year for travelers to that province, but it's also one of the places that was *not* chosen for a political demonstration. We've already arranged passage for Commander Matthias aboard the next shuttle. We could do the same for you and Ensign Tenmei, and you could obtain transportation to Zhevra from there."

Shar breathed out through his nose. Loath as he was to put himself any closer to Thantis, he was forced to admit that taking an indirect route to Zhevra made sense, as did seeing Phillipa safely to the surface. "Where are my friends now?"

"Commander Matthias has safely boarded her shuttle. She protested, but Ensign Tenmei convinced her to continue on to her destination, while the ensign remained behind to wait for you. She's just outside my office. You both still have time to catch the commander's shuttle. What's your decision?"

Risk my life going to see Zhavey, *or risk it going to see* Zhadi. *Interesting choice.*

"I'll go to Thelasa-vei," Shar said.

"Follow me, then." Zh'Nastha escorted Shar out into the gate area, followed closely by the *thaan* officer.

As promised, Prynn was waiting for them. Shar recognized her "there better be a good explanation for this" expression. Zh'Nastha led them out of the gate lounge and into the main thoroughfare, crowded with passengers coming and going, that followed the circumference of the station. Shar saw a few curious looks—mostly from offworlders who wouldn't know that staring was considered impolite by Andorians—but mostly, they passed without drawing too much attention. Prynn leaned closer to Shar so only he could hear her.

"What's going on?" she said under her breath.

"Change of plan," Shar said. "I'll explain on the way."

They found Phillipa in the main passenger cabin of the shuttle, where pairs of seats were arranged facing each other Andorian style, making groups of four. Persuading the passengers seated across from Phillipa to trade their seats for the aft-section ones assigned to Prynn and Shar wasn't difficult: a harried *zhavey,* next to the counselor—the creeping purplish pigmentation on her neck revealed she must be recently out of seclusion—had been struggling to comfort her unhappy infant. As Shar and Prynn arrived, the child appeared to be resting, but the former occupants of the facing seats—a pair of Vulcans—seemed grateful to leave.

While Shar and Prynn tucked away their luggage into a storage bin, Phillipa fussed over the *zhavey*—folding a stained blanket, closing a container of mashed *xixu* fronds, and holding her travel bag while she made herself comfortable in her seat.

Averting his eyes from the *zhavey,* Shar was grateful that a non-Andorian was available to help. On Andor, making uninvited overtures of any kind toward a *zhen* with child was unheard of. The unspoken rule emerged out of respect for *zhavey* and child's privacy, one of the rare times in Andorian life when personal boundaries were fanatically protected.

"Thirishar ch'Thane, Prynn Tenmei, this is Arenthialeh zh'Vazdi," Phillipa said when everyone had sat down. "Her clan has a keep close to Cheen-Thitar. She's a botanist returning from a month of field studies on Dramia."

The *zhavey* pushed aside a cluster of loose braids that had draped over the side of her face so she could better see Shar, offering him a flicker of eye contact before she politely looked away. Fingers spread apart, she extended her right hand, palm out. "I am honored, *Cha* Thirishar of the Clan of Thane."

Her Northern looks—the fine hair, delicately sculpted angular face—coupled with her youthful but serious expression triggered a white-hot piercing flash of Thriss as *zhavey;* the painful imagining stole Shar's breath. He dug down and found the composure to respond to her introduction with a proper shoulder bow. "I share the honor, *Zha* Arenthialeh. My familiar name is Shar." Mirroring her gesture, he raised his hand and pressed it to hers.

"For a supposed renegade, you appear to have been taught properly," she said dryly. "You may address me as Thia."

Renegade? Is that what I am now? Supposing that Charivretha wouldn't appreciate him having such a reputation, he found the label amusing instead of insulting.

The intercom loudly announced the shuttle's departure from Orbital Control, stirring Thia's infant into wakefulness.

Through the gauzy modesty drape over the *zhavey's kheth,* Shar saw the howling infant thrashing about in its nurture pouch, all knees and elbows, pushing the *zhavey's* pouch skin taut. The child poked its head outside the fabric drape, its unhappy face glistening with perspiration and pouch gel. The *zhavey* smoothed wiry curls, whispered soothing chants—and the sobs quieted. Until a shipwide announcement—a warning about possible turbulence—again startled him.

The infant wailed loudly, pressing a foot against the pouch

until the fabric drape came unfastened, baring the *kheth*. The out-line of the infant's toes could be seen through the *zhavey*'s nearly translucent white-blue skin. Blushing modestly, she quickly pulled the drape back over the infant, reattaching the fabric to her tunic. She scooped the infant out of the pouch, tucking his head in the crook between her head and her chest, and bounced, trying to soothe him.

Prynn turned toward Thia, and said politely, "Is all well with your child?"

"We have been traveling for several days and he has had to spend most of his time in my pouch. He's ready to wean, but I haven't let him because of our travels."

"A child that wants to wean?" Phillipa said. "How fortunate for you! My daughter—now two—still reaches beneath my clothes for my breasts in search of a quick snack."

Thia offered a smile of maternal understanding. She slid the child, still quivering with sobs, beneath the drape and back into her pouch. Reaching through the slits on each side of her blouse, she massaged her upper abdomen with downward strokes, stimu-lating the *zhiassa* let down. Slowly, the unhappy wails were re-placed by choked gulps as nourishment drizzled into the child's mouth.

After Thia's child was securely latched onto a teat, she re-quested Shar to make a formal introduction to Prynn. She hesi-tated only for a second when Prynn reached out to shake hands, human fashion.

"So you're a scientist?" Prynn said, initiating conversation.

Shar watched Thia's response carefully. Andorians tended not to make idle social conversation. Being in Starfleet had forced him to adjust, but most of his kind—particularly new *zhaveys*—didn't have as much interaction with other species. Her antennae tensing briefly, Thia received Prynn's inquiry coolly, but didn't become hostile as he might have expected.

"I am a botanist. Specializing in applications of synthesized plant chemicals."

"*Zha* Arenthialeh and I had a fascinating conversation about my own pharmacological project," Phillipa said, exchanging looks with Shar.

Noting Prynn's confusion, Shar quickly shifted topics. He

hadn't explained *all* of Phillipa's plans to Prynn, and this wasn't the place to discuss it. "Have you always lived in the Archipelago region, *Zha?*"

"My entire life," Thia said. She paused and looked long at Shar, studying him as closely as politeness would permit. "While my people are not known for being plainspoken with outsiders, I wonder if Shathrissía's Sending isn't the reason for your visit." Shar must have allowed his discomfort to project, because she added, "I apologize if I am causing you unease."

"How is it you know of Shathrissía's Sending?"

Thia tilted her head slightly to one side, her antennae angled back in surprise. Instead of answering his question, she offered an opinion. "You are very much Charivretha's *chei,* Shar."

Shar felt his own antennae tensing. "Am I then to be judged based upon political gossip about my *zhavey?*" he asked. "Whatever conclusions you've drawn are likely based on innuendo, not fact—"

Thia raised a hand, halting his diatribe midsentence. "I apologize. Clearly you don't understand my intentions. My comment was not about you personally or your *zhavey*'s politics—which I don't happen to agree with," Thia said. "It was about upbringing. Growing up in the South, you would have little understanding of how tightly bound the clans of Cheshras Island are. I know this because two of my bondmates are from the Zhevra region, where Vretha demanded that *your* bond be raised."

"There is no shame in being reared in Zhevra."

"Except for a cosmopolitan culture that encourages nothing more than a mere surface commitment to raising children with the traditions that have sustained our people."

"You generalize unfairly."

"Do I? Look around you, Shar. Are you not even the slightest bit curious as to why so many people are traveling to Andor at this time in the calendar?"

"I—" He had to admit that he had been surprised by the huge numbers of travelers he saw on the station; he also had to admit that he didn't know why they were traveling.

"Can it be that you have become so far removed from your people that you've forgotten the Spring Water Festival? Have you ever, in your lifetime, joined with the *shen* in your bond to plead for the Water Guardian's protection?"

Shar didn't have an answer for her.

"I thought as much." Her antennae flicked in disappointment. "So you wanted to know how a stranger would know of Shathrissía's death. If you had grown up in the Archipelago as *Zha* Sessethantis had wanted, you would know that there are few secrets between the Northern families. Since the days of the First Clans, our survival has depended on such closeness—my own house has farmed with the Thitars for twenty generations. There is little that happens in their keep that my clan is not aware of. In fact, I am on my way to reunite with my bondmates and our other two children so that we may together attend observances in Cheen-Thitar."

Shar's eyes narrowed. "We are not so slavishly modern in the South that we've failed to respect the old traditions—"

"That is hardly what I'm saying."

"—but perhaps if the 'Pelagos did not feel threatened by social evolution—"

Thia's abdomen shuddered. Her hands dropped down to cup her swelling *kheth* pouch, and she squeezed through the cloth of her tunic. A litany of soothing words interspersed with "shhh" and coos came too late; the infant shrieked into full wakefulness. "It is not reasonable to expect your journey to be disrupted by my *thei.* I will ask the steward if there is a quiet place to attend to my infant." With Phillipa's help, she gathered up her travel bags and climbed out of their row, into the aisle.

Thia took several steps before she paused; she turned back and looked directly at Shar. "Live up to the honor of your name, Thirishar." She then vanished with Phillipa into the compartment beyond.

When Thia was out of hearing distance, Prynn asked, "Is that what passes for meaningless chitchat on Andor?"

" 'Chitchat,' as you call it, isn't found on Andor."

"So what do you do at parties?"

"Parties?"

A long pause. "You do believe in parties."

"No."

Another long pause. "I get it. You're doing the Nog thing again."

"Yes."

She shook her head and peered out their viewport, watching his world spin past.

Knowing they would soon be planetside, Shar permitted the dammed-up emotions, stress, and frustrations of the day to wash over him. Later, he would have little to no time to collect his thoughts. *Violent political demonstrations and a terrorist plot . . .* he could not linger on such ideas. Leaning back into his chair, he alternately tightened and released his muscles, and closing his eyes, he cleared his mind, began a series of meditations. . . .

A warm hand touched his. Prynn.

Over the last two months, he'd discovered her to be a tactile, demonstrative person—so different from his own carefully culti-vated restraint; he enjoyed her spontaneity, how readily she fol-lowed her intuition instead of overanalyzing every minuscule decision as he was prone to do. For once, he followed an im-pulse, tangling his fingers with hers; by touch, he explored the knobby joints and the lines of her tendons; the process became a meditation of its own.

Comfortable silence filled the space between them. He lis-tened to the slow rise and fall of her breathing, subconsciously falling into the same rhythm. In the midst of the discord in his life of late, the time he spent with Prynn brought him a soothing peace that he'd come to depend on. And yet, if he was being hon-est with himself, there was more than comfort between them. Subtle undertones of emotions that he believed he wasn't capable of feeling again had begun to color his thoughts about this lovely, vibrantly alive woman seated beside him. He believed he was ready for their relationship to evolve, to become more than sup-portive, intimate friends; he mused on the thought, rolling it over in his mind and liking how it felt.

"Nice planet," Prynn said, finally. "What's the land/water ratio?"

Opening his eyes, he said, "Fifteen/eighty-five. Two major continents and a large number of islands."

"And how are the tides?"

"The tides?"

"For surfing," Prynn said. "I thought I might catch a few waves, but the guidebook I've been reading is crap, and doesn't say anything about aquatic sports."

"Ah. I believe there are some beachfront resorts, frequented mostly by offworld visitors. But my people generally use the oceans only as a source of food, industrial energy, and scientific inquiry. Not recreation."

Prynn *tsk*ed. Shar had learned to recognize the sound as an expression of disappointment. "I guess I'll just have to test the waters myself," she sighed.

"They can be uncertain," Shar cautioned.

"I think I can handle whatever your world throws at me." She looked at him and smiled. "By the way, I've been meaning to ask you—I grew up thinking the name of your planet is Andoria. But you always call it Andor. What's up with that?"

Shar shrugged. "I grew up thinking your planet's name was Terra. Then I went to Starfleet Academy and everyone was calling it 'Earth.' What is up with *that?*"

"Touché," Prynn said, her gaze returning to the view. Her smiled slowly faded. "It's a shame about the political demonstrations. Does that happen often? The violence, I mean?"

"It depends on the circumstances, and it's usually contained very quickly. Why do you ask?"

"I was thinking about that old generalization, about Andorians being 'a violent race.' I never took it seriously . . ."

"And you're beginning to wonder if there's some truth in it?"

"Is there?"

Shar didn't respond right away. *There are no easy answers to that, are there?*

"Shar?"

"There are many kinds of violence, Prynn," he said finally, hoping it would suffice.

She seemed content to let it drop, and after a few more minutes, she asked, "What did Thia mean, 'live up to the honor of your name'?"

"Thirishar was a mythological warrior—the greatest of all. He accomplished all the tasks given to mortals by Uzaveh and demanded a place in the Presence of the Infinite."

"Impressive," she said. "I'm named after an old friend of my parents. Though I half-suspect that a heroine named Prynne in one of my mother's books—an adulteress who dared stand up to overzealous human pilgrims—might have been an influence. So how does your story end?"

Shar said, "Thirishar wasn't granted a throne; he was split into four separate people because, in Uzaveh's judgment, he was not Whole."

"The four sexes," Prynn surmised. He expected her to inquire further about that, but apparently something else had piqued her curiosity. "I've heard you use the word 'Whole' before, but I thought it was just another way of referring to your people. The way you used it just now meant something else, didn't it?"

"Like many words, it has layers of meaning," Shar explained. "Using the term to refer to my people is one of them. But there are others. Telling another that they are Whole in your thoughts, for example, is an endearment of great intimacy, usually exclusive to the bond between parent and child, but sometimes to acknowledge the depth of feeling among bondmates. It can also be used to describe the sexual union of the *shelthreth*, in which new life is conceived."

"And in your mythology?"

"That's been a point of controversy among scholars, philosophers, and poets for centuries. Sometimes it seems as though there are as many interpretations of *The Tale of the Breaking* as there have been Andorians. The commonality among them is that we lack a crucial piece of self-knowledge that makes us unworthy of evolving beyond who and what we are."

Prynn frowned. "Wow, that's so . . . sad."

"Perhaps it is," Shar conceded, "to someone not raised in our culture, and especially in view of the present circumstances my people face. But among many of us, it's a motivational lesson. Our myths have inspired inquiry and exploration of ourselves, our relationship to the universe, our very natures."

"Are you saying *that's* why you became a scientist?" Prynn seemed delighted, as if it had been the last thing she expected Shar to reveal about himself.

"I was influenced by a number of factors," he clarified, "but it would be untrue if I said that, as a child, I was not drawn to the mysteries of those old stories, to the questions I discovered just below the surface of the metaphors."

Shar's gaze shifted to the viewport, to the blur of the planet's surface, now speeding past. "One of the interesting things about all this is that a growing number of our scientists think my people didn't even evolve on Andor. That hundreds of thousands—if not millions—of years ago, we were refugees from some other dying world."

"Why's that?"

"We haven't been able to find anything in our studies of animal and plant biology native to Andor that indicates the four-gender paradigm evolved naturally on our planet."

"You're unique then."

"Yes." *And alone,* he added mentally.

"That can be a good thing."

Can it? If he could definitively answer that, it might also address the other questions that nagged at him, eroded his peace. Ideas tossed back and forth in his mind, the theology, the science—and his hopes; he became lost in the currents of his thoughts.

3

Studying the fist-sized beetle perched on her plate, Prynn leaned down in her chair so that she was at eye level with the table and tried formulating an eating strategy; she didn't have a clue where to start. She scanned the cavernous waiting area of the shuttle-port, searching for other travelers who might have made a simi-lar food choice. Most of those milling around or lining the rows of benches gnawed on steaming bread pockets or fruits. Appar-ently, the "insect delicacy of the Archipelago" wasn't too popu-lar. *No wonder there wasn't a line at that kiosk,* she thought regretfully. *But I'm so hungry!*

The food vendor had handed her an elongated utensil with a smallish three-pronged head to go with the plate. She examined the utensil (that she'd started to think of as a baby pitchfork) and at the speckled exoskeleton, wondering if she should spear the beetle's underbelly, thus releasing any edible fluids or flesh. Or whether she should attack the beetle like a Bajoran tidal crab: first, the legs were ripped off, then the body decapitated before the fork was plunged into the tasty innards. Regardless of what approach she chose, Prynn didn't like the way the beetle looked at her with its prismatic eyes and ebony pincers. She looked around, hoping to spot a friendly replicator.

"Prynn," Shar said, tapping her on the arm.

"Oh, hi. Any luck on finding passage to Zhevra?"

He slipped into the chair opposite her and shook his head. "Travel was suspended just after we landed. No public shuttles or transporters until after the storm passes and the climate-control protocols are lifted."

"I was afraid you'd say that."

"We'll need to find shelter for the night. It's less than two hours to sunset and another seven before Deepening. I doubt circumstances will change before then."

"Deepening?"

"Midnight."

"So where do we go until we can head to the capital?"

"With Phillipa. To Cheen-Thitar Keep."

Prynn arched an eyebrow. "Really?"

"Public accommodations are full. Between the storm and the festival, we will have better luck with Thantis than finding space to sleep in an empty alleyway."

"I see. And you're okay with showing up without an invitation?"

"No," he admitted. "But it may be a preferable way to wait out the storm, the forecast for which is increasingly unfavorable for the next day, possibly two." He hesitated. "And . . . I've been thinking about the fact that there are certain rules of hospitality in my culture, rules that override personal considerations. These rules apply not only to the giver, but to the one in need."

"Meaning what, exactly?"

"Meaning that I would cause great offense if *Zha* Sessethantis were to learn that I was on Cheshras Island under these circumstances, and that I could have turned to her for help, but did not."

"Even though you're unwelcome there?"

Shar nodded. "To deny her the opportunity to be generous would only make the situation between our families worse."

"But so what?" Prynn asked. "She already shut you out. You don't owe her any—"

"This isn't just about me, Prynn," Shar said softly. "Or about her. Insulting the *Zha* of the Clan of Cheen also affects *Zhavey* and the political struggle here. It would affect Anichent and Dizhei, who have been hurt enough. I'm tired of making choices that hurt people."

Prynn sighed. She could see this wasn't an easy decision for Shar, and she wasn't going to make things any better for either of them by arguing about it from an alien point of view. That thought, however, brought up another question.

"How will Thantis feel about me coming along?"

Shar shook his head. "Again, personal feelings aren't relevant in this context. Meeting my obligation to ask for her hospitality obligates her to extend it to me and any who may be traveling with me."

Prynn nodded, but she was already imagining the awkwardness of being at Cheen-Thitar Keep while the whole clan was sitting shivah. *Maybe I need to stop thinking about this from a human perspective. Maybe they really don't have the same social hangups.*

No, she thought. *They have a whole different set of social hangups.*

"All right," she said. "You know this place, I don't. You're in charge. What next?"

"We need to meet up with Phillipa." He rose from his chair and she followed, carrying her travel bag over her shoulder and her beetle in front of her. "She's on an errand at a local marketplace right now, and isn't far from a leasing facility where we'll obtain an aircar for the trip to the keep." Looking at the beetle, he pursed his lips, clearly puzzled. "Why did you buy a steamed *shaysha?*"

"Oh. You mean this?" As they passed a recycler station, she casually slid the tray through the intake. "Someone left it behind. I'm just being a good citizen and throwing it away for them."

Marching double-time, Prynn struggled to keep up with Shar, who moved swiftly down streets and across avenues. Since this was her first time on Andor, Prynn hoped to get a feel for climate and culture; she slowed down intermittently, pausing to gaze at a brightly dressed *zhen* or read a sign. Hyperfocused Shar, however, was in a hurry and obviously didn't have time to play tourist. Keeping one eye out for interesting sites, and one on Shar so she wouldn't get lost, proved to be challenging.

Prynn had learned a little about the province of Thelasa-vei and the surrounding environs from an interactive holo program in an information terminal at the shuttleport. The primary city, Harbortown—Andor's oldest and third largest metropolis—was twenty kilometers away. Having been built in the largest natural harbor on Andor, Harbortown began modestly as a series of small fishing settlements dug into the mountainsides of the low-lying costal range that formed the harbor's perimeter. Over the centuries, the settlements had merged and extended out of the mountains and onto a land parcel situated between two of Cheshras Island's rivers. In modern times, Harbortown was an amalgamation of shipping concerns, oceanography research, geothermal energy production, and sea-life cultivation, to say nothing of its status as a revered cultural and historical landmark. "Living archeology" was the term used, implying that two thousand years of architecture and culture had been integrated into the world of computers, warp drive, and the Federation.

The hologuide had informed Prynn that the tip of the Thelasavei province was often referred to as the Hand of Cheshras because the four major rivers converged near Harbortown, creating five land "fingers." Harbortown was built on the largest peninsula between the Frost and Moss rivers. The guide had promised that the region's spectacular scenery could be found in and around the glacially carved harbor. She'd noted that the guide hadn't commented on the lesser villages' beauty—and now she could see why. Neither the scenery nor the inhabitants were distinctive.

Andorians, clothed in robes, tunics, suits, and dresses—similar to those one might find on any Federation world with humanoid inhabitants—went about their business, occasionally pausing at information terminals or stopping to talk with someone met on the street. But Prynn couldn't discern by looking what their interests or professions might be.

The neighborhoods themselves offered a bit more diversity. Row upon row of walls lined the avenues, some made of gray and brown stone and plasteel, others of clay and some of unfamiliar alloys. Ornate metal gates led within. As they passed, Prynn would catch glimpses of the buildings beyond, plastered in vivid hues—brick reds, creamy yellows, azure blues—and the steep peaks of sleek, burnished copper-sheeted rooftops. The effect was more of seeing bits of a mosaic without knowing the overall pattern. All of it appeared jumbled—disjointed.

"What's with this layout?" Prynn finally asked Shar.

It took Shar a moment to realize what she was referring to. "Each gate provides access to a neighborhood in the village. The residents live, work, and recreate within—they're self-sufficient, with their own markets, provincial transport systems, and schools," Shar said. "You'd see more activity out here in the open on feast days when the observant make their pilgrimages to the Guardian sanctuaries. You'll better understand when we enter the Shess neighborhood to meet up with Phillipa—"

And how anyone would know which of these many clusters of low-lying buildings was the Shess neighborhood escaped her. Aside from a complete lack of signage in either Andorii or Standard, gates appeared at irregular intervals; there wasn't a discernible organization to the village's layout. She hadn't expected the buildings to be so squatty—or appear to be. When she mentioned it to Shar, he explained that most of the shops were underground; only the upper sections of the first-floor walls poked above the surface. Each building was accessed through descending stairs. Reaching above her head, she could easily touch the rooftops without going up on her toes. From above, she imagined that the long avenues of roofs would look like the scaly back of horned reptile, especially with the last glimmers of the setting white sun glinting off the metal sheeting.

As they walked down the near-empty avenues, Prynn saw one of many gates marked with a geometric figure—four interlocking squares forming a quasi star—painted purple-black. *I know I've seen that before,* she thought, but she couldn't put a finger on where. Initially, she'd assumed that the figure was a kind of identifier like a house number or a coordinate, though she'd soon realized that virtually every gate they passed had been marked with the same symbol. Glancing over at Shar, she saw that he too seemed puzzled by it.

When Prynn asked what it meant, he paused before answering. "I'm not certain—we don't have old-style villages like this in the South. A visit to the capital and the surrounding communities would remind you of a visit to San Francisco or Ashalla." He walked over to a marked gate, crouched down, and scraped a bit of the black off with his fingernail. He raised the sample to his nose, sniffed; touched it to his tongue, swished it around, spat. "At least it's only paint."

His relief puzzled Prynn. Before she could ask about it, he resumed walking.

"I recognize the iconograph. I've seen it engraved on the doors of the Water Guardian's sanctuary—it's her symbol."

"Could she be the patron of this village?"

Shar's brow furrowed thoughtfully. "No. Each Andorian gender has its own patron—for example, mine is the Star Guardian. If I were observant, I would ask my own Guardian to mediate with Uzaveh on my behalf—not the Water Guardian. Maybe . . . There is one possible explanation, but there's a question of legality . . ." He drifted off, considering the matter. "The Visionists must hold more public influence than I'd guessed was possible."

"What do you mean?"

"The Visionists value tradition above all. This part of the world—the Archipelago—is the oldest inhabited region of our planet," Shar said. "Why our ancestors endured here for so long is hard to understand when you consider that nine months of the year, the rain, cold, and storms make for miserable living conditions. The only way we survived was the profusion of underground hot springs that allowed homes to be kept warm and humid, as most of my kind prefer."

"I suppose in a region where the weather is the biggest threat, the water god—"

"Guardian."

"—Guardian, then, would be a good one to keep on your side."

"Exactly. So every year, at the peak of the storm season, they had a period of fasting, prayer, and sacrifice to the Water Guardian, begging for deliverance. The symbol on the door was to remind the Water Guardian that true believers lived within and to pass them over. In the old days, it would have been painted in the blood of the eldest *shen* in the house."

Prynn blinked. "Excuse me? Blood?"

"Not for hundreds of years. Long before I was born, the celebration of the Spring Water Festival was heavily curtailed—some of its rites outlawed."

"Fasting and prayer dangerous? Someone should warn the Bajorans."

"Not that part. After the people felt like they'd been preserved from death, they celebrated. Eating, intoxicants," he paused, "*tezha* with strangers—I've read historical accounts of sentient sacrifices: *saf*-induced hallucinations leading to murdering a *shen* or pushing a child off a cliff into the ocean."

"You're kidding me," Prynn said dubiously.

"The finer points of our history—and culture—aren't widely known offworld," Shar said.

"History, I'll believe. But culture? Come on, Shar." His description of his fellow Andorians didn't track with what Prynn knew of them. "I had two Andorians on my floor at the Academy. They never went to parties. Ever. Hardly ever touched synthehol. Never once nibbled at a proposition for an illicit encounter. The phrase 'one-night stand' wasn't in their vocabulary. What gives?"

"Who we are as Federation citizens living among other species and who we are among our own kind . . . might be a bit disparate."

"Have you . . . ever been intoxicated? Out of control? Decadent?"

"Yes."

Intrigued, her eyebrows shot up. "Yes to intoxicated, out of control, or decadent? Or all three?"

Shar offered her only an obscure twitch of his antennae.

Prynn studied Shar with renewed curiosity, wondering how much of his true nature he held at bay—and what it would take to provoke it. To see him uninhibited, fully living in the moment . . .

"Left here," Shar said, turning off the avenue and in to an open gate. Through a gravel-paved courtyard, past several dark green buildings, down several flights of stairs, and through a damp, sooty hallway that smelled of mildew, they emerged into a massive subterranean marketplace. Rows of booths lined the four marble-block walls, with a center row bisecting the room. Rusting metal lanterns, hanging from hooks mounted into the ceilings, cast speckled light across the rock floor. Prynn saw glittering metal circlets, reed baskets, bolts of shimmering fabric, enormous rugs, decorative tapestries, and bins brimming with indistinguishable trinkets from data chips and padds to fruits. Cages littered with hand-size beetle exoskeletons hung from the open beams; Prynn guessed the orange speckled ones must be more *shaysha*.

As she walked, she kicked nutshells and bits of oily wrappers with her boots. "Andorians don't believe in the whole recycler-replicator thing either, I take it," Prynn said, following Shar down a crowded side aisle.

"Of course we do. Most every household has one. This is a place to trade or search for fresh foodstuffs, art, or one-of-a-kind items. The people of this region value and promote handicrafts—textiles especially."

"Right," Prynn said, recalling that Sessethantis zh'Cheen was a textile artist.

"Crafts aren't merely for creativity's sake or for personal pleasure. The process of doing the work is perceived as necessary to becoming a Whole individual."

"The artistry part I understand. But I suppose I don't get why, if you want or need something, you don't just ask the replicator for it."

"Sessethantis used to always complain about how we, meaning myself and my bondmates, didn't have to work for anything that we have. She expected Thriss to learn how to sew her own clothing, prepare meals from raw ingredients—develop skills that replicators have made, among many people, all but obsolete."

Prynn had a brief vision of herself, sleeves rolled up, hair tucked in a scarf, cranking the massive wood olive presses of old Toscana and collecting the precious droplets in green glass bottles to be sold at market. *Could I . . . ?* Shaking her head, she erased the picturesque thought of peasant Prynn tilling the rich soil of the Italian countryside. She was definitely a confirmed child of the twenty-fourth century.

Shar touched her sleeve, directing Prynn's attention to a stall some distance away where Phillipa was engaged in intense conversation with a vendor. Together they made their way around a peat grill sizzling and smoking with fatty fish steaks, then past a wide table where a cluster of Andorians were stitching together what appeared to be ornately woven sleeping mats.

When they caught up to Phillipa, she was finishing her transaction, sliding several credit chips across the table to the vendor. Regular visits to Quark's bar (which these days was ostensibly doubling as the Ferengi embassy to Bajor) had accustomed her to the use of such currency. Starfleet made provisions for its personnel who lived or worked in non-Federation locales where currency-based economies were still the norm. Usually it was just a matter of thumbing a bill that a vendor later submitted to Starfleet for some previously negotiated form of compensation. Credit chips functioned the same way, only anonymously. But it surprised Prynn to see such an exchange on a Federation world between Federation citizens.

Phillipa pocketed a smallish green satin drawstring bag inside her jacket. "You find us a way to the keep, Shar?"

"There's a vehicular leasing facility not far from here. I called ahead. They've reserved an aircar for us."

"What did you buy?" Prynn asked Phillipa, wondering what unique trinket she might have discovered here. "Something fun, I hope. Maybe for the kids? A souvenir?"

Phillipa cleared her throat. "Not exactly."

Prynn looked to Shar for an explanation, but his expression indicated that he wasn't going to offer her any answer either.

Damn. I should have replicated gloves, Prynn thought as they emerged from the marketplace into the early evening chill. She wasn't sure she had packed any either, having expected a trip to Andor's middle latitudes where temperate, summery climes prevailed. Withdrawing her hands into her jacket sleeves failed to fend off the cold, biting wind.

Once they moved out onto the open avenue, finding relative privacy in the nearly abandoned streets, Phillipa explained in a quiet voice that she'd transacted for multiple smears of *saf.*

Initially, Prynn thought she'd misheard her—the counselor's chattering teeth had broken her words into bits—and she asked Phillipa to repeat what she'd said.

With a brisk nod, Phillipa affirmed that Prynn had heard her correctly.

Prynn nearly swallowed her tongue. *Saf* smears were the stuff of Orion Syndicate black-market deals and other underworld crime. Not even Quark dealt in *saf.* She'd heard rumors of individuals who'd used the drug recreationally—but always on non-Federation worlds. Discovery of a *saf* smear in the possession of a Federation citizen . . . "Isn't—um—that—uhh . . ."

"Illegal? Yes. Which is why trying to obtain a sample with which I can conduct research can be difficult," Phillipa said. "Before I left the station, Dr. Bashir and I discussed collaborating on an analysis of the drug to see if there are any potential psychoactive benefits, so we obtained a special authorization from Starfleet Medical that allowed me to acquire it and transport it to DS9."

With visions of penal colonies and rehabilitation regimens dancing in her thoughts, Prynn said, "But Andorian Security—"

"*Saf* originated on Andor, Prynn. It's the only place in the Alpha Quadrant where you can legally procure it, because it's been part of the culture here for so long. Andorians have used it as part of their worship and their—" Phillipa paused.

Prynn followed Phillipa's glance over at Shar, who had flushed a deep blue.

"I'd be happy to discuss this later, Shar," Phillipa said. "Or desist altogether."

"Your sensitivity is appreciated," he said, brushing aside the counselor's concern, "but unnecessary. The role of *saf* on my world is a fact of our existence." Still, he averted his eyes from both of the women.

In quieter tones, Phillipa continued, "Andorians use *saf* in the *shelthreth*—as part of their mating process. At the appropriate time, the sanctuary priests and priestesses dispense it to the sealed bondgroup. After the *shelthreth*, *saf* is dispensed only by medical prescription. The vendor I was dealing with was a pharmacist."

"So why is it illegal . . . ?"

"For non-Andorians, it can be highly addictive, not just physiologically, but psychologically. I've counseled *saf* users who become chronically despondent when it's denied them, even though there is absolutely no physiological need for it." A faraway look appeared on her face. "We saw an outbreak of *saf* use during the war."

Shar looked up, puzzled. "I had not heard that."

"Most haven't. One of our dirty little secrets," Phillipa said, then went on: "*Saf* can also be fatal to non-Andorians. The overdose threshold is alarmingly low. Fortunately, *saf* is also one of those odd little organic molecules that doesn't replicate well, and the plant it's derived from can't be grown offplant. The upshot is that *saf* has never been widely available, and may never be. It can be processed only on Andor, and the Andorian government has always been very sensitive to Federation concerns about the offworld smuggling of *saf*. There are a number of effective voluntary safeguards in place, and these are revised and upgraded regularly. Unfortunately, determined people sometimes find a way around them."

"But what does it *do* that makes people willing to take the risks?"

Phillipa sighed. "Among other benefits, *saf* is a powerful aphrodisiac—"

Shar increased his pace, walking ahead of them.

"—that provides a myriad of benefits to all aspects of sexual function—"

"Oh. I see," Prynn said. For all his protestations to the contrary, their discussion clearly made Shar uncomfortable, and she had no desire to satiate her own curiosity at his expense. Although talking about Andorian sexuality, however scientifically, with Phillipa had nudged several carefully tucked-away ideas to the fore of her thoughts.

So she had sexual *thoughts* about Shar—she'd admit that much, the kind of thoughts that made a conversation about *saf* more intriguing to her than, say, your average human. More than just a strong emotional and intellectual bond attracted her to him, and unless she was completely obtuse, she believed Shar reciprocated her interest. Her *thoughts* hadn't yet wandered beyond the most innocent physical expressions like kissing—assuming Andorians even kissed. She really didn't know *what* Andorians did. Life hadn't required that her view of intimacy evolve too far beyond her own species' paradigm. But she was willing to explore other possibilities. Still, the thought of Shar's smooth lips on hers, however human that fantasy might be, nudged to life a latent instinct, an instinct she wanted to savor and explore. And as delicious as the longing felt, she consciously pushed it down, forced it away. . . .

"Are you all right, Prynn?" Phillipa said, her voice kind.

Prynn wrinkled her brow, questioning the counselor.

Phillipa touched her own cheeks, hinting for Prynn to check her own.

She clasped her face, feeling the burn beneath her chilled

hands. "It's nothing. Wind's kind of chapped my skin. You wouldn't have a moisture cream on you?"

Eyes twinkling, Phillipa shook her head no.

That Phillipa didn't believe Prynn's explanation was obvious from the knowing look in her eye, but the counselor didn't probe any further.

Prynn felt increasingly unsure of the emotions coursing through her. Maybe this supposed relationship was only in her head and she was becoming one of those stupid, giddy people that lived to be in the throes of infatuation. Yes, the possibility of a relationship with Shar intrigued her; but she also despised how dependent she'd become on her hopes for that possibility. How her chest would clench with anxiety until she knew he was fine with something that had happened or had been said. Or how a compliment—or touch—made her ridiculously happy. She didn't need bouquets or exotic wines or elaborate courtship rituals. But her attachment to Shar was leading her into making rash decisions: for a woman whose thrill-seeking tendencies sometimes made her reckless, adding another level of impulsiveness might land her in serious trouble. Not for the first time, she wondered what the hell she was doing chasing Shar halfway across the Federation.

You're doing it because you care. He needs your support and friendship.

And you have absolutely no idea how else to help him right now.

They reached the aircar facility faster than Prynn expected. Orange-pink sky had been pushed below the horizon by a rapidly descending canopy of night; advancing pewter storm clouds created a queer murky light that settled over the land like a spreading bruise.

Shar had procured the only available vehicle—a smallish saucer car—for their trip. All of them together with their bags would be a tight fit. The prospect of being crammed into a small space at the end of a long, stressful day wasn't pleasant; she felt frayed. Perhaps it was too much uncertainty or the nagging concerns she had about this last-minute decision to visit Thantis zh'Cheen. She wished she could figure out how to fix things with Vretha so that she and Shar could escape somewhere and relax.

While Phillipa joined Shar in the leasing office to negotiate the terms of returning the aircar, Prynn loaded their bags into the cargo hold, then hopped into the pilot's seat of the circular vehicle and began familiarizing herself with the instrument panel. She was disappointed to see that the console was of the offworld-friendly "universal" design that could be found in most humanoid civilizations in the Federation; she had been looking forward to seeing one that was uniquely Andorian. Running a brief engine check revealed that the antiquated vehicle had more kick that she expected. The navigation headset sitting on the passenger seat utilized an optical interface she hadn't seen since she'd hotwired her grandmother's clunky old aircar when she was twelve. Placing the headset over her eyes, she entered the coordinates Shar had given her into the instrument panel and the face shield lit up with the pale red gridlines of a map. She studied the route to the keep—about an hour's travel over rugged, uneven territory; narrow gaps between hills, rocky crests, and plunging gorges that would be especially treacherous due to night traveling conditions and wind velocity. Nothing a computer couldn't handle, of course. *But a nice challenge for a pilot unfamiliar with the lay of the land,* she thought. *Kinda makes up for the boring controls.* Prynn hit the starter, and with a rising hum the quadruple engines came on line.

On cue, the passenger hatch opened and Phillipa climbed into the backseat, while Shar rode shotgun. "We're cleared for departure," he told Prynn as she entered several custom settings into the console. "I see that you're familiarizing yourself with—"

"Buckle up!" Prynn said, and launched the saucer car away from the leasing facility at top speed, over the rooftops of Thelasa-vei and into the countryside.

Phillipa, who was trying to sit up after being slammed down and back into the cushions of her seat by the sudden acceleration, said, "I'd appreciate it if you'd warn me the next time you plan to do that."

"Sorry," Prynn offered, and shot a quick look at Shar, who was studying her with a peculiar expression, his antenna sticking almost straight up. Prynn flashed him a grin and a wink, then shifted her focus to the terrain.

The saucer car cleared civilization in less than a kilometer. A vast sloping wilderness spread before her. Without the nubs of brush and clusters of sedge to soften the landscape, the hillocks and hollows of the interior peninsula would have resembled a lifeless moon. Dark grasses bent and swayed, flattened by the intermittently violent gusts. Up a small rise, careering down a slope, swerving past marshy puddles and boulders the size of a shuttlecraft, Prynn raced along through puddles of shadow on the pale, moonlight-frosted ground, ignoring the path recommendations on her visor. Dark clouds veiled the starscape. Spying a hairpin turn where two hills joined up ahead, Prynn accelerated again.

Shar looked at her questioningly.

"I thought we should have some fun," she said, mustering the most innocent look she could manage.

And for the first time Prynn could recall in all the months she'd known him, Shar laughed.

The better part of the journey inland went without incident. Mostly. The saucer car had buzzed a herd of shaggy marsh bison, and their subsequent stampede had forced Prynn to bank the car at straight vertical; Phillipa complained once that her stomach had nearly lurched out of her throat. Otherwise, all was good.

The saucer car found turbulence and bounced through the last few kilometers of stark plains spread before the keep, now a dark hulking citadel on the horizon. Crowning a low rise in the landscape, the ancient towers, silhouetted against flashing storm clouds, grew more forbidding with every meter. Prynn's image of a pastoral agrarian manor proved false; rather, the keep was a fortress, built to withstand the assaults of time, weather, and enemy forces. She could make out the details of the brutish black bulwarks, rimmed with spikes and gargoyle-like statues.

Not exactly putting out the welcome mat, she thought, steering the saucer car down the long, flagstone road and over a bridge to a paved area abutting the front gates. "What's next?" she said, looking at Shar.

"Prynn, if you and Phillipa can manage the luggage, I'll secure the saucer car. Someone from the keep will come back for it later and make sure it's stored in the keep's vehicle hangar."

Prynn checked a weather readout on the dashboard before shutting down the engines. "Wind chill is plummeting. I suggest we move fast." She opened the pilot's hatch and hopped out. What had been a lively, spirited wind in town had become vicious, howling like a wounded animal. All her exposed appendages instantly numbed, the joints in her hands locked up. Once again, she cursed her failure to remember gloves.

Shar scrambled out of the passenger seat into the open air and stiffened. Prynn saw him shuddering against the cold as he opened a side hatch and unwound the thick cables that he would use to tether the saucer car to metal rings mounted near the keep wall—a simple but effective means of securing vehicles temporarily against the seasonal gales.

Gathering up the bags, Phillipa passed them out to Prynn; flexing her fingers to take the luggage sent bursts of frozen, searing pain through her joints. She hunched, holding the travel bags close to her body, threading her arms through the straps for fear of losing them. The wind beat relentlessly against her, a tidal wave of swirling and crashing air.

Phillipa climbed out of the saucer car and relieved Prynn of one of the bags, and together they hurried toward a slight overhang beside the gate. Looking up, Prynn noticed ornate relief carvings on the stone wall: animals' heads on humanoid bodies; snake forms sprouting multiple heads; monsters with moss-covered fangs; sword-wielding soldiers, their granite faces weather-stained and lichen-spotted. Deafening, ground-shaking thunder announced rain. Prynn shot a worried look over at Shar; he needed to hurry.

He seemed to be yelling instructions at her, but the wind roar in her ears made it impossible to hear. An exaggerated jerk of his head toward the two-story stone gate sent Prynn's attention to an elongated rectangular box jutting off one of the pillars: the call pad.

While Phillipa went to announce their arrival—she was, after all, the only member of their party who was actually expected—Prynn watched Shar until the last cable had been threaded and locked. *Come on, come on,* she thought, her teeth chattering.

Because she expected that he'd make his way over to them at once, concern flooded her when he stopped dead, staring for a moment, at a spot somewhere behind her. Prynn turned and followed his gaze to the wall beside the keep's gate where the mark of the Water Guardian loomed. Twice the height of any of them, the mark stained the stone with drips and drabs of indigo. Shar pushed against the wind and crossed to the wall. Reaching up with his finger, he scratched at the mark, touched his finger to his tongue and spat.

His expression told Prynn all: blood.

A small door in the giant gate slid open, expelling a gust of steamy breath.

What are we getting into?

Shaking with cold, they clutched their arms tight against their bodies and raced inside, through the arched doorway, and into a warm, low-ceilinged chamber that smelled of dried leaves and wet wood. Savoring the welcome pain of blood gushing back into her iced fingers, Prynn balled her hands and loosened them. The dull lighting, emitted by room-height pillars of glowing, opalescent white quartz, stung Prynn's dark-attuned eyes. She blinked, surveyed their surroundings, and gasped. Her hands tightened into fists and remained poised to swing.

Four armed Andorians, indistinguishable in their open-faced headgear with cheek guards, greeted them, drawn toothy daggers glinting. They were dressed identically: black chausses, black leather breastplates embossed with a silver-and-green crest that Prynn assumed represented the clan, worn over rough-woven red tunics that skimmed the tops of their knees. The tautness in their antennae betrayed their intentions.

Security, she wondered, *or a death squad?* Instinctively, Prynn raised her hands above her head, but then she realized the blades pointed not at her, but at Shar.

"I come in need," he said calmly, "seeking the hospitality of the *Zha* of the Clan of Cheen."

In near unison, the Andorians secured their blades in sheaths mounted at their hips and fastened to the breastplate with a square pin bearing the same silver-green crest. Each guard removed his headpiece, cradling it between arm and rib cage. Prynn hadn't seen Andorians with this appearance save in old holos from the early days of the Federation: crowns of straight white hair, close-cropped against the skull. Shar seemed like a different race entirely by comparison.

This is the part where they tell us to get the hell out of Dodge,
Prynn thought, dreading the prospect of facing the storm conditions outside.

One of the quartet stepped forward, extended a flattened palm
toward Shar. "We have not seen you for many cycles, Thirishar
ch'Thane. Welcome."

Shar reciprocated the gesture. "Your welcome is received
gladly, Vanazhad ch'Shal." He broke from the palm touch and
rested his hand on ch'Shal's shoulder.

Ch'Shal's relaxed antennae curled, and he mirrored the gesture, touching Shar's shoulder. "The *Zha* awaits you in the Enclave chamber. We will escort you."

"She knows I'm here?" Shar asked.

"She's known for some time," ch'Shal said. "Another visitor
to the keep informed her of your return to Andor. *Zha* Arenthialeh zh'Vazdi."

Thia. That made sense, Prynn supposed. The young *zhen* said
she'd be coming here after she met up with her bondmates.

Prynn fell in line behind Shar and Phillipa as they followed
the quartet of security guards—or assassins, or soldiers, or whatever the hell they were—another ten meters down the corridor,
which she assumed cut right through the keep wall. It opened
into a covered but open-sided path that bisected a wide cobble-
stone courtyard. Hearing the rain pelting against the steepled
stained-glass roof above their path, she braced for the elements,
but realized that forcefields held back the storm. Relieved that
she wouldn't be assaulted afresh by wind and rain, she relaxed
enough to study her new surroundings.

Twisting to look at where they came from, Prynn could see
that a command post was built into the keep walls. More than a
dozen security officers clothed similarly to their escorts patrolled
along the upper wall, protected from the weather by the same
forcefield technology being employed in the walkway. From the
intermittent lighted windows in the wall, she discerned there
were at least three occupied levels within. Considering that the
front wall was at least as wide as DS9's mid-core, she guessed
there could be hundreds, if not a thousand people inside. Once
upon a time, before Andor had been unified under one government and clans warred against one another, Cheen-Thitar Keep

would have been a formidable target. She wondered, doubtfully, if it had ever been conquered.

On the right side of the courtyard, extending the length of their walkway, Prynn saw a building complex sprouting interconnected milky domes and solar collectors, indicating an agricultural center. She knew that many settlements across the Federation depended on such artificially created environments for foodstuffs and to enhance oxygen generation. The keep's facility compared favorably with those she'd seen in other hostile or artificial environments, most notably the most remote areas of places like Mars and Titan. The other side of the courtyard remained open, save for a few scattered benches, and could be a gathering place during the temperate months. On all sides, Prynn noted many open oval doorways leading into more passageways; she imagined they were only seeing the barest surface of the keep.

Before she could ask questions, their escorts led them into an elliptical opening in the wall and down a steep stair into what appeared to be an elongated subterranean foyer. Windowless, the room's walls were adorned with tapestries woven in warm, welcoming colors. L-shaped benches were set into the corners of the foyer where they entered. Prynn noted another open oval on the far side of the room.

"Leave your bags here, then ready yourselves for Enclave," ch'Shal said. "We'll take you inside after you've changed."

Changed? Prynn turned a confused face to Shar.

He shrugged off his jacket, folded it neatly, and placed it on a bench. "You'll need to remove your clothing for the Enclave," he explained. "It's the custom."

Oh, is it? "So . . . when you say, 'remove your clothing' . . ."

"A cloth shield is provided for those who sit in Enclave with the clan," Shar explained as he sat down on a bench and pulled off his boots. "Traditionally, new visitors were received stripped of all their possessions and goods. The clan council would then evaluate them based on who they were instead of what gifts they brought or what they wore. These days, it's more a question of manners than security."

She then noticed that the walls over the benches were lined with hooks, with lengths of thin, vividly hued cloth in a myriad of colors hanging from each. No footwear.

"If you were carrying a weapon or smuggling contraband, you wouldn't be able to bring it into the presence of the clan council," ch'Shal said, clarifying further.

"I see," Phillipa said, reaching uncertainly for a garment of sunset orange.

What Shar called a "shield" was actually a long length of plain oval fabric with a slit cut in the center, presumably to pull over the head. Four finger-width strips of cloth dangled from the sides—ties. *Not too much there,* Prynn thought.

"After Enclave, you will have time to change into fresh clothes before attending the Deepening meal in the dining assembly," one of the other guards said. "Your bags will be delivered to the sleep hall."

Prynn selected a shield in what she thought was a flattering shade of violet, and stood waiting, clutching it to her chest, wondering why their welcoming committee hadn't left yet. There were, after all, people getting undressed here and they were the ones obsessed with manners.

The four guards remained where they stood, their antennae relaxed, chatting with Shar as he disrobed. Obviously they had no intention of leaving.

No nudity taboo. Wonderful.

Prynn exchanged looks with Phillipa, who, judging from the brightness in her eyes and her tightly pinched lips, wasn't thrilled about the situation either. And what was Shar doing? Didn't he sense their discomfort? His antennae allowed him to feel the moods in a room, didn't they? The counselor took a deep breath and began peeling layers of clothing. *Oh well,* Prynn thought, dropping her travel bag on a bench, *this wasn't exactly what I had in mind when I thought about Shar getting to know me better, but I'll deal.*

"Wait," she heard Shar say, and looked up to see that he was already naked. Prynn's first impulse was to look elsewhere. But her curiosity quickly got the better of her and she let her gaze drift back to him, allowing her eyes to linger and then roam discreetly over the lean cut of his body, gave herself a moment to study the differences between them. And he was different; outside her experience, sexually . . . but maybe not prohibitively so.

In fact, the more she looked, the more intrigued by the possibilities she became.

Shar, however, wasn't looking at her, or at Phillipa. He addressed the guards. "As a courtesy to my companions, who have different customs, will you absent yourselves while we change clothing and trust us to find our way to the Enclave as soon as we're dressed?"

"My apologies to your companions. Of course, Shar," ch'Shal said. "We'll announce your arrival to the *Zha*." The *chan* turned to his fellows and hissed a few short words in what Prynn assumed was an Andorii dialect her translator implant wasn't programmed for, and as one the four departed, leaving the three visitors alone. Shar politely kept his back turned to the humans as they changed.

"Shar, before we see Sessethantis . . ." Phillipa retrieved a small fabric pouch from a pocket in her travel clothes, spilled Shar's *shapla* into her hand, and passed it over to him. "You'll know what to do with it."

A soft sigh escaped Shar's lips as he placed the *shapla* around his neck, the locket disappearing underneath the "shield" garment. "Thank you."

Even in the chamber's dim light, Prynn could see the *shapla*'s shadow beneath the thin fabric. How long would it be before zh'Cheen saw it as well? And more to the point, what would she do then?

4

Phillipa pulled the sides of her shield's back flap forward, tucked them under her arms, and pinned them close to her body with her elbows. She had brushed up on Andorian anthropology for this trip, and wondered how she'd missed this custom. She could see how stripping away the clothes and trappings of rank would equalize all who joined together, as well as providing added security for the keep, but she wondered darkly if the intent wasn't also to make the guests feel so self-conscious they'd be as docile as a *sehlat* after a heavy meal. And she had reasons to be self-conscious. Sibias claimed he loved every divot and wrinkle created by her pregnancies. He might—but she didn't. She resolved to carve out enough time to take the occasional run around the docking ring when she got home.

But what Phillipa had the presence of mind to notice, as Shar led them down sloping arched passageways to the Enclave room, was the complete absence of doors inside the keep. Peering into archways, she'd found many spacious rooms with high, vaulted ceilings lined with the same luminescent white quartz that provided lighting elsewhere in the keep. Impersonal public spaces—but no private ones. She also noticed the complete lack of interest in their presence displayed by the keep residents who passed by. Not one sweeping head-to-toe examination, not even a furtive over-the-shoulder glance. Those residents who did acknowledge their presence evinced serene expressions and eyes that gazed not quite at them, as if they were focusing their attention on a point just beyond their guests' ear or forehead: eye contact without eye contact. Based on what she knew from observing Shar and his bondmates, and from what she saw here, Phillipa surmised that personal, interior space *was* privacy. Whereas among humans and many other Federation cultures, like those on Bajor and Trill, cordoned-off physical space created privacy, Andorians drew their circle of intimacy within their minds; all aspects of the exterior world—including the body—were seen as public domain. *They don't define me as the forty-five-year-old one-eighth Vulcan female that I am. In their view, what I am is what they can't see—it's my thoughts and feelings and experiences that only I can reveal to them.*

As they descended deeper and deeper beneath the keep, down a gradually declining passageway, the swelter intensified steadily until Phillipa discovered the reason for the muggy conditions.

The clan Enclave was composed of four diamond-shaped water pools framed by a deck paved in rough-hewn slate and granite. Water burbled up from a glowing opaque bottom, fizzing and foaming as it reached the surface. Sheets of steam peeled off the pools, saturating the room with fog and making it difficult to discern the octagonal chamber's dimensions. Through the veiling mist, she realized a full Enclave awaited their arrival. Along every pool edge, polite blue faces bobbed above the bubbling water, the colors of their sodden shields nearly indistinguishable.

From the minty-salt scent, Phillipa guessed that the peninsula's underground hot springs had been siphoned off to fill the pools. A flat, gray stone island rose from each pool's center, and from the goblets scattered about, Phillipa assumed the island was used as a table. Enclave participants sat along the edges of the pool, facing inward, enabling them to see all those seated around. Presumably, visitors could drink and socialize in this cozy environment, avoiding the inevitable bulk of furs, leathers, and boots required to move around comfortably in the drafty stone rooms that comprised most of the keep. Soaking in these pools and imbibing a favorite liqueur had the potential to be a relaxing experience; Phillipa hoped she had the chance to visit the Enclave under better circumstances.

As they entered, a decrescendo of whispery voices followed, fading to near silence. Condensation coated the mossy walls, water droplets drizzling down pillars and puddling on the floor. Phillipa walked cautiously, wanting to avoid an accidental slip, but she realized the stones had been roughed up, giving grip to her bare feet. Surveying those in the room, Phillipa identified Dizhei and Anichent, and was unable to suppress a pang of sorrow. She and her family had been stranded on Bajor during the lockdown caused by the parasite infestation, and Phillipa had been unavailable to the bondmates during their emotional reunion with Shar, or for their unhappy departure from the station. Now, weeks later, they looked better to her, healthier, no longer consumed by their grief. But their tension upon seeing Shar was palpable.

Then Phillipa's gaze found an older Andorian. Her delicate facial features, the willowy, almost swanlike carriage in the neck and shoulders reminded her so much of another . . . and her face . . . the face that had haunted her dreams for months. She met Sessethantis zh'Cheen's eyes directly and found no glassy politeness there, only pain.

They walked along the pool edges to the nearest empty spot. Shar sat on the edge, dangled his feet and, pushing himself off the side, slid into the water. Taking a place on either side of him, Phillipa and Prynn followed suit, discovering a built-in ledge to sit on beneath the water. Uncertain of the protocol for such a meeting, Phillipa watched Shar. Though his face remained impassive, his taut antennae betrayed his true mood; even she could feel the charge in the room.

Prynn didn't bother with a façade: she wore her suspicion like a drawn weapon, warning any who might cross her. Equally transparent was her attachment to Shar. The way she unconsciously touched his arm, his shoulder—the way she hovered protectively by his side—revealed an emotional attachment Phillipa wasn't sure a wiser woman would expose to this audience. Prynn needed to remember that in spite of the polite welcome they'd received thus far, the fact remained that Shar was uninvited. He had been deliberately excluded from the rites and there were reasons for that decision. But what troubled Phillipa most was how the clan would perceive Shar's response to Prynn. He allowed her to remain near him, he unveiled his expressions when he spoke with her, and when he occasionally brushed against her, the comfort and familiarity in his touch bespoke a connection that Phillipa wasn't sure that even Shar had allowed himself to acknowledge. *Zha* Sessethantis would not miss it, of that Phillipa was certain.

After several uneasy seconds of silence, a single hollow clang sounded, announcing the formal beginning of Enclave.

Sessethantis rose from the ledge, standing. "Welcome clan and friends to the Enclave before Deepening. We gather to join in the eternal quest to become Whole, and to celebrate the endeavor." She made a half-turn so she fully faced Shar and paused, willing him to meet her wide, lilac eyes.

Phillipa felt Shar tense, sensed his anxiety, saw it in his antennae.

"Welcome, Lieutenant Commander Phillipa Matthias of Alpha Centauri, who has come at my bidding to take part in the Rite of Memory. Accompanying her is Ensign Prynn Tenmei of Earth. We hope you will join us after Enclave for our Deepening meal in the dining assembly. May you find welcome in our keep."

A chorus of voices whispered *welcome*.

Phillipa bowed from her shoulders, and after a moment's hesitation, Prynn did likewise.

"And another comes with our Starfleet guests. Thirishar, long-lost *chei* not of my body, but of my heart, beloved of my—" She swallowed hard, her eyes bright and glistening; she dropped her gaze for a long moment.

The room stilled to utter silence save the gurgling of the pool, the drip-drip-drip off the ceiling beams. No one, especially Phillipa and Prynn, dared breathe as they watched Thantis approach Shar.

"Shathrissía. There. I have invoked the name of the dead," she said, her voice tremulous, husky with sorrow. "Thirishar was her true *ch'te*. He has long been away from us, walking a path apart. But he has returned to join us in our hour of grief. On behalf of the Cheen-Thitar clans, I bid you return to the Whole." She paused, surveyed her audience, then dismissed their attention. "Be about your business."

Thantis's welcome to Shar dissipated the tension. Phillipa hadn't been sure what the gathering thought would happen, but clearly, the situation had played out better than they'd expected. As the company relaxed, a low whispering resumed. No one appeared to care that neither Shar nor Thantis had yet to look away from the other.

A chill prickled Phillipa's bared arms and shoulders; she shivered. Ducking lower into the water, she settled where her chin hovered just above the surface. The sudden gush of heat saturated her senses. She continued shivering but she knew it had less to do with temperature shifts than with the charged emotional undercurrents she sensed around her. Phillipa expected the chill would remain until whatever gauntlets had been thrown down between Shar and Thantis were fought for and a winner decided. She didn't consider herself a betting woman and believed that was a good thing, considering that she had no idea—professionally or intuitively—who would prevail in their battle of wills.

Several hours later, Prynn stood on the threshold of the dining assembly, another octagonal room, searching for Shar and Phillipa among the hundreds of occupants. If she didn't find them soon, she was prepared to drop down wherever she could find an empty spot in an eating circle and start in on her dinner—or Deepening meal, or *whatever* the Andorians called it. The communal fashion in which the clan ate—seated on the floor on rugs, dishing their portions off platters and bowls onto plates, then using flexible *hari* bread as a scooping utensil—was dress casually, sit comfortably. The cleanup and serving chores seemed to be divvied up according to whoever was closest to the dishes and who had a free hand, not social rank. Practical. Prynn liked that.

In contrast, she remembered a ridiculous Starfleet-brass dinner party her parents had taken her to—one of the rare times they were all together, and her first fancy dress-up occasion, her hair tied up in a sparkling red velvet bow. Endless tables featuring more forks, spoons, and knives at each plate than she had fingers. After two hours of dangling her short legs off the Queen Anne chair, she'd rejected her bowl of rubbery escargot with cessar bean sauté, a sea fruit parfait, and a warm pumpkin soup, finding only a basket of rolls to her liking. She remembered being restless with hunger, her stomach yowling in such a way that she attracted the attention of an admiral her mother was conferring with. Tonight she had been similarly situated. The Andorian she had sat shoulder-to-shoulder with in Enclave—a *shen* named

Uthiri—had turned a bemused expression on her when the rumbles started. Now that she thought about it, Prynn couldn't recall the last meal she'd eaten. Probably something from the replicator on the *Viola,* or the mealy ration bar she'd tried on the Orbital Control Station. Yuck to both.

Finding her friends proved challenging. Not even Phillipa's humanness distinguished her from this crowd. In the wan white-yellow quartz light, the counselor's Scandinavian blond braid seemed to be nearly the same hue as most of the Andorian hair. She finally recognized Thantis, kneeling beside a member of her dining circle, a platter balancing on her forearms. Weaving in and out among the dining circles, she made her way across the room to a group situated close by a series of floor-to-ceiling windows. Even with the ambient noise of clanking plates and conversation, Prynn could hear the rain splattering against the panes, the reverberation of thunder.

"Sorry I'm late," Prynn said, squeezing in next to Shar and situating herself cross-legged. "The clothes I arrived in must have been misplaced along with my bag. I appreciate the loan of a *ceara, Zha* Sessethantis."

"No, I apologize, Ensign," Thantis said, walking over to Prynn's place. "The gatekeepers were careless. I hope our garb suits you. I know you are accustomed to uniforms, trousers, and such." She knelt down, providing Prynn access to the food platter. "By some, our traditional clothing is seen as quaint."

First retrieving a clean plate from a stack in the center of the circle, Prynn scooped the sour-grain pilaf off the proffered platter, the aroma of nutty citrus inciting more stomach growls. A seared marine animal of some kind and roasted *vithi* bulbs finished off the course. She bowed her head in thanks and then, in what she hoped wasn't too eager a fashion, dove in with a slice of *hari,* shoveling the pilaf into her mouth as delicately as she could. Between mouthfuls, she said, "*Zha,* I'm quite taken with your clothing. I'd like to take a *ceara* back home with me if it can be arranged."

"I would be honored to send several, Ensign, as a gift from my clan," Thantis said, placing the mostly empty food containers in the center of their dining circle and resuming her own place.

From the subtle twitch in Shar's antennae, Prynn could see he was gratified by her compliments. *If I can help Shar's standing with his mother-in-law by being a gracious guest, so much the better.*

But Prynn wasn't merely being polite—the three-piece *ceara* was warm and comfortable. The cloth—a fine-gauge fuchsia knit—feltlike cashmere but draped like silk, delicate and supple. With a sheer, formfitting neck-to-ankle body stocking as the foundation garment, the *ceara* top was a long rectangular piece of blue and gold fabric that she wrapped around her torso to cover her from waist to collarbone. At her neck, she crisscrossed the two ends, throwing one over each shoulder like a cape; then she pinned the ends to the undergarment with brooches bearing the clan insignia. On her lower body, she wore a pair of loose, wide-legged burgundy pantaloons, cropped at midcalf, with an elastic waist that sat at her hips. While Prynn wasn't sure she could wrap the top properly without more practice, the result was an easy-to-move-in outfit that was neither Starfleet androgynous nor the provocative fashion slavery that the Federation-dominating Risan designers tended to promote. She could sit cross-legged on a rug, hunched over her meal plate, in this half-underground two-story hall with its rock walls and musty draft and feel as relaxed as if she were skinny-dipping in the Mediterranean back home. This was fashion she could live with.

As her hunger was sated, Prynn shifted her focus to her fellow diners. The discovery that Anichent and Dizhei sat in their dinner circle troubled her—didn't Shar deserve more consideration than to be seated with his exes? On most worlds, such a move would be seen as a faux pas. Prynn imagined that Thantis was probably trying to make a point by seating the surviving bondmates together. The *Zha*'s class quotient dropped dramatically in Prynn's eyes.

She'd never met either of them properly. Their arrival on the station had coincided with the *Defiant*'s departure for the Gamma Quadrant, and they had returned to Andor so overwhelmed with their individual grief that there hadn't been an appropriate time for introductions. Prynn didn't want to appear to be ignoring them, but she couldn't think of a polite segue into a conversation. *Sorry we dropped in on your funeral. Great food.*

Excellent spa. Love the clothes. So, have you found someone to replace Shar yet? As that last thought crossed her mind, a mouthful of fish caught in her throat. Coughing, she covered her mouth. His face etched with concern, Shar abandoned his own plate, and massaged her back, patting her between the shoulder blades. Such a gesture was common in a Starfleet mess hall, but as she noted the expressions on the faces in the circle, she guessed it wasn't so common here. Thantis especially had an odd look in her eyes—not quite suspicion . . . something else.

Prynn recovered quickly, clearing her throat and blaming the spasm on a bone she'd forgotten to excise from her fillet. The incident passed and her fellow diners resumed their conversations and meals. But Prynn couldn't shake the feeling that the *zhen* had become aware of her in not so desirable a way.

Shar requested the platter of roasted bulbs, sitting at Thantis's elbow, to be passed to him. The *Zha* continued eating, dabbing at the sauce on her plate with the last of her *hari*. Another diner reached for the platter and passed it to Shar.

Without shifting her attention from her plate, Thantis said, "Weather controls will make it safe to travel out of the Archipelago by tomorrow Deepening."

"My *zhavey* expects me," Shar said.

"I will notify the Thelasa-vei shuttleport that you will need passage—but wait. You're not traveling alone, are you? You and your *friend*—" She nodded in Prynn's direction. "—will be traveling to the capital together."

"As you say, *Zha.*"

He calls her "Zha," not "Zhadi." Prynn's eyes widened at the implication. She understood that "*Zha*" was a polite form of address to a *zhen*—like "my lady." "*Zhadi*" was akin to "mother-in-law." *He's letting her know that she's not the only one who has issues with this relationship.*

"Commander Matthias will join you after she is finished here, though I understand she would like to make time to arrange meetings with some local colleagues before returning to Deep Space 9. Will you three meet up at the Orbital Control Station? Or perhaps in Zhevra?" Thantis's calm, unwavering tone belied the sharpness of her words.

Shar flushed deep blue.

Ouch, Prynn thought. *Drive it home that he's not welcome, why don't you.*

Before Shar could reply, Phillipa said, "I'm afraid that my determination to meet the Zhevra University faculty limits the time I'll be spending in the Archipelago, but I'd like to become better acquainted with this area. Perhaps you have time to show me around your home—review some of the clan history?"

"Indeed. We are finished here," Thantis said, adding her empty plate to the stack of used ones beginning to accumulate, "and I have political obligations later. The regional Visionist Party chapter is convening in the keep. Now would be a good time if you'd like, Commander."

"It would be an honor, *Zha* Sessethantis," Phillipa said, and stacked her plate with the others.

"Oh, and Shar, I believe you have something that belongs to me," Thantis said, a shade too casually for Prynn's taste.

Still munching on the roasted bulb, Shar didn't look up.

"There was obviously a misunderstanding because—" She leaned over, insinuated herself into Shar's personal space, and reached up beneath his collar to pull out the *shapla.* "Commander Matthias was going to deliver this to me."

No one moved. Prynn glanced over at Dizhei and Anichent, both of whom had tensed visibly.

Shar's calm was undisturbed. "Custom dictates that the bondmates return their weavings to the dead." Lifting the chain from out of Thantis's hand, he dropped the *shapla* back to its place beneath his clothes. "Before I leave, Thriss will be completed by me. I owe it to *her.*" Shar returned to his meal.

Kneeling down beside her, Phillipa touched Thantis's shoulder. "I apologize, *Zha.* I know that you had charged me to deliver the token in lieu of Shar. But when his journey here became necessary due to the storm, I assumed he ought to present the weaving himself."

"No matter," Thantis said, waving Phillipa aside. "You do not know our ways. You cannot be expected to understand. We shall leave now." Stiffly, she rose from the circle, with Phillipa following close behind, and strode away.

With the hostess gone—and considering the awkward moments before she left—even the most impersonal talk abruptly dried up. Prynn knew the parched silence resulted from the presence of Shar and his bondmates.

Dizhei and Anichent had never spoken during the meal—at least not since Prynn had arrived. From the apparent indifference between them, the three could just as easily have been mistaken for strangers rather than former lovers reuniting to commemorate a loss. Her own awkward encounters with Vaughn since their return home—some sad, some difficult—taught her that avoiding confrontation wouldn't help facilitate the healing process. Vaughn's insistence that he would be part of her life had started her gradually moving past her mother's horrific death. Shar, too, needed to mend. And her presence in the dining circle provided him with an excuse to avoid his bondmates.

"You know," she said to no one in particular, "I'm exhausted. Unless there's something else going on . . . ?"

"Dancing," someone said. "There's always dancing after Deepening meal."

"Oh?"

"Music. Several new compositions have been prepared for the—" The speaker stopped abruptly.

The Sending, Prynn finished mentally. *The funeral.*

"The kitchen will bring out sweets," said another. "Spring Festival begins tonight. Many delights have been made to celebrate the season."

The prospect of dessert and dancing appealed to her. She knew if she stayed that Shar would be her dutiful escort, showing her the dance formations, introducing her to the clan members he knew from earlier visits. He'd be the perfect, doting host, fully occupying himself with her welfare for as long as she needed him. *But this isn't about me. . . .*

"As much as I'd love to join the celebrating, I'm going to turn in. After all, I don't have your steely Andorian constitution—I do need to sleep occasionally." Prynn rose from the circle before Shar could appeal to her to stay. If he had asked, she wouldn't have been able to refuse him. "Who should I thank for this delicious meal?"

Her dining companions exchanged confused expressions.

"Never mind. I'll figure it out." Without a look back, she walked away, wondering how long it would take her to find the sleep room and, by extension, her bag—assuming it had been found. Not that her clothes would be of any practical use: shorts, string bikinis, and tropical-print tanktops wouldn't be appropriate keep attire. Her toothcleaner would be nice, though, and a favorite pair of fuzzy slippers. Before leaving DS9, she'd downloaded a few novels into a padd—a great way to pass a stormy evening. Shar could have all night; she would be there for him if he needed her.

And she had to admit: she really was tired. Andorians might be able to subsist on three or four hours of sleep, but as a human, she needed at least six followed by a large *raktajino* to be considered sentient.

Emerging from the dining hall into a domed central foyer, she realized at once that she should have asked for directions to the hall she'd been assigned to; she counted ten relatively indistinguishable arched passageways branching out from the foyer like spokes on a wheel. *I suppose I could just pick one . . .*

It took little time for Prynn to conclude she'd chosen the wrong passageway. After the first bend, she began to hear sounds from up ahead, like the echo of many soft whispers. Her curiosity piqued, she pressed on, and the sounds resolved into children's voices, becoming clearer as she went. United in rhythmic chants, they told the story of two people named Thirizaz and Shanchen who were calling upon a volcano to bleed lava into the sea, bringing forth a mist through which the duo could escape a wicked spirit that sought to keep the heroes separated. Prynn followed the voices through an archway and onto a cross-shaped path that allowed her to peer through the transparent ceilings of four classrooms.

Odd time for school, she thought, before the truth came to her: Needing to sleep for only one-eighth of their thirty-two-hour day, Andorians were neither diurnal nor nocturnal, but completely adapted to living and working day and night. That explained all the activity still going on in the keep, why they could eat comfortably at midnight, and why children would be at their studies in the hours following.

On one side, a dozen preteens clothed in coarse brown tunics squatted on rugs, hunched over large pads as a proctor/teacher strolled among them, looking over their shoulders at what Prynn guessed was an exam. Switching her view, she studied the chanting students in an adjacent class, who appeared to be on the young end of the primary grades—maybe six or seven. Seated in a circle, the students chanted their myth and illustrated the story with arm movements. All students wore a plain uniform in the same drab brown as the previous group. Prynn listened to catch a bit more of the story, gratified to learn that Thirizaz and Shanchen had made it, and had reunited with their companions, Zheusal and Charaleas.

Moving again, Prynn gazed over the railing at next class. Below her, two dozen older students had been organized into quads—presumably bondgroups—and each individual had been dressed in clothing that Prynn realized must denote gender. Recalling that bondmates were "given" to each other in their mid-teens, Prynn surmised that she was observing the keep's equivalent of pre-university studies. She drew closer and saw the instructor standing at the front of the classroom near a rotating holo of an anatomical diagram.

Prynn looked around and spotted some simple-looking speaker controls on the railing: four squares arranged two-by-two, matching the classroom arrangement. One tap on the right square muted the chanting from the previous classroom and accessed the biology lesson below. The instructor was in the middle of a sex-education lecture, currently specifying what nerve bundles on a *thaan* required stimulating to attain optimal sexual satisfaction. Her Federation cultural studies curriculum had taught that Andorians took their familial responsibilities—from parenting to lovemaking—seriously. Evidence of that assertion played out in the classroom below as Prynn followed what would have been considered an explicit, even titillating discussion in her own secondary-ed classes, but without witnessing any hint of prurient behavior—none of the snickering or lewd comments she'd experienced with her human peers. To the contrary: what Prynn sensed was reverence. She started to think that perhaps her cultural studies classes had understated the earnestness with which Andorians prepared themselves for the *shelthreth* and beyond; the society viewed sexuality as a serious component of the education one required to become a complete individual, and the students conducted themselves accordingly.

Most of them, anyway. Off in the corner of the classroom, Prynn noticed one student attempting to hide a padd within his tunic sleeve. His furtive glances at the padd followed quickly by a casual study of the hologram told Prynn he wasn't following class protocol. She smiled, remembering her own teenage misbehaviors—attempting to cram for tests in the fifteen minutes beforehand, hastily scribbling out an essay on Vulcan Poetics because she'd stayed out too late the night before hot-rodding with her friends in Rome.

Prynn wasn't the only one to notice the student's clandestine attempts to do outside work during the lecture. Shortly after she'd first observed him, the instructor stopped abruptly, directed the class's attention to the offender and called on him to stand.

Busted, Prynn thought, wondering what sentence would be passed down. During her school years, she had received the odd demerit or spent hours in after school academic servitude to do penance for her transgressions.

"Thezalden ch'Letha. You feel this lecture is unnecessary?"

"No, *Sha.*"

"Why, then, do you violate the harmony of our learning place?"

The young *chan* lowered his eyes. "I have an exam in geophysics, *Sha.* My institute placement depends on it."

The instructor moved closer to him, stopping when she stood in the midst of her students. "Truly, an important step in your life's journey. It is necessary to set such goals, and to devote oneself to achieving them."

The *chan* seemed to relax.

"But," added the instructor, "it is also necessary to keep those goals in perspective, to remember that they have no meaning outside the context of your bond. Why is that, Thezalden?"

The *chan* mumbled at the floor.

"Class?" the instructor said.

In atonal unison, the class recited, "With the bond, we are Whole. Without the Whole, there is nothing."

"Thezalden?"

Louder than before, the *chan* repeated, "With the bond, we are Whole. Without the Whole, there is nothing."

"Yet you dishonor your bond with your selfishness."

"I do *not*—"

"You have acted to satisfy your needs." The instructor circled the *chan* as she spoke. "Not theirs, and not those of the Whole."

"But—"

"One alone cannot be Whole—nor two, nor three. What one chooses, is chosen for all," the *shen* said, indicating Thezalden's bondmates. "What befalls one, befalls all. Their lives are yours. . . ." She paused to let her pupil complete the mantra.

" . . . My life is theirs."

"That is the First Truth. Never forget it."

"I—" Thezalden faltered, struggling for words. Even hunched over, his eyes fixed on the floor, Prynn could see his cheeks flush dark blue. Finally he whispered, "I'm sorry."

Prynn dabbed at her burning eyes with her fist and, breathing heavily, turned away and marched back the way she came. By the time she reached the foyer, she'd felt she'd regained enough composure not to attract attention. But she desperately wanted to find the sleep room now, put what she'd just witnessed out of her mind, and do her part to help Shar get through this and away from these people as soon as possible. Spotting two Andorians strolling together down a different passage, she decided to follow them, ask for directions—

"Unless you've just pulled your weaving off the loom and you're ready to dye it," someone remarked dryly, "I'd advise you to avoid that one."

Recognizing the voice, Prynn spun around. "Thia!"

Her cheeks painted with representations of insect wings in gold, red, and purple, Thia bore little resemblance to the harried *zhavey* she'd seen earlier. She'd discarded her travel robes for heavily embroidered teal green *ceara* with the addition of a gauzy drape over the top that Prynn had come to recognize as part of a *zhavey*'s clothing. Her braids had been wound up into a topknot behind her antennae with a half-dozen single braids looping out of the bottom; each ear was adorned with a series of earrings—several hoops, gem studs and a longer teardrop loop at the bottom.

She bowed slightly from the shoulder. "I am glad that you arrived safely, Prynn Tenmei. And wearing our traditional clothing, no less."

"Um, yeah. They misplaced my things, but I really like the Andorian style," Prynn said, grateful for the distraction. "I wondered if we'd run into you here, but I didn't see you at Enclave or at Deepening meal."

"I was taking a turn in the keep crèche, where our very young are cared for," Thia explained. "I heard about the travel difficulties created by the storm. Shar did the proper and sensible thing, bringing you here."

"I was afraid that under the circumstances—that is, with the preparations for the Sending that must be under way—this would be an inappropriate time to come here."

"The rites of the dead must be observed, once Shathrissía's clan has gathered," Thia acknowledged, "but so too must the traditions of the Spring Water Festival, including the welcoming of visitors such as you and me. The timing is unfortunate, but not unprecedented. You may be assured that all is well in that regard."

And now the awkward moment of silence ensues. Prynn looked at the floor; looked up at Thia—offered her a pleasant smile. The young *zhen* waited expectantly, though Prynn wasn't sure what she was supposed to do—bow, do the palm thing, ask about her child. *This might be a good opportunity to find out where the hell I'm supposed to be going.* "You want to keep me company while I get lost?" Prynn said, throwing up her hands in defeat. "I have absolutely no clue where I'm supposed to sleep."

Thia's eyes smiled at her, much the way Shar's sometimes did.

Prynn relaxed.

"Wouldn't you rather dress for the festival dances? I have many jewels you could borrow—and I could paint your face and body." Thia pushed aside her drape so Prynn could see that her empty *kheth* was made up similarly to her face.

For a moment, she was tempted, especially when she recalled Shar's explanation of the festival, but she declined, sensing that she needed to be cautious while at the keep. The idea of losing herself in a crowd of strangers here made her uneasy.

Thia seemed genuinely disappointed that Prynn wouldn't be joining her in the festival. "If you would like, I will escort you to your sleep hall."

This offer Prynn accepted gratefully.

Prynn's transparent motives for leaving the dining hall early simultaneously frustrated Shar and sobered him: Had he seriously thought he could sit side by side with his bondmates without so much as a word? Her choice forced him to confront the issue, without excuses. Of course, he had studied them out of the corner of his eye during the Enclave and Deepening meal, hoping to ascertain their feelings, but he was left unsatisfied. Both Anichent and Dizhei had been well schooled in the ways of protecting the interior world. He did not expect that he would know the truth until they chose to reveal themselves to him. Seeing them again reawakened his pain—and his love. Anichent's eyes were once again alert, having shed the tranquilized expression he wore at their last good-bye. He exuded the solemn solidity that Shar had always counted on. And Dizhei . . . she was definitely thinner, shadows beneath her eyes bespoke the stress of the previous months, but the gauntness in her face had vanished. Perhaps they had learned to live with grief. Had he? Or had he cut it out of himself, like diseased tissue, instead of learning how to *be* in this world without Thriss? What he had done was abandon his other bondmates. It had been the least egregious of his options. Or so he'd thought when confronted with the choice.

Noise continued in the dining hall, understandable considering the hundreds of people still eating.

"Thirishar." Anichent spoke first. Of course he would. Tragedy could not fully extinguish the relationship they had cultivated since childhood.

"*Th'se,*" Shar said, using the endearment. He needed them to know of his love for them. Of all that had changed, his feelings had not.

"You look well," Dizhei said, pushing food around her still-full plate.

"As do you, *Sh'za.*"

Silence: thick, obscure.

At last, Anichent said, "Will you come with us—to the arboretum? We should talk."

Shar nodded. He offered Dizhei his arm. Her split-second pause before she accepted stung, but what else could he expect her to do? Anichent took Shar by the hand. Together, they departed.

Prynn and Thia walked for what felt like half a kilometer or more, reinforcing the notion that the keep was more a small city than a manor or a farm. When they finally arrived at the sleep room, Prynn discovered it was yet another chasmal stone hall with a high-vaulted ceiling. Faded frescoes featuring winged creatures and fantastical knotwork adorned the longest wall. Folding screens composed of metal frames with dark-colored fabric stretched over them like canvas sectioned the room into smaller spaces; there were no personal "bedrooms" to speak of. Prynn watched a clan resident select a sleeping mat from among those stacked against the wall and unroll it on an open space on the floor. After stripping off her top layer of clothing, the *shen* folded it neatly and placed it beside the mat before crawling between the layers. No pillow. No lights out. No hint as to who might be sleeping next to you several hours from now.

Now, that's trust.

As Prynn strolled along the wall, wondering what criteria she should use to identify an adequate sleep bundle, she asked Thia about this lack of individual space—didn't it bother her? Did she ever want to be by herself?

"We've always lived by the axiom *When others are in need, I give,* meaning that whatever resources we have, we share between us," Thia said, selecting an especially bulky (and, Prynn hoped, warm) bundle and passing it to her. "Individuals in this sleep room need a place to sleep in order to meet a biological need that assures health and well-being. If a group is newly bonded and undergoing the *shelthreth*—or if a *zhavey* has recently delivered—there are secluded, isolated places where such sacred experiences can occur in privacy. Sleeping isn't a ritual."

In light of Thia's statement, Prynn considered her own bedtime routine, involving hot baths, novels, and pillow punching, and suddenly it all seemed a bit ridiculous. She followed Thia to one of the sectioned-off corners, where she discovered with some relief that her bag had been deposited. "This may sound like an odd question, but what about your possessions? Like, personal belongings?"

"Each family unit has rooms in the keep. Private family issues can be dealt with in those spaces, belongings stored, and so forth." Thia unrolled a bundle for Prynn, smoothing it out, loosening the layers. "But for the most part, the need to possess something exclusively doesn't figure into the Andorian way."

Prynn considered Thia's explanation for a moment, and then said, "You're all in this together, aren't you?"

"We're supposed to be," Thia said. She patted the bundle. "It's ready for you now. And lest you think we're entirely backward, take comfort in knowing that temperature regulators have been woven into the fabric. You'll stay warm."

Prynn laughed. "Am I that transparent?"

"Your skin. It's . . . bumpy," Thia said, pointing at the goose-flesh that prickled Prynn's arm. "And you're rather bluish for a species that ordinarily is not."

"Guess I've just gotten used to the chill—didn't realize I was becoming an icicle," Prynn said. "Say, if I needed to use the 'fresher . . ."

"Around the corner"—she pointed to the nearest passageway—"make a left, through the black stone arch." She paused. "If you're settled . . . ?"

Prynn nodded. "I'll probably turn in. We've had a long day. Where are you sleeping?"

"Close by. My *sh'za* has the children tonight. I will be taking my rest after dancing."

"I'll see you tomorrow?" Thia was one of a half-dozen people Prynn knew in the entire keep. She wanted to maintain contact with the *zhavey* if for no other reason than to have someone around who could show her the ropes.

"As you wish, Prynn Tenmei." She bowed her head politely.

Prynn prepared for bed, unwinding herself from the *ceara* and climbing between the covers as quickly as she could. Pushing aside her worries about Shar, she shifted her focus to her novel— a campy horror yarn about the early terraforming days on Mars—and to staying thawed.

*   *   *

"I recall our visits here with Thriss," Shar said, running his hand over the trunk of a blooming *elta* tree. Of all the rooms in the keep, the temperate arboretum with its profusion of plants and flowers reminded him most of their home in the southern continent. On their rare visits here during their youth, Shar frequented this place, especially when he felt homesick. "Is that why you chose it, Anichent?"

"In part. We shared happy memories here. I wanted to invite them to return, hoping that past joys might ease our present grief."

Shar nodded, agreeing with the wisdom of Anichent's choice. Feeling the peace in this place of ponds and delicate plant life, he was about to share his own memories of that occasion—shortly after their Time of Knowing—when Dizhei spoke.

"We have talked with many *zhen* and *chan*, Thirishar."

He swallowed hard, the now familiar ache suffusing his insides. "I hope you have found them suitable."

Dizhei sighed, her shoulders hunched as if weighted painfully. "In fact, we have not. We have found them—"

"They are not you, Shar," Anichent said, moving to Shar's side.

And before Shar could speak, Anichent leaned forward, touching his antennae to Shar's. Murmured endearments, words that Shar had not imagined he would hear again in this lifetime, soothed his raw emotions. He received Anichent, and felt alive with pain and soaring joy. Yet the familiar comfort of his *th'se*'s touch wrenched him, and he stumbled as if he had taken a blow. Reaching for Anichent, Shar gripped his shoulders, pulling him close. Anichent folded him in his arms.

"And they are not Thriss." Dizhei came up behind Shar, pushed his tunic to just above his waist and caressed his back with such tenderness that Shar was overcome. They stood together, touching, whispering words that had long remained unspoken. How easy it was, how natural, to step into their embrace and yield to their love for him—

Their love for him.

The love he had rejected for fear of hurting them.

Shar broke away. Though he felt that he was severing himself from a source of life, he forced himself to stand apart from them.

Not long ago, he had closed off this possibility, allowed himself to mourn the loss. He did not know if he had the strength to do so again. "What is it that you want from me," he whispered, saying it not as an accusation, but as a plea.

"It is not too late, *Ch'te,* for you to be *chan,*" Anichent said.

The old doubts reasserted themselves. Chan *for you? Or chan for us? Can we be together without forever being drawn into the past?* "Will there ever be a time when you don't blame me for her loss?" Shar said, his voice raspy.

Without hesitation, Anichent answered yes; Dizhei said nothing for a long moment. He most feared her silence.

"Forgiveness is not the issue," she said finally. "We—Anichent and I—hope that something might be saved. And whatever is past, can stay in the past. I cannot say that I will ever understand the choices you made, *ch'te,* but I can live with them."

Before Shar could answer, he glimpsed a figure in the doorway dressed in the ceremonial garb of keep security. He gestured for the *thaan* to come closer to deliver his message.

"You must come with me, *Cha* Thirishar," the sentinel said, politely redirecting his eyes. "It is urgent."

Shar frowned. "What is it?"

"*Zha* Charivretha is here."

Prynn had dozed off midway through chapter three. Disturbing dreams of the Martian terraformers in her book being possessed by the parasites they'd recently encountered on the station had yielded to an urgent need to visit the 'fresher. Parting the cobwebs of her dreams, she emerged from her sleep to discover the sleep room much as it was when Thia had left her. More sleep bundles had been spread out on the floor, more Andorians resting peacefully—still no sign of Phillipa or Shar, though. Drowsily, she stumbled out of her sleep bundle, felt around the floor until she found her slippers, and wondered in her half-awake state if she ought to cover up—find a bathrobe or something. Where was the 'fresher again?

Vague recollections of Thia's directions floating in her mind, she turned at the doorway, and shuffled down the hall. Surprisingly, she wasn't as cold as she thought she'd be, though she could see the storm winding up outside, the wind pressing brush and other flotsam against the window, sprays of water drizzling against the transparent aluminum, the incessant thrum of rain crashing against the roof and the outer walls.

Prynn made another turn through a dark gray archway, stepped into another passageway, and yawned. She was looking around for anything that would indicate where the facilities might be when she noticed a door left ajar. In her muddled mind, the door registered as unusual because she couldn't recall seeing a single door since she'd arrived in the keep. Hair prickled on her neck; her breath quickened. Pale light spilled from behind the door into the passage where she stood; the light beckoned her and she was helpless to resist. Gingerly, she opened the door. She had nothing to fear, nothing to fear. . . .

Upon stepping over the threshold, Prynn knew she should leave. She had no right to be here. But her need for understanding overcame her sense of propriety. She advanced further into the chamber.

Looking through the coffin's clear lid, Prynn saw her own face superimposed over that of Thriss.

Even in death, Shar's *zh'yi* was beautiful. Prynn brushed the transparent surface as if she were stroking the fine white-blond hair fanning out beneath Thriss's shoulders. Dewy and soft, her lips parted slightly in a breath never taken. *So much loss,* she thought, *so many lives broken.*

I can never have this moment with my mother. Prynn had no remains, no tokens, no mark to honor Ruriko's memory. *And Shar will be denied this!*

Placing both hands on the coffin, she leaned forward, rested against the surface, studied Thriss's silent face, and wished, for a moment, that she could wake Thriss from her death-sleep like a princess in a fairy tale: with true love's kiss. Her love for Shar.

She held the thought. Her love for Shar.

Is that what I feel?

Passing through the archway to the formal receiving room, Vretha discovered Thantis already within. The *zhen* stood with her back to her, hands linked behind her back, watching rain drizzle down the frosted panes. Even viewed from behind, Thantis appeared as unkempt and askew as she'd been six years ago—the last time Vretha had been in this room—the last time the two *zhavey*s had been allies.

Unified by a desire to encourage Shar to defer his Academy admission until after the *shelthreth,* they had hatched many plans, none of which had come to fruition. So Thantis had accepted the appointment to the Art Institute of Betazed and taken Thriss with her. Vretha had ascended to the Federation Council, providing her with easy access to Starfleet Academy and thus to Shar. Vretha hadn't spoken with Thantis since, save a few subspace communiqués exchanged between her and Thantis during her unsuccessful attempt to dissuade Shar from going on the Gamma mission. *Once again I'm reduced to depending on Thantis for help because of my failure to raise Thirishar properly.* Steeling her resolve, she took a deep breath, pushed her hood back from her face, and approached her old nemesis.

"I apologize for my intrusion at this sacred time of Sending." Standing beside a curio table, Vretha buried her clasped hands within the draping arms of her cloak and bowed deeply, waiting to be acknowledged.

"Somehow," Thantis began, turning about to face Vretha, "it seems oddly appropriate that your *chei,* who wreaked such havoc in my *zhei*'s life, should blunder into Thriss's final rites. He's always been a headstrong one, rarely willing to accept correction, ever insistent that his way was right. Then again, his present behavior proves how effective your teachings have been."

You would have been well suited for a career in politics, Vretha thought, smarting at Thantis's words. If she was planning on keeping her promises to the party council, she didn't have time to play word games with Thantis. She rose up from her bow and faced the *zhen* directly. Thantis's simple *ceara* and long silken tresses made her seem deceptively nonthreatening; Vretha had learned, through experience, that the artist knew how to target her barbs as skillfully as a seasoned parliamentary advisor. Still, an in-kind response was beneath one of Vretha's standing— after all, she was a Federation councillor, an elected representative of millions of Andorians; such an honor required that she know how to behave. This *zhen* had lost her child; Vretha would not return an attack on a wounded opponent. "I apologize also for Thirishar's untimely visit. Had the protests and the attempted bombing in the capital—instigated, I believe, by Visionist radicals—not interfered, my *chei* would be in Zhevra right now."

A hint of respect appeared in Thantis's eyes. "Well said." She turned back to watch the rain. The tempest's full wrath could hardly be known from within this protected space. Vretha's government-issue shuttle, the most current design available, had been tossed by wind and lightning like a pebble skittering down a path, adding to her seething frustration. Everything related to Shar tended to be complicated. Chasing him down through a typhoon was just the latest challenge he'd posed to Vretha. She clenched her hands into fists, burying her fingernails in her palms.

Closing the distance between herself and Thantis, Vretha stepped around a priceless settee carved from fossilized wood and assumed a place beside a series of tiered ceramic plant stands overflowing with filigreed ferns and striped cave lilies, a flower Vretha recognized as being rare, even in Andor's tropics. She cupped a bloom in her hand, caressing the luxuriant underside. "I heard of your injuries during the invasion of Betazed. I hope your work has not suffered."

"The biosynthetic arm was an adjustment, but I have resumed work on my art."

"Andor is blessed by your recovery."

"Your concerns are gracious, Charivretha." She paused. "But let us put aside the niceties and deal with the matter at hand. You will take Shar and his—friend"—she spat the word—"back to Zhevra with you. He cannot stay here, nor can she. It is unseemly."

Vretha didn't appreciate Thantis's insinuations. "Shar has duties to attend to. He will do so. As for his *friend*, Ensign Tenmei will do as she pleases. Her plans are of no concern to me."

Thantis lifted dark liquid eyes to Vretha. Their eyes locked. "The plans of Prynn Tenmei *should be* of concern to you, Charivretha. You have already paid dearly for naïveté where your *chei* was concerned." Thantis swished past Vretha, the scent of her anise-and-roses oil lingering in the air behind her. "Thirishar is on his way. Expect him shortly." She swept out of the room.

Vretha opened her fist and cast aside the crushed lily bloom.

5

"You will go back with me tonight," Vretha said. She was draped over the settee, her official parliamentary robes spread over the woolen coverlet like a rich crimson stain. The combination of the exquisite furniture and the fancy robes lent her an imperious air—an air, Shar imagined, such as a queen might have. A hand-blown glass carafe of wine sat on a low-standing wrought iron table beside her; she poured a goblet for herself, sipped from the rim, and plugged the carafe without offering Shar a drink of his own.

Not that Shar felt snubbed: he wouldn't have taken one if she'd offered. Standing before her, like a subject paying homage to his fief, he had to confess some surprise at her relative calm. Not once since the audience started had she raised her voice or hurled accusations. She'd understood his reasons for coming to Cheshras Island—even commended the wisdom of his choice. Fine. He still didn't trust her, nor was he willing to comply with her demands before his questions were answered. After a time, he said, "It isn't safe to travel. Between the demonstrations and the typhoons—"

"The demonstrations have been quelled," Charivretha said, polishing off her goblet of wine and pouring another. "Home-world Security has been deployed to restore order in the provinces where violence broke out, to keep it from reigniting. As for the weather, the route over the polar ice cap into the outer atmosphere in my government transport isn't as dangerous as piloting up and over the storm in the kind of passenger shuttle available in Thelasa-vei."

"What if I choose to stay?"

Vretha tilted her head to one side and regarded Shar with a look that bordered on pity. "Oh my naïve *chei*! Sessethantis doesn't want either of us here. If my visit didn't make it easier for her to rid herself of you, I'd never have made it within these walls. Right now, she's plotting my political downfall with her Visionist cronies." She shook her head. "No, you will come with me. I have too much to accomplish to squander hours humoring Thantis."

"And Prynn?"

Without hesitating, Vretha said, "Commander Vaughn's daughter probably ought to stay here with Counselor Matthias. For her own safety. Homeworld Security is spread thin right now, and emotions are heated. As my *chei*, you are a target. You wouldn't want her hurt, would you?"

She has an answer for everything—as if she has anticipated each of my responses. Narrowing his eyes, he studied the emotional energy his *zhavey* exuded; she was too calm for one who, under the circumstances, should be anxious. He probed carefully. "You seem surprisingly well-informed about my movements."

"I'm still Andor's representative to the Federation. I'm not without my resources."

Shar's eyes narrowed. "Resources," he repeated. "Then, they are, as usual, exemplary."

Vretha took a deep breath, rose from her chaise, and crossed to where Shar stood. Taking his chin in her hand, she tipped his face up so she could look directly into his eyes. "Let us put aside the games, Thirishar," using her gentlest voice.

But Shar sensed the tension rising in her. "Games? I don't know what you are referring to—" He twisted his head, ever so gently, trying to dislodge her grip on his chin.

She yanked him back and forced eye contact. Whatever technique she employed to shield herself from him dislodged. He saw—perceived—the resentment, the anguish consuming her.

"I had you followed, Shar," Charivretha said bluntly. "From Deep Space 9. I had someone aboard the *Viola* who kept track of you for me."

"You spied on me." He whispered the words, his muscles tensing.

"In my place, what would you have done? You haven't shown yourself to be one who honors his obligations."

"And have you honored the legal separation of me from my bondmates?"

"You haven't yet earned that right, Thirishar. When my seat on the Federation Council is secure, you can walk away. Not before."

"Is that what I am to you? A tool? A pawn?"

"You have made it abundantly clear that you despise me—"

"Hardly fair and not true—"

"—and everything I stand for—that I accept. What you refuse to accept is that you are where you are today as a respected Starfleet science officer with a prestigious assignment, because of me. I put you on this path, Shar. I provided you with the opportunities that gave you the life you wanted."

"So I am nothing without you. Would be nothing without you."

"I gave you life!" she hissed.

Standing close to Vretha risked ensnaring Shar in her seething emotions. He refused to be trapped by her. Striding over to the carafe, he poured wine into the used glass, and, throwing back his head, polished it off in one swallow, savoring the burn in his throat. Still, he couldn't relinquish his incredulity. "You had me followed."

Her back partially to him, she shifted, casting a long, enveloping shadow.

They remained encircled by silence for an extended moment and Shar wondered if perhaps the worst had passed.

A horrifying realization occurred, a thought so audacious he couldn't believe her capable of such a thing. "This isn't the first time, is it?"

Silence.

He could barely form the words, let alone think them. "Since I left for the Academy?" *Please let me be wrong.*

She slumped and she turned toward him, her face twisted. "I only wanted to protect you, Shar. You are so precious to me, my *chei*, you have to believe me."

Time stopped. Muted by shock, his rage found expression in his thudding heartbeat, in the ringing in his head, his trembling hands. He looked at his *zhavey*, seeking understanding, and found her graying visage unrepentant.

Refusing to look at him, Vretha said finally, "I have asked Zhende to collect your things. He is bringing them to my craft. We will leave before daybreak." As she passed by him on her way out the door, she patted his arm as she had when he was young and distraught, then brushed her antennae against his. He heard the solid, rapid cadence of her footsteps clicking on the stone floors as she walked away from him, leaving him alone. *Where can I go? Home?*

I belong nowhere and to no one.

Within him, darkness fell. What he believed, what he wanted, what he thought he knew became lost. Blindly, he searched the void inside him for answers—and found Prynn. He needed to be with Prynn; the realization came as naturally as breath. He needed her because she understood. She understood the black confused place inside him because the same place lived in her.

Without knowing where he was headed, he walked—and ran— losing himself in the crowds of painted faces. Instinctually, he found his way to the sleep hall. He saw her, seated on top of her sleep bundle, her face weary with worry; peace washed over him.

"Come with me," he said, reaching for her hand.

"Where?" she said, accepting him.

"Anywhere."

They left together.

On the other side of a silken partitian, Anichent slowed his breath to near stillness. He hoped his silhouette wasn't visible through the thin fabric. Forcing his emotions to remain steady was more challenging. He would not allow Shar to sense him, though in his *ch'te*'s agitated state, he couldn't be certain that Shar was aware of anything beyond his own turmoil. Listening between the lines of Shar's brief conversation with Prynn, Anichent's suspicions of this human's place in Shar's life were confirmed. More than Vretha or Thantis—or even Dizhei—he recognized the passionate impetuousness that characterized Shar's deepest emotional connections.

Once before, Anichent had witnessed such expressions between Shar and Thriss. He had chosen not to see them, but he could no longer afford the luxury of blindness.

Those individuals for whom Shar cared most were those he was slowest to let into his life. Why that was, Anichent couldn't say. He suspected that the deepest emotional places frightened him. Shar had never been comfortable accessing those parts of himself, reserving his most demonstrative affections for those who didn't threaten to take him to those deep places.

Hurt as he was by Shar's unintentional recklessness with others' feelings, however, Anichent's heart ached more for his *ch'te* than for himself. Because if what Anichent had begun to suspect was true, Shar was in very real danger, with no way to know who could be trusted, and no telling what their unknown enemies might do if Anichent tipped his hand too soon.

Anichent crept out of his hiding place and, easing along the walls, followed after Shar and Prynn.

"You're certain you can do this?" Shar asked.

Prynn didn't even look at him as she continued powering up the transport they'd chosen from those being stored in the keep's deserted hangar facility. With the weather getting worse, they needed something sturdier than the saucer car they'd arrived in. "I've flown under worse conditions. Remember that flight over the Prentara homeworld in the *Chaffee*?"

"Yes. We crashed."

"Shut up, Shar."

"I simply don't want you putting yourself at risk," Shar said, studying the navigational data as it scrolled up the console display. "I'll be fine if we remain at the keep."

No, you won't. And that's why we're getting out of here, even if means we have to bend the rules to do it. However, "borrowing" one of Thantis's shuttles for a little jaunt to Harbortown would definitely make things worse between him and her, not to mention between him and Vretha, probably between Vretha and Thantis, too—God, this was complicated! Small wonder if he was having second thoughts. She halted her check on the vehicle's engines and looked at Shar, offering him a reassuring smile. "As long as you're fine with it, this trip's a go. I'll take care of you."

"I believe that," he said simply. "And no, I haven't changed my mind. The longer I remain here, the more I feel buried alive."

"I understand that feeling," Prynn said.

"I know you do."

"Good," she said, tapping in the last series of diagnostic commands. "After everything we've both been through, what's a little bit of wind and rain?"

"More than a little." Shar began reeling off facts from the viewscreen. "We have seventy kilometers to traverse before we pass into the climate-controlled zone where temperatures are holding steady at a comfortable twenty-five degrees Celsius. Before we get there, however, meteorological data indicate we'll face winds of hundred-plus kilometers per hour and a wind chill of minus thirty."

"Stop worrying." She examined the power levels and energy flow, hoping that the temperatures wouldn't cause any systems to act up. Their crate really wasn't much more than an overpowered hovercar, engineering-wise. Shar's concern might not be entirely misplaced. She brought the engines online, and a low-pitched whine slowly wound up to a healthy hum. "Looks like we're good to go."

Shar strapped himself in. "Your orders, Captain?"

The promotion made her laugh. "Keep an eye on engineering. I'll handle navigation," Prynn said, and paused to call up a map of the keep's vehicle bay. She would have to steer the shuttle through a series of tunnels before reaching the launch doors just outside the keep's northern gate. Since the launch queue was empty, she didn't wait to begin piloting the shuttle through the metal-plated shafts, guided by long, thin strips of lighting embedded into the floors and ceilings, noting the steady gain in altitude as they approached the surface.

"Activating launch doors," Prynn said.

"We're clear to exit."

"Taking her out."

A gust of wind smacked into their starboard side. Instinctively, Prynn tapped in a series of commands to compensate for the rough atmospheric conditions, while Shar kept vigil over the stats being spewed onto his screen. The rough ride continued, however, as wind-propelled flotsam crashed into their vehicle.

The limitations of smaller craft designed only for lower atmospheric travel tended to annoy her. What she'd do for a zippy little Mark 10 shuttle right now!

Once they came within range of the weather-controlled zone
around Harbortown, they discovered that a clear spring night
awaited them.

It being three hours past Deepening, fasting and prayer had
ended; Shar suspected the festivities would be in full swing by
the time they crossed over the Nitra Bridge. Having grown up
with only a rudimentary knowledge of the ancient traditions, he
had no idea what to expect and he didn't care. It appeared that
Prynn felt similarly, showing no signs of apprehension about
their chosen course. She hadn't asked for explanations and Shar
hadn't offered. He had yet to fully share the circumstances that
prompted his run from the keep. The confrontation with Vretha
on the heels of his emotional encounter with Dizhei and Ancient
had left him feeling frayed; he had to escape. But, as with all his
decisions, there would be consequences. Shar had no doubt of
this.

So be it.

As soon as she discovered they'd left in one of her vehicles,
Thantis would undoubtledly alert the local authorities. He and
Prynn would eventually be found and brought back to the keep—
she had enough connections that there were few places on
Cheshras where they could hide. He'd explained this to Prynn,
who'd received the news in stride. Knowing the risks they faced,
Prynn had still supported his decision to leave and Shar had been
more grateful than he could express to her. She trusted him. He
couldn't say the same for his *zhavey.*

They managed to park without complication in a subterranean
public facility not far from the bridge. As they rode to the surface
in a lift, Prynn turned to him wearing a lively expression. "So
how does it feel to be an outlaw?"

"Outlaw?"

"Criminal."

"Truthfully?"

She nodded.

"Liberating."

Tossing back her head, she laughed, deep and throaty. "Me too. Have you considered what kinds of career options are open to us now that we're fugitives? Me, I'd like to be a pirate. Establish a base in the Badlands."

Initially, he wasn't sure how to take her comment. He cast a sidelong glance at her, looking for clues.

Stepping out of the lift into the crowds filling the plaza above the parking facility, Prynn strode forward as if she owned the ground she walked on; her confident demeanor drew stares from virtually everyone they passed. Her playful banter of being forced into a pirate's life notwithstanding, the possibility of being hunted by the Harbortown constabulary or incurring Vretha's wrath seemed not to bother her.

He'd chosen the perfect person to run away with.

"The Orion Syndicate is always looking for good pilots," he said, deciding to play along. He'd observed this kind of repartee hanging out in Vic's with Nog though he'd never had a chance to practice before. *Time to try something new.*

"Orion Syndicate? Why bother with them—they're yesterday's bad guys. We should go into business for ourselves."

"And how could a scientist help a pirate?"

"Are you kidding? Assuring the purity of whatever it is we smuggle. Devising clever new products to sell on the black market—genetically modified foods that make people grow taller or help them get thinner—"

"Make a contribution to civilization, in other words."

"That's the sarcasm thing again, right Shar?"

He quirked a corner of his mouth into what he hoped was a smile.

Pursing her lips in mock solemnity, she said, "Hmm. For now, I'd stick with the sarcasm. You haven't quite mastered the smiling part yet."

They followed the crowds heading over the first span of the Nitra Bridge. From a guidemap they'd found in the shuttle's database, he remembered that the Nitra was a kilometer-long pedestrian walkway spanning the Frost River, linking this land "finger" to the series of mountains encircling the ocean harbor, with the Moss River beyond Harbortown creating another natural boundary.

Her usual long, rapid steps gradually slowed to a stop at the first pylon. Shar caught up with her and stood behind her, leaning over her shoulder to take in her view.

"Oh my," she whispered.

Beyond the bridge's end, Harbortown's peaks rose like a series of dark jeweled monoliths out of the horizon; it was as if a painted starscape had fallen from the sky and crowned the city. Glints of every color sparkled in pockets between the buildings, while wavy ribbons of light snaked up and around the sides of the ramparts, creating elaborate curlicues and spidery bursts. Even at this distance, muted cheers, squeals, and celebratory shouts imposed over a percussive heartbeat of drums, cymbals, and gongs could be heard over the river waters far below, foaming and rushing toward the sea. On the other side of the bridge span, Shar could see the spiny profiles of the Guardian towers that kept watch over the crashing cataracts below them, and the city on the other side. In ancient times, Shar explained, he and Prynn would have been required to prove their worthiness to enter the city by engaging the watchtower guard in ritual combat. Today the darkened eyes of the empty towers—along with their distant siblings that watched over the other three ocean-bound rivers—presided over the revelry with nary a blink.

Prynn took his hand. "Come on," she said, and together they broke into a run across the span. She laughed as they snaked through the constantly shifting crowd, narrowly missing a few pedestrians who had veered into their path. Her jubilant laughter continued all the way across.

When they reached the other side, Prynn was panting and sweating profusely. "Are you all right?" he asked.

Bending from the waist, she flashed him a grin as she slowly regained control of her breathing. She pulled at her understocking, rendered nearly transparent by her sweaty exertions, separating the sticky fabric from her body. Between the exertion and the unexpected humidity, he assumed, she must be nearly soaked through. He knew he'd feel more comfortable if he could remove a few layers, though he wasn't sure how Prynn would react to such a suggestion.

"We could try to find you a change of clothes in town," Shar said.

"Nah. I'll just rearrange a few things before I suffocate. Don't you move." She ducked out of sight behind a wide *taras* tree. Minutes later, she emerged with the understocking bunched up in her fist and a reconfigured *ceara* top: she'd wrapped the length of fabric tight around her rib cage up to her breastbone. She'd then taken the two ends and tied them behind her neck.

Running her fingers through her short black hair, she ruffled it into its usual spikes, then smoothed a few wrinkles before spinning around so he could take in all views of her garment. "So is some Andorian purist going to assault me for wearing the *ceara* wrong or is this okay?"

He stared. The bare slope of her shoulder and the curve of her waist glowed warm in the moonlight. In the shimmering drape, her alien beauty was like something out of myth.

"Shar?" Her eyes narrowed. "I can always change it back."

Feeling transparent beneath her gaze, he looked away. "You are . . . lovely."

She blushed. "I wasn't fishing for compliments, but I'll take it."

He allowed her to lead him down the pathway from the bridge to the top of the Grand Staircase. Carved out of the mountain rock, the sharply descending stairs merged into the city's central canal street. Overhead, a clay-tiled roof, sides curled up to catch the rain, protected the stairs from the worst of the elements: the path ahead appeared to be dry. Bluish green tread lighting embedded into the steps would safely guide them. A sprightly ocean breeze, tinged with salt spray, teased the crooked trees bordering the staircase, sending their aging boughs creaking. Insect choruses, undeterred by Harbortown's noisy festivities, chirped and squawked.

Prynn linked her arm through his elbow. "There will be dancing, won't there?"

This time, there was no awkwardness in his smile.

Central Canal was nearly impassable, with revelers crowded into every space, pushing and shoving their way into the side streets that randomly branched off Canal. Prynn didn't notice; her face was turned upward, her eyes greedily soaking in rivers of lustrous purple drape over the street. Iridescent metallic threads had been stitched into tessellated patterns of winged creatures and eye-dazzling optical illusions of eternal circles. Beneath the awnings, row upon row of paper lanterns dangled, gleaming like tissue gemstones. And the noise! Grinding, crashing, singing, cheering, thudding, talking, screaming—all combined in a noisy fugue.

She could hardly absorb it all. Her stimulated senses drank in the salty humidity and pungent scorch of charcoal-roasted animal flesh overlaid with the lush honey-sweet ripeness she'd come to know as the scent of Andorian exertion. So dense was the air that she felt as if she drank each breath.

Laughing, Prynn spun around, taking in the scenery, her eyes alight with wonder. "I can't believe this place, Shar. It is absolutely astonishing! Why would you ever want to be away from here? I mean, besides your mom and all that. . . ." Her voice trailed off and she sighed. "Never mind."

"It's unfortunate that circumstances have to be complicated."

"Especially since you're giving up all this," Prynn said.

Shar steered her off Central Canal into a side street. A sunflower yellow fabric canopy enclosed the way, and Prynn felt gleeful at the prospect of wandering from street to street, saturating herself in vivid color. Ahead of them, she saw a darker throughway, with more lights and celebration past the dark. She soon discovered that they had to cross a shorter, narrower version of the river bridge to reach the adjoining street. Looking around, she saw Harbortown as a mosaic of black night and hot, wet color; a maze of cobbled streets, bridges, and façades embellished with garish sculpture and dramatic frescoes. Ornamented pillars sprouting blue-orange flames marked every corner. Wild-eyed, vulgar monster faces, fangs bared, stared down from their perches over every doorway. All around them, denizens from across the quadrant roamed, aliens Prynn didn't even recognize; many had painted their skin with Guardian icons or with nature motifs, wearing fanciful clothing or little clothing at all.

A misstep sent her stumbling into a tangle of writhing dancers with eerie clouded eyes who pawed at her clothes, pressed their faces into her neck, her stomach, clinging to her like tentacles. A few well-placed elbows released their collective embrace; shuddering, Prynn backed away.

Shar pointed out the yellow smudges on their arms and faces, explaining that *saf* changed color as it interacted with body chemistry. She watched their uninhibited gyrations with new understanding, but she clung more tightly to Shar's arm.

For the first time since they arrived, she saw Andorians wearing distinctive costumes other than the *ceara*—not the usual tunics or gowns that she'd seen at the keep or back at Deep Space 9. One Andorian she ran into wore a knee-length skirt and a loose, sleeveless mail shirt, with chunky brass bracelets bound around his upper arms. That individual was holding hands with another Andorian outfitted similarly to the guards she'd met at the keep with the chausses, tunic, breastplate, and gauntlets.

Noting her curiosity, Shar explained to her, while pointing out various examples, that those Andorians fully outfitted in traditional garb were likely observant and might be headed off to the Guardian temples to offer thanksgiving.

"The ones in warrior's attire—they are *chan*. My kind," he said. "The ones wearing the chain mail are *thaan*. You're already familiar with *zhen* because Thia's clothes are modifications of the traditional garb. A *shen* wears something similar to the *zhen*, except a *shen* visiting the Water Guardian sanctuary would reveal her entire back as a sign of her fertility." He drew Prynn's attention to a shorter Andorian walking past whose bare back had been tattooed with ornate iconographs and abstract patterns. Playing a version of I Spy, Shar would point out an Andorian and Prynn would identify whether the Andorian was *chan*, *zhen*, *shen*, or *thaan*.

Prynn rapidly mastered her task, but she had more questions. "What about physiological identifications? Like human females have breasts, Nasat genders have different shades of shell color . . ."

"Another time," Shar said dryly. "We only have a few days on Andor."

"Humor, Ensign. I'm impressed. First sarcasm, now wit. What will it be next?"

"I'll try to surprise you."

"Promise? I like my surprises wrapped up with bows."

"Bows?"

"Bows. Ribbons tied in loops that are ruffly and festive."

Eyes smiling, Shar sighed. "I fear that I failed to pack bows."

Walking in companionable silence, they passed through more celebrating, first pausing to watch a troop of gymnasts, then procuring a small bag of roasted sandbush seeds. Prynn was going to suggest they start figuring out a plan for when morning came, when she noticed a subtle change in Shar's demeanor.

"What is it?" she asked gently.

"I was just thinking . . . At Thriss's Sending, the mourners will be clothed traditionally," Shar said. "*Zhadi* will insist on it."

Silence.

"I saw her, you know," Prynn said after a moment. "In her coffin. I had no idea . . . she was beautiful."

"Yes," Shar agreed. "She was."

She sensed him drifting away from her, to that place he went when he remembered.

They had started across another bridge when Prynn asked Shar to wait while she looked over the railing. She'd noticed light and noise coming from below the level where they walked and she wondered what other surprises Harbortown held. Climbing up so her feet rested on the bottom rung of the railing, she bent over the top.

Vertigo assaulted her; she bobbled, tipping back. Pools of night and blinking lights blurred together, spinning into a whorl of color. Then Shar's hand was on her back, steadying her, and she leaned back into him, waiting for the wave of queasiness to pass. Once he helped her down off the railing, he guided her to the other side of the bridge to a curb, where he eased her into a sitting position. She dropped her head onto her lap, wedging it between her knees.

"That may have been a bad idea," he said philosophically.

"Now you tell me." She swung back up to a sitting position.

"From the base of the city to here is more than seventy levels," Shar said, stroking her back with the palm of his hand. "I should have warned you that it was a long way down."

"I had no idea we were so high up. . . . Help me up, would you?" Scrambling to his feet, Shar stood on one side of her, holding her shoulder and arm while she pushed herself up off the ground. She brushed dirt off her pantaloons and, testing her equilibrium, she started walking down the street. Shar, hovering at her elbow, was presumably there to help her should she feel faint, but Prynn believed that the dizziness had passed. She let him know that she was fine, but he continued to keep a hold of her elbow; enjoying his protectiveness, she wouldn't protest that kind of attention. They walked side by side, navigating the crowds for a few blocks, before the party thinned out and they could speak without having to shout. "I'm assuming there's a reason why your ancestors felt compelled to build their cities like this, one layer on top of another. Instead of like, spreading over the ground."

"Harbortown hasn't always had this elevation. Settlement began inside the caves that run deep into the adjoining peaks—a massive complex was excavated into the mountainside. As the populations grew, the settlers began building on the land around the harbor—technically where Harbortown stands now—and it was more like what you're accustomed to, sprawling neighborhoods and buildings over open territory. Canals were built to transport goods between the rivers. Thelasa-vei Province thrived. About thirteen centuries ago, a rash of mysterious deaths convinced the Guardian priests that the land was cursed. The harbor area settlement was abandoned, left for the demon spirits to claim."

"And the truth?"

"Excavating into the adjoining mountains released pockets of poisonous gases that were generated by chemical reactions between rock and hot water table. The gases seeped through the porous rock in and around the harbor—settlers had asphyxiated. But since the wind and water currents changed daily—"

"No pattern could be discerned from the deaths," Prynn said. "A child in one house would die and the neighbor would be fine. Once they figured it out, they sealed off the mountains . . ."

"Not quite. By then, the settlers had already started building up and over the first city. They became convinced that the higher up they built, the less likely it was that demons would follow. Since then, Harbortown has spread up the mountainside—an average of about five levels a century—until the present day."

"It looks like the other parts of the city are still habitable," Prynn said, looking—from a distance—into dark voids beneath them. "I'm certain I heard people down there."

"Harbortown residents and workers primarily utilize the top

fifty levels. But those who choose to live farther down, in the ancient areas, tend to be like more extreme versions of Thantis, if that makes any sense. They're Andorians who want to make a statement about 'the old days,' or nomadic clans who've given up their keeps. The lowest levels have been virtually abandoned, since the canals are no longer needed to transport goods. But the matter of the poisonous gases has never been fully addressed."

They had reached the end of the Central Canal district; another stretch of bridge lay before them. Shar shot Prynn a questioning look.

"I'll be fine. No more hanging off the rails, I promise," she said, walking backward across the bridge so she faced him. "See? I'm being good!" She dashed off a jaunty salute, then threaded her hands behind her back. If she read his antennae correctly, Shar was amused.

"I'm not overly concerned that you'll be catapulting yourself over the edge," Shar said dryly. "However, I am a bit curious about what other impulses you might have." He swept a long, languid gaze over the length of her body, coming to rest on her face. Their eyes met, held.

A giddy realization struck her: *He's flirting with me. If Andorians flirt. Do they flirt?* She stopped walking. He took one step forward; they stood, toe-to-toe, mere centimeters apart, but not touching. The activity swirling around—the drumbeats, the sizzling spits of roasting animals, and the swirling incense smoke—all receded into the distance, and her awareness diminished until it encompassed only the two of them. *I want him to touch me*, she thought, willing him to rest her hand on her hip, to cup her face . . .

Abruptly, Shar's attention shifted; his brow furrowed. "We have to get out of here." He grabbed her by the hand and dragged her toward a darkened archway on the opposite side of the bridge.

"What is it?" she said, worried.

"Look behind you," he said.

A rapid glance revealed a pair of uniformed security people making their way toward them. From appearances, they hadn't zeroed in on Prynn and Shar quite yet; the numbers of people milling in the street combined with the nighttime's limited visibility would make it difficult to find anyone. She watched for a moment as one of the police officers held up a padd for a *zhen* to look at.

"He's showing them our pictures," Shar said.

"They might not be looking for us."

"They're looking for us. I'm surprised we've made it this far. Thantis doesn't waste time getting what she wants—especially when she's provoked."

In that instant, the officer and the *zhen* he'd been questioning looked up from the padd and directly at Prynn and Shar. The officer tapped the comm patch on his neck.

Shar quickly drew Prynn back into the crowds and resumed moving. "We have about three hours before dawn. Do you want to try to elude the authorities?"

"I'm game if you are."

"We have about thirty seconds to make it through that doorway before they blockade the bridge," Shar said. "Once inside, we'll take the lift down as far as we can. Then, we'll start down the closest stairs." He squeezed her hand. "I suppose we're beginning our lives as pirates."

"Not funny, Shar."

6

"I can't find them anywhere." Phillipa waited in the doorway to Thantis's study. She suspected she brought old news, but she had been charged to track down the pair and she felt obligated to follow through. The dim quartz lighting in the dingy, windowless chamber made it hard for her to discern exactly where the *zhen* sat. She saw an armoire, a chaise with the stuffing popping through a fraying cushion, an unfinished tapestry hanging from a wall loom. Several yarn-wrapped spindles had been stuffed in a basket. Phillipa stepped into the room and peeked around a stone column.

Thantis was hunched over her desk, paintbrush in hand, embellishing a clay mask with a series of interconnected diamond shapes in black, green, and gold. Without looking up from her work, the *zhen* said, "It appears our young ones borrowed one of the shuttles we use to transport our textiles to and from market. They probably departed before we started looking for them." Twisting so she could see Phillipa, she gestured for the counselor to come closer. "Please take a seat." She rested her dirty brush in a vase of water. Retrieving a clean paintbrush from a tray, she resumed her work.

Of the several stools and chairs available to her, Phillipa selected a comfortably situated leather-upholstered armchair across from Thantis and waited.

"Have you started your mask of grief yet?"

"I wasn't aware—"

"Forgive me, Commander. You haven't even been here a day! I'll make a note to have one brought to you tomorrow. You'll need it for the Sending." Thantis leaned back and studied her work. "That will have to do for now. I'll be sending mine to the kiln day after next. You'll have time to apply your glazes before then." First stripping off a smock spattered with dried clay and paint, Thantis then wiped her hands on a towel and tossed it in the recycler before dropping into a chair across from Phillipa.

Resting her chin in her hand, the *zhen* studied Phillipa, her quivering antennae the only evidence of her being unsettled. She shifted, fussed with the drape of her red *ceara*, leaned back in her chair. In contrast to the immaculately coiffed Vretha, dried paint lined the creases of Thantis's fingernail beds, her cuticles ragged and fraying from being picked at; her braids, tied up in a scarf, skewed in every direction. The way she fidgeted reminded Phillipa of Thriss.

Phillipa offered her a neutral smile, but said nothing. Years of counseling had helped her cultivate a tolerance for silence. People usually spoke when they were ready to speak. She had been summoned to Cheen-Thitar Keep by Thantis; Thantis would tell her what she needed, when.

Finally: "Have you spoken with Charivretha?"

Aware of the tense relations between the *zhaveys*, Phillipa felt obliged to avoid placing further stressors on the situation. She chose her words carefully. "Yes. Her conversation with Shar ended badly. However, she still expected that he would travel to Zhevra with her. His leaving with Prynn surprised her."

"For all her finesse in politics, Vretha is as clumsy as a *klazh* when it comes to her *chei*." Thantis clasped her hands together in her lap. "And Ensign Tenmei. . . . A nice enough youth. Spirited." A long pause. "Tell me, Commander, are Thirishar and Ensign Tenmei lovers?" Her too-casual tone betrayed Thantis's deeper concern.

Now I find out what you really want. "I don't see how their relationship is relevant to the current situation."

Thantis shrugged. "Obviously you don't understand— whether they are or aren't involved romantically matters little to me. My *zhei* is gone. Her bond is not threatened. Speak freely."

If a therapist suspects a patient of lying, body language often provides the needed answers—one of the basic rules in Phillipa's studies on nonverbal communication. And Thantis's body language told a story in itself: rigidly held shoulders, tension in her jaw, a flinty set to her eyes. Phillipa knew what happened between Prynn and Shar mattered a great deal to Thantis, regardless of what she said.

But Phillipa vigilanty protected the secrets of her patients; for her friends, she did the same. Vretha had attempted to employ similar tactics to Thantis's when she'd wanted information about Thriss. Phillipa didn't take kindly to pressure. On her watch, more than a few overeager admirals with the authority to send her to the brig had been told—politely—to go to hell or *Gre'thor* or whatever place of eternal damnation best suited their culture. Resisting the demands of an overprotective mother would be a piece of Rigelian cream cake by comparison. "I tell you this not because I believe it's your right to know, but so the insinuations and assumptions can be put aside," Phillipa said, leaving no room for misinterpretation. "Shar and Prynn became friends on the Gamma voyage, during which Prynn lost her mother and Shar lost Thriss. Their friendship helped sustain them through a difficult time. When Shar decided to let Dizhei and Anichent seek a replacement for him in the bond, he was especially lonely. Prynn became a natural companion for him. Their relationship has progressed since then. I believe becoming more than friends would be good for them both."

Thantis's face softened. "Please believe me, Counselor. I do not wish ill for Thirishar. My *zhei* loved him with her whole soul. She would want him to be happy." She sighed. "But the confusion and turmoil that has accompanied his homecoming! Shar always walked a path apart from the others. That is what attracted Thriss in the first place."

"I know," Phillipa said. Memories of the many discussions she had with Thriss emerged from the recesses of her mind accompanied by a familiar hollowness—the guilt she'd felt since Thriss committed suicide. Sibias gently chastised her for personalizing her patient's self-destructive choices, but Phillipa struggled to separate what was her patient's free will and what were her own inadequacies. Many sleepless nights had passed since Thriss's death.

"Let us put aside Thirishar." Tucking her feet beneath her, Thantis curled into her chair. "Tell me about my *zhei*."

And Thriss used to sit just that way. . . . In a split second, Phillipa made a choice to lower her professional façade, allowing the words to come spilling out. "You have to know that I did everything I could. She had so much promise! I pleaded with Dizhei and Anichent . . . I suppose it doesn't matter now. And she had been doing remarkably well. Volunteering in the station's infirmary, renewing her applications for medical school. She was particularly excited about a possibility in the Cardassian territories—specializing in frontier medicine. There was such a life force within her . . . I don't understand where I went wrong."

Rising from her chair, Thantis walked over to a plain metal shelf where a row of holos sat among old folios, a piece of artwork—charcoal on canvas—sitting on an easel, several books. She fiddled with her holos, shuffling them around, wiping away dust with her finger. "You have to know, Counselor, that I read your report so many times that I memorized it. I hung on each word hoping that I'd find the answer to my question: Where did I go wrong as her *zhavey*? But you—you did all that you could."

"Did Thriss have a history of depression?"

"She was more sensitive to her environment than most Andorian children. Her happiness burned fervently—her despair became bottomless. She internalized criticism, praise, pressure. I know her hypersensitivity impacted her emotionally."

"But medically . . ."

"Nothing definitive. Her emotional variability seemed to be more circumstantial than physiological."

"I suspected as much," Phillipa said, feeling a little relief that she and Dr. Tarses hadn't made glaring misjudgments.

A long pause. Phillipa wasn't sure what she should say—or shouldn't say.

"Please tell me: How alone was she when she died?"

"Anichent and Dizhei were—"

Thantis turned back toward Phillipa, her hands flattened against her chest. "No. I mean in here." She patted her chest. "Within herself. Had all her connections with the Whole been severed?"

Tears welled up in her eyes; Phillipa couldn't help imagining

herself in Thantis's place. *Damn. This is so unprofessional of me.*
"I wish I could tell you that her last hours were spent being nurtured by those who loved her, but I can't. I believe that, for
Thriss, being disconnected from the Whole might have been
what pushed her to take her own life."

Shaking her head, Thantis offered Phillipa a sad version of
the soft, liquid gaze she'd come to recognize as an Andorian
smile. "Perhaps it was the Whole that smothered her."

"Wait," Prynn called out to Shar breathlessly, clutching her sides.
Two lifts and more flights of rickety stair gratings than she cared
to recall—taken at the speed of a crazed vole—had resulted in
side cramps. The smoky, incense-laden air didn't make breathing
any easier. The further they descended through the levels of Harbortown, the worse the air quality became.

"We'll stop here," he said, testing the lock on the stairwell
exit. A few solid pulls and the rusty fasteners holding the lid over
the security terminal gave way, exposing the inner mechanism.
Within seconds, he'd figured out how to override the door lock,
giving them access to level seven.

The lower city bore little resemblance to the manicured central districts above. Crumbling buildings and empty window
sockets lined the streets; gravel, plasteel chunks, greasy refuse,
and moldering fruit cores collected in the gutters. She heard the
skittering of small animals across the pavement.

Stepping out into the street after Shar, Prynn lost her footing
on the cobbled pavement, the cankered rocks slimy with algae
and filth. She stumbled forward, breaking her fall with her hands.
Doubling back, Shar knelt beside her and, after checking her for
cuts and bruises, offered her a hand. She wiped the brownish
sludge off her palms before accepting his help, and assured him
she was fine. "A woman can't live by adrenaline alone," she
joked weakly, blinking back fatigue, wobbling a little unsteadily
on her feet. "I need a break."

"As soon as I can find a safe place for us to stop. . . . I promise."

Surrounded by gaudy imitations of the decorations that embellished central Harbortown, they jogged past smaller groups of
body-painted revelers. Prynn nearly tripped over more than a few

who were passed out near doorways. The sour stench of fermented drink permeated the air. Compared with what they'd encountered earlier, this level was virtually abandoned. They moved swiftly, uncertain as to whether or not the security team still tailed them, ducking around corners, turning into dimly lit alleyways and over bridges, the slow, slurping shush of the canal waters the only constant.

In a not-so-distant block, the low drum rhythm of *pawm-puda-puda-pawm* hinted of habitation—perhaps an inn or a residential area where Prynn could rest for a few hours. Shar guided her in the direction of the music. As they grew nearer, shouts and singing joined the percussive beat, and soon an orange glow spilled onto the wet pavement, brightening the closer they came to the music.

Though she wanted to be a good sport, Prynn approached her limits. She needed rest, food, time to process what had happened and what might yet happen. A fatigued voice in her head admonished, *No worries yet. Tomorrow will come soon enough.*

As they emerged out of an alleyway into an open area, a barrage of noise and light and smell assaulted them. Circles within circles of dancers wove in and out with such speed that their costumes became a kaleidoscope of bright colors. Bystanders clapped their hands, waved their arms above their heads, mimicked the dancers' movements. *There must be a couple of hundred people here*, Prynn thought. Most of the dancers were Andorian, but she saw more than a few aliens mixed into the gathering.

Off to one side, the crown of one of the masonry torches that marked the street corners had been broken off and an animal corpse dangled over the flame, the crisping fat and skin hissing and bubbling as it cooked. As she walked forward, Prynn realized that instead of being an open plaza, this place had once been an enclosed building; centuries of weather and a lack of repairs had rendered the walls into disintegrating butts; sheets of painted plaster crumbled over the pavement, mingling with sludge and garbage.

"The Reiji," Shar muttered under his breath, his steps slowing to a near stop. "I didn't think they still existed. . . ."

"Did I hear that one still believes that the Reiji have passed into memory?" A hunched *thaan* in tattered clothes emerged from the shadow. Throwing back his head, he cackled, revealing a mouthful of glinting copper-colored teeth; then he turned toward Shar and Prynn, his eye sockets filled with knots of silvery scar tissue. "Come see for yourself! Come see!"

Ordinarily eager for new experiences, Prynn suddenly felt uneasy. Scanning the crowd, she noticed stained canvas tents and shoddy rugs thrown down in the food area.

"I think we'll be fine, Prynn," Shar said. "The Reiji are an old clan that long ago gave up their land and titles. They won't hurt us. We can probably find food and drink here—perhaps a place for you to rest. It will give us a chance to regroup. I'll go find their leader and see what I can negotiate."

"All right, then," she conceded, and wandered around the periphery of activity, looking for a safe place to wait. *Safety. Now there's a concept I don't consider often.*

Watching where she stepped never came naturally to Prynn. Stepping carefully implied "caution" and caution wasn't a word in her vocabulary. Either you lived or you were cautious. Prynn always chose the former, though as the knife blade came down through her sandals, between her toes, nearly shaving half the appendage off, a flash of reasonableness prompted a question of whether she undervalued caution. The knifepoint found purchase so close to Prynn's toes that she did a double take; her eyes flicked between the blade and her shoe, still incredulous that the weapon had missed. The slightest wiggle would draw blood. *Boy did I choose the wrong place to walk*, she thought, and shivered. Irrationally, she wished she were back at the keep in a sleep bundle having nightmares about parasite-infested Martian terraformers.

The Reiji onlookers seemed not to notice the near amputation, their gaze focused on the rodent-sized furball that squeezed past her ankle and scurried into the open street behind her. A collective gasp sounded, followed quickly by shrill, clattering conversation too rapid and slurred for the universal translator to parse entirely. The dozen gamers seated in a circle on the cobbled pavement directed their gazes and fingers at the escaping animal. Prynn surmised that losing the furball must be a setback. Should she chase after it? Step on it? Prynn wished she knew the rules so she could know where to stand the next time the knives came out.

Hissing what sounded like a vicious curse, the knife owner, a dried, shriveled Andorian, yanked the blade out of her sandal and sheathed it somewhere within his jacket.

Having the knife removed is a good thing too, she thought, backing away from the gaming circle. She searched the crowd for Shar, who didn't appear to be anywhere close by, so she stayed put.

The gamer gathered up a handful of brightly colored sticks—they reminded her of cocktail swizzle sticks—and passed them to a hefty fellow squatting next to him in the circle. The next player shook the sticks like dice and cast them to the clicking onto the street.

Gamers and onlookers cheered. *What the hell—I'm starting into that sleep-deprived delirium state anyway.* Hooking her cheeks with her index fingers, Prynn joined in with a whistle.

Grunting, the knife owner opened his mouth wide, and curled up his lip. He reached in with a thumb and forefinger, yanked a silver tooth out of his gums, and passed the tooth to the hefty fellow, who promptly pocketed the prize. The loser spat blood, spittle, and bits of mouth grit on the filthy paving stones behind him—where Prynn's feet had been. She added the instruction "watch where you step" to her list of things to remember for the duration of the trip.

Another member of the circle—a shrouded player with the saggiest wrinkled hands Prynn had ever seen—pulled a smallish metal box out of a pocket in his cloak. He slid up the grated side, dumping a furball similar to the recently escaped one, into the circle. The furry creature raced up and down the sticks, in and out and around, bouncing off the players' legs like a stray electron. The hefty Andorian, body taut with tension, unsheathed a knife and extended his arm, blade pointed downward, following the ricocheting rodent with his eyes. The other players shouted words of encouragement, urged their companion on. The frenzied animal raced around the circle, seeking escape until . . . a flash of silver, a death shriek, and a spurt of blood. Raising the speared animal on his knife above his head, the winner gloated, the other gamers and onlookers roaring with approval.

I bet he gets to keep his teeth, Prynn thought. A tap on her shoulder prompted her to turn around. Shar held out a tarnished goblet, which she accepted gratefully. Each swallow of the pulpy nectar coated her parched throat. A little sleep and she might reach nirvana. She said so to Shar.

"You said you wanted to dance, though." He inclined his head in the direction of the dancers. "Why not join in for a bit? I'll come get you when I find a quieter place for you to lie down."

"I suppose . . ." She smiled weakly, trying to convince herself as much as anyone that she was happy about their situation. *Trust Shar.* She clung to the thought. "As soon as I'm done with my drink, I'll see if I can find someone to show me the ropes. Do what you need to do, Shar. I'll be fine."

As she watched him leave, she thought, *So why am I worrying?* Shar, who was now talking with someone she suspected was the leader of this motley group, had procured a goblet of his own, and appeared to be comfortable making conversation. Before she could mull it over further, one of the dancers had pulled her into the circle. The driving beat—the exhilarating music—soon drove away her fears and her weariness; she lost herself in the celebration.

From the chrono on the desk, Phillipa could see that dawn was only a few hours away. She and Thantis had talked through the specifics of Thriss's final days; Thantis had shared stories from her *zhei*'s childhood. As she sat, listening to Thantis's remembrances, she couldn't help thinking of Arios—how he gnawed on his lip when he concentrated—and Mireh in slumber, her chubby, dimpled cheeks pressed against her stuffed bear Walter. Placing herself in Thantis's position, imagining the loss of a child, Phillipa shuddered, knowing what measures she would take to assure her child's well-being. A Tal Shiar assassin didn't stand a chance against an enraged mother. Admiration for Thantis's strength filled her. *How can Thantis even sit here—why hasn't she crumbled, become completely despondent?*

Her antennae no longer rigid with worry, Thantis sighed and said, "I have drawn comfort from your words, Counselor. Your offspring are blessed to have one such as you to guide them."

"And you are very brave, *Zha*," Phillipa said earnestly. "More brave than I believe I could be under the same circumstances."

Thantis clasped Phillipa's arm. "You have hints of an Andorian soul. I chose rightly asking you to come here to give your gift to the Rite of Memory."

"I'm honored that you see me worthy to be called Andorian, but I haven't advanced far enough in my studies of your culture to understand exactly what the Rite of Memory is," Phillipa said. "Help me?"

From a drawer in her desk, Thantis removed a glasslike object. Small enough to fit in the palm of her hand, the object, asymmetrical and multifaceted, looked like a clear natural crystal. "This is the Cipher created by my family when one of my parents—my *shreya*—passed away unexpectedly several cycles ago. Each of these facets contains a neuroimprint—a memory."

Phillipa's expression must have betrayed her surprise, because Thantis seemed to sense her thoughts. "It's not so strange, really. Vulcans still practice the transference of *katra* telepathically. And the human scientist Noonien Soong once devised a method by which memories could be encoded into an artificial intelligence. Other species throughout time have developed analogous techniques. This one, however, is new enough that we're still unsure if it will even work with non-Andorians." Thantis sat down at her desk and was tapping commands into her computer.

"If you aren't certain—"

"I know the process won't hurt you. But I'm unwilling to allow my *zhei* to go to her next life without as many pieces as I can possibly gather together for her Cipher. You are an integral part of that." A series of diagrams appeared on the screen over her desk. "I am not a scientist, Counselor, but I believe this information should answer your questions."

Phillipa leaned over Thantis's shoulder to get a better view. "Looks like a combination of neuromapping technology and organic computing that replicates the electrochemistry, extracts it, and stores it in a chip."

"Exactly," Thantis said, nodding. "Then the chips are fused together to make this Cipher, which is used in the Sending." She held up the crystalline sculpture. "All these facets are memories from different individuals in my *shreya*'s life. In this way, she can be fully known to us and remembered for many generations to come.

"My *sh'za*—she is a neurochemical engineer. She believes

that the procedure can be adapted to your neurosynaptic patterns. Your Vulcan ancestry provides you with a mental accuity that most pure humans don't have, not to mention a more highly evolved cerebral physiology."

"I'm only one-eighth Vulcan."

"My *sh'za* believes that will be enough."

Still processing the implications, Phillipa said, "And you really want me to be part of this family ritual, to combine my memories of Thriss with those of individuals like Dizhei, Anichent, and—" she was about to say Shar, but then she remembered that Shar would not be part of this process. The sudden silence in the room articulated what Phillipa wouldn't say.

"I have my reasons for excluding Shar," Thantis said quietly, turning off the monitor. "You do not need to understand them."

You invite a virtual stranger to be part of an important death ritual, but you won't include the person most intimately tied to the deceased? Phillipa intuitively sensed that Thantis withheld information from her, that Thriss's history was more involved than what had been revealed to her, but she was willing to wait.

A light flashed on her desktop. Thantis activated the com device. "Yes?"

"Harbortown police have spotted Thirishar and Ensign Tenmei. It appears they've escaped to the city's lower levels. The police are in pursuit."

"Thank you for your assistance, Magistrate. You will be honored for your service to my clan." Thantis switched off the comm. "At least that answers one of our questions." Turning to Phillipa, she said, "You must be exhausted. Take some rest time before Thirishar returns. I expect things will become very lively before dawn."

On her way back to the sleep room, Phillipa contemplated the night's events, examining the interpersonal dynamics she'd witnessed, and thought that, with the names changed to protect the innocent, this whole Shar/Thriss/Vretha/Thantis scenario might make a fascinating case study for a professional journal. The complex levels of subterfuge and interplay between the involved parties rivaled the Byzantine machinations of old Earth—and this in the twenty-fourth century!

With Thia's help, she'd prepared her sleep spot earlier, so when she arrived—yawning—at the sleep hall, she was inclined to go straight into her bundle without taking her clothes off. She'd pulled enough all-nighters to have learned how to sleep anywhere, anytime. Still, a nagging voice reminded her to attend to a modicum of personal hygiene before she collapsed.

As she fumbled around in her travel bag for her toothcleaner, Phillipa sensed that something was awry; she couldn't place a finger on what it was. Sibias was always teasing her about being so detail-conscious that she made herself crazy. *Could have sworn that when I left, my jacket was on top of my boots. Now it's draped over there. . . .* She paused. Looked around. In her duffel, her clothing remained in neat stacks, her padds in the same order she'd left them in. On a hunch, she unfastened the interior pocket of her travel bag. She reached in, felt the tiny, green velvet drawstring bag she'd acquired at the marketplace, and pulled it out.

Empty.

She dumped her travel bag out onto her sleep bundle. Checked every pocket, every corner. Nothing. Sorted through assorted trinkets, empty snack wrappers, a hardcopy novel, and "good-bye" notes from her children. Nothing.

The *saf* was missing.

In the temporary rooms loaned to her by Thantis, Vretha examined the latest folio of Federation Council memos transmitted to her personal database and had to confess that they seemed to be little more than garble to her preoccupied mind. The dust was still settling after the Trill debacle, Councillor T'Latrek had requested a hearing on the latest rumblings from the Romulan Neutral Zone. Councillor Rista had expressed concern that the Grand Nagus was turning a blind eye to Ferengi consortiums conducting illegal mining operations in disputed territories. All of it seemed so . . . trivial. Each and every one was a legitimate crisis, and yet she could summon no passion for any of them. Not today. Not now, when Andor's future seemed more uncertain than ever. As earnest as her efforts were to find proof that the rumors surrounding the Science Institute's alleged experiments were false, she had thus far come up empty. She looked through her message queue to see if her contacts at the institute had sent her anything new, but found nothing. In her growing desperation—and without Zhende's knowledge—she'd even made several off-the-record inquiries with Andor's less savory elements, like the nomadic Reiji. *We have to bring this situation under control as soon as possible. More serious consequences await if we don't,* she thought, wondering if unified Andor might fragment before this was over.

Of course, no one in the Federation would have a clue of how severe the rifts between the primary political movements were: Presider ch'Shelos would make certain that the Federation News Service carried several glowing reports about Andor's exemplary political process—its commitment to free speech and its gentle but firm zero tolerance of violence as a means of effecting social change. At least, Vretha hoped so. Part of her had begun to wonder if the Visionists even supported continuing Federation membership anymore.

How could we have come to this place where we are so fractured?

She checked her chrono. Admiral Nakamura had requested she sit in on a subspace conference he was convening to discuss his ideas for new starbase construction, and the meeting was to begin in a few minutes. She wished she had a polite way to excuse herself. The admiral didn't need her, he needed her clout; her presence lent credibility to his proposals. Why had she agreed to spend an hour of her valuable time listening to a group of admirals and engineers drone on? *I should simply cancel. . . .*

Footsteps padded across the floor behind her and she heard the soft taps of fingers at Zhende's workstation. Once again she gave thanks for her aide's efficiency in anticipating her needs so well. The subspace link to Nakamura must already be established, or nearly so.

"Zhende," Vretha said. She picked up several padds off her desk and turned to hand them back to the *thaan*. "Can you update my—"

A hand went over her mouth; another over her eyes. Before Vretha could scream, her world went black.

*   *   *

His appetite satiated, Shar pushed aside the plate piled with empty bones, and washed down his last bite with a swig of wine. He tapped his feet with the irresistible drumbeat, the kinetic bursts of color and constant rhythm of the steel sticks being struck stimulating his senses. Blood churned through him; his attennae twitched restlessly. He lay down on the woven grass mat, propping himself up on an elbow, and watched.

The chain of charms draped around Prynn's hips tinkled as she pirouetted under the raised arm of the quartet in front of her and passed through to join the next line of dancers. Grinning breathlessly, she grabbed the hands of a pair of *zhen* and began the basic footwork—heel to the left, heel to the right, turn to face your partner, lay your arm flat along the shoulder and walk around three times. Shar knew the dance—every Andorian child did: it was performed at the Time of Knowing when bondmates were given to each other.

When she continued on a fourth time around, she stopped midwalk, and laughed, dropping her hands to her thighs, before reaching out to take the hands of the partners in her line.

Prynn's skin glistened; he imagined he could see the heat rising off her body. As she moved to the next stage of the dance, he studied her, each sleek line from the hollow of her back to her throat, the swell of her chest. . . .

She caught his eye. Holding up her head proudly and maintaining eye contact, she swiveled her body in time with the music, a ripple of skin from her shoulders to her hips and back again. Inexhaustible, the percussion chanted—the shaking rattles, the thunder of the kettledrum, the thrum of the lap chimes. The rhythmic pulse became his; her rhythm became his.

Lights blinked; yellow, neon pink, and bloody blue reflections smeared together in the greasy rain puddles. The Reiji wailed, gyrating in tempo with the *pwam-puda-puda-pwam-puda-puda—*

Through a honeycomb curtain of dancers, Prynn beckoned, wild-eyed and bewitchingly beautiful. Laughing, she raised her arms above her head, linked her fingers and dropped her arms around a *shen* dancing beside her, pulling her new partner close, challenging Shar.

He stumbled to his feet, pushed away those preventing him

from being with the one who belonged with him. Roughly, he pried the *shen* and Prynn apart and claimed Prynn as his partner.

She placed his hands on her hips, his fingers gripping her lower back. Swiveling her hips, she guided him into the rhythm of the music, and he mirrored her moves, brushing warm skin to warm skin.

Thum-thob-thum-thob-thum-thob-thum—

The tempo quickened; the dancers became more frenzied. Throwing back her head, Prynn cried out, arching her body into his. She moved faster. Trapped in the dance, Shar held tighter, his thumbs pressed into her hipbones. Her hair in his neck, her breath on his cheek, her chest to his chest, and still the music moved faster. She tossed her head from side to side, the jewelry she wore jangling and flashing, catching the light from the overhead lanterns, hypnotizing Shar. And still faster until there was no thought, only rhythm that held them both as their limbs tangled together.

With an ear-shattering gong, the music ended; the dancers collapsed, panting, spent, Prynn among them. Wobbling, she wove back and forth, stumbling toward the mats. She raised a hand to her forehead; her head bobbed and dipped.

Dizzy from the heat, still reeling from the dance, Shar followed after her, light-headedness making it nearly impossible for him to focus. In and out, in and out—Prynn's form alternately came closer and receded as if he looked at her through a lens. His own hands trembled. In a fleeting moment of clarity, a thought occurred: *Something is wrong.*

Prynn was facedown on the ground, her skin rough with the small bumps humans tended to get when cold. He touched her shoulder—clammy—and rolled her over onto her back. She lolled bonelessly, giggling. She opened her eyes: white clouds over her pupils.

Drugged.

Saf. *It has to be* saf. He tried assessing himself, found concentration difficult, the white-yellow haze of euphoria blurring reason. But instinct told him Prynn wasn't fine. Bending over her, he gripped her shoulder. "Prynn. We have to . . . we have to . . ." His tongue felt thick and coarse. Shaking his head to blunt the wooziness, he looked around to see if any of the Reiji could help him, but saw only faces fogged in hallucination.

She pulled him down onto her, their bodies flush. "Shar," she whispered, her words slurred. "Please . . ." Hooking a leg around his waist, she pinned him, flicked her tongue along his neck.

Helpless to resist, he allowed her hands to roam over his back, into his hair, hungering for the sensations she coaxed from him.

He grasped a sliver of will.

Jerking her by the wrist, he pulled Prynn up to standing; she stumbled into him so they stood nose-to-nose. He hadn't intended to be so forceful, but he knew she could barely support her own body weight. His breath caught in his throat.

Her eyes, bright with exhaustion and need and arousal, swallowed any desire he had to speak. Cupping her face in his hands, he caressed her cheek. She turned her head to the side, pressed her lips into his palm; she clung to him. Her touch, her closeness . . .

You have to get her out of here. She is in danger.

Prying her hands off his shoulders, Shar secured his arm around her waist, put her arm across his shoulder, and staggered away from the Reiji encampment. He had no idea where he should go. A vague recollection of stairs—of a ramp—nagged at him, and then he saw it out of the corner of his eye.

Prynn needs help: He anchored his will to the thought.

Down a ramp. Switchbacks across and down, until his strength failed and he crumpled, crashing sideways into a wall, dragging Prynn with him. Rushing water roared and he pressed his palms against his sensitized ears to hold back the sound.

The canal. The canal led to a river. The river led outside the city. He had to get Prynn outside the city. A groaning from deep within the canal tunnels echoed and Shar remembered that banished demons roamed this place. Exaggerated shadows hid them from view—otherworldly or not. They could stay here, rest, wait, sleep . . .

Footsteps clicked above them, hollow, shuffling.

I have to get her out of here.

Summoning what little strength he had left, he dragged her along the canal front, guiding his steps by the marbleized lights on the water. She clung to him even as she drifted in and out of consciousness; her feverishly hot face against his shoulder, she mumbled delirious nonsense.

Hurry.

Though energy drained from his limbs, his senses had gradually become more acute. The rhythms of faraway skin drums thrummed in his pulse, as immediate as if they sounded from the cryptlike canal tunnels instead of far above, where heated revelry swirled in blazing color and light. He reached up, as if he could touch the lanterns dangling beneath the bridges, the delicate arches of scarlet and teal, until the vision vanished and he was thrust back into the cold catacombs of the demon city.

To propel them forward, Shar pushed off the pocked, corroded stone walls with his hand, though each push scraped skin off his palm. With what strength he could summon, he fought the seductive delirium. Their lives depended on him maintaining awareness—however slight—of their real surroundings.

An escape. I need an escape. Above him the smooth, curved tunnel ceiling offered no outlet. On all sides, the sharp rock walls were impenetrable; beyond the tunnels, the river, and then the ocean. The only way out was through.

Smudged in sweat and filth, Prynn lay flaccid in his arm, dying slowly, and it was his fault. *This is what I do to the people I love—I hurt them.*

He skidded on the algae-slick paving and stumbled, dropping Prynn. Spinning around, he found her: an unconscious heap at his feet, still as stone. He crouched down beside her, circled her wrist with his fingers, feeling her shallow pulse. Her skin felt clammy—she shivered.

Scaly membranes growing over his eyes leached color from the already monochromatic scenery. Water and rock. Slender shafts of moonlight reflected off the water's oily ripples, the light never piercing the black depths. Secrets hidden within the swift currents would remain secret. If he wanted to vanish, this would be the place he would choose.

I'm lost. We're going to die.

Shar's sight dimmed. His grip on consciousness slipped, slowly slipping away until he teetered to the ground.

7

Prynn opened her eyes slowly and immediately regretted it. Shafts of light gouged her eyeballs like phasers through unshielded hull plating. *Let's try this again*, she thought, starting off by wiggling her toes, her fingers, tightening her muscles and loosening them. Every joint smarted. She didn't need to open her eyes to know that a monster of a headache nested at the base of her skull, waiting to be provoked. One wrong move and the claws would come out, digging into her brain with punishing pain. She groaned.

"Prynn?"

Phillipa. "Yeah. I think so. But considering that I feel like my skin has been turned inside out and my organs are hanging on the outside, I can't be certain."

A soft laugh. "I've had other patients tell me the same thing after a *saf* overdose."

Saf. Saf . . . *I didn't take saf. Wait.* Memories of the previous night flooded her. Sharp flashes of color, drumbeats, the Reiji camp in the lower city, dancing with Shar . . . Her cheeks flushed hot. *Damn. What possessed me? I practically threw myself at him. Stupid, stupid, stupid!* Pressure on her neck. A subtle numbing of her throbbing head. Cautiously, she opened one eye and saw Phillipa, out of focus, sitting at her feet.

"Consider yourself lucky," Phillipa said.

Prynn almost laughed, but the shooting pain behind her eyes that the impulse produced shut it down quickly. "Yeah," she managed to say through her teeth. "Sure feel lucky."

"I'm serious," said Phillipa. "This level of toxicity wouldn't be easy to treat anywhere else in the quadrant. Fortunately, Andorians have learned how to deal with accidental overdoses, especially among their offworld guests. The treatments the keep physician gave you won't take effect immediately—maybe a couple of hours—but according to him, you'll recover quickly after that."

When she pushed herself up from the sleep bundle, a wave of dizziness slammed into her, and she eased back down with Phillipa steadying her.

"Take it slowly. *Saf* impacts your whole nervous system. Until your body rebalances itself, you might feel—"

"Like I've been hit by a stampeding *targ*? Yeah. That about covers it." Prynn closed her eyes, welcoming the blessed black of her eyelids. She burrowed deeper into her sleep bundle, burying herself in blankets. "Shar?"

A long pause.

The news must be bad. Please let him be all right. A faint tinge of panic.

Phillipa took a deep breath. "Shar's fine, but a lot has happened."

"I know. The shuttle, the police—"

"No. The shuttle was recovered. The Harbortown authorities brought you in. All that will be dealt with in due time."

"Then what is it?"

"Vretha's missing. She's been kidnapped."

Prynn jerked up—instantly felt like she'd body-slammed into solid ground—and cried out in pain. Cursing, she tried untangling herself from the sleep bundle, but Phillipa was pushing her back in, tucking the blankets around her. "You can't do anything about it. As soon as I have more information, I'll let you know."

Urgency pushed through her agony. "But I have to—"

"No," Phillipa said firmly. "You have to lie down, let the treatments work, and sleep off the pain for a bit longer. You're very lucky, you know, that you were found when you were. Both you and Shar had lost consciousness. If it weren't for Anichent, you, at the very least, would probably be dead."

How—what— "Anichent?"

"He followed you and Shar to the keep's hangar and managed

to put a tracer on your shuttle before you launched. He had Shar's biosignature on file, so he gave it and the tracer frequency to the Harbortown police to help them track you."

Warmth ignited in her fingers, burned down her hands, into her wrists and up into her shoulders and neck, devouring her aches like tinder. Phillipa's voice sounded far away—echoing—as if she were speaking through a funnel. Prynn tried opening her eyes, but drowsiness pressed heavily on her eyelids, forcing them closed and leaving her with one coherent thought.

Shar . . .

Phillipa left the sleep hall after Prynn had drifted back into a controlled sleep state. She hadn't told her, but the keep physician had also administered a mild sedative. Just as well: Once she learned about Vretha's kidnapping, Prynn would never allow herself time for her treatment to take effect. She would attempt to find Shar, offer him comfort, and ally herself to whatever course of action he chose. Such choices needed to wait until she felt better.

When they found her and performed a toxicology analysis, it was clear Prynn had consumed more than twice the usual *saf* dose—and not the same variety as the one Phillipa had purchased. That much she could take comfort in. The keep physician had explained that the Reiji ground their *saf* and stirred it into foodstuffs instead of following the usual skin application that allowed it to be absorbed more slowly—and safely—into the bloodstream. Phillipa wondered how she would ever explain any of this to Captain Kira—not to mention Commander Vaughn!—and quickly decided that particular problem would have to wait. The more immediate concern was Vretha's disappearance.

Elsewhere in the keep, Thantis's security staff were conducting their investigation, questioning residents, searching for clues. Phillipa hadn't been invited to participate, but that came as no surprise. She was an outsider. *Besides, no one ever assumes that the counselor knows much beyond what it means when you appear naked on a starship bridge during a dream, or how to overcome a fear of transporters.* Her report on the missing *saf* had been noted, but not immediately assumed to be linked to the kidnapping. Phillipa believed otherwise. And she thought she knew where to find answers.

Of course, at first she hadn't made the connection between the *saf* and Vretha either. Vretha was first reported missing, by her aide, roughly forty-five minutes after Phillipa had left Thantis's study. The councillor had been late for a subspace meeting with Admiral Nakamura of Starbase 219 and the aide hadn't been able to track her down.

Initially, there had been some question as to whether or not Vretha had been on the shuttle with Shar and Prynn. But the parking facility at Harbortown had recorded two passengers on the craft—not three.

Then the data chip had been found, ending speculation.

The chip had been left for Shar at the keep, and was waiting for him when he returned. Phillipa presumed the kidnappers had chosen him to be the recipient of their message in order to exploit the emotional turmoil it would create for him, maximize the urgency of meeting their demands. Whoever left it had been thorough: No DNA traces were found that might identify the kidnappers, and nothing in the chip or the message itself offered a clue as to whether it had been created on- or off-site. The demands were in text and unambiguous. Councillor zh'Thane would be returned only when the ruling Progressive Party launched a full-scale investigation into the unethical research that was claimed to be under way at the Andorian Science Institute. The government had a single Andorian day to comply with the demands, and to issue a public statement announcing the arrests of those involved in the alleged conspiracy. The kidnappers identified themselves as a militant faction of the Visionist Party who saw themselves as warriors fighting for the "true Andor." Assuming that Homeworld Security would eventually figure out where the councillor had been taken, the message warned against any attempts to transport zh'Thane out, or a rescue team in. Pattern scramblers had been put in place. Otherwise, the kidnappers had no qualms about becoming martyrs.

Documents attached to the message—the authenticity of which couldn't be verified—implied that experimentation involving the reconfiguration of Andorian chromosomal architecture was being conducted to eliminate the need to have four sexes to procreate. *Chan*, *zhen*, *shen*, and *thaan* would all cease to exist, presumably to be replaced by two new, reproductively compatible sexes.

Phillipa had been too shocked to speak when Shar let her examine the documents. Such experimentation was both biologically dangerous and culturally incendiary. She didn't need to be an Andorian to understand that. Gender issues typically rippled through all aspects of a species: social structures, family life, religion, politics. Some of the greatest internal upheavals in the history of many worlds had resulted from issues relating either directly to gender or issues ancillary to gender. Who and what the Andorians were, and how they thought about themselves and their relationship to the universe, was defined in large part by their unique biology. For the Science Institute to investigate such a radical solution to the breakdown of their reproductive process spoke to their increasing desperation, that they were willing to create what amounted to an entirely new species from the dying remains of the old. In that scenario, everything—good and bad—that had risen from the four-gender paradigm would be lost. It was easy to understand how many might view such experimentation as the equivalent of the horrors perpetrated on the Bajorans by Cardassian doctors like Crell Moset, or what humans like Josef Mengele had done to their own kind during Earth's Second World War. Bioethically, the forced reengineering of Andorian sexes could be considered a crime against sentient life.

Phillipa had questioned Shar about the claims, but he said he knew nothing about such a line of scientific inquiry. Nor, did it seem, was he inclined to spend much time dwelling on it; he was more concerned with formulating a strategy for insuring his *zhavey*'s safe return. Shar was already more or less fully recovered from his ordeal in Harbortown, but as his agitation following the news about the kidnapping increased, Phillipa feared for his frame of mind.

With Thantis's help, he had contacted the government and apprised them of what had happened. Whoever he had spoken with had promised to send investigative teams from Homeworld Security to the Science Institute, as well as to the keep itself, but with continuing concern about the possibility of more violence breaking out, the soonest anyone would arrive on Cheshras Island was three hours from now. In the meantime, keep security would continue its own investigation, hoping to have something of value to report when Homeworld Security arrived.

Several facts weren't in question. The kidnappers had been at the keep before Deepening—ch'Shal, Thantis's security chief, determined that much from the start. Apart from Charivretha herself, and her aide, no one had come to the keep since the arrival of Phillipa, Shar, and Prynn (until this morning, when the runaways had returned from Harbortown). Only the underground rail network connecting the five primary keeps on the peninsula had been accessed. But reviewing the security log data and tracking down eyewitnesses who might have seen something suspicious was painstaking work. At any given time, more than seven thousand people lived at Cheen-Thitar. Even if the obvious suspects—active Visionists or sympathizers, those who might have a grudge against Vretha—were culled out, the list still comprised the bulk of the keep with Sessethantis zh'Cheen at the top.

But Phillipa had her own theory. Armed with a double *katheka*—the local equivalent of stimulants like coffee or *raktajino*—she set out through the winding stone passages of the keep to prove it.

She quieted her steps upon entering the crèche. Save for a few *zhaveys* bathing their infants in basin stands, the snug room was virtually empty. Floor-to-ceiling tapestries depicting pastoral mountain scenes adorned the walls, a symphony of warm, soothing earth tones. Even the keep's chilly stone floors had been carpeted. Abandoned sleep bundles had been pushed aside. The sour tang of freshly mashed *xixu* fronds wafted from the rear—Phillipa understood the cereal was the first solid food infants ate when weaning.

She found the object of her search removing a steaming mug from the replicator. Before Phillipa could speak, Thia held up a hand.

"I know why you're here."

"Do you?"

She nodded, took a deep breath, and turned to face Phillipa.

The counselor didn't need to ask how the young *zhavey* had rested; Thia's normally lucent complexion had dulled to gray blue, her robes rumpled. She projected none of the composure Phillipa had come to expect.

"You believe that I know something about Charivretha's disappearance."

"What makes you think that?" Phillipa played along.

"Because . . ." She swallowed hard. "Because I do."

Vretha felt the *saf* wearing off; her muscles ached from the concentrated energy bursts that always accompanied its use. Even her bones hurt. *I'm too old for that kind of stimulation*, she thought, trying to recall the last time she'd used the drug, even with her mates. She understood its necessity to the *shelthreth*, but she hadn't liked the feeling of being out of control, the sense that her body was a separate thing from her mind, a physical entity that acted of its own accord and wasn't subject to her will.

Unfortunately, the *saf*'s hallucinogenic qualities made it nearly impossible for her to have any concrete recollections of what had happened to her over the last unknown hours. She'd been waiting at her desk, preparing for her subspace conference, when she'd heard footsteps behind her. Assuming it was her aide, she'd turned around, prepared to pass off a padd—after that, she knew only warped twisting impressions, color and sound filtered through a chemical prism. The hiss of a train, an aquacraft churning through the water, and now this place. She shifted her wrists slightly, discovering—not surprisingly—that they were bound; her ankles, similarly. She also suspected that the metal bands gouging into her upper arms functioned as transport inhibitors. Whoever they were, they intended to make it impossible for a rescuer to beam her out, forcing security into a face-to-face confrontation in order to free her. *A wise strategy*, she conceded. *It will buy them time to have their demands met.*

Allowing her captors to believe she was still unconscious, she lay still, her eyelids raised only enough to discern the barest details; she methodically analyzed her surroundings. Firm but shifting surface beneath her: sand. The air: no breeze, a damp musty cool. Craggy rock walls. The chill blue-white flood of artificial lighting. A cave. And deep enough underground for the temperature to be so constant.

"Welcome back, Councillor," came a soft voice from the shadows.

Unwilling to grant even the smallest acknowledgment that she was aware of him, she remained motionless, closed her eyes.

"Come now. Such theatrics might work during a council meeting, but not here, where there are only the three of us."

A boot nudged her leg.

Indignant at the crude treatment, Vretha spat on the ground in front of her.

"Temper, temper."

She looked up. A broad-shouldered *thaan*, wearing an all-weather pullover coated in pink dust, crouched next to her. In his eyes, accentuated by bushy brows, she saw none of the harshness she would have expected in a captor; his unlined face revealed his youth—he couldn't be much older than Shar. He thrust his chin forward, the aquiline line of his nose and cheekbones classically handsome and matched perfectly by the jauntiness of his posture. *He isn't a mercenary. This young one has a purpose,* Vretha thought. She sighed inwardly. *Revolutionaries are always young.* She recalled once, a long time ago, when she'd had the same fervor burning in her that she saw in this *thaan*. Now . . . now she understood the practical realities of the quadrant. She spent most of her energy trying to preserve what they had; she had little energy left over to improve circumstances.

"Are you going to kill me?" she said hoarsely. Vretha's throat felt scratchy; she cleared it, swallowed, but still felt sore.

Another one, a *chan*, pressed a water skin to her mouth, but she pinched her lips tight against it.

"It's not poisoned," the *thaan* said. Taking the skin from the *chan*, he poured a stream into his mouth. He then offered the skin to Vretha as the *chan* had before.

She drank more greedily than she intended, discovering she was drained from dehydration and hunger. When she was satisfied, she nudged the skin away with her cheek.

"The real question is, would killing you best serve our cause?" The *thaan* leaned in, his face coming close to Vretha's. "And the answer to that, Councillor, has yet to be determined."

Shar had been sufficiently dosed with analgesics and osmotic fluids to feel functional and coherent enough to endure ch'Shal's questions. While the Reiji drink had been doctored with far more *saf* than was healthy for him, his Andorian physiology was equipped to metabolize it far more effectively than Prynn's was.

Prynn. He couldn't think of her without experiencing more guilt than he had felt since Thriss's suicide. Memories of the previous night were murky at best, but he'd awoken, face buried in his sleeve, her scent on his clothes, and he'd flushed with both pleasure and embarrassment. Would she ever forgive him? She'd had an instinct about the Reiji encampment and he should have listened to her. Instead . . . they'd almost succumbed to drug-induced *tezha* before the overdose nearly claimed her life. He wouldn't blame her if she wanted to take the first transport home.

He'd stopped in to see her not long ago and found her sleeping peacefully. Sitting by her side, he'd watched her, the slow rise and fall of her breathing, how her dark lashes curled like a child's, and he was overcome with emotion. She'd come to mean so much to him. Allowing her to travel with him had been a mistake. He should have insisted that she remain at home, on DS9. If he'd adhered to his original resolve—to sever his ties to Andor—Prynn would have never been placed in danger and *Zhavey*—

Ch'Shal had shown him the security footage he had downloaded into a padd—grainy, muted recordings from the underground transportation network that held no meaning for Shar. Ch'Shal had proceeded to bombard him with requests for information: A chronology of his most recent communciations with Charivretha. An account of the circumstances that had brought him to Thelasa-vei instead of the capital, as he'd originally planned. Every word he could recall about his last bitter meeting with *Zhavey*. The details of his encounters with the other visitors and residents of the keep. . . . The questions went on, sometimes traveling in circles, it seemed, until Shar thought his antennae would break off from his mounting tension.

Seated at a reading table in one of the keep's libraries, surrounded by stacks of old scrolls and priceless crystalline sculptures, ch'Shal abruptly tapped his comm patch, apparently in response to a call. The *chan* excused himself, promising to return shortly. Shar sat alone in the vaulted room, feeling as if the overwhelming weight of his emotions would crush him. He looked down at the table. His right hand shook. He wrapped it tightly in his left and tried to calm himself. *Stay Whole. You're no good to her if you shatter. . . .*

Fifteen minutes later, ch'Shal returned, this time with

Thantis, Phillipa, and Thia. The sentinel resumed his place at the table opposite Shar, while Phillipa sat between. Thantis and Thia remained standing. All of them looked grim. Thia wouldn't even meet his eyes.

"Shar," Phillipa began. "There's something you need to know. . . ."

She's dead, he realized. *They've found her, and she's already dead. . . .*

"Arenthialeh zh'Vazdi has come forward and admitted that she's an accessory to the kidnapping of Charivretha. She's offered to help us in exchange for immunity from prosecution."

Shar stared at the *zhen.* He recalled their first meeting, wondered if it had been staged, whether he had played into the hands of his *zhavey*'s political foes.

Thia. Thia all along. . . .

"There's more," Phillipa said. "My *saf* sample was stolen. Only three people knew that I carried it. You, Prynn, and Thia. She—"

Before he was even aware of his own actions, Shar lunged, grabbing Thia by the throat with one hand, slamming her back against a stone wall. Whatever scream she might have released was trapped in his chokehold. He was dimly aware of Phillipa crying out, yanking at his other hand, which he had flattened and drawn back in preparation to drive it through Thia's eyes. He heard the metallic *shing* of ch'Shal's ceremonial blade being drawn, heard Thantis's shouted order telling the sentinel to stand down—

And Thia . . . Thia had one narrow hand clawing useless at the wrist of his choking hand, her other arm wrapped protectively around herself.

"Shar, stop it!" he heard Phillipa shouting. "It's not what you think—"

"It was you," Shar hissed at his enemy. "You used *saf* on Charivretha. That's how you got her. And you were behind what happened to Prynn and me as well, weren't you? *Weren't you?*"

"Thirishar, please," Thantis whispered in his ear, holding his face between the palms of her hands, forcing him to look at her, to see the fear and sorrow she wore. "You must listen. Do not do this thing."

A child cried.

Shar looked down in confusion, and for the first time it truly registered that Thia's *thei* was in her *kheth*, had been there the entire time.

Shar released her as if he had just been burned and stumbled back against the table, collapsing into a chair. Thia doubled over and gulped air hoarsely, Phillipa struggling to support her so that she wouldn't fall. *What have I done . . . ?*

Standing behind him, ch'Shal gripped his shoulder, as much to assert his control as to comfort him, undoubtedly. His blade remained conspicuously drawn. They had known each other since childhood, and that still had meaning—Shar had felt it when ch'Shal had first greeted him on his arrival at the keep. But he knew also that, as a sentinel of Cheen-Thitar, ch'Shal's duty to the safety of his clan superseded all else. In retrospect, Shar was surprised to still be alive.

Thantis knelt at his side. "Shar . . ."

"Is Charivretha dead?" he asked softly, watching as Thia's breathing steadied, as Phillipa checked her neck for bruising, as the baby slowly settled back into the slumber from which Shar's actions had ripped him.

"We have every reason to believe she yet lives," Thantis said. "But you must listen. Will you?"

Shar nodded.

"Arenthialeh did not take the *saf*—"

"No," Thia interrupted, straightening. "I ask your forgiveness, *Zha,* but I will speak for myself. The debt of truth is mine to repay." Shar could see she was trembling. Her hand rested on her lower abdomen, over her child. "My bondmates took the *saf* and used it on Charivretha. But it was because of me that they learned Commander Matthias had it. I told them about our conversation, the one we had aboard the shuttle from Orbital Control—that the commander intended to acquire a sample for medicinal research. She told me about it before you and I met. But my bondmates, my *th'se* and *ch'te*—" She said the words as if they caused her pain. Whether it was truly from anguish or the injuries that Shar had caused her, he didn't know. "They saw your visit here as an opportunity to make a political point. We all knew you were coming to Andor—the Progressives made sure of that. Your detour to Cheen-Thitar provided them with access they hadn't expected. But when Vretha appeared . . . she was just too appealing a target to ignore."

Phillipa's eyes widened. "Your bondmates weren't targeting Vretha, they were targeting Shar."

Shar's eyes moved to Thantis, who knelt beside him still. "Were you part of this?"

"No, Thirishar," she said. "Whatever else you believe about me, believe that. I knew nothing."

"Nor did I," Thia whispered. "Not until it was too late, when Charivretha and my bondmates were already gone. I did *not* conspire to kidnap you or Councillor zh'Thane. I don't agree with the Progressives or with what the Science Institute is doing, but I tried convincing my bondmates that there were other ways to draw attention to our cause. I truly believed it was just talk, that they would never take it this far. Clearly, I was wrong. Now I must make this right."

"Your cooperation will make a considerable difference in the consequences that you'll face, *Zha*," ch'Shal said.

She turned to him. "It is not the consequences meted out by the judiciary or the Parliamentary Council that concern me, Sentinel. It is what my bondmates will do when they learn I have betrayed them."

Shar felt Thia's eyes on him. At first, he resisted looking at her, but his anxiety overcame his anger. He saw regret. He saw apology.

He saw his own sorrow.

She wrenched her gaze away. "They've used my credentials and access to take Vretha into the Reserve."

Ch'Shal's eyes narrowed. "How do you know?"

"I kept extensive records of an expedition I made there three cycles ago. Those files have recently been accessed, and I believe I know where they have taken her."

"How far into the interior?" ch'Shal asked.

"Not far. Less than a day's travel by foot. But I suspect my bondmates had transportation."

"I'll need your data."

Thia nodded. "I warn you, it won't be easy to find anyone inside the Reserve. You could try isolating them by satellite, but I doubt you will have much luck. The latent radiation throughout the terrain tends to confuse biosensors. It's why we still perform scientific surveys there the traditional way."

"And with pattern scramblers in place, transporters aren't an option," ch'Shal mused. "An overt assault from the air will not go unnoticed, and likely cost Charivretha her life. If there's to be a rescue mission, Homeworld Security will need to go in covertly, on foot."

"When are they expected to be here?"

"In less than three hours."

"Too long," Shar said, rising to his feet. "I'm leaving, right now."

Ch'Shal frowned. "Consider what you're saying, Thirishar."

"I have," he answered. "I'm an experienced Starfleet officer, and I will not wait idly in order to entrust my *zhavey*'s life to another."

"I'm coming with you too," Phillipa said.

"Phillipa—" Shar began.

"I'm the ranking Starfleet officer here, Ensign," Phillipa snapped. "And I say this isn't open to discussion."

Shar blinked. "Yes, sir."

Phillipa winked at him.

Another voice, gravelly with fatigue, came from the archway. "Count me in, too."

Shar turned. Waxen and gaunt-faced, Prynn walked in and stood next to him. "You were right about those treatments, Commander. I feel like a new woman. My thanks and compliments to your physician, *Zha* Sessenthantis." She folded her arms and scanned the faces in the room alertly, but Shar perceived a slight swaying in her stance.

"Prynn," he said gently, "I think we can—"

"—use my help?" she interrupted. "Good. I knew you'd see it my way."

"Are you sure about this, Ensign?" Phillipa asked.

"Absolutely, Commander."

Once again, Shar found himself moved by Prynn. *She supports me in everything, even after all that's happened.*

"This is unwise and dangerous," ch'Shal reiterated. "I don't doubt your skills, but none of you has any experience in the Reserve, not even Thirishar."

"But I do," Thia said. "I'll guide them."

"Your *thei*, Thia," Thantis said. "You must think of him."

She shook her head. "My *sh'za* will take him. She was not part of our bondmates' plans, either. I must do this. My *th'se* and my *ch'te* might listen to me when they will listen to no other. I might be their best hope, as well as Charivretha's. I doubt any member of security would hesitate if forced to choose between Councillor zh'Thane and her captors. Perhaps I can assure that such a choice won't be necessary."

Watching Thia, Shar no longer knew how to feel about her. Moments ago he hated her enough to kill her. Now he felt relief for her willingness to help them, but also wariness at having to trust her.

As if she sensed him looking at her, Thia turned in his direction and their eyes locked once again. *She's right,* he realized at last. *She may be* Zhavey's *best hope.* He took a few steps toward her and extended his hand, palm out.

Her eyes went wide with surprise.

"Whatever happens, I wish to thank you for helping us," Shar said. "And to to tell you I'm sorry."

Slowly, Thia lifted her arm, and her palm met his. "As am I," she whispered.

He sensed the deep vein of strength flowing through her, and knew she would be a formidable ally—or opponent.

8

Kneeling in the beach sand, feeling the midmorning energy from the white Andorian sun warming her neck, Prynn checked and double-checked the four gear packs: tricorders, grappling hooks, karabiners, pitons, climbing cables, harnesses, field medical kit, canteens, ration bars to fuel them for the duration. . . . All appeared to be complete and in working order. *And then there are the three phasers*, she noted grimly. *The question is who I'm going to have to use this thing on*? she thought, glancing over at Thia, who was orienting Phillipa and Shar with a map of the Reserve.

Satisfied that they had all the equipment they needed, she touched her combadge, notifying ch'Shal aboard the aquacraft anchored off shore that the mission would be underway shortly. The team would maintain communications silence for the next twenty-five hours, unless they found Vretha sooner, or were forced to abort. Back at the keep, Thantis would be in the unenviable position of telling Homeworld Security what they had done, and reinforcing the fact that any interference with the rescue op would jeopardize all their lives, Vretha's included.

By dawn tomorrow this will all be over, one way or another, she thought, zipping the formfitting expedition suit up her neck. The suits were of the *Zha*'s own design and manufacture, created, she'd explained, for Thia's fieldwork. The second-skin feel of the unusual fabric took some getting used to—she felt practically naked. But it was flexible, breathed well and, according to

Thantis, would absorb impacts and even withstand blades up to a point. Phasers, Prynn assumed, were another matter.

Thia had wrapped her hair, turban style, in a long length of black cloth. When Phillipa asked her about it, she'd claimed that this remote nature preserve—an island roughly the size of the Indian peninsula—was "sacred" land and she would not "offend the Guardians" by appearing vain and disrespectful. Her back to the *zhen*, Prynn had rolled her eyes, inviting a withering glare from Commander Matthias. After that, Prynn had realized she needed a few minutes to herself, and volunteered to recheck their packs while the others discussed the journey ahead.

"So here we are," she muttered under her breath, "in the middle of nowhere." And other than the four of them, Prynn saw little life. Spindly deciduous trees clustered at the base of a waterfall provided a splash of vivid greens and maroons. Otherwise, the only observable plants were bristly brown-shrubs and clumps of yellowing, sun-ripened beach grasses sprouting from the dunes shushing in the late-afternoon winds. Small multipeds sunning on rocks and calls of unseen avians testified to animal inhabitants, but Prynn had no doubt about what held dominion here: sun, earth, and water.

The crescent beach of white-silica sand was enclosed by sheer layered cliffs of rust red sandstone, limestone, glassy crystalline gypsum, and grayish clay. The towering walls made it impossible to see the landscape above and beyond the beach. She knew, though, from the hour she'd spent studying the files provided by Thia, that this part of the Reserve was primarily desert, composed of dusty flats, water-carved peaks and canyons—some as deep as fifteen hundred to two thousand meters—and formations created by ancient volcanic activity. Prynn wasn't surprised to learn that Andorians chose not to live in this place: the Reserve had been beaten, kneaded, exploded, and reformed by plate tectonics and the elements for longer than Andor had known sentient life.

Across from where they landed on the beach was the waterfall where they would start their journey into the continental interior.

Satisfied that their gear was prepared, Prynn fastened up the packs, threaded two on each arm, and trudged down the beach to join her teammates, who had taken momentary refuge in the scanty shade offered by a defoliated tree. Thia had placed the padd on a flat boulder, allowing them reference to the terrain she was describing. Prynn slid in beside Shar, tried catching his eye, but his attention remained fixed on Thia's briefing.

Considering the stakes, Prynn tried not to personalize his behavior. But Shar had barely acknowledged her today, save with monosyllables and sharp nods. *Typical male "morning after" behavior,* she thought. Except that Shar wasn't really male, and there hadn't really been a "night" to have a "morning after." At least not one that she recalled. Though she liked what she could remember of the heated encounter. Which might be part of Shar's problem. Maybe he knew something she didn't and that was the source of the tension between them. Of course, she wouldn't know what he knew unless he deigned to speak to her. Prynn made a promise to renew her anti-relationship/anti-male stance as soon as all potential tragedies had been averted. It wasn't fair to resent Shar before that. But after? Once Vretha was safe, Thriss's funeral was over, and Thia's bondmates were in custody, Prynn would make him talk to her. Until then, she would tolerate his disinterested silences.

"We scale that rock formation over there," Thia said, pointing to a sheer-faced red rock escarpment, "on a path parallel to the waterfall. Midway up the falls, we will enter into a cave that's hidden behind the water. From there, we will go through the cave, tracing the path of a creek back to where it originates in a narrow slot canyon. The slot canyon opens onto the Great Wash. By then, it will be almost dark and we'll be able to move more openly. The mouth of the lava tube where I believe they've taken Vretha is a few kilometers past Temple Butte within the Coral Canyon complex."

"Why is it called the 'Great Wash'?" Phillipa asked, taking the padd off the boulder to examine it more carefully.

"Once upon a time, the wash formed the bottom of a primeval lake. Now, it's just a huge, relatively flat basin that is more or less a 'trunk' for dozens of smaller canyons that branch off it. It's still eroded by flash floods produced by torrential rainfall. Other questions?"

Taking the padd from Phillipa, Prynn studied their route, realizing that even if they moved quickly, reaching the lava tube would require an all-night hike. "We should probably stop talking and start moving."

"My thoughts exactly," Thia said. "Are we ready?"

Prynn snorted. "Of course." She passed each person their backpack. Shar carried the bulk of their climbing gear. Phillipa was in charge of their medkit and tools. The rest of their equipment was divvied up between Prynn and Thia. As Prynn hitched the pack onto her back and adjusted the straps around her waist so the weight was equally distributed, Thia watched critically.

"A resting spot will be available after we pass through the cave and into the canyon. Otherwise, I can assume part of your load. I assure you it would be no burden."

Instead of firing off a snappy comeback, Prynn counted backward from ten before answering. "I'm perfectly capable of carrying twenty kilos more than this."

"But after a *saf* overdose?"

Realizing that Thia didn't have the cultural reference point to understand that being called a female dog was an insult, Prynn let the *zhen*'s comment go.

"Let's be on our way, shall we?" Phillipa said, positioning herself in line between Prynn, who brought up the rear, and Thia, who walked behind Shar.

For a minute, Phillipa hung back so she could walk side by side with Prynn. "Don't make me regret allowing you to join this mission, *Ensign* Tenmei. You might technically be on leave, but as far as I'm concerned, you're an officer on Starfleet duty, under my command," she said, sotto voce. "Comport yourself appropriately."

"Yes, sir," Prynn said, taking a deep breath and neutralizing her expression. She owed it to Shar to be on her best behavior.

Studying the back of Thia's turban-swaddled head, Prynn decided that maybe she should avoid the rush and start hating the *zhen* before she exposed her traitorous inclinations. She would savor every I-told-you-so.

The climb up the waterfall face was straightforward; they could easily top rope and belay at the foot of the falls. The presence of a climbing anchor fastened near the top of the falls required only that Shar have decent aim when he launched the self-attaching cable. Not surprisingly, Shar made swift work of his tasks; the cable was secured and the belay device hitched up shortly after he started. The only question remaining was how the group would be organized. Thia volunteered to lead the team into the cave: after all, she was the only person in the group familiar with the terrain.

The mission is an hour old and I'm already forced to make a judgment call, Phillipa thought. Sending Thia first might be logical, but it also had risks: She didn't entirely trust the *zhen*—not for the same reasons Prynn might give—but the end result was the same. Thia had a conflict of interest when it came to Vretha's kidnappers. When faced with a choice between Vretha and her bondmates, Phillipa wasn't certain who Thia would protect or that she should be forced to make that decision. To keep an eye on their de facto guide, Phillipa decided that the team members would "buddy" for the duration of the mission. She would pair up with Prynn, while Thia would partner with Shar. Another risk, there, especially considering the incident back at the keep. As disturbingly savage as Shar's attack had been, however, both Andorians seemed to find it easy to put it aside, once an understanding had been reached. Once again, Phillipa couldn't help but be fascinated by the culture of this world, the seeming contradictions and subtle subtexts, the complex relationships among the four sexes, the unique stresses their biology-defined social structure put on each and every one of them throughout their lives. In that context, having Shar and Thia pair up seemed the safest choice. They understood one another; if Thia *was* up to something, Shar would likely see it before any of them.

In the end, Shar led out, fixing the karabiners and pitons for those who followed after. When Shar signaled that he'd completed his climb, Thia started off. Phillipa remained at the bottom, harnessed into the belay device, keeping an eye on the cable tension. Prynn paced as she waited her turn, kicking up dirt and pebbles.

Thia climbed, quick and nimble, vanishing behind a wind-carved palisade. A few minutes later, a beep on the belay device indicated that Thia had unfastened the harness. Shortly after, the harness came sliding down the cable, ready for Prynn to use.

Prynn slid the harness up over her thighs and fastened it around her waist. Phillipa double-checked her work, and once she was certain that the harness was secure, she attached the cable.

"I'm only looking out for Shar's safety," Prynn said quietly.

"Of course you are. So am I," Phillipa said. "But I'd advise you to examine your motivations more carefully—they might not be as selfless as you think." She took the ensign's phaser and de-activated the safety. "You need to be ready to use this," she said, reattaching the weapon to Prynn's waist.

Prynn said nothing, her resolve evident in her eyes.

As Phillipa watched the young woman ascend the rock, it began to sink in just how uncertain the outcome of their mission was, especially given the powerful emotional components. Thia was dangerously conflicted, and the closer they drew to their goal, Phillipa guessed, the worse it would become. Shar appeared to be focused, but he held himself apart—his aloofness could be problematic. On the other extreme, Prynn was an open conduit, her emotions surging so close to the surface that the merest provocation could initiate an overload.

Another beep from the belay device. Shar was ready for her.

Smiling wanly as she thought of her charges, Phillipa remembered how exhausting it was being in her twenties when each twist of life and love felt impossibly serious. And while she recognized that the two ensigns had developed much maturity in surviving their respective traumas, they were still young. Mistakes would be made and forgiven; they would live to love another day. She gave a good hard pull on the cable, and finding it taut, began her ascent.

Had the mission allowed for it, Shar would have indulged in a study of his surroundings. The feldspar cave-grotto flashed blue as it reflected the sunlight reflecting off the clear water. He could see smokefish streaking around the pools, scattering with each step he took. Once Phillipa arrived in the cave and they'd repacked their climbing gear, the hiking began in earnest. As they followed the creek backward, the beige sandstone walls revealed a dramatic geological history with fossils, cavern paintings, and petrified wood embedded in the bluffs.

The team followed along the meandering creek for hours,

emerging out of the cave into a narrow slot canyon—perhaps two arm spans across. Tall, water-polished walls closed in on both sides, squeezing out the sky and creating deep pools of shadow on the barren canyon floor. Stillness, unbroken save by the gurgling water, testified to the remoteness of this place; layer upon layer of rock compressed together had formed the canyon walls, revealing a history beyond living memory. He knew his ancestors had once sought refuge in this rugged country, but Shar felt as if he were among the first ever to walk this water-smoothed limestone path. None of them spoke. The desire to avoid detection would be the obvious reason, but he could sense awe from everyone—a sense of being small, of insignificance in the face of such majesty.

"Astonishing, is it not?" Thia said, so softly that the others couldn't hear.

"I had no idea . . ." Shar said. Near the top, gold-soaked daylight saturated the cream and rust and brown of the rock walls, exuding a glorious, cathedral-like solemnity.

"We've lost touch with our past and this place *is* where we came from. You're bound to connect with it."

"You really believe that? That this is where our species evolved?"

Thia nodded. "That's what the Codices say."

Shar was dubious. "But proof. Relics. Bones. Rock carvings. We know someone was here anciently, but how do we know that someone was what we think of as an Andorian?"

"Where is your faith, Thirishar? You believe that science has the tools to save our people, but you aren't so foolish as to pretend that you understand all of its mysteries. That is faith. Or perhaps that is your obstacle—that you believe the chance to save our people lies outside."

"Let me anticipate—you believe that the Infinite will save us."

"No, I believe that as we, as a people and as bonds, become one—become Whole—we will find our answers. Until then, the gates of Uzaveh are closed to us."

Shar sighed, shaking his head. Maybe once he would have agreed with her. Maybe now, part of him *wanted* to believe her. But he was too skeptical by nature to accept such an answer. While he had seen many inexplicable, even miraculous occurrences in his short life, Shar had yet to view any as attributable to a god of Andor.

Weeks ago, when the observant Bajorans on DS9 attended all-night services to thank the Prophets for once again saving Bajor from a threat and restoring their Emissary to them, Shar had wondered what Bajor had done to deserve such protection. Whether the Prophets were gods or nonlinear beings who existed outside space and time didn't matter: semantics, as far as Shar was concerned. What did matter was that these powerful entities cared about the Bajorans enough to influence the course of events so that Bajor would continue to thrive. Where were Andor's gods? If anyone needed divine mercy, it was the Andorians.

"How does going backward result in progress?" Prynn said, interrupting Shar's thoughts.

Glancing back at her, walking a few paces behind, Shar saw the challenge in her eye and was intrigued. He stepped closer to Thia so that they could walk three abreast.

"I don't accept your assertion that having faith is going backward," Thia said.

"I wasn't implying that it was. But from a purely outsider point of view, all this forcing together of bonds to be 'Whole' doesn't appear to be working out too well."

"Really, Ensign," Thia said, "I would have thought a Starfleet officer would be more inclined to withhold judgment of a culture she obviously does not understand." Before Prynn could fire off a retort, Thia continued: "The policy of forming bonds by design evolved only as a means of coping with our present circumstances, and only in the absence of a more permanent solution. Andorians are not able to produce enough children to sustain our species anymore. There are now less than ninety million of us left, in all the universe, where once we were almost three billion strong.

"But there was a time when our numbers were not so diminished, when having children was not so difficult. In that time, bonds formed freely, and we became Whole by choice, not by necessity. We hope to see such a time return, but for that to transpire, we must invest in the future."

"By sacrificing the present," Prynn said.

Thia stopped and looked at her. "I beg your pardon?"

"You're procuring the future by giving up the here and now."

The entire team halted. Thia glanced briefly at Shar before her gaze returned to Prynn. "We're fighting for our lives."

"No, you said it yourself: You're fighting for the future. You're *paying* with your lives. You've reengineered yourselves socially to believe that your first responsibility is to prolong the survival of your species. You indoctrinate yourselves with that belief from childhood. Your children think their highest purpose is to create *more* children. And to fulfill that purpose, they're raised to be the best possible partners, lovers, and parents—to want the bond, and to love bondmates they haven't even chosen."

Thia lifted her chin. "It is a responsibility we embrace, and we celebrate it joyfully."

"Well, *most* of you do, but that cultural mind-set leaves little room for failure, doesn't it? A single health crisis or fatality—hell, even a single voice of dissent—before children can be conceived, and *four* lives are essentially destroyed. The very thing you've been taught is your greatest purpose in life is gone, unless you find an unbonded stranger with just the right genetic profile to step in damn fast. But I suspect most shattered bonds aren't that lucky, am I right? One broken link in the chain, for any reason, and it all comes apart."

"That's enough, Prynn," Matthias said.

"How dare you," Thia hissed. "How dare you presume to judge us, you whose kind has never had to face such a crisis, or such choices. By what right do you condemn us?"

"I don't condemn you," Prynn said gently. "But I question any system that produces what I think are unexamined consequences. Maybe it's buying the time your species needs. But what I've seen—what I've experienced since I've gotten to know Shar, and since I've come here—makes me wonder if it also isn't killing you all inside.

"It's no wonder your people have gained a reputation for violence. All the pressure you put on yourselves, all the self-inflicted stress you endure throughout your lives, it's a miracle you aren't all suicidal."

As soon as the words escaped her mouth, Shar could see that Prynn regretted them and wished she could call them back. Eyes wide, she looked pleadingly at him. "Oh, God, I'm sorry . . . Shar, I . . ."

Shar stepped calmly in front of her. "Is that really what you think?" He watched Prynn struggling to decide what she should say, saw the calm settle over her face as she chose.

"Yeah . . . yeah, it is."

"Then don't be sorry. Never be sorry," he told her, and resumed walking. He could feel their eyes on his back.

"That's all you have to say?" Thia asked.

Shar answered without turning. "I suppose I could remark on the irony of hearing my own long-standing arguments with my *zhavey* replayed by two different individuals, but other than that, no."

"How can you allow an alien to speak of Shathrissía in such a manner?"

Shar stopped and turned to face her, frowning. "How can you, as a scientist, not even consider her arguments? True, Prynn will likely never truly know or completely understand the extreme circumstances that have led to what our culture has become, but she has, I think, accurately summarized the side effects of the steps we've taken to hold back our extinction. We may indeed buy the time we need to save ourselves as a species . . . but I have wondered if merely staying alive is enough of a reason to keep living."

"That's enough, all of you," Phillipa snapped, cutting off whatever response Thia was about to make. "Much as I understand the need for this kind of exchange, this isn't the time. It's counterproductive to our mission, and it's going to stop." Phillipa looked up. "We've got more immediate problems, anyway."

"Sir?" Prynn said.

"Look up."

The team complied. A swiftly moving dark cloud mass shrouded the sky. The low growl of thunder quivered the air.

Shar checked his tricorder. "Two air masses collided. The barometric pressure is dropping rapidly. A storm should be here any second."

"Run," Thia said, her steady composure belied by her admonition. "We have to get out of here."

* * *

They had cleared only a few hundred meters before torrents of rain poured into the canyon, rendering the smooth rock slick and dangerous; moving swiftly and safely became challenging. Prynn repeatedly lost her footing, twisting her ankles and bruising her knees. The rain fell faster than she could blink it away; she found her way by feeling for handholds in the canyon walls. The deafening clatter of the downpour drowned out all other sound. Stumbling, she crashed into a rock cluster; she tried finding her feet, but the slurping mud refused to release its grip on her boots.

A hand on her arm. Shar. Pulling her up, he towed her along beside him until they emerged out of the twisty narrows into a basin—the Great Wash, a cankered lunar landscape scarred with craters and broken stone. The shortest route across the bowl meandered in and around lava rock domes and rounded mushroom-like knobs. Prynn glanced behind and, satisfied that Phillipa and Thia could keep up, started jogging with Shar toward the other side.

Then she heard the crash. A wind gust raged through the basin; the ground shook.

Flash flood.

She exchanged panicked looks with Shar. *Higher ground. We have to find higher ground.* Through the curtain of rain, she squinted: on the opposite side of the basin she saw a series of thick, gray shale fingers splayed down a terraced slope of an ancient seashore.

They ran.

Throwing clots of mud and water spray behind her, she pumped her legs and arms as hard as she could, sputtering and choking on rainwater, her flight fueled by fear. She saw the dark shapes of her teammates off to the side as they struggled to reach the terraces.

The roar intensified as it ripped through the canyons. Prynn crawled over the top of the ledge first, braced her foot against a boulder, pulled Shar, then Phillipa, up to safety.

The deluge came. A rushing wall of muddy water, rocks, plants, and uprooted trees burst from the narrows where they'd been minutes before.

Below them, through the blurring gray sheets of rain, she saw black—Thia's turban.

She didn't wait. Leaping off the ledge, Prynn skidded down

the muddy silt of the terrace slope, using her feet to break the speed of her fall. She reached Thia and quickly ascertained that the *zhen*'s foot had become wedged in a crevasse. From behind, Prynn hooked her arms under Thia's and pulled; over the roaring water, she heard Thia's pained cries.

"Point your toes," Prynn shouted, her words barely audible in her own ears. "Flatten your foot!"

Gritting her teeth, Thia complied. Prynn pulled Thia straight-away from the crevasse, freeing her foot. She threw her arm around the *zhen*'s waist; Thia draped her arm over Prynn's shoulder. Allowing Thia to shift her weight onto her, Prynn pushed toward the terrace. Any hesitation and the greedy floodwaters would consume them. Each breath burned and her strained muscles quivered, but she pressed on toward the ledge—and safety.

Shar had thrown down the climbing cable and Prynn shoved Thia toward it, then lashed the cable around the *zhen*'s shoulders and under her arms. As Shar pulled Thia onto the terrace, Prynn, with help from Phillipa, dragged herself up next to her. The group sat in silence, watching the water rip through the basin, foaming and tossing, effortlessly ensnaring boulders, trees, and mounds of sand and dirt.

Then, as abruptly as it began, the rain stopped. The clouds parted, revealing the serene periwinkle face of night. Gradually, the floodwaters relaxed; the currents slowed. A few minor rapids had been created, but the worst of the danger had passed.

While they waited for the weather to stabilize, Phillipa mended Thia's sprain and administered some mild painkillers. Save a few scrapes on her face, Prynn was unhurt. Thia tried to thank her, but she shrugged off the *zhen*'s gratitude. What she did, she would do for anyone. Nobility didn't figure into it. And after their heated exchange, despite what Shar had said, she was feeling anything but noble.

As Shar passed out ration bars, Thia said, "Since we'd need a watercraft to navigate the basin, we can't follow our original route. We'll have to climb up this series of terraces and out onto the flats. After three or four kilometers across the plateau, there's a switch-back trail descending into the Coral Canyon via the Temple Path."

"Are you fit to travel?" Phillipa asked Thia.

She nodded, flexing her ankle.

Phillipa reassembled her medkit. "You'll have to lead, Shar. I'll belay after Prynn and Thia."

Coiling up the cable, Shar sidestepped out onto a ledge. Hands above his head, he felt the rock face, searching for the best spot to place a piton for the first belay station.

In order to avoid a tumble into the muddy floodwaters flowing through the basin, the climb proceeded slowly into the evening. Phillipa made only one misstep where she hadn't reset the tension on the belayer after Prynn. Too much slack resulted in her losing her footing, falling backward, and dangling in midair, swinging like a pendulum. She'd had the sense to right her body so that she took the impact of the crash into the rock wall with her backpack instead of her face. Shar, who had been supervising her climb from the top, had made the necessary adjustments to stabilize her position. After a few precious minutes (and a face full of gritty sandstone), she'd found a foothold to wedge her boot in and she'd resumed the climb. Now, she stood— gratefully—on the most secure ground she'd seen since the security aquacraft had transported them to the beach five hours ago.

A spiderweb burst of white light momentarily blinded her; she dropped her head, pinched her eyelids together, and blinked away the visual disturbance. She shook her head, discovering that her neck was sore. Massaging the muscles at the base of her head, she winced at their tenderness. Pebble-sized glandular lumps resisted her touch. *No time to worry about it, though,* she thought, betting that she suffered from a pronounced lack of sleep, tinged by dehydration and hunger. *So what's next . . . ?*

Shar, Prynn, and Thia knelt in a half-circle, the tricorder resting on a backpack in front of them. Phillipa listened a few moments as the three of them discussed the best path to take. *They have everything under control. I'll just work on prepping the gear so we can leave.*

As she stood upright, a burning flush surged through her skin and she put a hand to her forehead: hot. Looking down at her hand, she noticed clusters of red welts, some pustule-like. They itched. She rubbed them against her expedition suit. She had been exposed to plenty of allergens since they started off. *Damn. I'll have to get the ointments later.*

"You all ready to leave?" she said as she loaded the last of the equipment into Shar's pack. Her own pack felt binding and uncomfortable over her shoulders. She shrugged it off, adjusted the straps.

Thia nodded, and held up the tricorder for Phillipa to see. "I've mapped out the quickest route. If you want to pass me your tri—" She paused, her jaw dropped. She blinked. "Shar, hold up your wrist light."

"Where?"

"On Commander Matthias's face."

Phillipa winced at the beam being thrown in her face. "Is this necessary?"

"I see them," Shar said.

She heard the fear in his voice. "See what?" Phillipa said, rubbing her eyes with her fists. The bright beam stung and her eyes watered. And she suddenly felt prickly, crawling tickles on her cheeks. She swiped at her face with an open palm, saw black and red smudges on her hands.

"I see them too, but I don't know what I'm seeing," Prynn said. *"See what?"*

"Shax nests," Thia said. "You must have disturbed a *shax* colony when you crashed into the rock face. That's where they live. Some of them obviously found the exposed areas of your skin."

"Is this—" Phillipa slapped at her neck where the prickling continued. "—something I should worry about?" Peeling down the top of her expedition suit, she looked at her arms and chest, discovering that her skin had erupted in swollen welts.

"Only if we didn't have a medical kit," Thia said, taking Phillipa's backpack from her. Kneeling down, she unfastened the flap, and Phillipa watched her fishing around. "The *shax* prefer to nest just inside the epidermis of their host to lay their eggs; their saliva is toxic. One *shax* won't hurt you, but a massive infestation could make you . . ." Her voice failed.

"What is it?" Phillipa asked. She could sense the *zhen*'s apprehension. Imagining her skin crawling with insects, she shook her arms and hands, swiped at her limbs. The gushing hot sensation increased and she felt blurry, disoriented.

Thia sat back on her legs, took a deep breath. "The medkit was smashed when you crashed into the rock face. I can't generate the serum."

"Can you repair it?" Phillipa asked, louder than she intended, and the sound of her own voice reverberated painfully in her head.

Shar examined the damage to the kit, issued his verdict: "No. Not quickly enough, and not with the tools we have. We'll have to abort. I'm calling for an extraction." Before Phillipa could protest, Shar touched his combadge and attempted to contact the aquacraft offshore.

Shar's image swam before Phillipa's eyes as he moved. The bright, red-tinged sharpness of delirium was setting in, exaggerating all sensation. Swaying forward, Phillipa nearly collapsed. Prynn caught her, eased her to a sitting position.

"—pattern scramblers must be proof against comm signals as well," she heard Shar saying. "I can't get through, and I have no idea how far we'd have to travel to move out of their range."

Thia snapped into action, turned to Shar and Prynn. "I need one of you to find a plant for me. Look on the underside of any outcropping of rocks for small clusters—it would look furry, mosslike—with little yellow and white flowers growing on the top. I need as many handfuls of it as you can locate."

"I'll do it," Shar said. "Is it Shanchen's mantle?"

"Yes," Thia said. "Prynn, we'll need hot water, at least two liters. I'll also need a sharp, narrow piece of metal. Several if you can manage. The points will need to be made quite hot."

"I could slice up one of the karabiners," Prynn suggested.

"Do it."

To Phillipa, she said, "Take off your suit. I need to be able to see every welt."

Drops of sweat became rivulets drizzling down her face. "Tell me—tell me honestly what's going to happen," she said, her tongue cleaving to the roof of her mouth.

"Very shortly, you're going to feel pain throughout your body—as if someone were skinning you. If the poison progresses, you might experience some paralysis."

"And then?" She coughed.

"If I can't devise a poultice for you, you'll develop a high fever, the poison will break down the clotting factor in your blood, and you'll hemorrhage."

Mireh and Arios and Sibias flashed before her eyes. Their faces blurred, then dissolved as she passed out.

Prynn ripped open an emergency blanket, giving Phillipa a clean place to lie down. Together, Prynn and Thia undressed her, whereupon Thia unwound her turban and used it to cover Phillipa's fevering body. Prynn gathered together a pile of large rocks nearby, set a couple of open canteens among them, and then fired her phaser at the stones until they glowed red hot. The water quickly came to a boil. Prynn then went to work using her phaser to slice a karabiner into sharp narrow rods.

Shar returned with the plants. Thia confirmed they were the correct variety and added them to the water. Several ointments and analgesics from the remains of the medkit would augment the treatment. Once the plants had cooked together, the poultice would be applied to all the affected areas; Phillipa would have to ingest whatever remained. Thia readily admitted she didn't know how well her folk medicine would work, especially on a human.

Prynn quickly figured out what Thia intended to do with the metal pieces. Red welts indicated a midstage nest; the pustules indicated eggs about to hatch. A red-hot poker held over a welt would force the nesting *shax* out of the skin. The same poker pressed into a pustule would destroy the eggs before they hatched.

The first time she singed a pustule with the heated karabiner end, Prynn felt Phillipa's involuntary flinch; the smoke from the burning skin permeated her nose and eyes and throat and she wanted to vomit. A brief glance at Thia revealed the *zhen* felt similarly. They pressed on, working to stem the infestation. Dark red-purple capillary nets appeared on the surface of Phillipa's skin, indicating that the poison had already spread into her bloodstream at those places. Soon, Phillipa's torso was covered with oozing, black burns.

At last, when the plant concoction was ready, Prynn used her phaser to slice off the tops of the canteens. Shar peeled off his expedition suit to the waist and stripped off his tanktop, which he ripped into strips and tossed the pieces into the solution to soak.

He then applied the makeshift bandages to Phillipa's legs. Prynn and Thia wrapped her upper body. Once her exposed skin had been covered, Thia scooped the limp, shriveled leaves and flowers out of canteens and smeared them over the bandages.

After making Phillipa as comfortable as possible, the team seemed to be at a loss about how to proceed. "What do we do now?" Prynn said, running the tricorder over Phillipa's body. For now, her vitals had stabilized.

Thia sighed. "I think she's out of danger, but Phillipa needs to rest and heal. Fortunately, coming up to this plateau saved us time—we can afford to wait a while. We'll have to start off for the lava cave by second moonrise—sometime in the next couple of hours. At that point, we'll have to decide whether to abort the mission or split up." She shifted from side to side, twitching. Twisting her arm behind her, she scratched at her back.

"Thia," Prynn said, worried. "Your back . . ."

"It isn't *shax*," Thia assured her. "Since I started weaning my *thei*, my *kheth* is drying up more quickly than is comfortable. The sensation is—itchy. I will be fine."

Shar fidgeted. He looked uncomfortable. Prynn looked from Thia to Shar. Neither one seemed prepared to say more. She sensed subtext, but she wasn't Phillipa: reading people, especially Andorians who did their damnedest not to be read, wasn't her gift. *I'm too worn out to ask.* She slapped her thighs. "Well then, I'm going to try to freshen up."

"There's a little stream a few dozen meters from here," Shar said without making eye contact, nodding in the direction he'd gone to search for Shanchen's mantle.

"That'll do." She picked her way around the brush and the rocks. She could hear the water when she realized she'd forgotten her pack with all her hygiene supplies, so she turned around.

The low murmur of talk alerted her to activity. Not wanting to disturb them, she approached slowly. Her pack was propped against a prickly shrub. Reaching for it from behind, she stole a glance—

Heart racing in her chest, she hastened toward the stream. She would have run all the way back to DS9 if she could have.

*   *   *

"I am uncertain as to the propriety of this situation, Thirishar," Thia said, lying prone on the ground. She pillowed her head on her forearms.

I am equally uncertain, but such as it is, we do what we must, Shar thought. "I suspect you would not feel comfortable asking Prynn to help you in this way." Pushing up the fabric of her undergarment, he exposed Thia's lower back, feeling both intrigued and repelled by the crusting, scabbing lines of the *kheth* that wrapped her lower torso. Studying sexual anatomy and physiology, learning the processes of pleasuring a partner, of creating and delivering a child—none of these things had prepared him for the reality of a *zhavey's* body so soon after birth: her back mottled in purple pigmentation, the coagulated blood and *kheth* gel, the weeping gash, dark blue with irritation. His hand hovered over her back, uncertain as to whether he should touch her.

"You are uncomfortable. I know this forces intimacy between us that is not to be shared outside the bond." Thia pushed down her undershirt, turned on her side, and started to sit up before Shar gently pressed on her shoulder.

"No. I will help."

He poured a handful of fruity oil into his palm; he drizzled it onto her wound and the surrounding area. Pressing his fingertips into her skin, he rubbed the oil into the dry patches, feeling the roughness yielding to his ministrations. He felt Thia relax. Her breath assumed an easy rhythm, and he focused on making her comfortable.

"Though I do not regret allowing you to ease my discomfort, I feel . . . I feel that I have cheated you of the chance to share this first with a bond of your own."

Shar swallowed hard. "I have yielded my position in my bondgroup to another."

"I know you have lost Shathrissía, but why separate yourself from the chance to experience such joy with those you love?"

He sat in silence, poured more oil onto her back, kneaded it into her skin.

"I know that we see things differently, Thirishar. But do not punish yourself for Shathrissía's choice. Do not deny yourself your birthright—the greatest blessing of your existence: the *shelthreth.* There is nothing you can experience more majestic than when the four become Whole."

She was remembering, he could sense it, and he felt possessed with a longing to make those kinds of memories for himself, though he couldn't imagine how.

Abruptly, Thia rolled onto her back and pushed up into a sitting position. Her eyes were gray-green; he hadn't noticed before.

For a long moment, she studied his face, though Shar turned away from her scrutiny, still hiding, still protecting himself.

Thia reached for him, curled her hand gently around his chin and pulled his face back around so they were once again face-to-face. He felt her compassion, the comfort she offered. In turn, he released the sorrow, the fears that had been tormenting him for too long. He yielded as she enveloped him in her arms. Lying back onto the ground, she pulled him down onto her so his face rested in the V beneath her ribs, close to her heart. As she stroked his hair, curling her fingers in his locks, she whispered the soft chantings of his childhood.

He wet her skin with his tears.

Prynn waded into the gurgling stream, her discarded expedition suit folded neatly on a rock. The stench from Thia's treatment of Phillipa's wounds lingered in her nose. Nothing could purge it from Prynn's senses—the crackling hiss of burning flesh, the arch of Phillipa's back as she bucked from pain—and Thia had alternately held Phillipa's hand and burned out the *shax* through it all. As it was, Prynn couldn't summon the will to eat her dinner rations. She knew her body needed nourishment. Knowing what needed to be done and acting on that knowledge were two entirely different things.

Phillipa's going to be all right, she reminded herself. She clung to the thought like a lifeline.

In the moonlight, the white-pink coral sands glowed like the underbelly of a seashell. How pristine the scene appeared with the furry foliage of the unfamiliar bushes, the occasional fist-sized arachnid scurrying into the brush. Under better circumstances, this might be romantic. Instead, she'd taken refuge alone, behind a giant limestone boulder, stripped down to her skin, pretending that the person whose attention she craved most would be sneaking up to surprise her at any moment. He wouldn't be. She wasn't stupid. Idealistic, yes, but stupid, no.

Fact: Only yesterday, Shar had shown inklings of romantic interest in her. He might be an Andorian *chan*, but he was male enough that she knew the signs. At least that's what she'd believed at the time. Most of her recollections from the festival were murky, but undoubtedly, something had passed between them. Otherwise, why would he be treating her like she had the Marbagonian plague? Near the end, some of his response had been the *saf*—she granted that. But before the *saf*, she'd seen the looks, enjoyed the casual brushing up against her, felt the chemistry—because it was mutual! And except for that one moment of connection when she'd admitted her skepticism toward the Andorian way, he'd hardly made eye contact with her since they set out on this mission.

Initially, she thought he might be ignoring her out of embarrassment (which she shared) and/or guilt (which she understood). Seeing him with Thia modified her opinion somewhat.

Here, in solitude, she could indulge her jealousy. Biting down hard on her lip, she closed her eyes and replayed the scene in her mind. Thia had been facedown on the sand, arms flung above her head. Shar, oil bottle in hand, had poured some into his palm and began massaging her lower back where the *kheth* grew out of her spine. All right, having spent the last couple of days weaning her *thei*, her pouch was drying up, and the skin itched—she understood that. But couldn't the mated *zhavey* put the damn oil on without Shar's help? Or asked Prynn to do it?

Maybe not. Maybe Thia wouldn't ask her. Prynn wasn't *Andorian*. And maybe that's what this all came down to—the fact that Shar was *her* friend and Thia had made her feel like the outsider.

Prynn sighed.

Scooping up a handful of water with her hand, she poured it over her shoulders, relishing the sensation of the rivulets. She closed her eyes, welcoming the chill brought on by the night breeze brushing her wet skin. The second moon would rise soon enough. For now, she savored these few stolen moments of peace.

* * *

Pausing first to listen for aural clues as to Shar and Thia's status, Prynn cleared her throat as she approached their makeshift camp. She had no idea if the massage was an ongoing thing and she didn't want to intrude. Andorians might not have personal-space issues, but humans did and Prynn couldn't fully bypass her cultural programming. In spite of many summers spent on the Mediterranean rivieras where casual attitudes about nudity and sunbathing abounded, Prynn felt differently about seeing people she knew in "exposed" situations.

"So . . ." she said, her eyes sweeping up the trajectory of the second moon, over thousands of stars, brilliant and clear, and back down to earth. Taking a deep breath, she stepped into camp, if one could call a few backpacks and prostrate bodies "camp."

Thia tended to Phillipa, mopping her graying face with a ripped shred of cloth. She nodded to Prynn in greeting, but continued working. A study in calm, Shar sat propped against a boulder, intently studying his tricorder.

"Have we made any decisions?" she asked.

"Phillipa is in no shape to travel," Shar said, reattaching his tricorder to his hip. "Her vitals have improved, but her body will need to eliminate the poisons before she has the strength to move."

"I will stay behind," Thia said firmly.

"But you know where the lava tube is. You have more understanding of what we might expect," Shar argued. "You can negotiate with your bondmates."

"Once you descend from the plateau, the route is straightforward. The pathway is part of an archeological ruin—a temple. Traveling under cover of darkness protects you. Because of the radiological interference, my bondmates' ability to use sensors is just as restricted as yours." Thia eased Phillipa onto her side, peeled back her bandages, and studied her wounds. "Phillipa needs me far more than you do."

With obvious reluctance, Shar agreed with Thia and started assembling his pack.

Prynn guzzled water from her spare canteen, then nibbled on a ration bar. With little sleep, she would need the extra energy.

"Shar." Thia said. "Please . . ." Her voice trailed off. "My bondmates. Spare them if you can."

Shar flexed his palm, pressed it to Thia's; their eyes met. "I promise."

"Wait." Reaching beneath the neck of her expedition suit, Thia pulled out her betrothal *shapla*, pulled it over her head, and handed it to Shar. "Use this to prove that I travel with you. It may save you both—and your *zhavey*."

"Thank you," Shar said, bowing his head.

"Thank *you*," Thia said.

Something has changed, Prynn thought, unable to pinpoint exactly when the change had come, *for all of us.* A barrier had fallen. Maybe it was as simple as trust growing between all three of them. And for the first time since she'd left the keep—hell, for the first time since they left Orbital Control—her anxiety lessened. An instinct deep inside her reassured her that all was as it should be. Prynn felt amazed by the confluence of life-changing realities binding her to Shar, Shar to Thia, Thia to Phillipa. *One broken link . . .*

None of us will break, she vowed. "Let's get with it, Shar," she said. "Your mother's waiting." A thought occurred. *Time to be mature.* "And Thia?"

The *zhen* looked up from her ministrations.

Prynn walked over to where she worked and extended her flattened palm.

Wide-eyed, Thia raised her hand slowly, gingerly touching her hand to Prynn's. Their eyes met. She offered the *zhen* a slight smile. Thia bowed her head.

They stayed connected for a long moment before Prynn broke away.

Moving soundlessly across the flats, Prynn and Shar used the tricorder's positioning system to guide them away from camp, out onto the open plateau. The second moon provided them with light to see by, but forced them into the shadows of the rock outcroppings to avoid detection. As far as Shar could see, the deserted, nearly barren plateau offered little to no shielding. Protecting Thia and Phillipa from the eyes of their enemies would be impossible after sunrise.

So we will be finished before sunrise.

Thankfully, Prynn was as nimble-footed as he was, her light, swift steps making quick work over the occasionally unstable sand pockets (rendered so by the rainstorm) and through the narrow clearings between low-growing brush and rock. They moved in tandem, one occasionally extending a hand to the other if the stones were slick or steep. When they reached the plateau's edge, Shar discovered that they had missed the descent by a few hundred meters. Thia had warned them that the latent radiation in the geological formations interfered with sensors, and here was proof. He motioned Prynn beneath an overhang; he needed time to recalibrate his instrument to compensate for the interference.

"Shall we review our strategy?" Shar asked, wanting to broach the discomfort he sensed between them.

She sighed. "We follow the Temple Path to the base of the canyon. Lava tube entrance is approximately eight hundred meters due northwest from the ruins, behind a cluster of seep willows. Did I miss anything?"

He paused, sensing her tension. She had dozens of reasons to be frustrated with him. He didn't know where to start; considering what they had ahead of them, now wasn't the best time. "No," he said finally.

"Good." She sat down, peeled off her hood, took a swig off her water, and offered it to him. Not thirsty, he waved it away, but then he saw the look of hurt on her face and he realized that he *needed* to talk with her. Not transactional mission-related communications, but talking—the way they'd been talking for weeks. Time was short—this he understood. He also understood, especially after witnessing what happened to Phillipa, that unforeseen risks lay before them. He thought of Thia, of the kindness she had shown him, despite the rage he'd unleashed at the keep. She had given freely of herself, had admonished him to mend his life, to stop the endless cycle of self-punishment and regret. He had piled enough regrets on his conscience; he didn't want Prynn to be one of them.

As he tinkered with the sensors, he scooted closer to her. He didn't need to see her to know that she consciously avoided having to look at him. "Prynn?"

"Hmmm?"

He started the tricorder's reinitialization sequence: they had a few minutes before the instrument would be ready. "We have very little time and I've been wrong to avoid speaking with you before now. I've been unfair to you."

"What do you mean, exactly?" she said, her voice low and quiet.

"I mean that I felt responsible"—he sighed—"for what happened at the festival. I was angry at my *zhavey* and those things I do in anger are rarely good. I ran away and took you with me and in the process I compromised your safety. You could have lost your life."

"Damn straight," she said.

He hadn't expected that response. He searched himself, wondering what he had expected, but not that.

"You've been pretty clueless, period," she said, matter-of-factly. "I get that this is a difficult time in your life. More than difficult—impossibly bad. But I've been plenty supportive, and as far as I can tell, that doesn't seem to matter to you."

"What can I say? Without you . . ." His voice trailed off. "What can I say that will help you understand?"

She looked at him. "Why were you massaging Thia? What passed between you two?"

He blinked. She had seen him with Thia and had misunderstood. "Thia needed help. It's what is done."

"You were touching her in a very personal, very intimate way."

Trying to read Prynn in the half-light was futile; Shar wondered what, if anything, he should or could say that would make a difference. He thought back to his brief time with Thia and had to admit that he felt confusion. Not because he had developed an emotional attachment to the *zhen*, but because he had so naturally adapted to the role. He couldn't fathom how to explain this to her. Would she believe him if he tried? "Prynn, it was an obligation—what was needed."

"Needed?" She held up her hands. "What do these look like? Phasers? Why couldn't I have helped?"

"I'm *chan*. It's the *chan*'s obligation to help—what is expected of a *chan*."

"Since when does Thirishar ch'Thane adhere to the expectations of his culture?"

"I am part of the Whole whether I like it or not," he said, more sharply than he intended to. How could he explain to her what he himself was just starting to understand? The intuitive connection he'd felt to something larger than he or Thia or even his own bondmates. Until tonight, he'd always thought of the "Whole" in the abstract. Now he wondered if indeed it was more than an idea. Shar continued, "When I helped Thia, I connected with a part of myself that I never believed I'd have a chance to. I could not abandon *chan*'s obligation to *zhen*. It wouldn't be right."

Throwing her head back, she closed her eyes, exhaling raggedly. "So what does that mean, Shar? I would do anything for you—you mean that much to me. But is there a place for me—for us—in the 'Whole'?"

The tricorder beeped, signaling that the recalibration was complete.

"There will always be a place for you in my life," he promised.

"I want to believe that," she told him.

He could hardly blame her for her doubts; were he in her place, in this circumstance, he would feel similarly. They *would* work through this, because as much as he couldn't escape his Andorian identity, he refused to let go of his feelings for Prynn.

"We need to go," Prynn said, standing up and brushing the dirt, plant gum, and dried leaves from her expedition suit. "We're only a few hours away from daylight."

He couldn't argue with her logic. "Ready your caving gear. We'll make less noise if we're already outfitted before we reach the tube."

"Good thinking," she said, and removed her night-vision lenses from her pack.

Shar found their plateau position on the tricorder; they pressed on.

9

Deep in the mountain, night and day had blurred together for Vretha. She hadn't been neglected, being given adequate food and water. Having company while she relieved herself had become progressively less humiliating as the hours passed. Whatever motivation her kidnappers might have, making her suffer wasn't one of them. She had found them to be quite well mannered for criminals.

But having her hands and feet perpetually bound was starting to wear on her. Her muscles had knotted in her shoulders; her joints protested from being locked in the same position for so long. She wanted to know when and if there would be an end, so she asked.

The leader, the *thaan,* paused thoughtfully for a long moment before he spoke. "I believe that those of my political ilk have struggled, through peaceful means, to draw attention to the egregious mistakes being made by the Science—"

"It's already being dealt with," Vretha said dismissively. "These kinds of accusations are cyclical. Over the course of my political career, I've seen—"

"No. You don't understand. I've seen the documentation. With my own eyes," the *thaan* said, fervently. "I'm a security systems controller. I manage government accounts. I *know* that I speak the truth." He held a padd before her eyes, the pages scrolling rapidly. "See?"

Vretha squinted at the small readout, cursing her own limitations in science-speak. If Shar were here, all the diagrams and formulas would be explainable. Ordinarily, she counted on advisors to translate such documents into civilian. Vretha saw a model she could identify as a DNA strand, but she failed to see how the *thaan*'s accusations were linked to this diagram. "I'm sorry; I don't have much understanding regarding the technical points of genetics. But if you can give me a copy of it, when I get back to Zhevra, I'll see that it's evaluated properly."

Her captor snorted, slipping the padd into his jacket pocket.

He seems disappointed, she thought, *but he's maintaining a polite distance. I don't sense aggression from him.* She could see his frustration in how his hands clenched into fists, though his countenance radiated genuine concern. Part of being a politician required that Vretha learn how to read her opponents; as much as her logic told her that this *thaan* spoke foolishness, her instincts said he believed what he told her. *He speaks of a thing that isn't possible,* she thought, wishing she had the means to help him understand. Even the Enclave discussion had been theoretical: What if the Science Institute had chosen to take such an approach? For her part, she realized that the bulk of her recent work involved Europa Nova and Bajor. At present, she had little knowledge of Andor's inner workings.

"I will look into the matter—I would be looking into it now if you hadn't kidnapped me," Vretha said. "I promise I will help you find the truth."

"Promise? The way you promised that you would present our crisis to the greatest minds of the Federation in the hopes that a solution would be found? The way you assured us, repeatedly, that we would not be forgotten?"

"Federation scientists are as baffled by our dilemma as ours. To say nothing of the fact that the war has stretched resources to the limit. We have many worlds in far worse—"

"Politics!" The *thaan* hissed.

"Isn't kidnapping a high-ranking official a political point?" Vretha asked. "If you're so convinced of the legitimacy of your accusations, why haven't you gone to the press with your story? Why go to this extreme?"

"I tried. But the media wouldn't touch it. I could not verify the authenticity of my documentation, and of course the Science Institute denied everything." He narrowed his eyes and said calmly, "What do you know about a thing called the Yrythny eggs?"

Shar. Her stomach twisted, her antennae tensed.

"I see you've heard of them. I believe your *chei*, Ensign ch'Thane, provided these eggs to the institute for research."

"What of it?"

"The Yrythny eggs are the basis of this abomination."

She spat. "My *chei* has no part in any such research."

"Do I know that to be true? No. But let's say you're right. Your Thirishar is innocent. The truth remains: without his—*gift*—the evil wouldn't be possible."

Whether or not the *thaan* spoke truly of a link between the Yrythny eggs and the gender modification project, Vretha sensed danger in continuing this discussion. She had no idea what kind of contacts her captors had in the outside world. If they had decided Shar was the source of the problem, her *chei* might be at risk continually, no matter what direction her career took. The near-bombing attempt at the transport station hadn't ever been far from her mind. *I have to move this away from Shar.* She finally found a use for the contentious discussion in Enclave: the rhetoric. "You keep calling this alleged research heinous and abominable, but what about our plight? Our people are dying! If it is a choice between continued existence as two sexes and extinction, where *is* the choice?"

"In remaining Andorians or becoming something else entirely" he said. "The perversion of our biology is not how we were created. When we join together in the bond, the Whole becomes greater than the individual. Altering our identities as *chan, shen, zhen,* and *thaan* destroys the very foundation of our existence, for it says, 'I do not need the wisdom of *chan* or the blood of *shen*' to be Whole. I, the one, can be great without the others.' Such arrogance will destroy us."

Then they heard the explosion. Inky darkness extinguished the light.

A hundred meters away, Shar crouched behind a meter-wide stalagmite, hands over his ears, as the decoy device mimicked an explosion and emitted a low-level electromagnetic pulse that would knock out the kidnappers' tech—including lights. The decoy's phase two would begin any second; then Shar and Prynn would charge into the area where Vretha was being held and free her. With rebreathers fastened over their faces and night-vision visors over their eyes, moving around would be easy; their equipment was shielded from the pulse. The kidnappers could do very little to change what would follow. He'd heard his *zhavey*'s voice. He knew she was alive. That was enough for Shar.

A thick dust cloud rose up from the cavern floor, the decoy sucking flaking bits of obsidian and sand up into the air. Shar waved Prynn toward the chamber. Phasers drawn, they charged ahead, counting on the cloud for cover should the kidnappers fall back on torches. Their antennae would still give them a chance of triangulating on Charivretha and her rescuers, but it wouldn't be easy, especially if they kept moving.

As they came closer to the "room" where Vretha was being held, the outlines of three figures emitting variegated violet heat flashed up on his visor. He paused. Two figures ran from one side of the cave to the other; the third remained stationary. Assuming that his *zhavey* was bound, he moved swiftly toward the stationary figure, hunched over to avoid any dripping stalactites and unforeseen drop-offs: he couldn't be too careful. On their journey down, they'd discovered that the lava tube's geography varied; some sections, spacious in height and width, were easily traversed, other sections were narrow or featured irregular surface variations. The area he moved through to reach Vretha proved to be treacherous.

Blade-sharp mounds of obsidian created deadly obstacles as he squeezed between glistening points. Prynn, a few steps ahead of him, carried a rebreather in her hands. She would make sure Vretha was awake, alert, and ready to travel. Shar would free her from her bonds. His expedition suit protected him, but Vretha would have no such protection. They would have to carry his *zhavey* between them.

Through the misty dark of his lenses, he saw a glowing form—*zhavey*—shifting back and forth, presumably trying to figure out what was happening to her. He knelt at her side moments later, slicing through her ankle bonds with a knife. Before she could speak, Prynn had secured the rebreather over Vretha's head. Wedging Vretha between them, Shar draped one of his *zhavey*'s arms across his shoulders, the other across Prynn's. He felt Prynn stumble a few times—he stubbed his boot what felt like every other step—but they made rapid progress away from the kidnappers' camp.

"Shar?" Prynn whispered.

"Yes?"

"We need to see if we're being followed. There's only one way out of here and if they have the entrance covered . . ."

"Do it."

Shar felt Prynn stop and break away. In the half-light of his visor, the usually faint glow of her tricorder readout flared. He felt part of Vretha's weight shift back onto Prynn.

"Two behind us. And at least one in front of us. How do you want to proceed?"

Even aided by the night-vision visors, Shar had no idea precisely where they were in the sinuous lava tube's interior. He could sense the low-lying ceilings giving way to bell-like chambers; feel the drafty air from the plunging drop-offs on his left; knew that the often sharp, rough refuse left behind by the lava flow could slice through skin as easily as a *bat'leth*. They couldn't veer to either side without risking injury. Within twenty or thirty meters of the exit, they would gain enough light to better examine the terrain, find a hiding place and determine an escape plan. The EM pulse had given them a tactical advantage over those following behind them. But he had no idea what to expect from those up ahead.

"As soon as we have enough light, we'll see if we can get into a position where we can gain an advantage."

"I can draw them out. Claim that Vretha is injured. Say I want to negotiate. If you can double back and take out at least one of the guys coming up from the rear, I can manage the other. At that point, we can make a break for the canyon, then the Temple Path."

A few steps later and the dimmest hint of illumination spilled into the tunnel; Shar could make out the dark outlines of boulders, the jutting points of stalagmites. "We'll separate here," he said.

"Good luck."

Shar flattened himself against the cave wall, edging along the scabrous surface, feeling his way with his feet. He could hear Prynn and Vretha shuffling along and see their glowing forms shrink as they moved; back the way they'd come, two pairs of footsteps sounded.

Just before the mouth of the tube, the path that Prynn walked on narrowed. The trail rose at a steep pitch, twisting in and out of outcroppings that erupted like inky geysers out the swooping floor. Finding what he believed was adequate camouflage behind on the more towering pillars, Shar initiated a tricorder scan and confirmed that the kidnappers still trailed them. He also could now pick up at least one other Andorian positioned outside the cave mouth. Since the kidnappers could not be sure about the magnitude of the opposition they faced, their uncertainty would make them hesitate. Prynn could attempt her deception any time and he'd be prepared.

As if she read his mind, Prynn pulled the rebreather off her mouth, ruffled her hair, and took a deep breath. "Hey! I know you're out there," she called, her words echoing hollowly through the tube. Pausing briefly, she looked around, saw no sign of movement, so she resumed limping along, dragging Vretha alongside her. She stopped again. Cupping her hands around her mouth to magnify her voice, she shouted, "Councillor zh'Chane is wounded. I'll pass over my weapon if you'll help her." She eased Vretha into a sitting position. Shar could see Prynn whispering in his *zhavey*'s ear.

Returning to her feet, Prynn jammed her fists into her hips and turned from side to side. "I can't travel any farther! Please help me! I'll negotiate for our safety!" When the echo died away, silence, broken only by the faraway footsteps of their pursuers, resumed. She sat down beside Vretha, dove into her pack, presumably to further the illusion of Vretha's injuries. When Prynn's hands emerged, holding the smashed remains of their medical kit, he knew he'd guessed right.

Mere meters from him, a *chan* emerged from the shadows. *Have I been detected?* Shar took shallow, short breaths and stilled his limbs so that he didn't accidentally dislodge a stone. From his vantage, he had a clear view of Prynn; the *chan*'s attention was fixed on her, to the exclusion of all else. *But where is his partner?* "You're a fool, human," the *chan*'s voice boomed.

"I don't really give a damn what you think of me," Prynn said, turning to directly face her opponents. Dignified, she stood straight, her shoulders squared. "Councillor zh'Chane is wounded. We don't stand a chance of escaping. I'd like to avoid being a corpse."

"What leads you to believe we'll help you after the inconvenience you've caused us?"

"Because you have to know that if we're here, someone else knows *you're* here. Assume that if we don't reach our contact point at the designated time, Homeworld Security *will* come looking for us. And if they find us dead, you can pretty much kiss any chance you have of advancing your cause good-bye."

The *chan* whistled. Moments later, a long shadow cast by the diffused, coral backdrop of earliest dawn came from the mouth of the lava tube. Another *chan*, phaser in hand, blocked Prynn's escape. There would be no shortcuts.

"Drop your weapon!" the first *chan* ordered.

Prynn complied, placing her phaser on the ground and kicking it away. She slowly raised her arms above her head. "Okay, I've done what you ask. Help me, please?"

Descending from the mouth, the second *chan* retrieved her discarded weapon, shoved it into the pocket of his tunic, and kept his own weapon targeted on Prynn and Vretha while the other kidnapper took several long steps toward them and away from Shar. *Just a little bit farther . . . a little farther . . .*

Shar fired. For an instant, the phaser blast lit up the lava tube in neon orange. But the beam found its mark, not on the *chan* nearest Shar, but the armed one at the mouth of the cave. He crumpled where he stood.

Shar's attack on the second *chan* had distracted the first sufficiently to give Prynn time to act. She charged toward the first *chan*, grabbed his head between her hands and forced his face down hard against her upraised knee. He fell forward onto his hands, indigo blood gushing from his nose. Then Prynn was behind the *chan*, her forearm linked tightly around his neck.

"Bring him with us as a hostage. Let's get out of here," Shar said.

"Where's the other one?" Prynn asked.

Shar checked his tricorder and saw that once again the radiological properties in the Reserve were inhibiting its scans. "Unknown," he snarled.

"Shar," Prynn panted, giving the *chan* a hard yank when he appeared to be resisting her, "Help Vretha. She really has sprained her ankle. You'll have to carry her."

Yanking the rebreather off Vretha's mouth, he rapidly assessed her from head to toe. Other than her swollen right ankle— a natural symptom considering her injury—she appeared to be all right. "You're fine—you're fine," he said repeatedly, still unbelieving that he was in here in this place, with her, and that they were both safe.

Vretha nodded. A sob escaped her throat and she collapsed against Shar's chest, weeping. He enfolded her in his arms, rubbing her back soothingly. As he offered her comfort, the tightly wound tension within him unclenched, releasing him from a long-carried burden. "We will be all right, *zhavey*. We will. I promise. But we need to move now."

"Shar."

Prynn. Her voice sounded high and shrill. Shar turned toward her.

A *thaan* held a blade against her throat; the *chan* Prynn had been holding was crawling to the side, blood streaming from his face.

Shar pulled his *zhavey* tight against him. He couldn't reach his phaser. His eyes met Prynn's, locked. He expected fear, but found instead resolve, colored with anger.

"I'll kill her," the *thaan* said, pressing the blade just close enough to nick Prynn's skin.

Shar saw her flinch; a thin trickle of red on her throat. She blanched, closed her eyes. If he chose poorly now, it could cost Prynn her life. Or any one of them.

"Let them go," Prynn hissed. "You'll make them martyrs if you kill them. Do you want that?"

The *thaan* yanked her harder against him and Prynn cried out in pain. "You talk too much."

"She's right," Shar said. "Kill any one of us and you've handed victory to the Progressives. Isn't that what you're fighting against?"

"You think in such small terms, *chei* of zh'Thane. Our cause is greater than *politics*. This is about morality, about the barbarity of science—toying with Andorian biology and claiming it is in our best interests. It is about what you have done to help them!"

What do I have to do with this? "I saw the documents you left for me, but they seemed preposterous. I have nothing to do with them. Why would you think such a thing?"

"The Yrythny eggs, Shar," Vretha said. "He claims they're what's making it possible."

Shar froze, and all at once, he saw the documents his *zhavey*'s abductors had left for him, which he had dismissed so easily, in a new light. *Was it possible?* "Prove it," he demanded.

With one arm still tight around Prynn's throat, the *thaan* used the other to reach into his jacket pocket and remove a padd, which he passed over to Shar.

He quickly scrolled through the data, scanning it for the most relevant points, examining them in the new context he was being asked to accept. His breathing quickened, became more labored as he saw the truth, and his control faltered. *They used what I gave them. They've twisted the hope I tried to give Andor. . . .*

The padd slipped from his hands, clattered on the ground. As if he could force the revelation away, Shar shut his eyes, threw back his head, and screamed.

The echoes of his roar reverberated through the lava tube long after.

Prynn's worried voice cut through his anguish. "Shar . . . ?"

Shar opened his eyes and, still breathing heavily, looked at the *thaan*. "I'll help you," he panted. "But not like this. We'll go back now, together, and I'll find out if this is what it seems to be."

"You expect me to trust you?" the *thaan* said.

"The fact that you're asking suggests to me that you want to," Shar said. "I give you my word—and something else." Reaching beneath his neckline, he lifted out Thia's *shapla* and pulled it over his neck, offering it to the *thaan*. "I'm not sure who will recognize this token, but I offer it as proof that we can be trusted." The diamond-shaped locket, dangling from Shar's hand, glinted in the dawn light.

The knife at Prynn's throat fell to the ground; Prynn pulled away, pressing a hand to her bleeding throat. Shar sensed her anxiety—wished he could comfort her—but he remained focused on the *thaan*, whose expression of abject shock revealed him as Thia's bondmate. Whether or not the *thaan* accepted the *shapla* would determine what followed.

Teeth bared, the *thaan* lunged at Shar, wresting the *shapla* from his hand and breaking the chain. "You took this from her! You killed her to take this from her!"

"No. She gave it to me several hours ago," Shar said, silently blessing Thia's wisdom. "She awaits our return out on the plateau, where she tends to our wounded commander. Send your companion while we wait here. They will affirm the truth of my claims."

The *thaan* dropped to his knees, groaning, burying his face in his hands; his antennae rippled with grief.

Without interference, Shar and Prynn helped Charivretha to her feet and together they followed the twisting pathway among the lava pillars up to the mouth. They emerged from the lava tube, into a dazzling morning.

Shar almost relaxed.

The laboratory wing of the Science Institute felt more like home than anyplace else on Andor: he knew every stained lounge chair and smudged wall. Here, in the lab where he'd spent the last year before he left for Starfleet Academy, he would happily set up a cot and live without complaint. Shar would be perfectly relaxed if the interlude in the cave with Thia's *th'se*, when he'd made a disturbing assertion about the use of the Yrythny eggs, hadn't happened. He had told the others that he was visiting an old friend (which was true), but he also needed to find out whether the *thaan* spoke truly.

"So what did you bring me?" Dr. sh'Veileth said, receiving the pocket-sized canister from Shar. Stepping on the outer edges of her feet, she hobbled over to a lab table and studied the canister curiously, holding it up to the natural light pouring through a greenhouse window.

"When we were out in the Reserve, a botanist that we traveled with concocted this poultice using wild plants to treat one of our wounded." After the security medic had re-dressed Phillipa's wounds, Shar had rescued one of her old bandages from the recycler, at Thia's request. "According to the botanist, the plant is a different strain from the Shanchen's mantle that grows elsewhere on Andor. I knew you would know someone here at the institute who could run an analysis."

Sh'Veileth slid off the lid, sniffed, and choked on her breath. "Pungent. In a word, pungent. *You* were out in the Reserve? How'd you manage that? I've been trying for cycles. The committee's response is always the same: 'We believe you cannot prove adequate benefit to your research to justify the issuing of a permit at this time.'" She tipped back against the counter, hands on hips.

"I forget that the full story hasn't yet been released to the newsnets," Shar said, remembering that a sitdown interview with one of their chief correspondents was scheduled this evening. "My *zhavey* was being held hostage there. I was part of the rescue team."

"The mission was successful, I trust?"

Shar nodded. "We had our share of challenges. One of my teammates has been hospitalized. The other is keeping her company."

"The botanist?"

"No," Shar said, feeling the sense of unease he'd felt since the debriefing. "I lost contact with the botanist."

Since the rescue transport had brought them to Zhevra, he hadn't spoken with Thia; she'd been surrounded by a security detail as soon as the hatch lowered, and kept separate from the others. Her bondmates had been placed under arrest. Charivretha would be testifying against them, as would Thia.

The young *zhavey*'s fate was opaque: for her assistance in finding Vretha and saving Phillipa's life, Thia had been granted immunity from prosecution; she hadn't conspired with her bondmates, but she hadn't stopped them, either. Her *sh'za* had also cooperated fully while Homeworld Security conducted their onsite investigation at the Cheen-Thitar Keep. How Thia's choices would impact her career, her children, and her bondgroup had yet to be seen.

"My purpose in coming here was not to talk about my *zhavey*'s drama, Doctor. I was hoping you'd have news for me on the Yrythny ova," Shar said, redirecting the conversation as politely as he could.

"Oh yes! Absolutely," sh'Veileth said, throwing up her hands. "So sorry I didn't think to have it already waiting for you." She ordered the computer to organize and display the files relevant to her research. Outlined in red, a three-dimensional model appeared on her desktop.

Shar examined the model, saw that it was an Andorian chromosome—number seventeen. Most Andorian geneticists believed that the root causes of Andorian fertility issues resided in this particular chromosome's vulnerability to mutations. He shrugged.

"Now watch!" she said gleefully. A series of blinking yellow dots appeared, superimposed over the red DNA outlines.

"I am still uncertain precisely—"

"Inserting segments from the Yrythny DNA here"—she pointed to one of the blinking spots—"here, and here, changes the expression of the Andorian genes." Sh'Veileth's eyes widened, and she leaned forward as if she was sharing an irresistible secret. "For the better!"

Shar felt a familiar tingle—the rush of pleasure associated with scientific breakthroughs; *I knew it. I knew the Yrythny eggs might be able to help us.* "And?"

"While it doesn't resolve all our problems, this is a promising concept. Gene therapy developed from the Yrythny DNA has the potential to increase the window of Andorian fertility. I can conservatively estimate by one cycle, maybe two or more."

"More cycles, more opportunities to conceive."

Sh'Veileth nodded. "And now for the best part."

Stunned, Shar couldn't speak: More?

"A slight modification to the gene therapy has the potential to increase the numbers of viable gametes released by the individual partners—doubling or tripling the numbers. Healthy gametes too."

His mind raced through the implications. "More than one infant at a time? We have not seen multiple births on Andor in—"

"More than a hundred years. I know. This could dramatically shift the population dynamics in a relatively short time."

I want to be part of this research. "So how are the trials going?" Shar sat in front of the viewscreen, scrolling through the hundreds of files on the doctor's system, looking for the data.

She puckered her lips, twisted her mouth. "No trials. The Institute hasn't approved them yet."

He stopped cold. "Why?"

"Because the governing board doesn't believe I've done enough modeling. Too new. Too soon," sh'Veileth said with a deep sigh. "They want more tests, more models, more data before they offer the gene therapy to bondgroups."

"If Andorians knew the potential of this discovery, many would be petitioning to be used as test subjects," Shar said. "Hundreds—thousands—of bonds that believe that they had passed the window of conception would attempt to create more children. Since the newsnets are filled with the Visionists' accusations, you would think that the institute would be attempting to publicize a legitimate discovery."

"I know not how they work. Why they do as they do. I will be ready, though, as soon as the testing is authorized."

Shar gripped sh'Veileth's shoulder and squeezed. "You've done it, my mentor, my example. You've opened a window of hope for our people."

Sh'Veileth blushed, embarrassed, and extended her hand to Shar's shoulder. "I am honored to be the vessel of your faith and trust."

Not wanting to dim the glow of the moment, Shar spoke carefully. "I apologize for having to raise such an unpleasant subject, but I am curious. Are the eggs being used in research intended to reengineer our sexes?"

"You ask a difficult question, Thirishar," Sh'Veileth said. "Obviously you have heard the rumors, or you would not be asking. Other teams *are* using the ova—this is true. But I do not know the nature of their research."

Shar handed her the padd Thia's *th'se* had given him.

Sh'Veileth studied it for a few minutes, then looked back at Shar. "Let me see what I can learn."

Sitting at the desk in her office in the Parliament Andoria building, Charivretha stared at the padd in her hand, seeing but not seeing. She had no idea how long she had been sitting—it had been hours since Shar had paged her after his visit to the Institute. He had informed her that he would be by after he visited

Commander Matthias at the hospital. Now he waited in the vestibule.

I don't know if I can do it. For the first time in a lifetime of never accepting no, of always believing that her strength and determination could overcome every challenge presented to her, Vretha realized that simply because she could do a thing didn't mean she should. She touched her compad. "Send Shar in."

She swung her chair around so she could take in the view out her window, the ornate plaza with its elaborate fountains, its interlaid stone patterns. Tradition held that Thalisar had brokered peace among the clans there, and later died on that very same spot, leaving her people in the care of the representative democracy she'd created. Charivretha had believed in that system, believed that all others subscribed to its values as she did. *I was wrong.*

Head held high, Shar strode through the door. She hadn't seen him this confident in a long time. He exuded a strength that she recognized from his years at the Academy, from his first posting, but not since—

How much damage have I done, pressuring him to join in the shelthreth *with his bondmates? So many apologies,* she thought, sighing. She gestured for him to take a seat. *How do I say this, my* chei*?*

Shar didn't wait for her to speak, his eyes alight with enthusiasm. "I have an incredible report from Dr. sh'Veileth at the institute, *Zhavey*. She's made a breakthrough with the Yrythny ova . . ." His voice trailed off. "What is it? You have had news."

Her chest tightened. *I wish I could protect you from this.* "See for yourself," she said gently, pushing the padd she'd been holding across her desk to him.

"This too, is from Dr. sh'Veileth. Why . . . ?"

"She was able to track down both your answers and mine; she thought I should see it first. And she was correct."

Furrowing his brow, he studied the contents, his impatient scrolling gradually slowing until he sat, utterly still, his face just as she imagined it would be, a mirror of her own pained shock when she first read it. The padd dropped into his lap. He glanced at her wall with its plaques and awards commemorating many cycles of public service; dropped his gaze to the floor, her area rug—the one Thantis had woven it for her. It illustrated her favorite myth, the story of Thirishar, the great warrior for whom she had named her only *chei*.

"So it's true," he said, part questioning, part statement of fact. He looked at her with deadened eyes.

"Yes," Vretha said, her own emotions spent since receiving sh'Veileth's call. What had at first wounded so deeply had gradually numbed to a dull ache; Shar hadn't had the luxury of time to process the shock, the pain. "The Visionist accusations of a conspiracy are true. The research, authorized in secret by the institute board, was rationalized as being 'an attempt to pursue any and all options to prevent Andorian extinction.' That's how Dr. th'Saarash phrased it when I confronted him just moments ago. They believed if they could prove that their approach was valid that our people could be persuaded to embrace it."

Still dazed, Shar blinked, opened his mouth to speak, closed it, shook his head. At last he said, "And there is no question that—"

"None," she told him. "Our own scientists decided they should reengineer our species." The depth of their arrogance still stunned her. "And I was so certain that I knew our people better than my captors. That our scientists weren't capable of such a thing!"

"This is my fault," Shar said dully. "I provided the Yrythny sample."

"No, my *chei*. Do not claim this for your own. There have been many errors in judgment, mine not the least among them, but you are guilty only of seeking answers."

"What now, *Zhavey*?"

Sensing his anguish, she longed to offer him comfort, to soothe him as she had when he was younger and his disappointments were far less serious. But those times were long past. She remembered the presence of another, one who waited for Shar. *She is much better suited for this task than I. Prynn will be good for him.* "For Andor? Treachery will be exposed. Accountability meted out. For us? There will still be a press conference at Deepening. The people of Andor need to hear truth from me: that in their desperation, there were those among us who believed they knew what was right for our people, no matter what the cost.

Blinded by their devotion to Andor, those convictions led them to make wrong choices."

"Do you speak of the scientists—" He paused, looked hard at her. "—or yourself?"

She closed her eyes, wished she could answer differently. "Both. I will face our people and I will inform them that while it has been a great honor to serve them, I will request that my party nominate another to replace me as Andor's representative to the Federation. I am resigning from the council."

He knew, of course—better than anyone, even her bond-mates—that serving Andor on the Federation Council had been her dream. "*Zhavey*, are you certain?"

"I have grown far from those I love—including you, my *chei*—and I need to rediscover my people, to find where I became lost." She pushed her chair away from her desk, circled to the side where Shar sat. "If you choose not to stand with me, I will accept your decision."

After a long moment, Shar stood. He reached out his palm and pressed it to hers. "You could be speaking for me as well, *Zhavey*. I will face them with you. It is not the way of our people to be alone."

As soon as the press conference ended—and when he was satisfied that his *zhavey* no longer needed his companionship—Shar slipped away with Prynn. It was well past Deepening now and he hadn't seen her since he'd visited Phillipa in the hospital. Prynn hadn't left the counselor's side since they returned from the Reserve, and her first order of business had been to facilitate a subspace message to Sibias back on the station. Prynn wanted to make sure that Phillipa's children knew their mother was safe.

After that, it had only been a matter of waiting for the results of Phillipa's final round of tests before she was released, and the two women had, at *Zhavey*'s insistence, relocated to her penthouse in the center of the capital, where Phillipa would rest comfortably. There, they had received word from Cheen-Thitar: Thriss's Sending was to go forward in three days' time, at Deepening . . . and Thantis had asked that Charivretha, Shar, and Prynn join Phillipa when she came. Evidently, Vretha's candor during her press conference had mitigated the strain between her and *Zhadi*.

Now he and Prynn walked side by side through the lighted city. From her cautious expressions, he could see Prynn had ascertained that all was not well with him, but she refrained from asking probative questions and he had yet to offer her any answers. Too much had happened between them over the last few days for him to assume that all had returned to normal between them. Strains over the festival night's intimacy, the Reserve mission—even her perceptions of what had happened between him and Thia—still required mending. And sh'Veileth's revelation had stirred much turmoil in him.

They crossed an avenue busy with foot traffic, past the news kiosks and restaurants—including one featuring Vulcan fusion cuisine—until they reached a residential district of stately private homes. Flower boxes mounted at nearly every window overflowed with sea ivy, black-throated conch flowers with furry yellow branches. Where the keep's relief sculpture depicted violent monsters and dramatic geometric designs, Zhevran architecture focused on nothing more threatening than twining vines and pastoral forest scenes. Shar explained that these complexes primarily housed members of parliament and their immediate clans, how his *zhavey* had moved into her high-rise when she had ceased cohabitating with her bondgroup.

Prynn listened, studying him intently out of the corner of her eye. She walked with her hands linked behind her back, maintaining an arm's length between them, but Shar could sense her concern for him, even as she kept her distance. "So is that what happens to bondgroups? They raise a child and then it's over?"

"Some bonds invoke the Whole Vessel Law and break apart completely. Others simply dissipate as the individuals pursue their careers—such was the case with my *zhavey*. My *thavan* and *shreya* stay with her from time to time—she is closest to my *thavan*—but she primarily lives alone."

Her brow wrinkled and Shar couldn't read her; he asked what she was thinking.

Smiling wistfully, she said, "Honest? It sounds lonely. To grow up, knit with these individuals you love, only to drift apart. Where's the longevity? The lifetime commitment?"

"In the creation of children," Shar said, his own answer surprising him. He was reluctant to admit that this trip had prompted him to reevaluate his recent decisions, specifically to invoke the Whole Vessel Law and officially separate from Anichent and Dizhei. Seeing them again, followed later by the intimate moment with Thia in the Reserve, had started him thinking, wondering about what it might be like to be part of a mated bondgroup, to create a child. But he *had* made his decision to start a new life, a decision that felt right.

And then there was Prynn. She was hardly a consolation choice. He owed it to her—and to himself—to allow their relationship to evolve.

As they passed through the archway into Therin Park's east entrance, a hush descended over them; the noise and confusion of the city receded far away, replaced with the musical burbling of flowing water, the rich fragrances of herbal plants. The only noticeable noise was the quiet tap of their feet on stepping-stones. As though moving through a series of rooms, they strolled past terraced waterfalls and water gardens embellished with saucerlike leaves; among airy ferns, waist-high woody stems were sticky with nectar and dunes of bright blooms. They encountered few visitors as they walked; Shar enjoyed the solitude.

Prynn appeared to be delighted with the Water Guardian's sanctuary. She stopped to gaze at hundreds of clear baubles with enclosed flames bobbing in the water near their footpath; watched as melon-colored fish with winglike fins rose to the pond's surface and jumped at swarming reed flies. She walked over to a vine-covered arbor, leaned over a railing, and watched scarlet and yellow slips of fish dart in and out of swaying water grasses, their scales flashing bronze when they caught the light of the rising moon.

Shar followed, assuming a place beside her.

"I could stay here all night," Prynn said, resting her head in her hands. "Peaceful."

"Peace has been hard to come by."

"Shar—"

"No." He touched her arm. "I will say this. I would understand if you regret your choice to come to Andor. That *I* have disappointed you."

"No, no," Prynn said with a soft chuckle. "How can I possibly hold you responsible for all the crazy things that have happened to us?"

"Because many of those things have happened because of me."

"Yeah . . . But I wouldn't have been able to see all this"—she gestured at the surrounding gardens—"without you either. Your homeworld is astounding and vibrant and who could help but be crazy about it? And spending time with you was the best part."

"All of it?"

"Most of it." She shrugged. "Except for the *saf*, obviously, the festival was amazing. I loved all of it—the smells, the lights, even the running-away part. Okay, especially the running-away part. And I loved it more because you shared it with me. I just— no." She shook her head, turning away from Shar. "This isn't the time for that conversation."

Taking her by the shoulders, he turned her back so she faced him. "What conversation?"

"The conversation about us—you and me," she said, studying the ground. "How this works—if it can work."

He reached for her hand. "Do you want that? You and me— together?"

She lifted her gaze; her eyes shone. "We've just started, Shar. There's so much we can share with one another. . . ."

Shar closed his eyes and allowed her words to settle. He hadn't even dared to hope that she would want a relationship after all the mistakes he had made. That she, who was so beautiful and so *real*, wanted to share his life. He saw her laughing eyes, her expression open and forgiving, and he reached for her face, touching her cheek with a light caress.

She sighed and leaned into his hand.

"When this is done," he said, tracing her ear, the cord of her neck.

"When this is done . . ." Resting her hands on his shoulders, she closed her eyes and pressed her lips against his. He tensed briefly, uncertain of how to respond until the pleasurable sensations she coaxed out of him pushed aside his fear, replacing it with a dizzy tingling in his chest; he yielded.

Shar liked the taste of her, how her teeth grazed his lips when she moved her mouth; he allowed her to guide him, matching pressure for pressure. When he bit down on her lower lip, he felt her startle and he quickly broke off, apologizing . . .

"No," she said huskily, pressing her fingers to his lips. "No. That was fine. That was *really* fine. You learn quickly and you surprised me, that's all." Her eyes became very bright. "We should go away after the Sending, for the rest of our leave. Phillipa still has friends here she wants to look up. It can be just the two of us."

"I like the sound of that. Suggestions from the native? I've investigated, and there's a private, remote resort on one of the southern islands. I visited New Guinea once when I was on Earth—it is like that."

"Surfing?"

"If you insist."

"Perfection, then."

"This is perfection too," he said, leaning in and touching his forehead to hers.

10

"So how does this work again?" Prynn asked, sorting through an assemblage of white mourning robes. "An hour before Deepening, we meet in the plaza by the front gates, dressed in our funeral clothes. We join a procession up to Tower Hill, where a bier has been readied. There's a ritual. Then we come back and eat?"

"More or less," Shar said. Nervous energy had kept him jittery since they landed at Cheen-Thitar Keep. The last time they'd presented themselves at these gates, he'd been received as a hostile intruder. Today had been a study in contrast. In the hour since their arrival, he'd paid his respects to Thriss's *shreya* and her *charan*. Both of them had received him warmly, treating him as a long-lost *chei* of their own, embracing him, asking about Vretha and his Starfleet posting with genuine interest. More curious: As soon as he was finished helping Prynn, he was expected in Thantis's study. She had requested the meeting. Her messenger had joined their greeting party. Shar was uncertain of his feeling toward the summons.

Growing up, Shar had always had a cordial relationship with *Zhadi* even when her disagreements with Vretha were at their most contentious. Still, she'd left no doubt that she believed Shar was complicit in Thriss's suicide. Her help in saving Thia from his rage, even in rescuing Charivretha, didn't change that. Why would she want to see him now? Perhaps he had spent too much time around other less trusting sentients because he couldn't shake his suspicions that somewhere behind the words and gestures truth lived. He could hardly be surprised. Didn't his people spend a lifetime cultivating the ability to erect a nearly impenetrable façade as a means of self-protection?

Prynn pulled a robe out of the pile, held it up to her shoulders, and checked out the length: midcalf. Too short. Tossing it aside, she resumed her search, settling on a hooded caftan paired with a braid rope belt. She pulled it over her head, discovered the long sleeves didn't dangle past her wrists, that the caftan swept the floor, but didn't drag. It would do.

Shar thought she looked beautiful, her tan skin warm against the cool white, and young—far younger than her twenty-six years. He was possessed with a desire to remain close to her.

She rolled up the robe, tucked it under her arm, and looked expectantly at Shar. She touched his sleeve. "It'll be fine, you know."

He stirred. "I know."

"Have you heard from Dr. sh'Veileth?"

"Thank you for reminding me. I noticed that I received several new messages in my database this morning, but I didn't have time to go through them."

"I could check for you. Thia would appreciate knowing the results, no matter what the doctor says."

Shar raised his eyebrows. "You've changed your opinion about Thia?"

"I dunno. She did risk her life for us, and she saved Phillipa," Prynn said pragmatically. "And she's not here. It's much easier to like someone when they aren't around. My people say, 'Absence makes the heart grow fonder.' "

"Interesting. My people warn that absence makes the heart forget."

Prynn had no response for him.

With Prynn now outfitted for the Sending, his last excuse to postpone visiting Thantis evaporated. He needed to face *Zhadi* and told Prynn so.

"I can walk with you—I'll even stay if you like," Prynn said. "Thantis wouldn't dare try anything with me there." She forced a half-smile. The effect was more worrisome than reassuring.

Her protests to the contrary, he could sense how nervous this situation made her. She was the only one in attendance with no direct ties to Thriss; she had come only for him.

"No," he told her. "This is something I must do alone."

Many long hours remained before the Sending and Prynn had no idea how to fill them. Phillipa was finishing preparations on her mourner's mask. Prynn's belated invitation and distance from the deceased assured that she wasn't required to make one, though she almost wished she were. At least it would keep her busy with a useful task. *Besides checking Shar's messages,* she reminded herself.

Spotting a public computer station in a corridor alcove, she keyed in the codes to access the Starfleet comnet, entered Shar's ID, and waited for the message queue to appear. Scrolling through the list, she discovered that Captain Kira had sent station announcements to all personnel databases, Quark had transmitted his weekly specials, and the Promenade Merchant Association had sent out a notice welcoming a new Replimat manager. She found sh'Veileth's message wedged between a note from DS9 facilities maintenance and a news summary from the Bajoran comnet. After scanning the contents, she couldn't repress a smile. "I have to find Thia," Prynn said aloud. And recalling that the keep where she resided was close by—probably local to the underground train network—Prynn decided she'd found a way to stay busy until the Sending.

As she approached the foyer she'd mentally dubbed the "hub" room with its many spoking hallways, she thought she recognized a *thaan* crossing the marble floor from one passageway to another. She narrowed her eyes. Yes, it was him. Had he noticed her? She worried that he might not welcome an intrusion, but she and Shar owed him their lives. Swallowing hard, she walked up close behind him.

"Anichent."

Startled, he stopped, turned around, obviously puzzled. His face softened upon seeing her. He bowed from his shoulders; Prynn reciprocated. He asked how he could help her.

The words tumbled out in a rushed stream. "I don't know if it's appropriate for me to say this, but among my kind, acknowledging a debt of this magnitude is what we call good manners.

The truth is, I—and Shar—we would have died from the overdose if you hadn't—"

"I did what was required. One alone cannot be Whole—nor
two, nor three."

His words prompted a flash of memory: the classroom, the
chan's discipline. A sharp twinge twisted in her chest.

Anichent continued. "Even under present circumstances, Shar
remains a part of my Whole." The emotional timbre shaping his
words found a sympathetic vibration within Prynn. That
Anichent still loved Shar didn't surprise her; the quality of that
love did. Perhaps she had expected bitterness or regret. She had
no reply for him; instead she raised her face, willing him to sense
what she could not say.

Antennae curling, his eyes smiled. "My feelings for Shar remain constant. Shaded by tribulation, yes—but enduring."

A realization stabbed her: Anichent's loss had opened Shar's
life to the possibility of Prynn. Compassion swelled within her.
Unthinkingly, she touched his tunic sleeve. "I'm sorry about
Thriss. . . ." she whispered. "And Shar."

Anichent bowed again. "As am I, Prynn Tenmei. But I rejoice
for my mate and any who bring him happines."

"I am here, *Zhadi*," Shar said, crossing the threshold into Sessethantis zh'Cheen's study.

Without looking at him, she motioned for him to sit down.
She had already dressed in the mourning robes; her finished
mask sat on her desk. Freshly scabbed-over scrapes on her forearms testified of her ongoing grief. *And I have never hurt myself
in the way Anichent and* Zhadi *have,* he considered, not for the
first time, and wondered what made him different from the others. He took a seat on an ottoman, a respectful distance from her.
As a young *chei*, he had liked this room, with its cozy clutter and
its earthy scents of soil and dried plants. On their rare visits during his youth, he and his bondmates would often sneak in here to
hide from their elders. It seemed appropriate that he would begin
his farewell to his old life in this place. He sat patiently, waiting
to be addressed.

Thantis said at last, "I have asked you here to take part in the
Rite of Memory."

Shar swallowed hard, blinked. Had he heard her correctly? "What?" he managed to choke out.

"Though I have allowed all to believe that I have excluded you from the ritual because I hold you, in part, responsible for Shathrissía's suicide, permitting this lie to masquerade as truth does nothing but—" She stopped as if fighting back tears. "I am punishing my *zhei* for the sake of my own pride. To send her into her next life without you, you of all, Thirishar, is a most cruel, most selfish act. I plead for your forgiveness."

Openmouthed, Shar sat helplessly, confused as to what he should say or do. "Forgive you? It seems to me that your acceptance of responsibility for my mistakes is wrong, *Zhadi*. This all began when Thriss and I stepped out of the bond to consummate our desires. In so doing, we severed a connection to the Whole. I blame no one but myself."

"No," Thantis said, still seething with emotions she could scarcely contain. "I have kept something from you—and from Anichent and Dizhei. And while I believe that your bondmates understood my *zhei*, no one—no one knew her as you did. If I allowed you to share the memories—my memory—you would see what the others would not: that I knew how to save Thriss and chose not to."

Before Shar could speak, Thantis led him by the hand through a door in the back of her study. "Judge for yourself, Thirishar. Examine my offering to the Rite of Memory. You will then know who truly bears responsibility for Thriss's death."

"Thank you for letting me stop by without notice," Prynn said, taking a seat at one of the unoccupied workstations adjoining Thia's. She had resolved to be as polite as she could. What was the point of bearing a grudge? "I can see you're already busy at work."

Acknowledging Prynn's arrival with a brief, impersonal glance, Thia returned her attention to the padd in her hands. "I haven't yet had the time to compile the notes from my trip to Dramia," she said, without looking up from her viewscreen. "The botanical society wanted a paper proposal before they planned their next volume." She slipped her padd into a slot in her desk and initiated the upload.

Nice to see you too, Prynn thought, only somewhat surprised that Thia's cold, almost haughty demeanor had returned. She didn't know what she'd expected, but maybe a "Hey, how's Phillipa doing" might have been a polite gesture. The *zhen*'s help in rescuing Vretha, however, at least earned her Prynn's tolerance. Otherwise, Prynn would have had no patience for the prima donna act. Reminding herself that she was doing a favor for Shar kept her on task. She cleared her throat. "Shar received some interesting data from Dr. sh'Veileth this morning. And he wanted you to have it as soon as possible."

Thia arched an eyebrow. "Yes?"

"See for yourself." She slipped the data chip out of her jacket pocket and passed it over. "The way I understand it, the variety of plant you used to help Phillipa was a different strain from the one found in other places on Andor. There weren't any matches to it in any standard databases."

Thia clicked the chip into place and tapped in a series of commands, and the diagrams Prynn recognized from sh'Veileth's message appeared on her desk screen.

Prynn continued. "What appears to make this particular strain unique is—"

"—the existence of a four-gamete fertilization process," Thia finished for her, her mouth open in incredulity. "This is incredible. We've looked for evidence like this for centuries."

"Apparently you weren't looking in the right place, or as sh'Veileth hypothesized, it's possible that this particular strain has a different life cycle from its relatives. It might have longer periods of dormancy or require a narrow set of circumstance to germinate," Prynn said. "Of course, the Science Institute wants to send in a survey team to collect their own samples. It's possible that the combination of plants you used in the poultice created a false positive analysis—"

"But the result is promising. The first real lead that we have indicating that nature does indeed support a four-gender paradigm. This is unbelievable."

"And from a believer, that's saying something," Prynn said, offering Thia a friendly smile. *Truce. Come on, take it, Thia. Let's not part as enemies.*

Reaching toward her, Thia touched Prynn's hands. "Thank

you. I have been less than gracious to you and . . ." Her voice trailed off.

"Thia?"

Color drained from the *zhen*'s face, and she teetered forward, sending her padd spilling onto the floor.

Catching her by the shoulders, Prynn pushed her back into her chair; drooping, Thia slumped down, her mouth half open. Prynn grabbed her wrist to find a pulse and found nothing; *Dammit I don't even know if an Andorian pulse registers in the wrist.* She discovered a dark blue blood smear over her hand. Muttering swear words, Prynn pushed up Thia's sleeves and discovered forearm-long, irregular gashes oozing blood. *What the hell—!*

Heart racing, she slapped Thia on each cheek; the *zhen* bobbled and swooped with each slap.

Bleary-eyed, Thia jerked to alertness. She steadied herself with her armrests. Prynn lent support with a hand on her shoulder.

"Are you still feeling dizzy?"

"I don't—maybe—" She teetered slightly to the side.

"Maybe's enough for me," Prynn said, and helped Thia out of her chair and onto the floor where she could lie down. Crouching down beside her, Prynn cursed herself for not keeping her tricorder handy. She studied the *zhen*; other than the wounds on her arms, Prynn couldn't see anything else critical. Of course, medically she had no idea what she was dealing with. "Can I get you food—a drink? A wet cloth for your face?"

She rolled her head from side to side. "I am fine. I assure you."

"You've been hurt, have you eaten?"

Thia looked abashed.

"Anything at all? Or slept?!"

"It has been a difficult time since we returned from the Reserve. I have been occupied with many concerns."

"You Andorians—could you make it any harder on yourselves?" Prynn said under her breath, wondering how someone like her, who eschewed personal melodrama, found herself in the middle of all this intrigue. "I'm calling a doctor—"

Thia grabbed her arm, gripped tightly. "No. Don't."

"But those wounds on your arms."

"No. I can take care of it." She covered her face with her hands. "Leave me," she pleaded. "Please."

Prynn remained confused. Thinking through conversations she'd had with Shar, anecdotes about Andorians—Thriss—and came up empty as far as answers were concerned. *Why wouldn't you seek help for such an injury—?* Then she knew. "They're self-inflicted, aren't they?" Prynn sat back on her haunches, staring through narrowed eyes at the *zhen.* "You did this."

Curling into herself, Thia keened softly, rocking back and forth. "They left me," she chanted over and over again. "I am alone."

Prynn tried coaxing Thia into talking with her, but the *zhen,* trapped in the wake of her own pain, ignored her. Prynn went to the desk where Thia had been working when she'd come in. She searched for hints—clues—anything that would help her understand what was happening. A jacket had been thrown over the chair; Prynn searched the pockets, found them empty. She scanned her desk, pulled open drawers.

And there it was, in the upper right-hand corner of the desk drawer. Prynn removed the coiled chain bearing the *shapla,* and opened the locket.

Empty. The hair weaving, created by joining the locks of the four bondmates at the Time of Knowing, was gone.

"I am alone . . . alone . . . alone." Thia's chant grew fainter, her voice became hoarse.

Prynn looked on helplessly. *I have to help her. I can't leave her here.* Pulling Thia up off the floor, Prynn held her by the shoulders. "You're not alone. You're coming with me."

"Why?" Thia said through her sobs.

"I don't know, but I'll be damned if I'll leave you here." *Shar will know what to do.*

A cloud of plaster dust burst from the ceiling.

Shar—and not Shar—opened his eyes and found he was in a strange, darkened place of teetering tall marble columns and echoing halls. He saw silhouettes of headless statues, heard the frantic scree-scree-scree of birds trapped in bowed steel cages. Flowering plants denuded of petals and soil had been crushed beneath chunks of wall. He saw a placard in standard: Betazed

Art Institute. The Dominion War. Betazed. I'm in the middle of the invasion! *He tried pivoting his head in the other direction, but discovered that a cold weight held him down. Flames could be seen outside a window. A series of thunderous concussive blasts shook the hall. Smoke, like a dense particulate fog, crept through every open orifice.*

Shar moved his hand. Moved it. He fingered the flowing green of the ceara *pantaloon and knew that he was not in this place and he was not moving these fingers. That he was within another. Then he remembered: the Rite of Memory.*

By touch, he found his way to his waist, to his ribs, to the cold, heaviness on his chest. He tried, in an act of futility, pushing it away, knowing it wouldn't budge. A cave-in.

A clanging behind him. The metallic twang of a phaser blast. Shuffling footsteps—probably at least a half-dozen.

And then a warm hand on his shoulder. "Zhavey! Zhavey!"

Shar's heart skipped. He peered through the mist, searching for her face.

Thriss had dropped down beside him. "We heard the art academy was hit by the last Jem'Hadar assault. I ordered this team together. I'll get you out of here." *She took his hand in hers and called out,* "Reshus! Leilo! Over here!"

Soldiers. Or not. One was Bolian. The other, unknown. Shar couldn't tell in the haze. The pressure lifted; he started sitting up, coughing clots of phlegm and blood and spitting them on the ground.

"Oh no you don't," *she ordered, forcing him back down.* "Not until we can free your other arm." *It was then Shar realized that a round, dense weight remained on his upper arm—a statue had toppled, trapping him. He could see blood pooling beneath his elbow; above the puddle of blood, a laceration, pumping spurts with the rhythm of his heart.*

Thriss yanked a field tourniquet from her medical bag and wrapped beneath his shoulder, cinching it until the bleeding slowed to a trickle. Medical tricorder in hand, Thriss scanned the injured limb. She frowned, blew out a hard puff of air, took his hand in hers.

Shar loved the feel of her hand—he always had. She had the most graceful, long, slender fingers. . . .

"Zhavey," Thriss said gently. "Your arm. I . . . I cannot save it. If I were a physician—if those who came with me were more than orderlies, perhaps."

Cold sweat prickled on his brow; nausea overtook him. The full meaning of her words sank in: amputation.

Pressing her cheek against his, she whispered in his ear, "I will explain the procedure. I assure you, you won't feel any pain."

Before he could respond, a deafening blast shook the gallery, releasing a cloud of dust. Thriss threw her body over his. Shar wanted to push her away, plead with her to leave this dangerous place, but she would have none of it. He could sense it. In his lifetime, he had never seen this Thriss—her focused determination in the face of horrific stress.

"Reshus! Get over here, Leilo! I need your help!" Thriss shouted.

The Bolian huddled against a pillar, weeping softly; the other sprawled lifelessly on the ground. Shar tried to tell Thriss that shell shock was common among those unexposed to combat, but his mouth wouldn't form the words.

He felt her fussing with the tourniquet, and then she leaned close so her face hovered above his. "I'll be right back, Zhavey."

At first Thriss spoke kindly, showing Leilo sympathy in hopes that he would help her with the procedure. Her gentle tones gave way to gruffness until at last she barked orders, demanding that he focus. Could this be Thriss? Blood loss made it steadily more difficult to focus—and he wondered if he was hallucinating. Then he felt Leilo sitting beside him; she must have won him over. The Bolian attached a series of sensors to Shar's forehead with quivering hands. Shar saw the sweat beading on Leilo's face: fear.

Not Thriss. As she coolly removed a laser scalpel from her bag, Shar saw her mouth move, but heard nothing save his thudding heart. He felt slight pressure against his neck, then numbness. Time elapsed in elongated warm minutes until the acrid stench of burning skin choked him and he knew the limb was gone.

Thriss cried quietly. She lay down on his chest; he could feel her fine, soft hair tickling his neck. "You are my Whole, Zhavey."

Shar's vision blurred. He felt his time with Thriss slipping

*away and deep within Thantis's memory, he cried out, longing
for more time. . . .*

*"Leilo, help me lift her," she ordered. "We have to get her
back to the hospital for a transfusion!"*

The smoke gave way to darkness. He opened his eyes.

He was back.

Thantis helped unfasten him from the playback system. When
the final wire was removed, he stood before her, their heads
bowed.

"I never knew she was so strong," Shar whispered at last.
"She had a powerful will, yes, but the commanding, confident
zhen I saw in your memory . . . A Dominion siege would have
broken the Thriss I knew." He paused, thinking about what he'd
seen in Thantis's memory. "At least I thought I knew her."

"Her medical colleagues respected her, trusted her. Among
them, she flowered, became stronger. Away from Andor, she
could have continued to be the Thriss you saw in my memory. I
should have encouraged her to return to Betazed, to be with me,
for the duration of your voyage to the Gamma Quadrant. Instead,
I let Charivretha persuade me that she belonged with her bondmates." She paused, reconsidering. "No, that too is not a full
truth. I wanted my *zhei* to be like Andorians were supposed to be.
I was too proud to admit that the demands of our world were too
much for her."

Night had fallen at the keep.

An hour before the Sending summons, Prynn was to have met
Shar and Phillipa at the sleep hall so he could walk with them to
Tower Hill. Now Thia had been added to their group, even
though Prynn wasn't sure she had the right to extend the invitation. The problem was, no one had seen Shar since he'd gone to
see Thantis, and she feared now that her only hope of finding him
was waiting until the mourners gathered at the gate. Not wanting
to risk offending Thantis, she absolutely needed to tell him about
Thia before then.

Not that Thia was in any danger of behaving rashly; the initial
shock of her bondmates breaking from her had numbed somewhat. While mending her wounds, Prynn had tried to comfort her

with the reminder that their bond had produced three children. Her obligation to the Whole was fulfilled.

But as Shar had loved Thriss, so Thia had loved her *th'se* since childhood; she had cherished hopes that they would remain together through many cycles to come. Such a possibility had remained open to them, once Charivretha, as one of her final political acts, had called for her kidnappers to be pardoned.

Thia's *th'se* had met with her. He had simply felt that their trust was irreparable, based on Thia's choices, and asked that she be excised from the bond. The remaining three bondmates would stay together for a time to raise their children, then go their separate ways. Using the Whole Vessel provision that Shar had cited to separate from Dizhei and Anichent, they legally executed their decision. Thia was devastated.

Before she'd started looking for Shar, Prynn had procured a mourning robe for the *zhen* and found a relatively private place in the sleep hall for Thia to prepare for the Sending. Thankfully, Phillipa had shown up, and Prynn was able to search for Shar without having to worry about Thia.

As she made her way through the halls, which were bustling with activity, she saw white mourning robes being donned with more frequency. The gate summons would come soon.

A thought occurred about where he might have gone. She set off running, unconcerned about the odd looks she might get or the complaints that some keep residents might make.

She found him where she thought he might be. At first she mistook him for another *chan*, but when he lifted the bronze headpiece with its ceremonial mask from his head, there was no question of his identity. Clad in the traditional garb of *chan*, he had little resemblance to the lean, wiry Starfleet science officer she knew. The person standing before her was a warrior, with supple arms wrapped in leather and metal. His unknotted hair flowed freely over his shoulders—she'd never seen it loose before.

Allowing the heavy door to ease closed behind her, Prynn walked across the darkened chamber to where Shar stood beside Thriss, her coffin aglow in incandescent white.

"I almost didn't recognize you," she said. She touched the breastplate with her fingertips, traced the bold *chan* iconograph engraved on the leather, sensed the strength in the lines she touched. "I thought you might be here."

"I had one last task." He opened his palm and Prynn saw he held the three hair weavings. The betrothal symbol. He held them as if he had no idea what to do. And why should he? A lost, life-time promise rested in his hand. She probed his face and found the paralysis of grief etched in each beautiful angle and curve.

"Can I help?" she asked quietly.

Seeming relieved, he nodded. He breathed as if a weight had been lifted from him.

She found a touchpoint on the side of the coffin and pressed. The clear barrier slid back into the bier. She stepped away, feeling like an intruder on this private, sacred moment, but Shar reached for her hand.

"Stay."

Prynn's heart caught in her throat and she could barely breathe for the pain of it. She squeezed his hand, tangling her fingers with his.

Shar held out the hand cupping the hair weavings; he trembled, emptied his offering, and then his hand dropped to his side. They stood side by side, unmoving.

The keep bells sounded: five, sonorous baritone rings, summoning the mourners to the gate.

Prynn heard the door creak open behind her and she turned to see Anichent in the chain mail of *thaan*, Dizhei's skin painted in the flourishes of *shen*, and Thantis in the white *ceara* of *zhen*. All carried masks beneath their arms. When Dizhei recognized Shar, she drew in a sharp breath, clasping a hand to her mouth. Anichent walked toward his *ch'te*, arms open.

Prynn let go of Shar's hand and withdrew into the shield of shadows at the edge of the room, watching as Anichent and Shar embraced, joined by Dizhei. She looked on as the group linked hands and, with tearstained faces lifted, chanted in their whispery voices words in Old Andorii that Prynn could not understand.

She slipped out a side door.

"Where have you been?" Phillipa hissed, pulling Prynn out of the cluster of mourners milling around the agricultural buildings. She had remained inside waiting for Prynn as long as she reasonably could before deciding that she, Vretha, and Thia should leave. Ever since they'd come out to the plaza, she'd been searching for Prynn, but the darkness had complicated matters. With most of the mourners hooded and cloaked, distinguishing one individual from another was nearly impossible. From one end of the keep's front plaza to the other, she'd searched hundreds of faces, hoping that one would be Prynn. At last, results!

Dazed, Prynn blinked, looking at Phillipa as if she were a stranger. "What?" She clutched her white caftan as if she didn't know what to do with it. "Oh. I'm sorry. I came straight here when I heard the summons. I hope you didn't wait too long."

"Never mind. You'd better get ready," Phillipa said, indicating the robe Prynn had tucked under her arm. "And where's Shar?"

Pulling her caftan's hood over her head, Prynn said, "He should be along shortly. But he's not walking with us."

"What does that mean?" As they walked across the plaza to join the others, Phillipa activated the pale beacon on a handheld lantern and passed it over to Prynn; Thia and Vretha already had theirs.

"I don't know. I guess we'll find out," Prynn said absently, hanging the light over her wrist.

Prynn seems lost, Phillipa thought, though she couldn't discern why.

When they met up with Vretha and Thia, only Vretha acknowledged them with a slight nod. Thia was a ghost of her former self: sullen, distracted—moving like a wisp that could be swept away by the wind in a blink. Phillipa feared for her. With their group assembled, Phillipa fixed her mourner's mask—a solid scarlet red with no embellishments—over her face, pulled up her hood, and waited for the processional to begin.

Hundreds of wrist lights flashed on the sooty, metal-gray keep walls as more mourners crowded into the waiting area. Even the windows of the guard halls in the keep wall were darkened in consideration for the solemnity of the occasion. Beneath the weathered skulls mounted along the tops of the walls, towering relief sculptures of gorgonlike creatures seemed to follow them with their hollow eyes; *Mireh would have nightmares.* Phillipa looked forward to moving outside. Presently, she had her wish.

Wind, scented with wildflowers and highland marsh grass,

flooded in as the two story steel gates groaned open, bellowing protest with each meter. Phillipa, Vretha, Thia, and Prynn hustled to get out of the way as a platoon of security guards established a throughway for the processional. A drumbeat started, establishing a slow, steady rhythm.

The keep bells sounded again, signaling the arrival of the bier. Heads swiveled back as Thriss's coffin, like a palanquin on poles resting on the shoulders of six shrouded bearers, was carried out of the studded interior fortress doors and down the staircase. Silently, the crowd looked on as four mourners, clad in the traditional garb, walked at the head of the coffin. Phillipa understood the four mourners to be the First Kin, each representing one of their mythological forbearers. The First Kin were accompanied by a robed figure in tawny brown wearing a resplendent gold mask: the priestess of the Earth Guardian, Thriss's protector. Following behind the coffin were three masked mourners that Phillipa presumed were Thriss's parents. As the First Kin passed close to them, Phillipa startled with surprise, looked hard—narrowing her eyes—and realized she hadn't been wrong. "Shar is with Dizhei and Anichent in the First Kin," Phillipa whispered to Prynn. "Why didn't you tell me?"

From the expression on Vretha's face, Shar's appearance as First Kin had apparently shocked her as well; she waited expectantly for Prynn's answer.

"Because I didn't know," Prynn said under her breath. "It all happened too quickly."

Phillipa could see that Vretha had more questions, but there was no time to ask them. As the coffin passed, the crowd filed in behind, walking to the drumbeat rhythm. Phillipa, Vretha, Prynn, and Thia settled into place several rows behind the palanquin.

Stepping out into the rugged, barren land outside the keep, Shar became Thirishar.

The night felt cold and vast and absolute; he accepted his utter insignificance as one small life walking beneath a canopy of watchful stars. With his own strength and ability, he could do nothing. He could not create light as could a star. He could not waste mountains as could the angry earth. He could not command the power of the oceans. He could not lay waste, as could fire. But with *zhen, thaan,* and *shen* beside him, they could bind their natures together and, in becoming One, challenge the powers of the universe.

Moonlight frosted stones upon which they walked, keeping the drum rhythm. Save the whispering grasses, crackling and hissing with each wind gust, they walked silently.

He raised his gaze to Tower Hill, saw the obsidian table upon which they would offer Thriss to the Star Guardian. He looked at Thantis, who carried the crystalline Cipher created from the Rite of Memory, which she would use to send their beloved. The winding pathway through the grasses and brush was not long. He moved forward, closer to the end of the only life he had known. He clung to the remnants of that life, reaching for Dizhei and Anichent.

The priestess sang of the beginning of the Whole, when all life was One. Her plaintive song stirred Shar. His mind retreated to childhood. Memories of the liturgy flowed into his mind and he mouthed *The Tale of the Breaking* as the priestess sang it, her words being carried on the winds.

Behind him, a choir of mourners sang with her.

Each step toward Tower Hill brought them closer to the place in the story when Uzaveh broke Thirishar into four. Now Shar grieved as he fully comprehended what was lost. His steps grew heavy. He looked up at the final twists and turns of their road, feeling too weak, too sorrowful to make it. He sagged.

Anichent lifted him.

Dizhei lifted him.

With shared strength, they walked until the last curve was rounded. They stood atop Tower Hill, surrounded by earth's offering: the fragrance of fresh soil, green grasses, and mounds of trailing flowers. The First Kin stood at the head of the table as the shrouded bearers placed the palanquin on the obsidian table.

Soon, the mourners filed in around them, their white clothing unifying them in common purpose. Thirishar saw many masks—personal expressions of grief—many bowed heads and covered faces; heard the muffled sobs. When the last row of mourners joined them, the priestess assumed her place opposite the First Kin.

"Who comes, seeking safe passage for Shathrissía?"

Together, the First Kin said: "We, her Whole, do."

The priestess opened her arms to the sky. "As we return Shathrissía to you, the great Guardians of the Night, we plead for her safe passage to her next life. From you, Mother Stars, came the substance of her life, which you poured into the vessel of her parents to give her form. To you, Mother Stars, we return her. Who will send Shathrissía home?"

Thirishar expected Thantis to step forward, for she bore the Cipher. She remained fixed where she stood beside him, unmoving. He could sense her pain and touched her arm reassuringly. Raising her masked face to Thirishar, she pressed the Cipher into his hands. He knew without being told that she was incapable of finishing the ritual: her grief was too great.

For one long moment, he gazed upon Thriss for the final time. Memories deluged his mind, raising an emotional torrent that threatened to swallow him. He imagined he could hear her voice in his mind, the music of her laugh, feel the touch of her skin against his, and he knew he would miss her as long as he drew breath.

And he needed to let her go.

"I, Thirishar, hold the Cipher, and will send Shathrissía," he said, willing his voice to sound strong and clear—for the sake of the First Kin who stood behind him.

Shar fitted the Cipher into a notch carved into the table just below the head of the coffin. When he felt the Cipher locked into place, he gave two hard turns to the Cipher and stepped back with the First Kin.

At first a low crackling sounded from deep within the table. With a burst like a rush of wings, a soaring pillar of blue fire ripped out of the table, burning with the brilliance of captured sunlight; the hilltop glowed like midday.

Staring deep into the flames, Thirishar watched Shathrissía vanish. Where once there was one that he knew and loved, there was no more.

The flames raged on: crackling, leaping, flowing.

And a voice, clear and pure, sang out. A mourning hymn, a song of loss and grief so poignant that none within hearing could doubt that the singer knew suffering. Thirishar joined the crowds in searching for the singer, and saw no one. The crowds parted, admitting a slight, white-robed mourner to the inner circle around the table. Her hood fell back.

Thia.

Opening her arms to the sky, she continued singing her pleas for Uzaveh's mercy. A halo of fire light had fallen around her and she glowed. She sang as if she knew Uzaveh, as if she believed he had the power to save her.

Without knowing why he did so, Thirishar, holding the hands of his bondmates, stepped toward Thia. Neither Anichent nor Dizhei resisted. They could not bear that she grieved alone. Welcoming Thia into the circle of their arms, they joined their voices with hers and continued singing Thriss on her journey to the Stars until at last, the fire dimmed. The obsidian table was empty. The mourners departed.

Slipping away from Phillipa, Prynn huddled into the granite hollow beneath the summit of the hill, waiting for the last of the mourners to begin the trek back to the keep. She wanted to be alone, needed to be. Once again, her world had realigned its orbit and she needed to understand how to live in this new place.

Deepening had come and gone. The darkest hours of night were yet ahead of her. She was not afraid of being alone in the darkness. She had spent most of her life battling the middle-of-the-night nightmares on her own; Vaughn had always been on assignment, Ruriko often summoned away to San Francisco for meetings at Starfleet Command. For one brief moment, she'd believed that she had someone to endure the darkness with her. *Not yet.*

She heard her name being called, but chose not to answer. He would find her soon enough without her help. She thought about what she would say when she saw him. For him, she felt joy. He would have the chance he believed had been taken from him. More than that, he would *choose* the *shelthreth*. Without Vretha. Without Thantis or a computer or some governmental institution choosing for him. He hadn't yet discovered that he had the choice, but he soon would. For him, at this time and place in his life, choosing his birthright was right for him. She knew this.

She wouldn't stand in his way.

Shar hiked up the steep, grassy slope toward her. She was still taken aback at how handsome he was in his warrior's clothes, his long hair blowing loose. Tonight, he had transformed before her eyes; she loved the person he had become. She was sorry that their journeys would separate here: she would have liked to have been with him from the beginning of his new life. Perhaps someday, there would be a place where their lives would rejoin.

"Prynn," he said, breathlessly. "You didn't go back with the others."

She shook her head. "I wanted some time to myself. Before I have to leave."

"That's not until tomorrow. Come with me now. We can walk together."

"I'm not done yet. I'd like to stay a bit longer."

Shar took in her view. "This is beautiful." In the distant horizon, beyond the endless rise and fall of the foothills, they saw gashes of lightning dancing on the ocean, illuminating patches of night sky. Mists rolled in off the waters, crawling into the grass, slowly blanketing the hills; by morning, Tower Hill would be bathed in fog. "I'll stay with you," he said, moving to stand close to her.

"No, you're needed back at the keep," she said softly. "Anichent and Dizhei will be looking for you. And . . . and Thia will be looking for you too."

At first he looked puzzled; gradually, understanding illuminated his face. "No, Prynn, you are the only—"

She touched her fingers to his lips. "No. No words. I understand. Honest I do. And I'm prepared to be very selfless and tell you to go to them. But if you stay here much longer, I might not be able to let you leave. Go to them. Go now."

Gentle as a whisper, he kissed her fingers. She closed her eyes; felt his fingertips brush her cheek.

When she opened her eyes, he was gone.

Epilogue

Phillipa held a hand up to her eyes and squinted out across the lagoon where schools of swimmers clustered around a floating grass-roofed bar, then surveyed the beach. While there weren't many sunbathers, the glare off the ocean made it difficult to make them out. She stepped off the shaded veranda, out into the sand, and beads of sweat instantly erupted on her forehead and nose. Trudging through drifting sand mounds, she circumnavigated a ruffled sun umbrella and a pile of wet, sandy towels before detouring down closer to the water where the lazy tide had compressed the sand, finding the passage much swifter.

At first, Phillipa wasn't sure she'd found the right person, considering how many humans and near humans with whip-thin bodies and tanned skin soaked up the Andorian sun. But the bright orange surfboard painted with yellow orchids planted in the sand was a dead giveaway.

Hair still wet and water beading on her upper arms, Prynn had stretched facedown on an oversized towel, arms pressed tightly to her sides. Her tan looked positively brown against the white stretchy tanktop she'd pulled over her bikini. Phillipa wasn't surprised that she sunbathed alone, but she'd privately hoped that Prynn might have found a new friend or two over the last few days that she could at least gossip and carry on inane conversations with. Nursing freshly inflicted emotional wounds would be part of her life for many months to come—a temporary reprieve would have been a healthy escape for her. Tomorrow, they would be on the transport headed back to Deep Space 9—without Shar.

Rolling over onto her back, Prynn pushed up onto her elbows as Phillipa approached. Sunglasses dropped down her nose, she looked at Phillipa. "I have a swimsuit you could borrow." She dove into a loosely woven grass bag and sorted through a tangle of a towel, a chrono, a few padds, and what Phillipa guessed, based on the scent rising off Prynn, was a bottle of coconut-frappé sun-protection lotion. She tossed over a wad of skimpy scraps of cloth.

Phillipa examined the bits of string and fabric. *You call this a swimsuit?* "And lose the chance to wear this old thing?" Phillipa said, indicating her uniform. She threw the suit back to Prynn. "Wouldn't think of it. Besides, if that bikini you're wearing is any indication, I doubt your suit would make it over one of my thighs."

"Suit yourself. But I think you'd look quite fetching in red polka dots." She sighed. "You've come to take me back?"

"You have a few more hours of sun. Then we could eat dinner out. I read in one of the brochures that there are a few nightclubs that feature magicians and singers."

She pushed the sunglasses back flush against her eyes. "I'm kind of tired. I'll go out if you want, but I might just replicate something. This resort has a great in-room selection available. Lots of fruity drinks with umbrellas in them."

"You can't hide forever."

Prynn retrieved her towel from the ground and wrapped it around her waist, sarong style. "That sounds like something a counselor would say."

"You're allowed to wallow for a few more days, but then you'll have to start figuring out how you're going to make it."

"Make it without my almost-boyfriend, you mean?" she said, resignedly. "How is he, by the way, and his new bond?"

"Probably the only fact relevant to his current relationship that I'll share with you is that Dr. sh'Veileth received permission to use her gene-therapy treatment. Since the group wasn't pre-matched, this could be a test to see if reproduction can be made viable among freely chosen bondmates."

"Lucky them. They get to have each other, make babies, and make history. Not a bad package."

"Prynn—"

"I know. I know. You don't have to tell me. But you have to know that I'm investigating any and all religious orders that mandate celibacy. I think it's my destiny."

Seeing that there was no reasoning with her, Phillipa decided that now was as good a time as any to do what she'd come here to do. She reached into her jacket and pulled out a small, wrapped giftbox. "Shar said something about how you liked things wrapped up in bows."

"He remembered," Prynn said, amazed. She took the proffered gift from Phillipa.

"I'm going to leave you alone to open it."

"It's not that big a deal. You can stay."

"Nah. I need to get out of this uniform and into something more appropriate for the beach."

"The offer of a suit stands."

"Pass," Phillipa said, and left Prynn for her moment with Shar.

She found a private sitting place on a sun-warmed boulder above a tide pool. Through the glassy green waters, she saw waddling crustaceans, the feathery fingers of anemones, and the vivid-hued sea plants fanned out like peacock feathers. Breakers slurped, slapped, and hissed below, and for a long moment she was lulled into stillness by the rhythm.

She undid the bow—an azure blue satin—and tied it around her wrist like a bracelet. Peeling back the folds of the wrapping paper, she shook the contents—a tarnished pewter box—into her palm. Caught between apprehension and curiosity, she studied the box for a long time before unfastening the latch.

Ignoring a slip of hardcopy tucked into the lid, she looked at the *shapla*. The painfully tight weight in her chest released and the tears came. She unfolded the slip and discovered a single word.

Someday.

A slight tremor in her hands made opening the *shapla* clumsy. Inside, she discovered a lock of white hair.

The wind changed; Prynn shivered. Soon, the sun would set, the waves would rise. She gazed out at the horizon, the wash of coral and lavender and blush washing together over a canvas of blue sky.

With her finger, she twisted a tendril of her hair into rope; she removed a pocket knife from her beach bag and cut off a short length. She carefully braided the white with the black and closed the locket.

Someday.

Undoing the catch, she draped the chain around her neck, and fastened it, adjusting the chain until the locket nestled against her skin. Through her shirt, she touched the diamond-shape outline with her fingers, feeling the locket press into her breastbone.

Someday.

GLOSSARY OF ANDORII TERMS

In our interpretation of the Andorians, the species is comprised of four sexes. This is loosely extrapolated from Data's line in the *Star Trek: The Next Generation* episode "Data's Day," in which he states that Andorians marry in groups of four. While the authors and editors of *Star Trek* fiction freely acknowledge that "A" doesn't necessarily equal "B," we decided to go with that particular interpretation simply because it afforded us what we felt were the most interesting storytelling opportunities.

None of the Andorian sexes is truly male or female as humans might define them. Andorians do, however, accept male or female pronouns in order to simplify their interactions with the various two-sex species that dominate the *Star Trek* universe, and to avoid unwelcome questions about their biology.

The sexes break down as follows:

zhen ("she")
shen ("she")
chan ("he")
thaan ("he")

The dominant language on the world of Andor (or Andoria, as it is sometimes called) is known as Andorii. As with many terrestrial languages, certain words in Andorii are gender-specific. What follows is a short list of those words and a few others established in *Deep Space Nine* fiction set after the TV series.

sex:	zhen	shen	chan	thaan
polite form of address:	Zha	Sha	Cha	Tha
beloved (bondmate):	zh'yi	sh'za	ch'te	th'se
parent:	zhavey	shreya	charan	thavan
offspring:	zhei	shei	chei	thei

sibling:	zhi	shi	chi	thi
parent by marriage:	zhadi	shidei	chada	thadu
child by marriage:	zhri'za	shri'za	chri'ze	thri'ze

OTHER ANDORII TERMS

ceara: traditional clothing among *zhen*

challorn: a sweet-smelling flower

eketha: a hardwood tree

elta: a floral tree

grelth: an arachnid

hari: a flatbread

katheka: a stimulant analogous to coffee

kheth: the temporary pouch that grows over and around the lower abdomen of a *zhavey* for the final phase of Andorian gestation

klazh: an animal known for its careless way of moving

saf: a psychoactive chemical refined from an Andorian plant, used in the *shelthreth* and generally available only by medical prescription on Andor. Possession of *saf* is illegal off Andor

shapla: a betrothal symbol; woven locks of hair from bondmates

shax: a poisonous parasitic insect that nests under the skin of its host

shaysha: an edible beetlelike insect

shelthreth: ritual consummation of marriage for the purpose of conception.

taras: a kind of tree

tezha: sexual union outside the *shelthreth*

vithi: an edible flower

xixu: a marine plant whose fronds may be mashed and used in baby food

zhiassa: a *zhavey*'s milk

zletha: a flower